SUN DANCE

"Good God, Skye, when does this end? Will he die?" asked the viscount.

"When he pulls himself free after dancing the rest of the day, mate. The skewers must work throught the muscle."

The viscount watched, disturbed. Both Diana and Alexandra fled, the viscountess sobbing as if something inside her had been violated.

"Skye. What did that chap say just before he began that dance, eh?"

"He asked Sun to honor his sacrifice of undergoing torture, and to give him the strength to fulfill his vow."

"But what did he vow, Skye?"

Barnaby Skye wondered whether to tell the viscount, and finally decided he would. He lifted his silk hat and settled it again in ritual gesture. "To kill me because I once killed Hunkpapa in a battle. And all white trespassers."

Tor books by Richard S. Wheeler

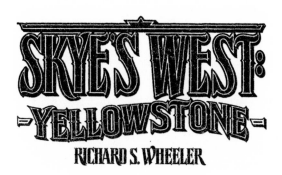

SKYE'S WEST: YELLOWSTONE

RICHARD S. WHEELER

TOR®

A TOM DOHERTY ASSOCIATES BOOK
NEW YORK

YELLOWSTONE

Copyright © 1990 by Richard S. Wheeler

A Tor Book
Published by Tom Doherty Associates, Inc.
49 West 24th Street
New York, N.Y. 10010

Cover art by Royo

ISBN: 0-812-50894-7

First edition: October 1990

Printed in the United States of America

0 9 8 7 6 5 4 3 2 1

For Michael Seidman

Chapter 1

The trouble in Mister Skye's lodge really began with Victoria's medicine. As spring progressed, the old Crow woman turned inward and slipped into a stoic silence. Sometimes she squinted at Mister Skye intensely, as if measuring him for a grave, and then turned angrily to whatever task lay at hand. He didn't press her. When she was ready to tell him, she would. And he would listen. He didn't hold with Indian religion, but he respected it, and sometimes found it uncanny.

His other wife, young amber-fleshed Mary of the Shoshones, was affected by Victoria's gloom too, so Mister Skye's lodge was filled with sighs and sorrow as the bluestem poked through moist clay and leaf buds formed on the cottonwoods along the Platte.

Once he questioned Victoria.

"What is it?" he asked on a blustery March night when gusting winds drove smoke back down into the lodge, making them cough.

"Don't do it," she said. "Bad. We'll all weep."

But that was all she would say, and turned industriously

to resoling one of Mister Skye's winter moccasins with buffalo rawhide, fiercely jamming her awl through tough leather.

But he would do it. The draft for five hundred pounds, two thousand five hundred dollars, sealed it. His usual guiding fee was five hundred dollars, but expenses always ate into that. True, he would spend much of this on harness drays for Frazier's carts, and saddle horses, all gathered from trading posts along the Platte and tribesmen, but there would be a thousand left over if all went well. Enough to comfort Mister Skye and Victoria and Mary for years.

In spite of all that wealth, which had been delivered to his agent, Colonel Bullock, the sutler at Fort Laramie, Mister Skye thought long and hard about accepting the offer. When his head quit working he tried to resolve the matter with a jug of whiskey. But when he emerged from that winter hegira he had even less notion of whether to do it than he'd had before he'd soaked his brain in spirits. He'd never guided Britons before, and didn't ever want to. They stirred memories in him. Even less did he want to guide this hunting party, formed by Viscount Gordon Patrick Archibald Frazier, a great landlord near Bury St. Edmunds, Suffolk. No, he didn't relish it at all, in part because of a seething rage toward his fellow Britons that hadn't abated in decades— and in part because in British possessions he was a wanted man.

"Take it, suh," advised Colonel Bullock, the retired Virginian who was waxing rich selling grog and tobacco to the small garrison at the new army post, as well as calico, shoes, fresh oxen, and sundries to the summer hordes en route to Oregon and California. "There's no danger I can fathom. Take them to their buffalo and elk. Show them the geysers, and pocket it."

"There'll be a lot of them. Enough to drag me north across the line, Colonel. And besides that, every bloody Briton I meet starts me boiling again. Especially the titled ones, the ones called Lord and Sir, and Your Excellency and Mister."

Colonel Bullock looked amused. "They'll have reason to

respect Barnaby Skye," he said. "God knows, they made enough inquiries."

So he would do it. Through the winter he bought horses, and when new leaf lifted the cottonwoods to a mint-colored haze along the Platte, Mister Skye's wives unlaced the small buffalo cowhide lodge, loaded the slender lodgepoles on travois, gathered their few belongings into parfleches and loaded them on Skye's bony black Missouri mules. They struck due north, herding forty-two half-starved and winter-weakened nags, plunging into the land of the Sioux and Cheyenne, deadly enemies of Victoria and Mary's people, and every warrior among them a famous horse thief.

He'd agreed to be at Fort Union, six hundred horseback miles north near the confluence of the Missouri and Yellowstone, on the 15th of June, 1850, along with forty horses, twenty of them broken for harness. Frazier's packet, the *St. Ange*, owned and mastered by Joseph LaBarge, would arrive on the June rise, as the rivermen called the second annual flood of the Missouri. From there, they would start directly up the Yellowstone on the great hunt.

April had always seemed to him the worst month to travel. The grass had 'barely peeked from the icy earth, and wouldn't support hungry horses. He would need to keep them alive with cottonwood bark. Rivers roared, and innocuous creeks turned into torrents or lakes, forbidding passage. Late blizzards descended, locking the country in a cold blanket. Ponies plodded and slipped and stumbled through gumbo, making heavy work of what would be easy going on drier turf. Game was hard to find, and poor, reduced to bones by winter starvation. Moist cold earth clawed up through buffalo robes. Chill winds chapped flesh and triggered fevers. Haze and icy pellets and sheeting rain worked into his old percussion lock Hawken, dampening the powder so that he sometimes had to claw caked DuPont out of it, pour in fresh, and jam the galena back down the muzzle, riding a patch. Often there was not a dry stick of firewood to be had. But it wouldn't all be bad: the very things that would make his journey an ordeal would keep horse-hungry Sioux and Cheyenne, not to mention Assiniboin, Blackfeet and Gros Ventre, in their lodges a few weeks more. He had forty horses to deliver, and only himself, Victoria, Mary, and Jawbone, to do it.

Jawbone. Mister Skye sat comfortably on the bony, scarred blue roan as they herded the winter-whipped horses out of the Platte Valley and onto endless broken plains, rough and empty and filled with hidden menace. His yellow-eyed evil horse had become a legend among the northern tribes. The terrible stallion bore the scars of arrows and knives, battle axes and clubs. Mister Skye's training, and the beast's own rude intelligence, had given Jawbone an uncanny grasp of danger, making him a splendid sentry. Every warrior of every northern tribe knew the roman-nosed beast was a medicine horse, capable of murder. The thought pleased Mister Skye. They all knew Jawbone as well as they knew him. And when they spotted the medicine horse, or the burly man wearing his battered silk tophat, the unblinking bleached blue eyes, and a nose as thick as a keelboat stem, they thought twice. Or thrice.

For weeks they furrowed the gumbo north, leaving a trail of horses and travois traces behind them like a wake behind the taffrail. Mister Skye studied the bleak brown lands and saw nothing but contentious crows and an occasional hawk nesting in the rigging of the sky. They camped in silent cottonwood bottoms whenever he could find them, and there he slashed bark for his gaunt animals, and studied the country, and sat glare-eyed through long nights beside his picketed ponies, keeping Jawbone loose-saddled and ready.

His weathered sits-beside-him wife watched him, muttered, and then slid into indignant silence. She'd seen visions, he knew. But she'd say nothing about them. He thought Mary might comfort him with her smiles and the trifles of her bold hands, but she rebuffed him too, until they'd become silent strangers on an endless voyage.

They pierced up the sodden grassy ditch of Old Woman Creek, pushed on to the swollen Cheyenne River, cut across angry creeks to the Beaver, skirted the brooding slopes of the Black Hills, sacred ground of the Lakota people and their *Wakan Tanka*; struck the gloomy gorge of the Inyan Kara and then on to the Belle Fourche, past the dark terror of Devil's Tower, which set Victoria to muttering death songs; then on over a pine-crusted divide to the Little Missouri, which took them to the great Yellowstone. They had not seen a mortal the entire distance, even though the mark of their passage rolled behind them as indelibly as sin in the judgment books of God. Mister Skye took it as a great omen, and thought his luck had soared. But Victoria muttered, placed carmine riverbottom pebbles she'd toted a great distance atop Lakota medicine cairns, for reasons Mister Skye couldn't fathom, and refused to sleep in the lodge as long as they traversed this land of the enemies of her Absaroka people.

They struck the roiling Yellowstone in late May, beneath black-bellied thunderheads that soon boomed down the wrath of the One Above upon their passage. Swiftly Mary and Victoria erected their lodge, deep in the cottonwood bottoms back from the river, and waited for the Spirits to descend and drive them back to Fort Laramie. Mister Skye shot a wolf that evening, ending a two-day fast in the very heart of a game-rich land. He gnawed soft gray wolfmeat, while his wives sniffed dourly and starved. Whitemen, he thought, will eat anything. He'd even eat cooties and grubs.

"We're almost at Union," he announced maliciously. "And not a pony lost. Three lame, all gaunt and poor, but not a beast lost. Oh, we're bloody rich, ladies. I ought to shoot one, just so you can say you knew it all along. Haw!"

Victoria glared and muttered. "You'll see," she said. Those were her first words in a week.

They toiled down the Yellowstone, heading northeasterly on a great tribal highway where anyone could encounter anything, usually lethal. But no hunting party or band of horse thieves beset them, and Mister Skye grinned at his silly women, and began bellowing sailor ditties, and bawling at hail, prancing hairy-chested in showers, and blaspheming Victoria's medicine, asking her how eagle claws and moose eyes and red pebbles could affect their passage and Fate.

"You'll see," she said.

They forded the boiling ice-green river badly, taking a cold bath and risking the weary horses. Even Jawbone swam listlessly, letting himself be carried a half mile in the flood. But they lost nothing, and Mister Skye gloated.

"Try frog medicine," he said. "Frogs got better medicine than anything. I always seek my brothers the frogs for counsel."

But Victoria didn't, and didn't smile, either.

They traversed a thin neck of land, hungry again, and raised Fort Union a day later, across the mighty Missouri. It glowed on the north bank, its sixteen-foot palisades golden in the late sun, the heart of empire, the crown jewel of American Fur Company, Barnaby Skye's erstwhile employer. Small figures boiled out of the fort like grapeshot, launched pirogues, and an hour later Mister Skye, Victoria, Mary, Jawbone, and forty-two dripping and shaking horses rested safely in the lee of the great post, an island of comfort in an aching sea of nothingness.

The Viscount Gordon Patrick Archibald Frazier had become a fixture in the pilothouse, but the master, Joe La-Barge, and the pilot, Renfrew, didn't seem to mind. Lord Frazier had discovered that the pilothouse, which perched atop what these Americans called the texas, or officers' quarters, afforded a spectacular view. He also found the packet's bearded master affable but too familiar.

Day after day, the little *St. Ange* had wrestled its way up the boiling Missouri, at first through forested lowlands and then between grassy bluffs in a mile-wide ditch cut through endless steppes. Lord Frazier had devoured every account he could find of the passage up the great Missouri, including those of Audubon and Catlin, and even Prince Maximilian zu Wied-Neuwied and his artist Bodmer in translation. But not even these keen recollections prepared this English lord for what his bright protruding eyes beheld. The distances and magnitudes were beyond his fathoming. His entire Suffolk could lie in some dusty corner of this vast continent, unnoticed.

He was a man of landed estates, a squire lording over a dozen hamlets, but like most Britons his heart lay close to the seas and the vessels that plied them. At first he had eyed the *St. Ange*, which LaBarge had named after Governor St.

Ange de Bellerive, as some sort of Yankee nautical claptrap, and had twitted LaBarge about it. The low flat hull that lay on the water like a lilypad and had so little cargo space in its low hold, for instance. Or the great superstructure that lay upon this makeshift raft, making the vessel topheavy and unworthy of Neptune's wiles, and likely to capsize, like a fat man on stilts.

"This is a mad thing you run, LaBarge," he ventured early in their passage. "Are you sure it's quite safe?"

"It's never safe," LaBarge answered suavely, letting that riposte sink into Lord Frazier's skull.

"I should say not!" the lord cried.

"But it suits the river admirably," LaBarge added. "The Missouri knows not where it runs. One day its main channel lies starboard; the next day to port. Underwater demons build sandbars one day and wash them away the next. The river's awash with logs and trees eroded from the banks, which we call sawyers, and they can poke a hole in a hull faster than we can maneuver. Our firebox eats twenty cords of wood a day, and even at that we barely make enough steam to do the rapids, especially when a stiff wind runs against us. We stop for wood each day, sometimes twice a day, and risk our lives fetching it when tribesmen are around."

"I suppose you strike sandbars, then. What do you do once you're grounded?"

"Why, wait for a rise, or grasshopper over them."

"I say. Grasshopper? You'll have to translate, LaBarge. You Yanks contaminate the tongue."

"See those booms and spars, sir? And that capstan on the foredeck? Well, sir, we lower those spars until they rest on the sandbar, and then my men start twisting that capstan until we lift the boat up on those spars, like a grasshopper lifting its carcass, and then the paddles and the angle of the spars propel the boat forward. We repeat that until we're off."

"I think you're joshing me, LaBarge," Lord Frazier muttered, but some time later, in a barren country they called Dakota, he found LaBarge wasn't joshing at all. In fact—though he hated to admit it—he found the vessel admirably suited for its strange locomotion up a river that was about half mud.

He'd spotted the first tribesmen at a place LaBarge called Bellevue, not long after the river had erupted from a dense bankside forest into grasslands with occasional copses of trees along the shores. The half-naked bronzed men watching the passage of the fireboat excited Viscount Frazier.

"What are they, LaBarge?" he cried.

"Omaha, most likely."

"Are they a menace?"

"Usually not. The tribesmen up and down the river rarely trouble us, we are careful. They are subject to excitements now and then, so one never knows. We've had scrapes with the Yankton Sioux recently."

"Trouble?"

"They beg. Want trinkets for the firewood. Shoot their flintlocks as we pass by. Attempt to board. We don't let them, except maybe a headman or two."

"Shoot at us?"

"Oh sure. Most trips. Look," LaBarge said, pointing at perforations in the white enamel. "We dug the lead out."

Lord Frazier felt himself going giddy and tried to hide it.

"I say. Shall I call my men to arms?" He had thirty of them below, and a whole cartload of fine English pieces made by Manton, Dickson and son, James Purdey, Charles Lancaster, and John Rigby over in Dublin. Even his two cooks, wine steward, and taxidermist could fire them after he'd instructed them back in Suffolk.

"Hardly. Lord Frazier, as master of this vessel I'm in command, and that includes its defense. We'll have no trouble unless we make it with rash conduct. Most difficulties can be resolved with small gifts—a twist of tobacco or some vermillion. I'll want you to heed closely, though. The Rees, up in Dakota, can be a trial. They incline to treachery."

"You're addressing a lord of England—" Viscount Frazier cut himself off abruptly, thinking he'd never accustom himself to American democracy and the insolence of servant classes. He smiled, then. "Of course, of course, my good master."

Down on the main deck, Lady Alexandra had spotted

them, and had squealed her terror. She had excitable humors, he thought, in spite of flaxen hair and a steady gaze. Too delicate for this, but she'd insisted on coming. He'd rather hoped she'd stay in Bury St. Edmunds, so he could booze with Diana and shoot bison and play tiddlywinks—their private name for carnal delights—in their tent. But Lady Diana simply would not be put off.

"Will we live?" she cried, waving a soft white hand at them far below. "Are we to meet our Maker?"

"Not quite yet," yelled the viscount, uncertainly.

LaBarge laughed, which seemed altogether rude to Viscount Frazier. These Americans, he thought. Not a bit couth.

But the *St. Ange* toiled up the turbid river without troubles, although Lord Frazier discovered astonishments at every bend of the treacherous flood. They rammed into frequent spring showers, which drove Lord Frazier to the men's lounge where he whiled away time with his ladies. These puritanical Americans consigned all female passengers to a separate cabin far aft, and even wives travelling with husbands were compelled to bunk there. But since he'd chartered the ship, except for some American Fur Company cargo, no rules were observed.

They usually anchored nights at islands or sand spits for safety, and Lord Frazier came to admire LaBarge's prudence. Whenever they stopped for wood, the master posted a rifleman atop the texas as a sentry. A shot would hurry wood cutters aboard. But no excitements disturbed their peaceful passage up the muscular river.

One gray day at a place LaBarge called Crow Creek in Dakota, they came upon buffalo, and the viscount and all his men rushed to the rail to study the huge beasts drinking at river's edge.

"You may shoot some," said LaBarge, "and I'll send a yawl. You'll find buffalo hump and boss rib a feast you'll remember."

His lordship wanted the honors, so he had his two Mantons brought him, and banged away without effect. It puzzled him. The beasts took the balls and scarcely shivered.

"Sir, if I may," yelled the master from above. "Aim

back of the shoulders, sir. A ball in a certain area there will drop them.''

But the shaggy beasts had taken alarm and lumbered up the grassy coulee, and vanished. Except for one that stood quaking and spraying blood from his nostrils. Lord Frazier took another Manton handed him by his armorer, peered down the barrel again, squeezed, and the beast shuddered and fell. That night, he found LaBarge's estimation of buffalo meat was as good as his word.

They pierced into a land more and more arid, with tufts of silvery grasses that upholstered the yellow clay, and finally LaBarge told him they'd make Fort Union the following day. At once the viscount began to think ahead toward the unloading, and the great hunt. And of course, about Skye.

''Tell me, LaBarge, is this chap Skye to be trusted with our lives?''

LaBarge didn't reply, but stared dreamily up the aquamarine river at white rifts ahead, and paused so long that Frazier thought he didn't hear the question.

''Lord Frazier,'' said the master softly. ''If there's any man on earth who can keep you out of harm's way, who knows the northwest, who knows the tribesmen, who knows every menace, it's Skye. Skye and his amazing ladies, and that horse of his.''

''Horse?''

''Jawbone. An army in himself.''

''Are you quite sure?''

''You'll need him,'' LaBarge said. ''Heed his every word, or face doom.''

Lord Frazier thought LeBarge's advice perfectly extraordinary, but it pleased him that this barbarian would serve.

Chapter 2

Mister Skye watched for Victoria amid the throngs that
erupted from Fort Union to celebrate the arrival of the *St.
Ange*. She'd vanished, after a sullen silence all day. He
couldn't fathom her dread, but he respected it. Never before
had she refused to meet his clients, but now, as the twin-
chimneyed riverboat slid past the wooded point below the
fort, and the welcoming roar of the six-pounder up in the
bastion shivered the air, he knew she couldn't bear to meet
these British clients of his. He suddenly shared her dread,
and wondered whether he'd gotten himself into something
disastrous.

But his jet-haired Mary stood beside him, solemn and
determined. She was with child, he knew, and in the winter
he'd see the first of his progeny. That would be seven months
and a long summer's hunt away. He smiled at her, though
she didn't return the smile, wanting only to cling to his arm.
Victoria's medicine had afflicted her too, he thought. He
pressed her warmly, a burly arm around her, letting his
steady strength calm her. She wore her ceremonial clothes
for the occasion, white doeskin tanned to the texture of

velvet, a bright red-beaded headband, bone necklace, and soft summer moccasins poking from under the fringes of her skirt. It melted him. Her incredible beauty always awakened something in him that he called The Glow.

Around them shouting engagés thronged toward the levee, along with tribesmen of every description, but mostly Assiniboin and Cree, with some Blackfeet and Crow too. Here on the neutral ground surrounding the old fort, ancient enemies jostled but did not war. Mister Skye stood quietly in the hubbub, resisting the flow of humanity racing to river's edge. The white vessel carried the annual resupply for the fur company, and in a few hours robe and peltry trading would begin. But it also carried Mister Skye's destiny in the cabins on its boiler deck.

The *St. Ange* answered the fort's booming welcome with its own whistles, shrilling steam into the dry summer air. The pulse of the great riverboat slowed, while tribesmen gaped at this magical thing, and the splashing wheels at each side quieted as the boat nosed toward the levee. Mister Skye could see two blue-suited men high in the pilot house, the bearded LaBarge and his pilot. And another. He studied the other one, faintly startled by the man's wine-colored waistcoat and broadbrimmed green hat. Probably Viscount Gordon Patrick Archibald Frazier, he thought. A fine rill of distaste ran through him. Half the lords of England were fops and dandies; the other half arrogant blockheads. Maybe Frazier was both. He suddenly regretted it, regretted ever being tempted by all that money, and wished he could ride quietly home with his dear women and forget all this.

Too late, he thought somberly. He'd do what he'd agreed to do. The gleaming boat slid the last yards to the bank, riding stilled paddles, and rough deckmen tossed hawsers to the fort's engagés on the bank. Skye watched it all with professional interest. The *St. Ange* looked to be loaded to the scuppers, but all riverboats had that appearance. Two women on the boiler deck caught his eye: a slender flaxen-haired one in a nankeen dress and ostrich-feather hat, the other a glossy-haired stocky brunette in a lavender velvet suit and white jabot at the throat. It amazed him to see women dressed like that. It amazed the savage crowd, too.

Mister Skye surmised that his clients were in no hurry to disembark. At least none of them clamored at the rails while the deck hands dropped long planks from the gangway to the levee, enough planks side by side to afford the passage of a wagon. The foredeck was covered with vehicles, two-wheeled carts mostly, which the hands easily maneuvered down the planks. The mob had turned silent at such strange sights. Rarely had they seen a wheeled vehicle of any sort, and here were dozens being dragged off this ship. Frazier's carts, Skye thought. All of them neatly loaded and battened with canvas wagonsheets or wooden covers.

Then they wrestled a cart with iron-barred sides and a roof, full of squirming dogs that were raising an amazing racket. Frazier's dogs! The lord had mentioned he'd bring some, but Skye had scarcely expected a cartload of them. A squat rumpled man in a liverish suit followed this baying cargo to the levee, and Skye perceived something slavic about him, maybe in his Mongol eyes. Assiniboin women stared warily at the dogs, ready to run. The hound-master trudged to the rear of the cart, pulled a pin that anchored two doors, and dogs spilled out, a blur of brown and tan and black. Everywhere around him, engagés and Indians fled as a wave of dogs whirled and eddied and exploded outward like grapeshot, yapping and barking. Bulldogs! Not a hunting hound in the lot, as far as Skye could see.

He heard wild nasal laughing, and discovered Frazier—it had to be Frazier—wheezing up there at the sight of his mutts bowling over Indians and engagés like tenpins. Skye found himself grinning in spite of his better judgment. Maybe Viscount Frazier had a nasty sense of humor, he thought.

The next cart, enameled white with his lordship's crest blazoned with green and gilt on its sides, the deckhands treated as something holy. Eight of them gathered along its shafts to ease it gently down the planks, and Skye wondered about it, while booting at growling bulldogs that threatened to nip Mary's trim ankles. Reverently, as if unloading the Ark of the Covenant, men rolled the cart downward under the watchful eye of what surely was Frazier's own crew, many of them dressed in some sort of simple black livery.

Behind this cart wobbled a vast, corpulent man Skye instinctively knew was a Briton, square-faced, ruddy, John Bull-shaped, who watched the progress of this glossy cart distrustfully. Mister Skye sidled over, wanting to peer inside to discover whatever precious cargo it contained, and he was not disappointed. As soon as the crewmen had chocked its fine spoked wheels, the cart's steward unlocked the rear doors with a huge brass key to see if anything was amiss inside. Wine! Whiskey! Scotch! Gin! Barnaby Skye gaped at hogsheads of whiskey, and row upon row of bottles fitted tightly in racks that pinioned them firmly. A faint glow built up in Mister Skye, and visions of rendezvous danced in his head.

"Is that stuff booze, Mister Skye?" asked Mary, faint hope illumining her features.

"The world's best, I'd wager."

"Ah. It will be a good hunt."

Next the hands freed a sturdy blue-enameled cart that had been anchored to the foredeck with cleats and cables. This, too, bore Frazier's coat of arms in green and gilt on its sides, and Skye thought the two-wheeled vehicle seemed unusually heavy as he watched sweating men ease it down the gangway. This too was followed by some sort of specialist in Frazier's employ. Once the wagon rested safely on the levee and out of the way, the man unbolted the rear doors, revealing rack after rack of glowing rifles. And below, kegs of powder, pigs of lead, and other paraphernalia. An armorer, the man was Frazier's armorer, thought Skye. He gaped at the chased and engraved weapons, the glowing stocks, and knew he was seeing a fortune in arms. Tribesmen gawked, thunderstruck, at the weapons, and jabbered among themselves about it. Arms to wage an entire war!

Other carts followed bearing nameless burdens beneath their canvas covers. Kitchens, Mister Skye surmised. Provisions. Mess gear—though he knew Frazier wouldn't call it that. Tents and awnings, quarters for Frazier's large staff. One cart seemed to contain nothing but bagged grain; fodder for horses, Skye supposed. Then at last the weary crew tackled the remaining vehicle, this one no cart at all but a yellow-enameled four-wheel wagon of some sort, with what appeared to be a collapsible duck cloth top. A mobile palace. Surely Frazier's home away from home. For himself, no doubt, and those two ladies, whoever they might be. Frazier had not mentioned women, but the presence of two didn't surprise Mister Skye, who well knew the lords of England. That one would take four big harness horses, he thought, wishing he had some clydesdales or percherons. But he had only the mustang stock of the west, trained to drag carts. Plus some big mules he might break to harness en route. The black mules in his own herd might just do, he thought. But they'd take training.

"Mister Skye, I want to go home," whispered Mary. "I don't like this."

"Don't know that I do, either."

How out of place all these gorgeously enameled wagons looked in this rude place, he thought. Behind them vaulted the silvery cottonwood palisade of Fort Union, and surrounding it were the earthy lodges of countless tribesmen and the gaily bedecked savages. The garish carts didn't belong.

Well, this was Viscount Frazier's lark. At last the great hunter and his party congregated on the main deck, as colorful as peacocks except for one gaunt gentleman in funereal black with a frilled white shirt at his throat. Mister Skye knew they'd spotted him, no doubt because Joe LaBarge had pointed him out, and now they hastened down the gangway to earth, looking as alien in this tawny land as hottentots. And dazzling, too. Cree and Assiniboin gaped at the slender blonde woman with her ostrich plumes and squash-colored nankeen skirts. Never had they beheld such a sight! And at the other woman, built of rectangles, with glossy brown hair and mirthful brown eyes, and wearing a lavender velvet suit that rippled sensuously as she walked, as if this lady lived for one thing that every male could instantly discern.

Barnaby Skye held his ground, finding himself wary and afraid. Not since he'd jumped his majesty's vessel of war long ago had he suffered the company of Englishmen. And never a lord.

Frazier turned out to be a portly man, square-faced,

sandy-haired, with those bulging eyes so common among
the British nobility and a cool assessing gaze that missed
nothing. He carried a handkerchief in hand and dabbed at
his bright nose with it, a beak reddened by the expanded
capillaries that told Skye of excessive imbibing of spirits.

"Skye, I presume," he said nasally, not offering a hand.

"It's Mister Skye, sir," Barnaby replied, iron in his voice.

"Well, whatever. Have you done your duties?"

"Duties? Ah . . ."

"The drays. The saddle horses. Good stock I trust."

"The ponies, yes. Uh, mustang blood and mules, small
but hardy." Mister Skye found himself stammering and defensive before this august lord of England, and hated it.
Frazier's very presence here seemed to rob the land of liberty.

"Well, fetch them, fetch them."

"Now? This afternoon?"

"For me to see how you've rooked me."

Barnaby Skye burned, but held his peace. "This is my
wife Mary," he said, an edge on his words. "She's a woman
of the Shoshones, the Snakes."

"Yes," the lord said, examining Mary cursorily.

Mister Skye waited. Before him stood two ravishing
women, dressed for a promenade in Picadilly, whose names
he didn't know. But Lord Frazier did not introduce them,
and Mister Skye realized he didn't intend to. The old class
divisions he'd hated so much slapped at him here, in the
middle of the north American wilds.

Malcolm Clarke, the bourgeois of Fort Union, pushed
through the gawking crowds to greet his guests. Lord Frazier eyed him wearily, seeing simply an unkempt long-haired
man in a baggy black suit and open shirt.

"Viscount Frazier," Clarke said, proffering a hand. "I'm
Malcolm Clarke, in charge of operations here for American
Fur. Please accept the hospitality of the company, and make
yourself at home. I'm at your service."

"Yes, of course," the viscount said, reluctantly taking
Clarke's hand and dropping it instantly. "Very good, Clarke.
This is Viscountess Frazier"—he waved at the flaxen-haired
woman—"and this is Lady Chatham-Hollingshead."

Both women nodded but did not proffer their hands. Mister Skye waited to be introduced, but knew it wouldn't happen. Nearby, engagés and deck hands were offloading the annual resupply of tradegoods, but for once the tribesmen weren't gawking at bolts of cloth and iron pots. These amazing Britons and their bright wagons riveted them, and they huddled around Viscount Frazier and his party, wide-eyed.

"I must see to the shelving of the trade goods. This is our busiest season, but Mrs. Clarke and I would like you and your ladies to join us for dinner in an hour. Mister Skye and his Mary and Victoria will also join us."

Viscount Frazier's gaze settled on Mister Skye briefly. "Really? How extraordinary. With your kind permission, I'll alter the list a bit. This man here"—he waved at the saturnine one in black, with evasive brown eyes that studied people when they weren't looking at him—"is my steward, Aristides Baudelaire, who's responsible for everything. And also, the man there, Colonel Boris Galitzin, master of hounds and horses and the hunt." He waved a languorous hand toward the slavic man in brown tweeds. "We'll all pester you with a few questions at table, eh?"

Clarke nodded. "I must tell Kakokima to set two more—"

"No, no, no, Clarke. Set one less. I'm sure Skye and his squaws will excuse us tonight."

"It's Mister Skye, sir."

"Whatever. You, my good man, will report to Monsieur Baudelaire. He's responsible for all matters, my personal aide and secretary. Fetch us the game, and take us up the Yellowstone to the geysers, and that'll be the sum of your duties."

Baudelaire gazed blandly at Skye from moist brown eyes that hinted of raw power and utter ruthlessness.

Malcolm Clarke refused. "I think, Viscount Frazier, that you would be wise to listen to Mister Skye, and place him in overall command. He and his ladies will share our table."

"Ah, yes. American democracy," said Frazier, unhappily.

Mister Skye listened closely. He had always refused to

guide any greenhorn party that would not heed his counsel. Their lives and safety and comfort depended on it, as well as the lives of his own family and himself.

"Not democracy, sir. Safety," said Clarke. "You've taken pains to employ the best man available in all the American west. It's a dangerous land, sir. Things happen, things that a seasoned man of the mountains can deal with best."

"Yes, of course, Clarke. I've an army, you know. Thirty stout blokes with the world's best arms to fend off a few savages if need be. We'll be quite all right."

Mister Skye said nothing, but he was swiftly coming to a decision.

"I'll ask my wife to set additional places, then."

"Begging your apologies, Clarke, but we'll decline. I've a splendid field kitchen to put to the test tonight; a trial, you might say, eh? I'm sure all your little tales of savages and furs are quite rich, but we'll hear them some other day, eh?"

The bourgeois of Fort Union was taken aback. "As you wish, Viscount Frazier. If American Fur can be of any service—"

"Why, yes, yes. A buffalo. Have you a fresh carcass hanging? We thought to sample it. My chef, the Abbot Beowolf, there, has some notions about a proper herb for the beasts."

Clarke looked nonplussed, but recovered swiftly. "Our hunters brought in two this morning. Yes, I have one hanging."

"Capital, Clarke! I'll send a man. Now you go put your trinkets on the shelves, eh?"

Clarke stared, locked eyes with Mister Skye, and winked. Then he strode off to the trading room to supervise.

Mister Skye peered around him uneasily, missing Victoria acutely now. A knot of Cree squaws collected around some bulldogs. The women were squealing and exclaiming, clapping hands to mouths, at the sight of dogs with the ugliest snouts they'd ever seen. The bulldogs yapped and snapped, triggering shrieks and nervous giggles. Some roamed the levee, sniffing the carts and lifting legs.

"The horses, Skye. Take me to the horses, and fetch me your bills of sale so I can see the rooking I took." He waved at the master of the hounds. "Galitzin, come look."

"Penned behind the fort," Mister Skye muttered.

"Gordon, dear, I think I'll go in there"—the Viscountess pointed toward the fort—"and sit. My toesies are killing me."

But the other lady, the blocky brunette in lavender velvet, chose to join them and walked with an easy stride as they rounded the east palisade of the fort, deep in shadow, and headed toward some pens at the rear. Just what her relationship was to Frazier, Mister Skye couldn't fathom, but he entertained some educated guesses drawn from a London childhood.

"Twelve-foot palisade, wouldn't you say, Galitzin?"

"More than that, your excellency."

"Keeps the savages at bay, eh, Skye?"

"Trading posts are rarely beseiged, sir. The tribes need the blankets and pots and gunpowder too much to risk it."

"So you say. Galitzin here was a cossack colonel for Czar Nicholas, but I filched him a year ago, eh? He's my man in all matters of combat, and you'll take direction from him on questions of safety, the hunt, and care of the beasts."

"Perhaps you didn't read the terms in my letter, Viscount Frazier," rumbled Mister Skye. "I wrote that I'd insist on overall command because your lives and safety, out among the wild tribes and beasts, depend on my experience."

"Of course, of course. I showed it to Galitzin here, and we thought it a bit cheeky, my good man. We're toothed and fanged and all that, Skye."

"It's Mister Skye, sir."

They reached a pen that had been cobbled together from weathered, silvery cottonwood logs. Within, forty-odd wiry mustangs and mules peered at the visitors, many of them small, misbegotten, and mean. They ranged across the spectrum from coyote duns to blacks. Some were ewe-necked. Most roman-nosed. Their enormous tails swept the manure. The croups of some were lower than their withers. Only a few topped fifteen hands.

Viscount Gordon Patrick Archibald Frazier stared, clucking with his tongue. Galitzin sighed. Lady Chatham-Hollingshead laughed heartily. And that ghost who shadowed Frazier, Aristides Baudelaire, watched blandly, his brain obviously calculating advantage and profit.

"Rooked. I knew it." He pointed at a linebacked dun with a forelock so thick it blinded the animal. "Who's the sire and who's the dam?" he asked, and laughed shortly.

"Mustangs, sir," Skye said. "That's all that's to be had in this land. They endure. They've got hard hoofs that will give you no trouble. They're small but tough. The métis—French and Cree or Assiniboin breeds up in British possessions—use them to draw their Red River carts, which are heavier than yours."

"There goes my dream of racing over the prairie on a noble white steed," said Lady Chatham-Hollingshead.

"Patience, Diana. We'll buy others from that chap who runs the fort, whatever his name. Proper mounts. Rooked. You, Skye, have rooked us. I knew it. The cunning of your class. I saw it at once in you."

"And what would my class be?"

"The sailor class. See it in your gait. You manned a British ship—I can tell from your speech. The rogue and ruffian class."

Relief flooded through Barnaby Skye. "Viscount Frazier, the bills of sale are in my kit, some, anyway. Indians don't write bills. If you want the horses I'll draft you a note for the remaining balance, on account with my agent, Colonel Bullock at Fort Laramie. If not, I'll refund the entire amount. I'm sure you'll find another guide here—just ask Clarke—more to your liking."

"But—" sputtered Frazier. Galitzin hawked up spit. Baudelaire smiled gently. Lady whats-her-name pouted. A black-headed bulldog wet cottonwood posts.

And Mary squeezed his arm and peered up into his eyes, her own aglow.

Chapter 3

Viscount Frazier gaped. "But you can't do that. You're in bond to me, Skye."

"I'm doing it."

"You bound yourself."

"I agreed to guide you if you'd agree to certain terms."

"Terms? Terms? Whatever are you talking about, Skye?"

Barnaby Skye grinned. "You read my letter, mate."

The enormous lout gazed insolently at Frazier. The viscount had scarcely taken the measure of the man, but now that he stared into that alarming, uncouth, scarred face he recoiled. Skye had a nose such as Frazier had never seen, an amazing beak, twisted and bulgy, which rose like a hogback between two obscure blue eyes. The ruffian wore his graying hair shoulder-length, and on his head perched a ludicrous black silk tophat, tilted rakishly. He encased his hairy torso in a fringed buckskin shirt, and square-toed boots poked from under buckskin leggins. The sight was so comic that Lord Frazier cackled.

"I say, Skye. I know your type, and I'm glad to be rid of you. I'll send my man along and you give him your draft.

He'll parse your arithmetic and your bills of sale for those jades you call horses, so let's have none of your cunning, man."

"Those ponies are tough, and you'll come to admire them," Skye rumbled. "They're safe enough penned here by day, but you'll want to put a night watch on them when you pasture them yonder. The tribesmen think it's a great honor to snatch a horse."

"I'm sure we'll manage, Skye. Galitzin has managed horses and hounds in places you don't know exist. I've read all about the dubious habits of these natives."

"It's Mister Skye, mate."

"There you go." He chuckled nasally. "Mister Skye. Baron Skye. Lord Almighty Skye, peer of the realm."

Lady Chatham-Hollingshead thought that was hilarious, and laughed gustily, which pleased Frazier.

"I think I'll examine zese beasts," said Galitzin. "Zey interest me."

"Halter's on the rail there," Skye said.

"Yes, Boris. Sort out the rubbish. Keep the rest, if any are worth it. And let me know. I'll have to arrange with that chap—the one that operates this post—for some decent ones."

"Clarke's got none to spare."

The viscount glared. "Stuck with these, am I?"

"Best I could fetch, mate."

"Mind your tongue." He sighed noisily. "Very well then, I'll accept your draft for the balance."

Lord Frazier let the oaf lead them back to the narrow portal at the front of the fort. Skye had a sailor's rolling gait, no doubt about it. But that squaw of his was comely enough, if one were inclined toward dusky savages. Good riddance. He'd fetch another of these rustics, one with fewer airs and a map of the country etched in his thick skull, and that would suffice nicely. There'd be no quarrels with Galitzin about who would be in charge. And he'd cost less too, no doubt.

They rounded the side of the fort, into tangerine sunlight, and found bedlam everywhere. Rivermen and engagés still toted bundles of trade goods from the bowels of the steamer

into the fort, sweating and cursing. Everywhere, half-naked
bronzed Indians gaped and pointed at bolts of scarlet tradecloth, black iron pots, kegs and crates, shining fusils and
spools of bright ribbon. Lord Frazier watched his bulldogs
whip through the hoi polloi, yapping and growling and scattering squaws and children.

Skye and his squaw threaded through the gawking crowds
and into the yard of the compound, while Frazier, Diana
Chatham-Hollingshead, and Baudelaire tagged along. Inside, the raucous sound fell away suddenly, and they found
themselves encased in a deep quiet. The factor's spacious
house looked as if it had been plucked from someplace back
east and shipped up the river. All the rest was easy to iden-
tify: offices, a fur warehouse redolent with acrid robes, a
kitchen wafting scents into the yard, employee barracks,
storage rooms, quarters for a few married couples, a mor-
tared stone magazine near the far bastion. Snug, he supposed. No doubt the Hudson's Bay posts were much the
same. A fortified village.

Skye led them across the dusty yard toward a small pen
that contained the ugliest horse Viscount Frazier had ever
set eyes upon. The distrustful blue roan whickered a greet-
ing at Skye, and Frazier knew at once that this demented
animal, with evil yellow eyes and scars crosshatching his
lumpy body, was Skye's own beast of burden. It fit, he
thought. A lout of a nag for a lout of a man. The horse
lifted its head, bared yellow teeth and shrieked, a note so
shrill it pained Frazier's tender ears.

"I prefer bagpipes," quipped Diana.

"It fits, it fits," Frazier muttered. "His lordship Skye
has got himself a blooded mount."

Baudelaire laughed softly. He always laughed softly, Frazier thought.

A small, crabbed squaw sat on a mound of gear next to
that demonic horse, glaring at them. Lord Frazier was pinioned by the sheer force of her glare, which lanced from
her eyes with some sort of power that made the viscount
uneasy. She'd drawn her jet hair back from her seamed face
and into two braids that tumbled over a shapeless brown
calico blouse.

Skye's other squaw. As rough as the oaf himself. "That's Skye's first wife. He's got two, you know," Frazier said to Diana. "Only decent thing about him."

Lady Diana chortled. "Two's never enough," she said. "Three can be amusing, especially at tiddlywinks." She winked broadly at Frazier.

The viscount found it convenient not to meet the glare of that fierce woman, and watched Skye instead as the guide silently dug into a hide case of some sort—a parfleche, he remembered from his reading—and pulled out a fist full of papers.

The guide squatted down and began totting up figures with a pencil. Obviously he could do figures, which was more than most of his class could manage.

"The horses and mules cost, in dollars, fifteen hundred and forty-three," he rumbled. "I owe nine hundred fifty seven." He dug a nib pen and an inkpot from the parfleche, along with a blank sheet of foolscap, and drafted a note, poking his nib into the pot frequently. So the guide had written his own letters, Frazier thought. It astonished him. He'd been sure, from the fine copperplate, that someone competent had drafted the letters.

Wordlessly the guide stood and handed the draft to Frazier.

"Read this, Aristides, and check his figures against those bills. No doubt I've been rooked."

"If you can't prove that, don't say it," Skye said. "If you say it again, defend yourself."

"I say—" said Frazier, alarmed. This man might lay hand to him. "You're talking to a peer of England. You're asking for a whipping. Have you no manners? I suppose not."

Skye laughed. "It's Mister Skye, Lord Frazier."

"Oh my yes, I quite forgot!"

Diana chuckled.

Aristides Baudelaire studied the draft casually, and yawned. "I suppose it's quite proper, your lordship. It's for the balance, payable by Bullock, the sutler at Fort Laramie. Insured by bloody nose with fist as collateral. Maybe the bourgeois here will honor it."

"If you're satisfied, then we're done," Skye said, still looming like a volcano beside them.

Why was it, Lord Frazier thought, that the man could seem a blooming menace just standing still?

"Oh, I suppose," he said.

Skye's women beamed suddenly, and the old squaw hugged the rustic fiercely. "Now we go? We can go?" she asked, and Lord Frazier discovered a wetness on the woman's cheeks.

"Touching sight, eh, Diana?"

"Where's the scotch?" she retorted.

The guide never looked back. He tied a rope around the jaw of that appalling horse while it squealed and butted him, and then threw on a primitive pad saddle of some sort, and added other gear. Then he opened the gate and led the monster into the yard.

"Stand back, mate."

"I suppose he kicks, eh, Skye?"

"No, he kills."

With that, Barnaby Skye and his squaws threaded through the crates and barrels in the yard, and through the portal into the vast freedom beyond. The lunatic horse clacked its teeth and laid back its ears. As they plunged through the gates, the yard seemed to shrink and become alien, as if Skye's party had filled it with their very presence. It puzzled the viscount.

"I say, that's something for Alexandra's diaries," Frazier muttered. "Wherever she got to. She gets ethereal this time of day. Odd how that brute came so highly recommended, not once or twice, but by everyone. Even Chouteau himself, down in St. Louis. Everyone. Amazing. He's pulled the wool over a lot of eyes, I'd wager. Imagine Pierre Chouteau touting him. And Robert Campbell down there. And that Senator Benton—who's as wild a beast as this one, I hear. And all the rest. It's perfectly astonishing."

Only golden dust and a faint odor of buckskins lingered behind. Viscount Gordon Patrick Archibald Frazier peered about the shadowed yard, wondering what was missing. Something impalpable had departed, gone from the very air.

"Let's find that chap—the one who runs this place. We'll sup with him and his savage bride after all," Frazier said. "I'll want him to fetch us another bloke who knows this country. Aristides, go tell our chaps to try out the field kitchen, and we'll find whatever his name is, the one in command of this place, and tell him we'll favor him at his board."

Bedlam reigned in the plank-walled trading room. A dozen sweating clerks in shirtsleeves pried open crates and untied bales, shelving a year's trading stock. Over the next months this mound of goods would vanish through the small trading window, an aperture between the inner and outer gates of the fort that permitted only one or two tribesmen at a time to dicker.

The mountain of bright blankets and iron pots didn't astonish the viscount so much as the spectacle of the bourgeois—whatever his name was—in shirtsleeves, engaged in menial labor like his underlings. The chap scarcely understood his own position in life. Even as Frazier and his party gaped, clerks stuffed bold blue and red and green blankets, some of them bearing black stripes, onto plank shelves, while one pale clerk kept inventory and checked goods against cargo manifests. Another clerk lifted shining smoothbore fusils from a crate and stood them on a long rack. Others shelved bright ribbons and poured sacks of glass trade beads the size of peas into bins, and set shining knives, awls, axes, hatchets, lance points, cast-iron kettles, fish hooks, and hawk bells into cases.

He cornered the bourgeois as the man stuffed a bolt of striped cotton ticking onto the shelf.

"I say, my good man, we've changed our mind here. We'll sup with you shortly, eh?"

Clarke stood, winded, absorbing that, his glance taking in the viscount, Diana, and Baudelaire. "Well . . ." he muttered, uncertainly. "Viscount, I've told my lady—" He stopped. "I tell you what. I'll have her entertain you all. I can't attend. The trading season opens tomorrow, and this is the busiest moment of the year—we'll be at this almost to dawn. And then we'll have to roll out and start the ceremonies—a shot or two from the six-pounder, some speeches, some gifts to the chiefs, and all that. I beg your forgiveness, sir. But I'll send word over to Kakokima—my wife—''

"But, but, my good man. We need your counsel, eh? We've discharged that lout Skye and want you to fetch us another. Someone more tractable."

"You what?" Clarke was plainly astounded.

"Discharged him. Pitched him out on his ear. Worst ruffian I've ever seen."

Clarke paused, catching his breath. Around them swirled clerks toting trays of pocket mirrors and other gewgaws.

"There's more to this," Clarke said carefully. "Barnaby Skye doesn't suffer fools gladly."

"What? What? Are you saying I'm a—"

"I'm saying that Skye no doubt turned you down. He never risks his life and those of his wives on—well, certain types."

"Whatever. Find us another guide, eh? Any of your company men, eh? They all know the country. We'll pay his wages for you while he serves us, and you'll be ahead."

The man stood silently so long that Frazier wondered if he'd heard. "I don't have a man I'd spare you, Viscount."

"You've men all over here! If you can't spare an English-speaking one, we'll settle for one of these brute French. We speak the tongue."

"None I'd post to your party, sir. Now if you'll excuse me—"

"See here, now, chap. We need a guide."

"You had the best of all," Clarke said wearily.

"A dishonest scoundrel. Those horses—those ill-made nags—why, we were rooked, sir, rooked."

"Barnaby Skye's as good as his word, always, Viscount. And those horses he bought for you—they're something! They'll keep on kicking through trials that would kill domestic ones."

"Oh, pshaw, I know good horseflesh when I see it. Tell you what, my good man. We'll trade these to the company, and you sell us some real horseflesh, eh? We'll add a few quid to make it come out."

"Don't think you heard me, Viscount. Now if you'll excuse me—I'll send word to Kakokima . . ."

"Never mind, never mind. I can scarcely imagine sitting at table with a red woman of the plains. We'll go try out our kitchen and find a guide to place in our service. La-Barge should know of a dozen."

"By all means ask him," Clarke said, returning to his toil. "See me tomorrow afternoon if the company can help you further."

Viscount Frazier wasn't used to being dismissed, but he took it amiably, and they wandered through the narrow portal. Behind them, some clerk swung the heavy gates shut and bolted them, and the lord found himself locked out of civilization and on a treeless steppe with a thousand or two savages milling around conical buffalohide lodges. It alarmed him faintly until he spied the blessed *St. Ange* docked right there and manned by a doughty band of rough rivermen.

"Hudson's Bay would have treated us differently," sniffed Diana. "Where's the scotch?"

Lord Frazier found his entourage camped under the very palisades of the fort in an area that contained no lodges of the savages. He supposed the company insisted on some well defined distance between the skin teepees of the savages and its walls. Galitzin had organized the camp in his usual competent way, with the bright enameled carts parked to one side and tents erected in orderly rows within, most of them at the foot of the palisade. Several of his men had been detailed to roasting quarters of buffalo over two fires.

"Had a devil of a time finding firewood," Galitzin said. "With all zese savages about, we couldn't manage a stick. I finally bought some from some squaws."

The thought of so many savages camped around them made Lord Frazier uneasy. In the low sun he could see an endless forest of amber cones and black lodgepoles, pulsing with life, a pall of cookfire smoke hanging bluely over a huge village of Crees, Assiniboin, and heaven knew what others. He scarcely knew the tribes, in spite of all the bloody reading.

"Where's my lady, Galitzin?" he asked, not seeing Alexandra about.

"Why, she wandered through, poked around in your parlor-wagon zere, and I haven't seen her since."

No sooner had he asked than he spotted her running wildly toward them, weaving among the lodges west of the fort, clutching her yellow nankeen skirts and screaming. Trouble with the savages, he thought.

She stopped before them, gasping, her cheeks wet and her flaxen hair in wild disarray. "Chesterfield," she gasped, trying to catch her breath. "Where's poor little Chesterfield?"

The lady's bulldog. It spent more time in bed with the viscountess than did Lord Frazier, and made twice as much gas.

"In a savage stewpot, I hope," the viscount said.

At which Lady Alexandra sobbed piteously.

"Here now, the pup's about somewhere. Galitzin, where's that pup?"

"Why right zere, gnawing on a buffalo rib, your lordship."

"Chesterfield!" she shrieked, and plunged toward the bewildered bulldog, snatching him from his meat.

Frazier waited patiently. One had always to be patient with Lady Alexandra, especially in her dreamy phases. "Tut tut, Alex. Whatever is troubling you?"

"They eat dogs!" she said, waving a slender arm vaguely. "I saw them. I saw a bulldog's head in a boiling stew, its poor eyes peering out at me. Oh, these bloody beasts!"

"The dogs or the savages, Alex?"

"The savages! Eating our dogs. How could they?"

"Why, it's convenient I suppose. Meat right there on their doorstep."

"Oh, Chester," she cooed. "I won't let them eat you. I'll have them before the magistrates." She carried the wiggling pup to Frazier's parlor-wagon, a bedroom of his own devising that he'd brought clear across the Atlantic, and vanished within.

"Galitzin, we've a little difficulty. That rude fellow who runs this place—can't remember the name—won't trade

good horses for that rubbish back of the fort. And he won't
spare a man for our service, either. These Americans!''

"I've been looking at the horses, your lordship. Zey seem
sound and healthy, and as Skye said, their feet are a marvel.
Hard and solid. Zey're small creatures, but I suspect the
American mustang is more than it seems. I even see some
Arab qualities in them, dished heads, short-coupled bodies.
Ze Spaniards brought them here, you know. And you know
how Arabs fare even in deserts!''

"You're simply excusing Skye and his vile beasts, Galitzin. But I suppose we're stuck with them.''

"I made inquiry about pasture, your lordship, and found
zere's none closer than two miles from here, with all the
tribesmen and their ponies about. Not unless we cross the
river, anyway. So I fed them some oats from our stores, to
get them by, and tomorrow we'll be off. I've posted a night
guard. They'll be safer here within sight.''

"Capital, Boris. Now I've got to track down LaBarge—
is he aboard that packet?—and have him post a guide to our
service. I imagine any riverman will do who knows the land
and where the buffalo are hiding. In fact, the dumber the
better. Never say I learned nothing from dealing with Skye,
Boris.''

But when Frazier pressed Joseph LaBarge to find a suitable guide, the bearded master refused so violently that an
ill-concealed tremor ran through him. In fact he seemed
astounded that the viscount thought so little of Skye.

"Well, LaBarge, we'll go without one, then. It's simple
enough. We'll follow the Yellowstone up to the geysers, and
then come down here again. We don't need a guide when
we have a river, eh?''

"Viscount Frazier—you need Skye.''

"Oh, we know about the savages and all that. I've read
the blooming books. I have trinkets to give them and thirty
well-armed men. Now one more thing, LaBarge. Would
you ferry us across the river tomorrow?''

"You need Skye,'' said LaBarge. "Yes, I'll ferry you to
your doom, if I must.''

Chapter 4

In the blue of dawn, Frazier's men wrestled the carts and wagons back aboard the *St. Ange* while LaBarge's crew built up steam. A mob of Cree and Assiniboin in gorgeous festival dress watched silently. Then the deckmen loosed the packet from its moorings and LaBarge's pilot steered it toward the south shore. No sooner had they cleared land than the fort's cannons boomed sharply, a Yankee flag scurried up a pole, and the fort's bourgeois and clerks, in black suits and shining boots, emerged for the ceremonies preceding the new trading season.

"They could scarcely wait for us to be off," Lord Frazier said to Baudelaire as they stood at the foredeck rail.

"The Americans are fond of money," Baudelaire replied.

On the barren south shore of the Missouri, just above its confluence with the Yellowstone, LaBarge's deckmen jury-rigged a gangway to a gentle bank. Frazier's men unloaded the carts and the wagon once again, then drove forty-two mustangs and mules to shore. Baudelaire settled with

LaBarge—the price was ten pounds—while the party trooped down to the bank.

Galitzin set to work at once, shrewdly guessing which mustangs were saddle horses and which were trained to harness. The packet's whistle shrilled, and a thunderous vibration and splashing drew the ship out into the main channel. LaBarge waved amiably from the pilot house, and in a few minutes the *St. Ange* had crossed to the north shore.

Not even the hubbub of neighing horses and rattling harness and shouting men allayed the sudden dread that raced through Viscount Frazier as he stood on the hushed and alien shore. Across the wide Missouri lay the only safe harbor in a wild unknown land.

"I say, Aristides, I rather miss that vile place."

"We've brought our amenities with us, my lord. Would you and the esteemed ladies care for something cold and wet?"

"This shore. There's absolutely nothing. Even the Opposition fur post a few miles down is across the river. I have the strangest sensation, Aristides. As if swarthy men will rise out of the sagebrush and send arrows into us."

One by one, Galitzin and his men backed wild-eyed mustangs between the shafts of the carts and hitched them. Other men settled light English saddles over the bony backs of the little horses. One or two of the ugly brutes humped and bucked, but most accepted their burdens calmly.

"You see? Skye sold us better horses than they look, your lordship," said Galitzin. "And more than the forty we required. Two spares, including those mules. I can't fathom what ze mules do, but I fear zey're pack beasts. I've a notion to break them to harness, but I have to see how the teams zere pull your wagon first."

"Quantity for quality," the viscount quipped. "Spares. Have you found a nag suitable for myself? And Lady Diana?"

"Not yet," Galitzin said, returning to his labors.

"This place makes me shiver," Diana said.

"There's nothing amiss," Lord Frazier replied. He peered closely at distant red bluffs magnified by transparent air, at silent steppes lifting upward from the great river, at silvery bunchgrass. A raptor circled far off to the south; eagle or hawk, he thought. "It's because we don't have the fort's protection now," he said.

"I dreamed of riding a charger so fast he'd leave any savages far behind," she said. "But I suppose I'll be riding a mule."

In fact, that's what Lady Diana Chatham-Hollingshead ended up with for a mount. Galitzin discovered the four mules were saddle animals. The lady, wearing bold yellow riding attire with brown velvet trim, bounded up on a long-eared black beast, and howled. "Here we go," she said, steering the wily creature into reluctant figure eights.

Galitzin selected a good fifteen-hand dun for Lord Frazier, and then they were off. The viscount rode out to the right to see his gaudy caravan, bold scarlet and blue and green carts creaking over land where no wheeled vehicle had ever rolled. They made a gorgeous picture, gleaming enameled carts strung in a long line, each with his family coat of arms on the side, a stag's head caboshed on a barry-bendy ground. He watched the yellow parlor-wagon, driven by a coachman with a postilion riding to the left and forward, while his thin blonde viscountess peered from a window. Perfectly gaudy, he thought, against a desert land hued dun and gray and ochre, and a bleached blue heaven. It'd be a splendid hunt.

That afternoon they angled across a humped nose of land just above the confluence of the great rivers, and coiled down a sudden grade to the wooded bottoms along the west bank of the Yellowstone, which flowed due north just there. They found a well-worn trace along the bank and pushed south, up the turbid river, encountering no difficulty of any sort. With each passing mile, Lord Frazier grew more exuberant. For a day or two they'd travel up the river, getting his company accustomed to the daily drill. And after that, he'd hunt. He gazed keenly at the mysterious brown ridges, seeking the black giants of the North American plains, but saw none. He knew he would soon.

Behind him the carts rolled effortlessly, well organized by the valuable Colonel Galitzin. They wouldn't need a guide! They wouldn't stray far from the great river, going

out or returning, though he wasn't sure just where the geysers were up near the headwaters. No matter. He'd find
some savage to take them. A lot of them spoke a bit of
English, he'd read. The lord counted it a blessing to be rid
of that bounder the Americans thought so highly of. A
blessing not only to his purse, but to his entire company.

Their riverbank passage took them on occasion through
gloomy groves of cottonwoods, rising to majestic heights
above them, leaving the earth littered with shaggy bark and
branches. The stuff burned with a foul odor, he'd noted
back at the fort, but seemed plentiful, and would fuel their
cookfires all along the way. The shade of the giant trees
cooled them, and kept the fierce sun—why did it burn into
flesh so intensely at this high altitude?—off their faces and
hands. Up on the rocky steppes he spotted yucca and prickly
pear cactus, and down along the river grew chokecherry and
hackberry, willow and box elder as well as the shimmering
cottonwood trees. Along much of the high Missouri they'd
spotted white-rumped antelope and mule deer, and an occasional elk as well, and now along the Yellowstone they
found the same species in great abundance. Capital, he
thought. They'd feast on venison tonight.

He summoned his armorer, Gravesend, and had a Manton rifle brought him. The next stag, he thought, would turn
into a roast. Bucks they called the males here. The next
buck. The fine British steel felt sweet in his dry hands. He
clasped it, and the burnished maple stock, with sensuous
delight. Suddenly his dread lifted, the dark anxiety that had
hung over him like the queen's displeasure since the fort
had vanished behind them. Fondling a loaded piece fanged
a man and drove fear out of his skull. He peered back and
found his retainers subdued and fearful, just as he had been,
and knew at once the solution.

"Gravesend," he commanded. "Hand out arms to those
who want them. We'd best have a few in hand anyway, to
deal with the savages."

"Very good, sir. I've those Colt Dragoon revolvers we
purchased from the chap in Connecticut. They'll feel good
tucked into a man's belt, I imagine."

"Tell the men they'll be docked if they lose them," the

viscount cautioned. "You'll be counting them each evening, I trust, Gravesend?"

"Of course, sir."

No sooner were the weapons distributed than the viscount felt a great wave of relief among the men behind him. Their silence melded into hearty conversation and occasional laughter. Who needs a guide, he thought. A little common sense, a little muddling through, a little applied intelligence would see them along. Why hadn't he thought of that earlier? Why hadn't Galitzin?

They would make six or eight miles that day, enough for the first time out. He didn't want to gall those scruffy mustangs or chafe men's feet in new boots. Diana joined him, cussing her black mule, even though she had taken to admiring its huge rotating ears. She had her chased damascus fowling piece sheathed on her saddle.

"Let's fetch us our supper," he said.

"I'm game."

"That you are, and I'll cook you later," he rejoined. "But now we've got to get ahead and drop some stags."

"Bucks."

"Whatever. There you go, sounding like Skye."

He kicked his wiry dun into a bone-jarring canter, but she fell behind at once, cussing her dainty-footed black steed.

"I don't think he likes to run," she said. But she whipped the surly mule into a trot, and in twenty minutes the two were a mile or so ahead of the caravan, walking their mounts silently through a grassy park surrounded by giant trees.

"I've seen the harts all day, scampering one way or another. We'll find some, eh? I don't suppose you plan to shoot one with that piece of yours."

"Gordon, it's your piece that drops things," she said, laughing bawdily.

They were enjoying that, and working themselves toward some tiddlywinks in the grass, when eleven brown savages in breechclouts emerged from river brush, each of them pointing a bow with a nocked arrow at the viscount and his lady.

* * *

Old Victoria's spirits lifted when they left Fort Union behind them. All the time they'd lingered there, waiting for the strangers from across the great water, she'd felt a weight on her bony chest heavier than a cast-iron kettle. Her medicine, the magpie helper, had shown her clearly what would happen when those people from Mister Skye's own land employed him. It would be something worse than death for her, Mary, and Jawbone. Much worse. It had made her weep in the night, and resist her man for the first time ever. It had darkened each day and made each rising and setting of the sun a thing that took them closer to the doom that awaited them.

Magpie had come to her in the moon of falling leaves, long ago, strutting boldly about her as she drew water from the Platte River. Magpie had alighted directly on her head, and pecked her once. Then Magpie had flown away, far into a distant tree, and made raucous noises. Victoria had known at once Magpie had a thing to show her, so she had left Mister Skye and climbed a bluff and spent three suns fasting. Her vision had come with a frosty dawn that lay gray and icy over the naked land. They would hold Mister Skye like an eagle with clipped wings, hold him among them and then take him far across the waters to the land where he was born, and keep him there. Keep him in a dark place until he died, longing for his family, for his sits-beside-him wife, his Mary, his medicine horse, Jawbone, and the feel of an open land without fences about him. And that is how life would go on, not only for Mister Skye, far away, but for Victoria, who would never hug her man again, never feel him warm beside her in the buffalo robes, in their own lodge; and the same for Mary of the Snakes, who would never again see Mister Skye. And all the worse for Jawbone, who would pine for Mister Skye, not eat, not drink, not run over the hills, and die.

All these things she saw, and knew they were more terrible than death because they were a living death without end. She could not tell Mister Skye she had seen this; he would scoff, and say it was only a phantasm and not the real world where the sun rose and set. But she knew anyway, knew Magpie had shown her the turning of the circle, and so the old woman had slid into a deep mourning, a widowhood that lacked only death.

But now she witnessed a miracle. Here was her man, Mister Skye, riding Jawbone out of Fort Union, leaving these countrymen of his behind him. He rode through the portal of the fort, and she felt some tension within her ebb away, as if she was leaving a prison behind her. Outside, Mister Skye peered into the lavender twilight of the June night and turned Jawbone east. His women followed. He rode straight past the encampment of the Britons, past those bright wagons and men in identical dark britches and shirts, past the thin blonde woman in the squash-colored cotton dress. The woman waited for him to stop, to say something, to become their guide again, but he didn't. They gawked at him as he rode past, saying nothing, keeping all their dark thoughts to themselves. And Victoria felt joy.

She knew where he was going, and followed behind gladly. He steered the terrible horse gently through the lodges of her people's enemies, the Assiniboin, while the people around them stared at him and Victoria and Mary. They all knew of Mister Skye, and of his medicine horse. Then at last they came to the end of the lodges and he rode eastward across barren clay stripped of every blade of buffalo grass, and finally turned north up a broad coulee with broken sandstone ledges along its periphery. Mister Skye's two black pack mules and Victoria's and Mary's ponies would be there, along with their lodge and possessions, guarded by two Cree boys who were eager to serve the man with the terrible medicine.

Mister Skye found them and the ponies, and paid the boys with a packet of precious gunpowder and six lead balls apiece, a handsome reward. The boys grinned, and danced happily back toward the fort two miles distant.

"Well, ladies, we're far from home and unemployed," he said, a gleam in his obscure blue eyes.

"I am glad!" Victoria cried, speaking up for the first time in many days.

He eyed her affectionately, aware of her feelings. "Is that your medicine barking at me?" he asked amiably.

For an answer she beelined to him as he clambered down
from the blue roan, and hugged her man fiercely.

"That's more than medicine," he said, hugging her.
"Whatever was troubling you, it's past, old lady."

"I don't like this place," she said, her voice muffled by
his pungent elkskin shirt. "It is the place of our enemies.
The river Absaroka come here, but not my people, not the
Kicked-in-the-Bellies. Let's go to Absaroka, Mister Skye.
Let's swim the Big River and go. Right now."

Something of her terror lingered in her and she could
think only of flying, of breaking camp and riding down to
the great river and making a raft of their lodgepoles and
swimming their horses across, away from those people from
across the sea.

"Right now!" she cried. "Right now!"

"Belay yourself, Victoria. I've a mind to do something
else. We haven't a dime in our accounts with the colonel
now. Gave the whole amount back. It's a hard month of
travel back to Fort Laramie—bad time with war parties running. And when we get back there, end of July or so, it'll
be too late to pick up a client."

She listened quietly, wondering as she always did why
Mister Skye needed clients, wondering why he guided
whitemen at all, when all he needed was a little powder and
ball, which he could buy with robes she and Mary tanned.
They could live out their days with her people in the heart
of Absaroka, the most beautiful land at the middle of the
earth.

"But maybe we can fetch a client over at Fort William,"
he went on. "Opposition boat isn't in yet. Who knows
who'll be looking for a guide when it comes? I'll see what
Joe Picotte has to say. We'll camp there a few days anyway,
until the boat comes. It's the one chance we've got for a
client this season."

The Harvey, Primeau and Company adobe trading post
lay down the Missouri a mile or so below the confluence of
the rivers. Only a half hour's ride. The companies opposing
the giant American fur had come and gone, she knew. The
great Rocky Mountain Fur Company had tried it; later, Fox

and Livingston. But none had weathered the ruthless competition of Pierre Chouteau's Upper Missouri Outfit.

"Mister Skye," she pleaded. "I still got damn bad feelings. We got to go away from here."

He patted her affectionately. "One quick stop for a talk with Picotte."

She turned silently to her packing, not liking it a bit. That sinister vision still haunted her, piercing every corner of her soul and aching old body, not leaving her as it should now that he'd escaped from the ones with the bright carts.

They left in a blue dusk with a green streak of light still lingering in the northwest: Mister Skye, massive and comforting on Jawbone, his senses reading the twilight; Mary on her light gold pony, young and vibrant; old Victoria, hunched over her rail-thin bay mare; and the two pack mules, each carrying a heavy burden in panniers on pack-saddles.

With each step eastward, Victoria's spirits revived. She wanted distance and more distance between Mister Skye and his childhood people, before they came with snares and brass collars to capture him like a black bear in an iron cage. They rode a short distance along the shore on a well-hammered trace, and soon the adobes of the opposing post loomed up at them. This one had fewer lodges gathered about it, but across the flats were eighty or a hundred, the bands of chiefs who'd been successfully wooed by Picotte or Harvey, usually with extravagant gifts of tobacco and whitemen's suits or blue soldier uniforms, which the chiefs loved as a mark of their warrior status.

The towering plank gates had been shut for the night here too, but Mister Skye's sharp hammering brought young Picotte himself, a lantern in hand.

"Want company, Joe?" Mister Skye asked at the eye peering through the cracked door.

"Barnaby Skye! Sure do, you old coon. I haven't a thing to wet your whistle, but the *Mary Blane*'s overdue. It's above Fort Clark, and that's all I know. They're badly overloaded."

"That's what I heard," said Mister Skye. "I'm looking for a client, if any are wanting a guide."

"Well, come in and we'll palaver," the bourgeois said.

A few minutes later they were ensconced in one of the guest rooms, and the horses and mules were safely corraled in a corner of the yard.

"We're out of coal oil and candles, except what's in that lamp, so I guess we'll just talk in the dark," Picotte said.

Which suited Victoria fine. She loved the soft June night with its restless, eddying air.

"I'm busted," said Mister Skye to his host. "We turned down some porkeaters that would have got us butchered."

"I know about them. Went over myself this afternoon to gawk at those carts and saw how the stick floats. I think maybe you done right, Mister Skye."

"It didn't help my Big Dry any, Joe. Are you sure you don't have—"

"We can't bring the stuff into Indian country, Mister Skye."

Picotte laughed. Mister Skye bellowed. In a moment the pair of them were roaring and bawling like sore-toothed grizzlies, and Victoria glared at the two giants, not understanding whitemen.

Her dark vision refused to leave her mind.

Chapter 5

Savages. Lord Frazier peered wildly about him, and knew he would die. A great sob erupted from him. He, the seventh viscount, a peer of the realm, would feel arrows pierce deep, deep through him, through his vital parts, and that would be the last he'd ever know.

Beside him, Diana burst into tears. He could no longer choke back his own, and that added to his terror and shame. These savages wore paint, greasy black and white chevrons across their wide cheeks, slashes of vermilion on their foreheads. A war party. He knew that much from his readings. And he would die. He flinched, feeling the arrows pierce his tender flesh even before they were loosed.

"I'm going to die," Diana cried. "They'll kill us. Talk to them. I'll do anything, anything—"

Resignation flooded through Lord Frazier, and he felt himself sagging in the saddle, his soul half departed from his doomed body.

One of the savages, a six footer with his jet hair in two braids and a single eagle feather stuck at a rakish angle in his tightly bound hair, walked toward them, the arrow in his drawn bow never wavering from Frazier's chest.

Here it comes, he thought wildly. Not even time to make peace with God. Here it comes!

The savage was a giant, with shoulders as wide as an ox, arms like mizzen-masts, and hands the lord knew could rip him out of his saddle and pulverize his soft flesh in an instant.

The savage spoke in a rumbling voice. Harsh, peremptory words the viscount couldn't fathom. Oh, for a translator, one of these rustics who knew the tongue of this one—whatever tribe he came from. Frazier realized he hadn't the faintest idea which tribe. The savage barked something and the viscount gaped, utterly lost.

Then the savage motioned violently, his arms describing harsh arcs, and this time Frazier understood. He eased out of his saddle, trembling, and slid toward the grass, almost collapsing because his legs refused to prop him. So they'd march him off to a tree and fill him with arrows, he thought.

The savage barked at Diana, some explosion of words, and she crept down, weeping all the while. "They'll have their way with me," she cried.

The leader herded them away from the dun pony and the mule, and then several savages pounced at the animals, grabbing reins, snatching at the sheathed rifle and shotgun, exclaiming at the beauty of the burnished stocks and chased barrels and locks. Swiftly they probed everything else, the scrimshawed powder horns, the pouches of shot and wadding, the mercury fulminate caps, the lord's splendid hunting knives—

The knives. Surely they would scalp him, he thought, his terror ballooning. They'd grab his sandy hair and run a knife brutally across his forehead, and over his ears and around the back of his head, then pull violently; and he'd feel his hair popped from him and his skull naked to air, and a ghastly pain.

And Diana. They'd lift her glowing chestnut locks while she screamed, and they'd run the tip of a knife around her skull, an act so disfiguring she's go berserk, then leave her heaped on the ground, her remaining flesh bleeding.

The tension gripped him so severely that his body ceased to work; his lungs refused to pump, his heart pulsed faster and faster until its rhythm disappeared and he felt only a hum in his chest and a deepening paralysis. Death, then.

But it didn't come. Not quite yet. The leader, the giant savage, cat-footed to Diana and snatched her hat from her head, exclaiming in his strange tongue at the creamy ostrich plumes curving majestically back from the brown crown. He drew a plume through his fingers, exclaiming, grunting, waving this strange trophy before the others, who flocked around to see this exotic thing.

Just then yet another warrior, this one on a spotted gray pony with chalky handprints pressed into its chest and stifles, rode out of the river brush. He wore only a breechclout, like the others, and bore the scars of battle on his bronzed body: long puckered scars slashing across his ribs and arms and creasing one calf. This one spoke something sharp, and pointed back on the river trail. Lord Frazier knew at once this one had discovered the caravan, perhaps two miles back, and was telling the others.

The caravan! If only he could survive until it arrived, until his thirty men and his Cossack colonel could drive these beasts away! But he knew it would never happen. A half hour separated him from that plodding column. Still, he had to try something, anything . . .

"Do you chaps speak English?" he asked, his voice squeaky and unnatural. Oh why couldn't he act like a proper Englishman, like a lord, like a peer of the realm?

They stared, saying nothing. If anyone understood, he didn't reveal it. Frazier desperately wished he'd learned the finger language of the plains. He'd read that all these tribes could talk with it, and most of the rough fur trappers and traders knew it too. But he lacked even a rudimentary knowledge. He'd been hasty. Oh, for a guide. For any brute who could placate these savages! Oh, for a company of kilted pipers, screaming out the fierce bloody howl of a hundred bagpipes, a sound that sent shivers through any auditor, civilized or barbaric.

The leader took hold of Viscount Frazier's fine knife,

with its Sheffield steel blade glinting in the dappled light, and approached him.

It's coming, my own blade into my bowels, he thought wildly. The savage stopped just before the peer of England, smiling faintly.

"Anything. I'll give you anything!" the viscount croaked.

But the warrior simply motioned. He wanted the viscount to do something, but Frazier couldn't fathom what. Then the savage flicked the knife at a button, terrifying the lord. Others of these brutes swirled around Diana, fingering her velvet riding habit while she whimpered piteously.

"I'll bloody well have you whipped," he cried.

The savage patted the lord's hunting jacket, a plum-colored tweed with leather elbow patches and sleeves, and motioned.

The coat, the coat. The brute wanted his coat. The lord swiftly shed it with trembling arms that wouldn't work right, and handed it to the beast. Lady Diana fared no better. Two of them wrestled her beautiful velvet coat off her while she shrieked and struggled.

"They're attacking me!" she cried.

He couldn't help that. He watched, frightened, as they wrestled her to the grass and pulled her velvet split skirts off, leaving her in white drawers, and danced around with the handsome skirt. Next they tugged at her soft boots, of finest English leather, and popped them off while she groaned, awaiting her fate.

The powerful leader slid Frazier's jacket on, but found it too small, and pulled it off. He pointed at the lord's shiny boots, and Frazier sat in the grass tugging them off. The savage examined them curiously and tossed them aside, and pointed at the lord's britches.

"Not my pants," he cried, but he had no choice. The Sheffield blade waved ominously under his nose.

Moments later he sat naked in the grass, as white as a fish belly, while the savages swiftly gathered everything he had possessed and divided the plunder among themselves. Beside him huddled Diana, equally bereft, but with flesh not so pale.

"They're looking at me," she muttered.

Lord Frazier thought wickedly that on other occasions his lady rakehell would not only have been amused, but probably would have approved and been eager for whatever came next. But now she clutched herself with arms that hid little, and sobbed.

The one on horseback barked a sharp command and the savages fled with their booty, leading away the horse and mule as they vanished silently into brush.

Lord Frazier gaped. Alive. He and Diana lived.

But she had spotted something, and her pointed finger steered him to an awful spectacle. On the sunny bluff above stood a line of horses, more than he could count, scores of them, and on each pony sat a brown warrior, some wearing little more than a breechclout and feather. Several others wore magnificent war bonnets of eagle feathers, with long tails of feathers reaching clear to the ground at the feet of their restless ponies. Frazier shuddered. Never had he witnessed, or imagined, such barbaric splendor. He was too rattled to count, but knew instinctively he saw hundreds, hundreds of savages on ponies, bearing bows and arrows, rifles, lances, and lethal-looking warclubs. Enough well armed warriors to overwhelm his little caravan, toiling along back there somewhere.

He stared, frozen, expecting the crack of rifles and the hoarse cries of battle. Instead, a leader, one of the bonneted ones, lifted an arm, and the whole column of savages wheeled westward, away from the river bottoms and out of sight.

Lord Frazier felt terror drain from him like ale from a keg. Alive. Both of them. Even if the devils had snatched everything they possessed, and he and Diana were as bare as Adam and Eve in this paradise. She grinned at him from a face wet with tears, and he marveled at her pluck.

"Go fetch me some clothes, Gordon, and don't let those bastards see me. I'll have them whipped if they stare."

"But I can't walk up to the carts like this—I can't even walk at all on these sticks!"

"You'll have to, Gordon. You can wear a leaf or two if you wish." She laughed wildly, her guffaws sounding like sobs.

He rose and began his march to the rear, mustering whatever dignity he could manage, knowing he'd bloody well
find that Skye and tell him to guide them.

Under a flat gray sky that threatened a drizzle, Mister
Skye worked downwind of a small herd of buffalo, about
ten miles from Fort William. He and his ladies would make
meat while they waited for the *Mary Blane* and whatever it
might bring for a client. They'd spotted the herd to the
north, black dots grazing a still-green swale in an endless,
empty land, and had hastened eastward at once because the
beasts were directly downwind.

Victoria rode her bay pony beside Skye, while Mary
herded the two packmules which had been brought along to
cart much of the meat and the summer hides back to the
fort. Victoria's spirit lay as gray as the low clouds. She
didn't want to be here in this land of the Lakotah, Cree and
Assiniboin, her people's enemies. The blackness that had
settled over her with her medicine vision refused to lift,
even though the people from Mister Skye's land across the
waters had left. She wondered at it, why her spirits remained as dark as before. She squinted angrily at horizons
and ridges, seeking out menace along them, but didn't find
any. The land slumbered through a chill, sullen afternoon
without even a wolf or coyote to disturb it.

She'd resigned herself to his will. She always felt proud
to be the sits-beside-him wife of Mister Skye, and wherever
he went, there would she go also. But she'd never known a
time when her heart lay so heavy within her, and she glanced
at her man often, wondering when he would be snatched
away from her forever.

He circled around the herd and then approached from the
southeast, well out of the wind. They topped a ridge and
spotted the small herd grazing quietly two hundred yards
ahead, and hastened back down the slope, keeping out of
sight. Mister Skye drew his Hawken from its beaded elkskin
sheath, gathered his tied shooting sticks and possibles, and
crept back up the slope and over it on hands and knees while
Victoria waited in the humming quiet. A few moments later
the Hawken boomed once, and not again. Mister Skye rarely

wasted a shot, she knew. His head rose above the ridge and he motioned them forward. She and Mary topped the shoulder and saw a downed cow, still spasming, and the remaining buffalo trotting away.

She and Mary set to work at once, cutting out the tongue and peeling back the hide. She wanted a whole hide this time, not a split, to repair their lodge, so Mister Skye and Jawbone helped them roll the big cow over so they could peel hide from its underside. They cut out the humpmeat along the boss ribs, and the backfat, and the valuable sinews that ran down the back. Then they sawed tender meat from the front quarter, until they had all that the two mules could carry. They'd feast at the fort that night, she knew. And she'd have a light hide to scrape and tan and sew into the lodge, and a worn, smoke-cured hide from the lodge to turn into fine moccasins that would turn water.

But she didn't rejoice at this bounty as she normally did. She labored silently beside Mary, who had learned not to try to cheer Victoria while they lingered in this land of their enemies. She would not be cheered. Done at last, they abandoned the red carcass to the two coyotes and circling raptors that had watched and argued, and rode through a somber afternoon to the fort, Victoria's spirits as gloomy as the low heavens.

She knew, even before they walked their ponies through the massive gates, that Mister Skye was lost. Her medicine told her so; a powerful knowing so intense it wracked her small body until she hurt badly. But Mister Skye knew none of it, and steered Jawbone easily into the trading post.

She saw them at once, the two who had come from across the great water, whose names were almost unpronounceable to her: Boris Galitzin and Aristides Beaudelaire, standing beside the factor, Joe Picotte.

"Ah, there you are, Skye," said Galitzin. "We've been looking. Zey told us at the other post you were here."

"It's Mister Skye."

"Yes. I forget. We've urgent business, Mister Skye. We've had a little brush with some savages—not the body of us, actually, but his excellency—in which zey made off with his horse and embarrassed him. He's gone quite daffy about it, though we scarcely see what all the trouble is. At any rate, sir, he sent us back at once with his commission. He wants you and your ladies to guide him at any price, under your terms.''

"No."

Victoria heard Mister Skye's resolute reply, and dared to hope a bit. In all her days, she'd never stared at other mortals with such pain and dread.

"Ah, I have a note from his lordship." The colonel dug into the pocket of his new hunting jacket and produced a scrap of foolscap. "It says you are to be in charge."

Mister Skye read it, frowning, while Victoria tried to read his thoughts.

"And this, of course, sir. He's returning your draft on Bullock's account," Galitzin said.

Mister Skye took it. He seemed lost in thought.

"Let us go to Absaroka at once, Mister Skye. My medicine helper speaks."

He turned toward her, his obscure eyes searching her brown ones with an intensity she'd never experienced. "Aye, I've always heeded that, Victoria . . ."

His very gentleness saddened her.

"We're camped a dozen miles away, on the west bank of the Yellowstone," Baudelaire said hastily.

"What happened?"

Baudelaire smiled amiably. "Why, a minor fright. His lordship rode ahead with the lady, and a few savages stopped him and took a few things. He felt the need of someone who could translate."

Mister Skye didn't answer for some while. "What do you wish, sir?" he asked the man in the prim black suit.

"It'd be helpful. Of course it was all exaggerated. His lordship took it too seriously."

Mister Skye turned toward the colonel. "Galitzin. You're a colonel, used to command. How do you feel bearing a note that places me over you?"

"I don't know that it does, Skye. You'll be dealing with the savages is all."

"You've both made light of what happened."

"Why, we both think Lord Frazier's quite unbalanced,

and calmer heads ought to prevail. Now if you'd rather not, we'll head back and tell him that you've turned us down, and—''

"I'll talk to him."

Victoria felt herself go faint. She glanced at Mary, who stood tautly, taking in all this too. Already she felt a kind of widowhood settle over her, saw in her head the vision she'd had of Mister Skye being carried off, never to return to her arms. Her man stared at her unblinkingly, and for once she couldn't meet his eye because her own spirit groaned inside of her.

"I'm sure you know the tribe that stole the horse from the viscount, Colonel?"

"We haven't the faintest idea, Skye. His lordship says that the chiefs wore eagle-feather bonnets with long tails of feathers that reached clear to the hooves of their ponies."

Lakotah, thought Victoria at the description of her people's ancient enemy.

"Sioux," said Skye. "I wonder which." He stared at the two men solemnly. "You've not told me everything. You've made light of this, although I imagine the viscount came to the edge of death. Something changed his mind about the value of my services. You've come here on his instruction, but you're doing your duty half-heartedly, eager for me to refuse. You both are disloyal to your employer, then."

"Why—why—you've put a twist on it," said Galitzin. Baudelaire merely smiled and nodded.

"I hear," said Skye.

Victoria loathed them both, but she knew Mister Skye had discerned their true nature and would not be fooled.

"We'll go talk to Frazier presently," he said. "You go ahead and tell him how it went here. How truly you described his ordeal to me, and how hard you struggled to persuade me."

Baudelaire nodded and smiled.

"—And I'll correct matters when we get there," Skye added.

Baudelaire smiled blandly again, but Galitzin glared.

Victoria knew Mister Skye was politely calling them liars, and worse, disloyal men. They enraged her. No warrior of the People would betray a sacred trust like these whites.

"Oh, Colonel Galitzin. Your safety doesn't depend on rifles, but on diplomacy. Any of the tribes can gather well-armed warriors by the thousand, and form them into the best light cavalry in the world. Perhaps you were unaware of that. Surely your men are. One reckless shot, and they'll never see England again."

"I'm sure your melodramatics will have their effect on Lord Frazier, Skye, and you'll be our general."

Victoria watched them trot out of the fort, and knew Mister Skye had accepted. He would have to deal with those conniving men all the time he guided them. Dourly, she watched him give some of the meat to Picotte as a gift, and then they took off. They would reach the viscount's camp four hours after Picotte's engagés ferried them across the Missouri. She'd lost, but she knew she would never speak of it again. In the few days remaining of her life with Mister Skye, she would watch over him fiercely, as she always did. But she would not sleep in his lodge. Mister Skye's lodge would be dark.

Chapter 6

When Mister Skye, Mary, and Victoria rode into the camp the Britons had made on a grassy flat along the Yellowstone, Viscount Frazier saw them through different eyes. Barbaric splendor, he thought, discovering safety and comfort in the guides he had supposed he could do without. Mister Skye and his women had not followed the river trace at all, but had emerged as silently as stalking panthers out of a long coulee above the camp.

Galitzin and Baudelaire had returned hours earlier, telling him they'd found Skye and had engaged him. They seemed amused about it, and Lord Frazier scented mockery in Baudelaire's attitude. Both of them had treated the episode as a bloody joke. But it hadn't been funny. He'd limped along toward the caravan, waving a box elder branch before him like a figleaf in the Uffizi Gallery, the rubble along the way biting at his naked feet. He'd worried too about leaving Diana behind, fearing the savages would return and diddle her. Then at last, as the caravan hove into sight, snaking through a grove of looseknit cottonwoods, he'd dodged behind a hackberry bush.

"Galitzin!" he had cried, waving a bare arm and peering around the tree.

Galitzin had reined up, stared, and snickered. "Would your excellence like me to hold up the column while you and the lady, ah—"

"Galitzin, the savages! They stripped us and stole our duds. Go fetch clothing for Lady Diana and me, eh? And stop the men. I'll—I'll have words with you if you let this be known."

It had taken Galitzin an hour to stop the column, fetch clothing, and rescue the viscount and Diana, who'd grown snappish while slapping deer flies behind a chokecherry thicket. The story had raced through the column in spite of Lord Frazier's interdict. Everywhere the louts he'd engaged were smirking. And no one simpered more than Baudelaire, who'd hinted that maybe his lordship's horses had drifted off while his lordship was enjoying the attentions of his lady.

Not even his own Alexandra believed him. "Gordon, dear, you shouldn't indulge yourself in the middle of the morning," she'd lectured.

But now Skye approached, some palpable barbaric force emanating from his solid body. It was that ineluctable presence again, the thing the viscount had felt at the fort. The man seemed to own this wild land and traveled through it like some lord of the wilderness, that silk top hat jauntily perched over his shoulder-length hair and that black Hawken cradled like a firstborn in his massive arms. Gladly, gladly, would Lord Frazier entrust his life to such a man.

They halted before him, Skye and his women, the old one glaring ominously straight through him, and the two pack mules, one dragging a travois of lodgepoles.

"Will you meet my terms, sir?" Skye asked without so much as a hello.

"Gladly, Mister Skye. I've had a scrape that taught me a bit."

"Did it teach the rest?"

"Lady Chatham-Hollingshead, yes."

"Tell me exactly what happened."

Odd how the man addressed him without a *please* or a

your lordship. "Ah, later, eh?" he replied, peering about at Alexandra, Diana, Galitzin, and Baudelaire, who smirked beside him near the yellow parlor-wagon. But Skye's stare, striking him like pikes, changed his mind, at least a bit.

"Ah, the lady and I rode ahead a mile or two, intending to shoot a stag—ah, buck—and all of a sudden there they were. Savages! A swarm of them. They snatched everything, ah, quite everything, and rode off. And up on the bluffs were a whole army of them, more than I could count."

"What did they take?"

"Horse. Mule. My Manton. Her Purdey. Ah, the equipage."

Mister Skye said nothing for a moment, apparently pondering it. Then, "Your story seems to amuse people."

"That's right!" snapped Diana. "The beasts made off with every rag we wore. I thought they were going to do me, but they didn't."

"You sound disappointed, Diana," said Alexandra.

Lady Chatham-Hollingshead laughed. "Too many for me, but maybe not for you."

"Mister Baudelaire and Colonel Galitzin appear to take the matter lightly," Skye said.

"Not at all. It's a serious matter," protested the colonel.

Baudelaire smiled blandly.

"I assure you, Skye, it happened, and I never want to see a dozen drawn bows, a dozen arrows pointing at my middle, ever again. Not ever."

Skye nodded. "Painted?"

"Terrible white and black stripes, sir, and red on their foreheads."

"You told Galitzin the chiefs wore bonnets with a long feather tail?"

"Yes."

"Probably Sioux, then. They do that. Maybe Cheyenne who take their ways from the Sioux. They're after the Assiniboin that were trading at the fort. You're lucky."

Galitzin nudged Baudelaire with his elbow, and the viscount caught it. "I'm afraid, Skye, some of my men don't quite believe me—or you."

Mister Skye nodded, and fixed that unblinking stare at the colonel. "You'll learn the hard way, if you live," he said. "All right then, I'll take you. But if you and your men don't heed my counsel, I'll leave you to your fate. That must be understood."

The man sat his battered yellow-eyed stallion, waiting.

The viscount nodded. "Done."

"Colonel?"

"Whatever my private wishes may be, I am in his excellency's service," Galitzin said.

Mister Skye looked faintly amused, and turned his gaze toward Baudelaire, a question in his eyes.

"I am at the service of all masters," the viscount's aide purred. "Set me to a task, Mister Skye, and I will be delighted to do you the favor. Yes?"

Skye grinned suddenly, startling the viscount with the warmth of it. "Well then, we'll be off in the morning. Buffler wherever we find them. Good elk, royal elk, along the river. Pronghorn, mule deer, coyotes—bear. Even an old silvertip grizzly now and then."

But Lord Frazier wasn't really listening. He gaped at the younger squaw, Mary, astounded at her exquisite beauty. Skye's younger woman had flesh the color of honey and peaches, smooth and unblemished. Her face formed a wide oval, with an exotic cast from large, almond eyes set above prominent cheekbones. Her slim figure, barely visible beneath a soft tan doeskin blouse, seemed voluptuous, and the brown calves bared by riding astride her pony were smooth and young and perfectly formed, disappearing beneath her hiked red calico skirts. Why hadn't he noticed her before, he wondered. A peach, a plum, a dusky fruit! A lady made for wooing! A savage damsel—dame, he corrected himself—awaiting his attentions! He had to have her. Surely he could woo her, this exquisite child of the wilds—Snake was she? Yes, Snake. An enchanting Shoshone, snared like some bird of paradise by this brute of a guide who sat his evil beast before him. Woo her, a simple task: he a lord of England, and she a simple child of nature. He'd set Baudelaire to it . . . Ah, Baudelaire. The chap had his uses even if he was French-born.

Skye surveyed the orderly camp that Galitzin had laid out with military insight, seemed satisfied, and turned that blue roan of his into the twilight. He stopped well outside of the camp's perimeter; there Skye and his two squaws slid off their mounts and in the lavender dusk made their own camp, placing some unspoken distance between themselves and these lords and ladies of England.

"Baudelaire," whispered the peer of England. "I want the young one, called Mary."

The frock-coated man smiled, saying nothing.

"You'll give us all cooties," snapped Diana.

"You have such evil habits," said Alexandra.

Lord Frazier laughed softly. "Despicable," he agreed. "Hurry, Aristides. Begin tomorrow. Even tonight. There's a reward in it for you."

"Mister Skye'll kill you," Diana said.

The viscount hadn't thought of that, and it disturbed him. But not for long. What could the brute do, after all? With thirty retainers watching his every move? Nonetheless, he resolved to be cautious. Baudelaire watched him expectantly, nodded, and smiled.

Mysterious Baudelaire, he thought. The man smiled even when being eaten alive by mosquitos. Which in fact were biting the viscount's tender hide. He swatted unhappily at them, wondering if the ferocious things would torment him the whole trip. Some of his retainers had gathered downwind of a campfire, coughing in the smoke they hoped would drive the things off. But his parlor wagon was armed with netting.

"Good night, my little ladies," he said, his voice an invitation.

"I think I want to visit Skye's camp," said Lady Diana. "He's such a manly animal."

Mary wished she could go out with Victoria each day, but her task was to herd the mules for Mister Skye and stay close to the whitemen's carts. Often she rode alone on her lineback dun pony, driving the mules before her and keeping a sharp eye out for the dangers these blind whitemen never seemed to see—except Mister Skye. He had Indian

eyes. The big dark mules didn't need much herding. One
drew a travois of lodgepoles, with their small cowhide lodge
anchored to the poles. The other packed the rest of their
things in panniers on a packsaddle her man had made from
canvas duck.

Mister Skye usually rode well ahead on the river trail,
often with the soldier chief called Galitzin and the great
chief, Frazier. His name and title confused her. Sometimes
he was Lord Frazier, sometimes Viscount Frazier, and he
had other names too. But she'd never heard him called Viscount Gordon, or Lord Gordon. So each day she rode alone,
keeping her own counsel, usually just a little ahead of the
carts and the big yellow wagon. That was her duty, and it
didn't occur to her to complain to Mister Skye, her man,
about her tasks. When they camped each evening she swiftly
erected the lodge by herself, intuitively putting it up in the
best place to shed rain water, feed Jawbone, hide the fire,
and minimize surprises from woods and brush and dangerous coulees. At Mister Skye's insistence, it was always a
little distance from the camp of the ones from far across the
waters.

She didn't really trust them. She'd been influenced by
Victoria, who'd turned silent and angry in the presence of
these odd white people. Victoria had confided her medicine
vision to Mary—the magpie's vision that had foretold what
was to come: these people would take Mister Skye away,
far away across the waters, and neither she nor Mary would
ever see their man again. She believed it, and watched the
Englishmen closely, trying to discover the secret things inside their minds that would make them do what Victoria
saw in her vision.

That terrified Mary, but still she could see not even a hint
of such evil in these strange ones. Instead they treated her
politely, though some of the men gazed at her too long,
with eyes that told her they wanted her. She ignored that.
Among her own Shoshones she'd been celebrated for her
beauty. How they all doted on it, exclaiming about it to her
mother and father. Many of the young men had courted
her, leaving small bone rings where she would find them
and playing their love flutes outside her lodge, to steal her

heart. But after her eighteenth winter, Mister Skye had visited among them with his sits-beside-him wife, and he had eyes for her. She scarcely dared believe her good fortune: every one of all the Peoples of the plains knew this great white man, his medicine horse and strong wife.

She'd been named Blue Dawn in the tongue of her people, but after Mister Skye had heaped many good things, blankets and rifles and powder and shot and knives and calico and ponies, at the lodgedoor of her rejoicing father, he had taken her to his own lodge and she became Mary in his tongue. He had told her it was a name of great honor among white people. She'd rejoiced in Mister Skye's love. Old Victoria had rejoiced, too, to have another woman to help with the endless toil of making camp, tending ponies, gathering breadroots, wild onions, and camass, braintanning robes and hides, and keeping them all in good summer and winter moccasins. She adored the other wife, and rejoiced in old Victoria's company.

Now she wished she could ride with Victoria, far off on the high broken prairie above the river bluffs. Victoria could slide through open country unobserved, like a spirit-fox, seeing but not being seen. And so she always scouted for Mister Skye, off forward and to one side or the other, like cat's whiskers, probing for whatever lay just over a rise or hidden in a swale. Each day at dawn, Victoria sternly tightened the small pad saddle over her bony mare and rode out into the gray sea of land, her disapproval of this hunt and these strange people plain to Mary and Mister Skye, who watched with sadness as Victoria rode away. It was not good, Mary thought, but nothing could be done about it. Victoria and Mister Skye disagreed about these Britons, and this time he was ignoring her medicine.

They'd found no buffalo after three days of travel up the Yellowstone, but Mary knew they would, and then the viscount would shoot some, and they'd all enjoy great red feasts. What strange people they were! The great chief had two men who did nothing but cook. Another who did nothing but walk beside the cart carrying all those spirits, and pour them for the lord and his ladies. And another who was going to tan hides like a woman, and clean and tan the heads of beasts too, and fill a cart with them to take back across the waters. Back there he was going to make bones from wood, and stuff the hides full of his wooden bones and straw and sew them up. And still another man did nothing but look after the lord's guns and walk beside a whole cart full of them.

The one called Baudelaire, who were nothing but black, like a warrior coming back to a village after a great victory, often walked beside her as she rode. He seemed friendly, but she didn't like him much. She didn't dislike him, either. She watched him catch up with her once again, this time riding a pony. He wasn't much of a rider, and bounced painfully as his horse trotted toward her. But soon he caught up and settled his mount into a fast walk beside her, smiling gently but saying nothing. She liked that in him, not talking all the time. Some white people never knew silence and the seeing and hearing of the world.

"Well, our beautiful Mary herds the mules all alone again," he said perceptively.

"It is my duty."

"But not always so pleasant, I imagine."

"I don't mind. See what a fine day it is. Sunny and not too hot. It could be very hot now."

"You're a fine patient woman to serve Mister Skye so well."

"There is no man that walks upon the breast of the earth mother like Mister Skye. It is only an honor to do his bidding."

"You are not only beautiful but brimming with virtue," he said.

"I do not know the word virtue."

"Goodness."

She smiled, knowing otherwise, and saw him observing her closely.

"His lordship would enjoy the pleasure of your company today, Mary. He mentioned it to me. It is a great honor, being invited to ride with our chief. He stayed with the carts this afternoon, just so he might entertain you."

She knew she must refuse. "This is where I must be, with the mules, ahead of your carts and men."

"Oh, oh. Why, I'll post a man to drive Mister Skye's mules, and you can go back and ride with his lordship and enjoy his favors—and gifts."

"No," she said. "I am here to see the things you don't see."

"See?"

"Yes. White men don't have good eyes. So I am here to give you eyes."

"But—Mister Skye and the colonel ride ahead, watching. And your Victoria rides far to one side, seeking buffalo. And the river protects us on the other side—"

"No, it doesn't, Mister Baudelaire. See there, that wall of brush near the water? It could hide a hundred of the enemy."

Baudelaire peered nervously at the spit of river brush, seeing nothing. She watched him curiously. "Ah," he said at length, "you and Victoria and Mister Skye guard us well, Mary. I must commend you for watching, and for the eyes that see what we don't. Truly, you are a rare and beautiful woman."

She smiled. All her winters she had known of her beauty, and when Mister Skye had given her a looking glass she could hold in her hand, she saw it herself, better than in the mirroring waters of ponds. But she'd always known it, seen it in her firm, smooth, honeyed flesh and the shine of her brown eyes. "It is true," she agreed. "Mister Skye has eyes only for me, and no other. And I am his."

Baudelaire nodded gently. "A beautiful and faithful woman, a crown for Mister Skye," he said. "I'll suggest to his lordship that he come forward and ride with you. He will be honored by your company, even as you will be honored by the attentions of a great chief, a chief above chiefs, of the British."

She nodded. "That is where Mister Skye came from long ago," she said. "But he would never go back."

"No, I'm sure he wouldn't, with a woman like you to keep him here."

"It is more," she said. "He is as big as these prairies and this sky above us. Back there he would not be so big."

"Very well said, Mary. I'll suggest to his lordship that he join you after our nooning."

"That would be fine, as long as he doesn't keep me from looking. I see and hear the things that tell of danger."

"I'm sure there's little danger, Mary. Three days now, and we've not seen any of it. And Mister Skye is just ahead."

She didn't reply. She lacked the words to tell things to someone who would not understand.

"Very well, Mary. You'll be honored by his lordship's company by and by. He rarely favors a woman, so consider it a great honor."

She nodded, wondering.

Chapter 7

Day after day, Victoria rose before the rest of the camp stirred, and rode off to find buffalo. And night after night she slid back about dusk, and reported she had seen none. She ranged far north and west of the Yellowstone, ghosting up coulees to peer over the ridges ahead upon a vast, silent land populated by nothing but an occasional antelope and jesting crows.

Something within her was saying that the sacred buffalo weren't there, north of the river, in the widening triangle of treeless slopes between the Yellowstone and Missouri. Still she tried, ranging farther each day than she would admit to Mister Skye. She needed that distance, and the long lonely hours upon her gaunt bay mare, to prepare herself for what was to come. Soon she'd be alone, an old Crow woman without a man, and the hard solitary hours helped her prepare for the darkness to come. In camp at night. She rarely spoke to her man, and when she was forced to, the answer came in harsh gusts.

"The viscount's growing impatient," he said one night. "He came for buffler and we haven't fetched him any. Says

I ought to be out hunting them too, but I told him you have eyes twice as good as mine, and know the way of them far better than I do.''

"Not here," she replied dourly. "Not anywhere there." She waved a bony arm in a great northerly arc.

And so they toiled up the river, never sighting the four-foots they had come to hunt. Lord Frazier sometimes made meat because the bottoms teemed with deer, and once he shot a small cow elk. But the land died under the fierce July sun, and gradually even the deer vanished, bedded down somewhere and grazing only in the dark of the night. And the harder it got to feed his large party, the more the viscount complained and accused Skye of failing to do his duty.

They passed the confluence of a braided stream rolling up from the south, the Powder River was what Mister Skye called it, and more and more Victoria knew inside of herself that the sacred buffalo were across the Yellowstone, out there in the lands of the Sioux and Cheyenne. The peoples of the prairies, like her own Absaroka, didn't draw sharp property lines the way whites did, but had homelands nonetheless that they considered their own, often demarked by an important river. And now she knew the buffalo languished down there, across the river, in the heartland of her enemies.

These whitemen and their strange carts mystified her. They talked as if they were all great chiefs and other peoples of the world were bugs. Never before had she avoided the people Mister Skye guided, but these were different. So she roamed far. She really didn't know what happened among them each day: whether they killed rattlesnakes or saw an otter or shot a hawk or got sick and died. They had bad medicine, like the spirits of under-earth creatures.

She had to find the buffalo. She eyed the shimmering river contemplatively one moonlit eve, and knew she'd cross it the next morning. It had dropped steadily since the spring flood; now its green flow coiled around long bars of sand and gravel, and the waters didn't rage as they had earlier. And she'd spotted a great buffalo trace into the water, probably a place where they forded.

She reined her little pony into the cold water before dawn, and found solid footing and a shallow passage. The water never reached her mare's belly, though it tugged at her and threatened to upset her as she splashed slowly across, wary of a channel and dropoff. But just as the dawn blued the northeast she led her mare up a shallow bank and let her shake loose water off. The south bank. She sat in the gloom, feeling a palpable change. The north bank had been country almost without owners, hunted by Sioux, Cheyenne, Piegans, Assiniboin, Cree, Gros Ventre, and her Absaroka. But now she sensed she was invading, though all those tribes hunted here as well, and claimed this country too.

This bank too had its river road, but she chose instead to retreat to the hills south and east, staying away from lethal traffic, war or hunting parties who could easily capture on old woman of the Absaroka and enslave or kill her and steal her pony.

The country here was rougher, and off to the south she could see dry prairie ridges, forested with yellow pine, country where the Cheyenne loved to summer because of its abundant wood and shade and sheltered grassy bottoms along ever-flowing cold creeks. To the west lay another great river the whites called the Tongue, that rose far away in the Big Horn Mountains, and some instinct told Victoria she'd find the buffalo there, scattered through the cottonwooded bottoms and parks of the river, escaping the terrible heat.

By mid-afternoon she struck the Tongue a few miles above its confluence with the Yellowstone. From the ridge she peered into a shallow trough, an emerald streak almost a mile wide running between tan bluffs. She paused cautiously in a crevass, studying the empty country and absorbing its menace. Anything could be hidden in the brown shadows of the giant cottonwoods that speckled the bottoms. And indeed something was. The buffalo, shaded up on a fierce day, hiding from merciless sun. More than she could count. Her man always used the word *thousands* but that wasn't enough. She saw thousands of thousands snoozing in the shade, occasionally rising up, rump first, turning around, and settling down again until blessed darkness and its cool would permit them to graze. She'd never seen so many in a wooded place, though out upon naked prairie she'd seen black rivers of them, the sacred provider of meat, tools, lodging, clothing, and so much more for all the peoples. But this herd lay concealed in dappled shade, and she knew the heat had driven the animals to shelter. She felt the heat also from her own terrible thirst, and the whited tongue of her mare, and the sopping wetness of the mare's back under her little pad saddle.

But she did not ride into the shallow trough toward the Tongue and its water. Instead, she turned the reluctant pony toward the Yellowstone, not far away, where she hoped to intercept Mister Skye. This time she would have news. She reached the great river when the sun lay low, yellowing the west sides of ridges and bluing the east, until the land seemed toothed and fanged and ready to strike at her. She chose a broad, gravelly place and forded easily, though the mare dropped briefly into a deep channel and out again so fast Victoria scarcely noticed the wetness of her moccasins. Nothing disturbed her passage, though she set a flock of black and white mockingbirds into a raucous furor, a dangerous thing always because it was a sign.

She studied the trace along the north bank and saw nothing, no linear tracks of cart wheels, or fresh hoofprints in dust, or manure, and knew they had not come this far this day. So she turned downriver and found them after a while, camped early because of the wilting heat that made men sweat and dry at the same time. These people lay about indolently, waving fans of sedge or leaf, gulping spirits from sweaty tin cups. All were dark-tempered because of the oppressive sun that lay over them like fired anvils. How strange that none of them slipped into the cold river to cool down, she thought. Did these whites know nothing about comfort?

And there was Mary, a cup in hand, sipping spirits along with Frazier and the rest and smiling, sitting crosslegged on the grass, her blue calico skirts hiked and her honeyed arms bared. Victoria frowned. She did not see Mister Skye there. She found him at their lodge, lying on a robe within, the lodgecover rolled a way off the ground to permit the breezes to cool him.

"You are not with her," Victoria said.

"If I touch spirits, I'm lost. No one over there with the bloody sense to deal with things. I can't. No buffler. Bad spot here, on a dozen horse-thief trails . . . and me parched worse than ever."

"I found them."

He peered up at her in the buttery light of the lodge, absorbing it, beginning a question.

"Many. Hiding from Sun in the bottoms of the Tongue. More than I've ever seen, I think. What a fine eye I have. I looked a long time at nothing but shadow."

He grinned slowly. "I suppose his lordship will be pleased. We found what he come for. Any sign?"

"No. Maybe people are far away. Not even old tracks."

"Suppose I ought to tell Frazier," Skye said, rising.

"Tell him when the sun comes back," she replied crossly. She had no reason at all, and simply felt like keeping her secret a few hours more.

"They'll want to do some preparing, Victoria—"

"Sonofabitch, you do what you want," she retorted. "You go over there and they'll give you spirits."

He grinned slowly. "Not now. But I got a powerful dry on me, Victoria. Powerful."

She glared at him. "You gonna get plenty dryer when they take you away."

"What are you talking about?"

She glared. "You know damn well."

"I don't, woman. Is this your medicine vision?"

She refused to answer, and turned crossly to the tasks at hand. She wanted food, but Mary hadn't built a fire and she doubted that the party had made meat. She'd make a stew, then. The bottoms were full of breadroots and sego lilies and she still had time to dig some before dark.

"Don't know what you're jabbering about, but it's just hoodoo," he muttered.

Buffalo! The camp was in a perfect frenzy that dawn as word swept through it. The viscount had abandoned his soft berth in his parlor-wagon and now danced about outside, giving nasal commands to everyone within earshot. Diana Chatham-Hollingshead thought his voice had risen at least an octave, and if it kept going up he could join the Vienna boys' choir.

She eyed Alexandra, who lay awake languidly, but probably wouldn't abandon her blankets until mid-morning. That was the way the viscountess lived. Diana knew she was made of other stuff, and plunged through her days like a clipper in full sail. She couldn't stand being left out of anything, especially not the forthcoming hunt. She'd shoot her share of the black beasts and then some. Her head ached a little from the boozing, but some tea would cure that. How amusing that had been, with poor Gordon sniffing around that dusky savage, and Baudelaire smirking about, and Skye's wife sipping scotch and giggling, quite unaware.

She'd frustrated his lordship in the end.

"Mary," Gordon had said huskily, drooling upon himself. "Mary, let's repair to the wagon."

She hadn't understood until he made himself clearer, and then she had giggled and said, "Ask Mister Skye. If he says I should go to your robes, I will. That is the custom."

Poor Gordon had been nonplussed at that, and muttered something. And Baudelaire had listened intently, smiling.

"I will ask Mister Skye," Baudelaire had said blandly, and Lady Diana knew exactly what was coming. In a day or so Baudelaire would tell Mary that Mister Skye approved. And that's how the evening had ended, with the savage wending her wobbly way back to Skye's lodge. It had amused Diana then, and amused her now to recollect it.

Lady Diana drew up her pink silk drawers and then pulled on her hunting attire, split twill skirts for riding, and a loose silk blouse just right for the hot day ahead. Even as she finished her toilet, she felt the wagon lurch as a team was being hitched, and heard the coachman and postilion going about their work. Lord Frazier wasn't even waiting for breakfast!

She stepped out into a cool, dry morning and discovered that the fat wheezing Abbot Beowolf had at least steeped some tea, something to repair her aching brain, but that would be it. Crossly, she took the cup he handed her and watched Gordon play with rifles like a schoolboy, aiming and dry firing, and wiping every last mote of dust off the stocks.

"You ignored my pleasure last night," she accused.

"Ha! Buffalo! I want a trophy bull."

"Gordon, you should *be* a trophy bull, not shoot one."

"Ha. That's all you think about."

"It's what I do best," she said. "And now I have a headache. I always get a headache when you ignore me."

"They say cow's best to eat. Not so tough. The hump of the cow."

Diana refrained from comment, and found that a groomsman had saddled a pony for her. How she detested these bony, stupid beasts, and longed for a fine thoroughbred with a flowing canter, such as she rode after foxes.

"Buffalo, my lady," he said, helping her up by making a stirrup of his hands.

"Tiddlywinks," she replied crossly. She took the reins and whirled the cold-mouthed little mare toward the front of the column, wanting to see Mister Skye. She detested him, especially since he didn't seem to notice her advances. But at least she could get proper information about the hunt, since Gordon was sputtering gibberish.

She couldn't find him or his dusky tarts. Already the caravan of carts careened up the Yellowstone with the soaring sun white at their backs. She cantered ahead, scarcely remembering the lessons she'd absorbed about leaving the safety of the caravan, and in a while she discovered Mister Skye, Mary, and Victoria, all waiting at a gravelly place beside the wide, glinting river.

"We'll ford here," Mister Skye rumbled, a gnarled hand lifting and resetting his silk tophat at its usual rakish angle. "You'd better wait with us, Lady Diana."

"Where're the buffalo?" she demanded.

"Ahead a few miles. Up the valley of a big stream called the Tongue."

"I want a big bull," she said, glaring at him.

"I imagine you'll see a few."

Then she surprised him. "Where are you from?"

Something changed in his scarred face. "Lots of places, Lady. Fort Laramie in recent years."

"You don't talk like the Yankees. I think you're from Canada, and a subject of the crown."

The older squaw glared at her.

"I've never crossed that line," he said enigmatically.

His small blue eyes seemed to study everything but her, focusing on the far shore, the flight of a magpie, a sudden shiver of cottonwoods leaves in a breeze, and even the sullen rock-crusted bluffs that held no secrets at all. His lack of attention annoyed her. She had a gorgeous face and figure; slightly blocky, true, but lushly colored. But he didn't seem to notice, or else he was a lot more clever—or stupid—than she gave him credit for. Stupid, probably. He didn't know a gift when it was laid naked in front of him.

"I think I'll cross," she said, spurring her little mare.

"Best wait," he said.

She ignored him, kicked the horse into the swirling water and felt it step daintily, feeling for a solid bottom with each step.

She heard a splashing behind and an instant later that evil blue roan, Jawbone, plunged beside her with Skye in the saddle, and he grabbed her bridle with one of his ham-handed fists.

"I think we'll wait," he said gently.

She quirted him across the chops, and he jerked back, losing his grip. That weird horse of his shrieked, reared up, and snapped at her, almost biting her thigh. But she spurred her mustang mare forward, not stopping, feeling the restless tug of the river push her pony downstream. In the deepest channel it threatened to topple her pony, suck her hooves out from under her. But a moment later the mare crow-hopped up the far bank and shook icy water in a fine spray that made rainbows.

Nothing happened.

"See?" she yelled, waving triumphantly at the three Skyes from a hundred fifty yards away.

The caravan hove into sight, and she watched the gaudy carts, bright greens and blues and reds, and the yellow parlor wagon, snake down to the river bank and stop. Mister Skye instructed the cartmen about crossings, his voice rumbling clear across the wide flow. Victoria started across the

river, her rifle in hand, while the first cartmen whipped their
reluctant drays into the boiling river, followed by the next,
and then the others, and finally the yellow wagon, drawn
by four skittish drays that looked ready to panic. She
watched fascinated, wondering if the water at this ford
would reach the bottoms of the carts, or invade the yellow
wagon. It crept higher on the wheels, pouring between
spokes. The sheer force of the river threatened to overturn
carts and horses. Creaking hubs vanished in the flow and
still the throbbing water climbed up spokes and wet the
bellies of the drays, twisting the horses downstream and
hammering the topheavy carts. But then the wheels and hubs
and forelegs of horses reappeared, spilling water.

Victoria arrived first, glaring at Lady Diana while her
bony old bay shook off water, and then the old woman froze,
her squint locked on something behind Diana, who turned
to look.

Standing quietly in the shade of a giant cottonwood was
an Indian youth, eighteen or twenty, Diana thought. A
handsome young man, slim and brown, with a diamond
face and coal hair carefully braided. He held a bow, and a
quiver was slung over his bare back, but he had no arrow
nocked and no paint smeared across his face or arms. He
observed the fording of the river by the bright carts almost
hypnotically, drinking in sights he'd never seen or imagined
in his young life.

"Lakotah," hissed Victoria, swinging the muzzle of her
battered rifle around a bit, as a sort of warning. The Indian
observed her and made no response.

"Dogs!" she whispered. "Enemies of the Absaroka!"

The youth did not abandon the shade of the cottonwoods,
and for that reason the cart-men and others wrestling the
muscular river didn't notice him. But his face remained ex-
pressionless, without the faintest revelation of curiosity, anger, fear, or anything else. At last he slowly made signs,
his powerful brown arms and fingers spinning the prairie
language.

"Hunkpapa!" Victoria cried, though Lady Diana hadn't
the faintest idea what that meant. She eyed the approaching

carts yearningly, wanting protection that still lay in the middle of the broad river.

"Big village!" Victoria snapped. "Came yesterday and found buffalo on the Tongue. Camping over there." She pointed up the Yellowstone.

Victoria herself began flashing her ancient arms and fingers, until the youth nodded. "I made the sign of the sky, the heaven," she said. "Now he knows. He sees Mister Skye! And Jawbone!"

Indeed the guide had spotted this, and was splashing his roan through the boiling current. He rode straight toward the youth, letting Jawbone clamber up a steep bank and stand, ears flattened and body dripping, before the young man. Something hardened in the youth's eyes, though Lady Diana couldn't fathom what had changed. The youth stood his ground, even against the menace of Mister Skye above him. Then, in motions so small his fingers scarcely seemed to whisper, the youth conveyed something to Mister Skye.

"He says his name is Sitting Bull. You'd say Sitting Buffalo Bull," Victoria explained to Lady Diana. "He's one of the village wolves—guards. And we must visit the village of these dogs."

Chapter 8

Lady Alexandra discovered that she was not a viscountess but a queen. Of all the wonders that smote the eyes of the Hunkpapa, she plainly excited them the most. Her flaxen hair, pale chiseled features, jade-colored eyes, and tall willowy figure captivated them, so that these Sioux swarmed around her, wanting to touch her silky hair or peer into her gentle dreamy face.

Not even the enameled wagons, gaudily colored and bearing the viscount's crest on their sides, or the nickel-trimmed black harness on the drays caught their eye half so much as her own pale hair and flesh.

After they'd all crossed the Yellowstone, their guide had talked with the young Indian waiting there, sometimes using strange words harsh to her ear, other times swiftly gesturing with fingers and hands that somehow communicated. They had all watched, the cart-men clutching their rifles and revolvers.

"Put up your weapons," Mister Skye had rumbled at last. "We're making a peaceful visit. This young man's not wearing paint, and the Hunkpapa aren't on the warpath. In fact, it's the time of their sun dance—big religious doings this time of year—and some buffler hunting, I suppose.''

They had all listened carefully to the guide, grateful for his expert advice, and then nervously returned rifles to Gravesend, the armorer, though some men were reluctant about it.

"Fetch your gifts, Lord Frazier. Tobacco and a little powder and ball. We'll smoke with the chief and headmen, and they'll welcome us. You'll be safe enough in the village—they treat their guests the same way most folks do. Nothing'll be stolen. Not inside the village, anyway.''

The guide's squaw, Victoria, had glared at him and looked like she didn't believe a word of it.

"You'd better not give them spirits, though. Give them spirits and there's no saying what'll happen. Just don't do it and don't let them know you've got a cartload. Some Sioux chiefs won't permit spirits in their village. They've got wiser heads than we do.''

Poor silly Gordon had looked upset, but his lordship was hiding it as best he could. Alexandra had gazed at the young Sioux, not finding anything menacing about him, and discovering a grecian beauty in him that attracted her in ways she couldn't put in words.

The Hunkpapa youth had led them upriver toward the village, and before long other warriors appeared out of nowhere—she couldn't imagine how they could rise up out of the earth—and shortly the carts and Englishmen were flanked by a score or so of these Sioux, all of whom wore very little in the fierce heat.

So many! The youth hadn't frightened her, but the others had. She had feared for her life, and so did all the rest, except for Mister Skye, who rode that broken-down horse of his as serenely as if he were going on a picnic. But that old squaw beside him glared fiercely about her, looking murderous herself, and Alexandra remembered that the old woman's Crow tribe and these Sioux—Mister Skye had variously called them Tetons, Lakotah, and Hunkpapa—were enemies.

She wore another of her squash-colored nankeen cottons today, this one with split skirts so she could ride. She didn't enjoy the riding much, but she enjoyed even less the rocking, jarring wagon, so now she rode toward the village, staying close to her postilion and coachman. She also wore a wide-brimmed straw hat gauded with feathers, to protect her vulnerable white skin.

How fierce they looked, she thought. Scores of warriors formed the escort, with more joining the procession as they approached the village. Mostly they stared, sometimes riding close to gape at her hair. And then at the bulldogs, especially at her pugnosed ugly Chesterfield, who trotted along faithfully ahead of her little pony. Some of the warriors were at least six feet tall, with angular features, and the scars of battle puckering honey-colored flesh. Several had peculiar slashes on their chests, and she wondered about them. The older ones didn't have the serene handsomeness of that young Adonis called Sitting Bull, and their corded muscles and scars and flat stares gradually evoked dread in her. They progressed up the south bank of the Yellowstone, with serrated rocky hills to her left and thick river verdure on the right. Even before they rounded a great bend, she spotted a layer of blue smoke and sensed she was about to see the village.

Ahead lay a broad flat, still green and lush even though nature's alchemy had turned the surrounding bluffs to gold. Cottonwoods massed near the river, but on the grassy meadow yellow cones rose like beehives, each topped by a small forest of poles. A barrage of gray curs howled toward them, and she feared for her little Chesterfield, but the village mutts and the bulldogs simply chased one another in wide spirals rather than tangling. People boiled toward them too, people in leather skirts and loincloths and fringed leggins. But most of the stocky women wore calicos they'd traded robes and pelts for—bright reds and greens and indigos, sewn into billowing skirts and loose blouses that left arms bare.

Gordon, riding just ahead, looked pale, and she saw sweat rivering down his neck in spite of the dry heat. Even Diana looked subdued, and Baudelaire positively terrified. She found malevolent pleasure in his pale terror. One never saw Baudelaire baring any emotion other than bland amusement. It was like seeing him naked, she thought. Near Skye and his squaws rode Boris Galitzin, ramrod erect in the saddle, trying to look serene in spite of the twitch spasming his lips.

She'd expected an uproar, but except for the whirling dogs, there was none. Instead these Hunkpapas gaped, blotting up sights too astonishing to exclaim about. The procession pierced into the village itself, wending among cowhide lodges, smoke-blackened at their tops, golden below. Many had been rolled up part way to let summer breezes through. Some women had been erecting brush arbors, shady places made by planting four poles in the earth, tying crosspieces to them, and then laying leafy branches across the tops to keep the sun at bay.

There were so many things she didn't understand, such as the tripods before each lodge, each dangling feathers and small animal skulls—and scalps. She recognized the human hair, most of it black, and she shuddered. The lodges had been raised in concentric circles, their oval doors facing eastward, and she supposed there might be some religious aspect to that. But now the crowds pressed so closely about her mare that she could scarcely see the village and all its strange sights. She knew she was a cynosure of a lot of brown and black eyes. Girls gaped and clapped their hands over their mouths. Children peered upward with blank faces.

Her hair. She smiled and undid her wide hat, and pulled a brooch out of her locks, letting them cascade over her shoulders, and knew she'd done something that fascinated the Hunkpapa. She sat her saddle regally. Let them gawk, she thought.

Strange scents thickened the air; woodsmoke, roasting meat, leather and sweat, and less pleasant odors rising from the offal of dogs. And horses! Everywhere she saw restless ponies picketed near lodges, the acrid sun-pummeled scent of them strong in her nostrils, along with the sharp and not unpleasant fragrance of their manure.

Mister Skye halted before a lodge somewhat larger than the others, with feather-bedecked lances struck into the tan clay before it. He peered behind him, studying his clients for signs of folly and finding none. He knew the Britons were much too uncomfortable to do anything rash. Still, the guide's gaze settled steadily on Galitzin, and then the armorer, Gravesend, and others he seemed to have catalogued in his mind as trouble.

Whoever was within that lodge certainly took his time, she thought. Crowds of these Hunkpapa pressed silently around them now, blocking all escape. They pointed at the bulldogs, some giggling or covering their mouths at the sight of creatures so ugly and fierce-looking. One crevassed old man with a buffalo-horn headdress and a dreadful necklace of dried human fingers—she thought he might be one of the medicine men she'd heard of—eyed the ugly dogs with obvious displeasure, as if the creatures had profaned an altar by coming into this village.

Then at last a man emerged from the honeyed darkness of the great lodge, and she watched enthralled. Never had she seen such a beautiful body, tall and perfectly formed, with deeply defined sinews cording through it, and all of his near-naked flesh the sienna color she'd first seen in Italy near Florence. And upon his powerful neck sat a chiseled head with prominent cheekbones, an aquiline nose, and gray eyes with a gaze so observant that she felt chilled as he took her in, and the others, one by one. Nor was that the end of it. He wore an eagle feather bonnet of such wanton savage luxury she could barely fathom it, feathers bound in red tradecloth with ermine pendants dangling from either side, and a feathered tail that extended to his bright quilled moccasins.

Dizzily—for something percolated wildly within her—she met his intense gaze, which lingered on her once again until she was certain of his keen interest in her. She scarcely knew what malady had beset her, and clung to the low pommel of her saddle. But his attention slid swiftly to other things, especially when Mister Skye began making the signs of these lands with his burly arms. This noble chief would fill pages in the journal she was keeping, she knew. Pages!

"*Pte,*" the chief replied, nodding, and spoke in a soft tongue Lady Alexandra couldn't fathom.

At last the guide turned to his clients. "We're welcome, and we'll be guests of the village," he said. "We'll have us a smoke now. His name's Bear's Rib, and he's an important chief of these Hunkpapa. Lord Frazier, you'll join us for the smoke. Bring your twists of tobacco and your gewgaws and follow what I do. Colonel Galitzin, you'll join us also. And Lady Alexandra, he asked that you join us too. After the smoke, we'll have a feast, and at dawn tomorrow we'll join the hunt for Pte, the sacred buffler. That's their name for it. They spotted that herd too. They're camped here because it's upwind. And after the hunt they'll have their sun dance, but I think maybe that's something not for your eyes.''

Lord Frazier found the chief's lodge more commodious than it appeared from outside. The buxom young squaws—or perhaps daughters—had rolled the hide lodgecover up a foot or so, like most others in the village, turning the lodge into a kind of chimney that drew air upward and out the smoke vent at the top. The chief seated himself at the rear, opposite the door, and motioned to Skye to sit at his right, then the viscount and Galitzin. Two village headmen settled themselves at the chief's left, one of them the fierce chap with the ghastly necklace of fingers. Alexandra was seated separately, near the door and close to a small stack of firewood.

The viscount settled himself on a soft buffalo robe, wishing it might be a chair because he was going to be uncomfortable shortly sitting crosslegged. He had supposed the inside of one of these nomadic tents would be dreary, but instead color rioted at him. Along the sides were bright-dyed parfleches with intricate geometric designs in green and yellow. Above him hung the chief's bow and a quiver festooned with red-dyed quills.

Methodically the chief—Frazier thought him an ugly brute with grossly large cheekbones—pulled his calumet from a soft-tanned bag and tamped tobacco in it. Its bowl was of a rose pipestone, and some sort of burnished hardwood comprised the long stem. Even as he tamped, one of his squaws laid an orange ember wrapped in some large green leaves before him, and the chief nimbly dropped the coal into the bowl and sucked until the tobacco burned, its pungence filling the lodge. Frazier sensed that this would take a while, and that the tribesmen would not be hurried through ceremony.

Bear's Rib lifted the pipe with both hands, saluted the cardinal directions, the sky and earth, and puffed slowly.

"I know a parcel of Sioux, and I'll translate for you," said Skye. "He's saluting the spirits that lie in each direction, *Wakan Tanka* above, and the Earth Mother below. Now I'll do it."

The guide completed the ritual and handed the pipe to Lord Frazier, who took it, wondering if he was going to do something heathenish and sacrilegious. But Skye seemed to read his doubts.

"He's honoring the spirits and expects you to. Best not to violate the medicine of his house, mate."

So the viscount imitated what he'd seen and handed the pipe to Galitzin, who followed. The next, seated separately, would have been Alexandra, but Skye intervened.

"Hand it to the headman," he said.

Galitzin did, and when the pipe had run the circle it was sent around a second time, until the whole charge of tobacco had been burned. The viscount's knees hurt, and he grew impatient.

"Tell him who I am," he whispered to the guide. "The queen's blood runs in my veins."

Mister Skye stared at the viscount as if he were daft.

"Your excellency, I am Lord Gordon Patrick Archibald Frazier, the seventh viscount, Bury St. Edmunds, Suffolk."

Bear's Rib stared blankly.

"Tell it, tell it, Skye."

"It's Mister Skye, mate."

"Whatever, whatever. I won't stand for insolence."

Bear's Rib returned the pipe to its pouch as deliberately as he had pulled it out, and then began some sort of welcoming oration. Mister Skye listened, and occasionally resorted to sign language, so the viscount supposed the lout of a guide lacked a full understanding of this tongue.

"He's welcoming you and urging you to stay in the village and share the big doings. Tomorrow they'll hunt the buffler. They've got some fine buffler runners—fast ponies trained for the hunt—and we're welcome to join them, make meat. I said we'd be pleased to do so, and you have some gifts. Now's the time."

"Ah! Yes!" he said, digging into the commodious pockets of his tweed hunting coat. He handed Bear's Rib two twists of pungent tobacco, some gaudy ribbons in rolls, and the powder and shot, each in a canvas pouch. Then, sighing in the silence, he withdrew another twist and dropped it before the chief. How they all sucked his blood, he thought.

The chief accepted these amiably, and began once again talking to Skye, this time jabbing a finger at Alexandra. Then Skye muttered a while, his burly hands slicing the air when words didn't come.

"He asked about the lady, and I said she's your woman, and that you both are from across the waters. He said he's never seen a woman with hair the color of aspen leaves before they fall, and he wondered whether the color is rare. I told him not at all; lots of people in your land have the color. Then, ah, he said he'd give you ten fat ponies for her—"

"Oh!" exclaimed Alexandra.

"—and I said I'd ask you. That's some price, ten ponies. Does her honor."

"Why, she's my wife, Skye! I can't give her to a savage."

Mister Skye nodded, and said something to the chief, who listened and talked to Skye at length.

"Bear's Rib says he knows that, but he's got two beautiful fat young squaws he'll give you for, ah, Lady Frazier. Plus the ponies. I said it's against your religion, but I'd ask."

"No, no, unthinkable!"

"It's not unthinkable," Alexandra said. "Tell the gentleman we'll take him to England and I'll introduce him to society."

Galitzin was grinning like a well-fed coyote.

The chief tried again, talking animatedly to Skye.

"Bear's Rib says he'd like to borrow her while you're here. Give you a fat pony," said Skye, solemnly.

"Borrow me!" she cried. "The brute! I'm worth two ponies. I'm worth five. I'm worth—Tell him I said yes."

"Why, Alexandra—"

"Try one of his fat squaws," she retorted.

"But, Alexandra—it might lead to—Are you sure he's quite clean?"

"Lakota bathe in a creek most every morning," Skye said, amused. "Is it settled?"

"Settled! See here, Skye, you've gotten us into something—"

"I got us into it," cried Alexandra.

"It'll scandalize the men—"

Alexandra giggled. "Let it," she said. "I'm going to, whether you get a squaw and a fat pony or not."

Skye turned solemn. "He might want to keep you, lady. Chiefs live by whim, same as any bloody king. I'll tell Bear's Rib no—"

"Say yes or I'll discharge you."

Galitzin grinned. "Is this how you got ze ponies for us, Skye?"

The viscount was shocked by the quiet ferocity of Skye's response: "Every pony was bought and paid for with the pounds you sent, Colonel. And no man touches my wives."

"Bear's Rib reminds me of Adonis. I saw the naked Adonis all over Italy," she said dreamily. "He has a beautiful soul."

Lord Frazier sighed. "There's no stopping her when she's being ethereal, Skye."

"Tell him I'll come to him tonight, Mister Skye."

The guide and the chief conferred in that muttering tongue, and then Skye said, "He is pleased, and will bring a fat pony to the chief shortly. As for the lady, he desires she stay and cook him a supper. He's curious about the food a woman with hair the color of the sun cooks. He will lend her a kettle."

"I don't cook! I have servants."

Skye consulted again with Bear's Rib. "He says if you don't cook, you're lazy. But if you are the wife of a chief of the people, he can understand it. He wishes to know what you do."

"I keep a journal. And just what does he do, Mister Skye?"

"He'll tell you he listens to the shamans—the medicine men—and listens to the elders, and then decides things."

But Bear's Rib was clambering to his feet and dismissing them. Lord Frazier followed the others out into a slanting sun and a blast of heat. Outside the lodge, his retainers waited quietly, still surrounded by curious Hunkpapa who were fingering the carts, poking and probing everything except Jawbone. Around that brutal horse lay a wide circle of emptiness. Apparently the beast was known to these people, the viscount thought. Capital. He'd somehow hired a guide and a horse and two squaws who'd smooth everything over.

Skye's squaws, he noticed, stood solemnly near Jawbone, and the old Crow woman glared angrily at the crowd, daring them to come closer to her. Even the evil horse stood with ears laid back and lips distended, baring teeth that could rip flesh apart.

One of the village wolves, or policing society, nodded at them and gestured that they should follow him to a place at the edge of the village, which would become their camping ground. These people didn't seem so bloody frightening now, the viscount thought. Just friendly people like any other.

He was much put out with Alexandra and intended to have a word with her privately, even if she just laughed as she always did. Pleasuring with a savage! Unthinkable! Almost, anyway, he thought, glancing covertly at Skye's young Mary. But of course Skye's woman was half-civilized, and that made the difference.

Well, the buffalo tomorrow. He'd sailed across an ocean for this, and it excited him. These savages seemed to have ponies trained to race among the beasts, but he couldn't imagine why. Surely those lumbering giants couldn't run fast. He intended to have Gravesend drive the cart to the herd, and hand him loaded rifles, one after the next, and bang away. He thought he might shoot a hundred buffalo before growing weary of it.

Chapter 9

Mister Skye awakened to the bustle of men and animals outside of his lodge. He peered upward through the smoke-hole upon an iron sky that told him it was not yet dawn, and very early this July day. His ears registered the hubbub of a rising camp, men coughing, the clank of cookpots, and more: the nasal voice of the viscount like a tolling bell, rousing men to action. The hunt, Mister Skye thought. It'd be only minutes before the eager man came banging on Skye's lodge, sundering the guide's rest.

He peered about in the gloom, sensing the warm presence of Mary in a buffalo robe to his left. But not Victoria. She slept apart most nights, or disappeared long before he went out to greet the sun and make water. His lodge had not been a happy one. He thought to crawl over to Mary's robes and fondle her, but he didn't. She would push him away, just as she pushed him away whenever things weren't good between them. So the two of them lay alone in their robes, as alien and distant as strangers.

He rolled out of his robe, fastened his leggins to his belt, and pulled a patterned red calico shirt over his thick chest.

Then he lowered his grizzly bear claw necklace over his head and settled the polished long claws on his shirt. Big medicine. He normally shaved when he could and happened to have a ball of soap, but this morning he didn't bother. He had always scraped away his cheek-bristle for his women, but for days his women had avoided him, so stubble collected on his jaws and forested his face. It was his way of saying his lodge had darkened.

Mary feigned sleep but watched him, he knew. He yawned, driven by the racket of the viscount's camp outside, and pulled his square-toed boots over his white feet. He'd never surrendered to moccasins, though he wore them often enough around camp. He liked boots, and the feel of half an inch of sole under him like the thick hull of a man-o'-war.

Then he stood in the sable gloom, completing his toilet by anchoring his holstered Colt's dragoon to his heavy belt and screwing his silk tophat over his graying shoulder-length hair. An odd collection of rags and leather, he supposed, but it suited him. He ducked through the small lodge door and into a crisp dawn, marked by a yellow streak fissuring the northwestern sky.

He peered about him at the large village of silent cones that caught the pale light on their eastern slopes and looked like fangs against an indigo western sky. Over in the Sioux lodges no one stirred. No smoke from cookfires rose and flattened in the air. He turned to Jawbone as he always did at dawn. The young blue roan nickered. He never had to picket the animal. After it had grazed its fill, it drifted back to Skye's lodge and stood sentry through the long night.

Mister Skye scratched Jawbone's ears, and the beast replied by butting him with his massive roman nose. It had become their morning ritual, an act of love. The stallion had known no other master, and had met Mister Skye the first day of its life. Its sire had been a roan mustang, uniquely large for the feral horses of the American west. For years Mister Skye had tried to trap and tame the noble animal, which roamed the high valleys of the Pryor Mountains in the land of Absaroka. He never succeeded. But he did have a tall roan mare from somewhere back in the States, a lady of difficult temperament, always half-rebellious under saddle. So Mister Skye decided that if he could not capture the stallion, he'd borrow its fire, and arranged the match, picketing and front-leg hobbling his big mare at a place the stallion haunted. He used chain, knowing how hard the stallion would try to steal her. He feared she'd kill herself struggling with her bonds, but she didn't.

Eleven months later Jawbone was born, yellow-eyed and evil, biting the hand that held him. From that day forward Mister Skye shaped his colt into a terror of the plains, a medicine horse so brave in battle and canny as a sentry that he became a legend among all the tribes, something magical, as awesome as Mister Skye himself. Even now Mister Skye's thick fingers probed along the horse's flesh, discovering gouges and pits and puckered flesh where Jawbone had felt the searing pain of lance and arrow and battle axe, and once a ball from a fusil that raked his stifle. The horse squealed and whickered, welcoming Skye even when his wives didn't. Skye curried, inspected hard hooves and hocks and fetlocks, pulled a burr from Jawbone's mane while the stallion nipped and butted and squealed.

"Ah! There you are, Skye," said Frazier. "Let's be off, eh?"

"I think we'd better wait for our hosts."

"Well, let's just shoot a few now."

"The shots might start a stampede that would put the herd twenty miles away. I don't suppose that would please Bear's Rib a bit."

"Well, wake them up. It'll be an inferno soon. I've never felt a heat like this. Over a hundred every afternoon."

Mister Skye had been mulling it since yesterday, when the chief had invited them to join the hunt. The viscount expected to be led up to the herd to shoot them while they grazed or stood, but the village warriors planned to saddle their prized buffalo runners—horses especially trained to race beside a running buffalo so the hunter could loose an arrow or fire his fusil into the heart-lung area just behind its shoulders. The runners were amazing animals, as fast as warhorses because buffalo could gallop at surprising speeds; and fearless, willing to edge close to those wicked horns, dodge them if the great beast hooked toward his tormentors, and go on to the next, guided only by knees because the hunter needed both hands for the killing.

"I'm afraid we'd better wait, sir. It's a courtesy required of a guest here."

"Well, when will they—"

"Later. Mid-day. Who knows? Indians don't live by ship's bells. And they don't get up early, either. That goes double for males, whose entire life is hunting, war, and sport, mostly gambling. The women toil. They cook, sew, dress hides, gather firewood, take care of children, make lodges, cut poles. But not the hunters."

"But it'll be roasting. The sun's barely up and I can feel it burning—"

"They're used to it. When they do get ready, they'll saddle their buffler runners and ride downwind to the herd. The buffler are hunkered in the woods up the Tongue, and the breeze is out of the southwest, so the Hunkpapa'll stay east and north and then start the herd running. Victoria says the buff are pretty much on this side of the Tongue. I thought to take you upstream a way, to an eastern bluff overlooking the valley, and you can shoot from there."

"A bluff? Why can't I be on the level instead of shooting downhill?"

"Safety. Stampeding buffler are frisky."

"I don't like it, Skye."

"It's not our hunt. You don't have a buffler runner. I've never seen them run the buffler out of a woods. It's bad enough out on grass, going a gallop over chuckholes with beasts as heavy as a ton, hundreds, even thousands, boiling by, ready to turn you to pulp if your horse stumbles or you fall. But cottonwood bottoms—I can barely imagine it. Getting brained by every passing limb, running into trunks and thickets."

"Well fetch me a buffalo runner."

Skye shook his head. "On the day of a hunt you couldn't trade for one. And I wouldn't let you ride one through those bottoms without a lot of practice."

Lord Frazier looked annoyed. Lady Diana Chatham-Hollingshead joined them, curious about the day's events.

"Our guide and these bloody savages have conspired to ruin the hunting," the viscount said.

Mister Skye contained the anger lancing through him and explained the whole business once again. He stopped short of saying that if they ruined the Sioux hunt, they'd be in big trouble, worse trouble than Frazier could imagine. That old medicine man—Eagle Beak—had been plenty unhappy about the whitemen arriving just as the hunt was to begin—and then the sun dance.

"Where can I get a buffalo runner?" asked Diana.

"Don't suppose you can today, lady. After the hunt you might try trading."

"I'll run one of these mustangs you got us, then."

"I wish you wouldn't, lady."

She laughed. "That's why I will."

Around noon the village warriors finally collected their ponies and weapons and rode off toward the south. They'd awakened at various hours, made their medicine, usually a morning prayer facing the sun, this time accompanied by a lengthy song about the forthcoming hunt, and finally gathered their weapons and mounts. Each took two ponies, one to carry him to the herd, and the other his prized buffalo runner, kept fresh and unridden for the great race.

"It's afternoon!" cried Lord Frazier. "And so hot I can hardly breathe!"

At Mister Skye's prompting, only the viscount, his armorer Gravesend, and his taxidermist, Will Cutler, came along. Gravesend and Cutler rode the arms cart, while the unhappy lord rode his sweaty pony. Skye took them southeast along a ridge that formed a divide between the Tongue and a creek to the east, and once they topped the grassy ridge they could see the thin green streak of the river bottoms winding through arid prairie. The cottonwoods had thinned here, upstream from the Tongue's confluence with the Yellowstone. Mister Skye led them down a long coulee to a point of land that pierced into the bottoms, and suggested that Lord Frazier shoot from there along with Gravesend, while Cutler waited with their cart out of sight in the draw. And there they waited and sweated, while the

ruthless sun and furnace winds sucked the juices out of
them all.

Gordon Patrick Archibald Frazier was in a sulk. Had he
sailed clear across the Atlantic, suffered the cinders and
smoke of barbaric railroads from Boston to the confluence
of the Ohio River and the Monongahela, and camped on
grimy bed-bug packets from there to Fort Union, months
on end, all for this? The heat was suffocating, beyond anything he'd ever experienced in cool England. The sun hammered at him until pain gripped his eyeballs. His shirt
dampened until he could no longer tolerate his tweed jacket,
and he tore it off in spite of the indecency of shirtsleeves
and handed it to Gravesend. That stopped the sweating, at
least. But nothing stopped the searing heat that sapped energy from him like a leech dining on his blood.

And that was only part of it. That brute of a guide insisted on joining him on the promontory, and had taken to
calling him *mate*, a term common sailors used. That or
matelow, British slang for a seaman. Whenever Lord Frazier's noble ears suffered that form of address he winced,
but there seemed to be no educating this oaf to the niceties
of civilization.

What is more, the guide had lectured him, and couldn't
seem to still his tongue.

"Not the best spot, mate, but we're guests. Now I don't
expect the buffler to be moving fast. Not in this heat."

"Skye—it's Lord Frazier, Sir, your lordship, or if you
must, Viscount Frazier. But never Gordon. No retainer shall
address me familiarly."

The big oaf grinned.

"Furthermore, you needn't stay here. My man Gravesend will reload, and that'll be quite sufficient."

"I'll be watching out for Hunkpapa. They'll be coming
along with the buffler."

"Gravesend'll watch."

"He'll be loading and you'll be aiming. And I'll be
watching. Shoot a Sioux hunter, and maybe your scalp will
hang from a lance tonight."

The viscount glared, but said nothing. The barrel of his Purdey scorched his fingers when he touched it.

"Buffler drop fast with a heart-lung shot, spot the size of a hat just behind the shoulders. No sense wasting powder on anything else. Another thing, mate. I'd suggest you lie down, set up some shooting sticks, rest your piece in them. You'll have a better shot than just standing here. Take your time, follow a good 'un—"

"I don't intend to take my time. I intend to shoot as fast as Gravesend can reload. And as long as I'm retaining you, you can reload also."

The guide shook his head. "I'm your eyes, mate," he said.

Lord Frazier stared. Was this man uncivil deliberately? "Skye, you push me to my limits."

The man grinned again, insolently, too.

"Buffler's sacred animals to the Indians," Skye continued. "They're downstream making medicine now, thanking the spirits of the ones they'll take. They make meat and shelter and clothing; make moccasin soles. Tallow makes soup and grease for their clay paints. Bedrobes, tools, and a whole lot more. Hair gets stuffed into saddle pads, children's dolls."

The viscount began to develop a headache, and a terrible thirst in the exhausting heat.

"I say, enough, Skye."

"Trophy buffler, now. You look for a light colored bull. They're mostly lighter in summer. Some even tan and buff. A few famous ones albino—sacred ones to any tribe. A few cinnamons too. Look for the odd color and you'll have a trophy."

"I say, Skye—"

"Mister Skye, mate."

The viscount felt a change come over the land, something not palpable, like thunder too distant to be heard. The earth beneath him seemed less secure, and he gradually perceived a vibration in it, an earthquake under the clay. He peered to the north, staring wordlessly, seeing nothing running the bottoms or dodging the massed cottonwood along the distant river.

"You're right. They're coming now," Skye said.

Then a brown mass, a wall of chocolate, poured into view, and above it a whirling haze of chalky dust that whitened the brass sky.

"Best lie prone, mate. Still have a minute."

"I'll shoot as I will, Skye."

The beasts lumbered closer, not running fast, and he knew he'd drop fifty, a hundred. It enthralled him, this sight of a river of running flesh, flooding around trees, appearing and vanishing as the cottonwoods thinned and thickened.

"Hunkpapa in there, mate."

"I don't see any."

"That's why I'm here."

He aimed into the chest of a distant leader, and fired. The heavy piece jolted into his shoulder, and he handed it to Gravesend, who handed him a John Dickson and Son. This too was so bloody hot he could scarcely touch it, but he swung it toward another leader, two hundred yards to the right, and well below. He aimed the wobbling sight on the beast's chest, and squeezed again. The boom rocked him, set his ears to ringing. He peered into the roiling dust and saw nothing stagger.

"Better to wait for a broadside shot, mate. Shoot midships, not the fo'c'sle."

"You mind your manners!"

Buffalo straggled by, these first lumbering faster than the main body of the herd. The viscount banged at them, feeling the butt of his rifles punch his aching shoulder again and again, and dropping nothing.

"You brought me to a bloody poor place to shoot, Skye!" he cried.

"There's Hunkpapa in there now. Hold up, mate."

"I don't see—" But then he did make out several, racing their dark ponies right through the thundering mass of beasts. Not a one held a rein, yet the ponies seemed to know just where to go. He watched one pony and rider veer tight against a cow, watched the man's corded arms flex, and the cow stumbled at once, tumbling over and over, a thin shaft, feathered and broken, projecting from a place just behind its shoulders.

"More of them, mate. Better hold up."

"I see them, Skye!" he retorted testily.

The hunter who'd dropped the cow never paused, but plucked another arrow from the quiver bouncing on his bare back, and nocked it while his pony closed on yet another cow ahead.

"How can they tell who shot what?"

"Each man's got his own medicine mark on his arrows. And each tribe's got its own way of making and marking the arrows."

Five more warriors swept by, their ponies nimbly cutting and dancing between the buffalo. Briefly he admired them, and grasped the importance of the buffalo runner. Those trained ponies meant food and wealth for any tribe.

"That's the last of the hunters for a bit, mate."

Lord Frazier steadied himself. Odd how his heart banged in his chest, and how his arms trembled under the weight of the rifle. He felt parched, and his dry tongue stuck to the roof of his mouth, as much from thirst as from wild exhilaration.

He swung his wobbling barrel toward a bearded bull that limped slowly by, a trophy beast perhaps, and fired. His aching shoulder stabbed pain once again, and the beast limped by, unscathed. Surely he'd hit it! He watched, waiting for it to slow, to leak blood, to fall.

And still they came, a river of animals, more four-footed creatures than he'd seen in over forty years of living. He could scarcely imagine a herd this size, or the fodder it required each and every day. He fired a Boss and Company piece at a nearby cow that veered closer and closer, but she never faltered, and he watched enraged as she trotted relentlessly up the river bottoms.

"You've ruined my hunt, Skye. Bringing me here. How can a man shoot running animals?"

"Hold up, mate. More Hunkpapa in there."

He saw them. Eight or ten knotted close, weaving their ponies through the black torrent, effectively dropping cows until the valley before him was littered with kicking carcasses.

He shot anyway, picking a cow that looked wounded and

slow. His new piece boomed, spewing blue powder smoke, and he sniffed the acrid odor, mixed with sweat and the stink of manure, buffalo, and alkali dust.

The rifle flew from his grip, some jarring blow wresting it from his trembling hands, and he realized Skye had ripped it from him.

"When I say hold up, you hold up," the guide said in a low voice that somehow pierced through the rumble.

He had never been addressed so rudely by a retainer. A rage burst in him like a lanced carbuncle.

"They're gone. You can shoot now," Skye said, as if nothing had happened.

And Viscount Frazier obliged, again and again until his shoulder could suffer no more. When the last of the great river of buffalo trotted by, the viscount surveyed the carcasses below, and knew every one had an arrow, or arrow wound, in it, and not a one had dropped with one of his lead balls through its lights. He turned a grimy face toward his guide.

"Enough of you. You're discharged, Skye. I came for a hunt, not a stampede."

The insolent guide grinned.

Chapter 10

Alexandra thought she discovered nobility in her chief. They couldn't speak a word to each other, and maybe that was best. He sat in the lodge, eying her, and she found wisdom in his gaze. He seemed to be waiting for something. It thrilled her, seeing these splendid traits in this leader of his people. Everything about him was perfect, even the scars of war, one puckered slash disappearing under his breech-clout, another angling across his ribs into his back. She wondered about those peculiar scars on his bronze breast that she'd seen on others of these Hunkpapa. Bear's Rib. A noble name, no doubt, like her own maiden name, Heddonborough, in England. She thought him a royal presence, a majesty, a sceptered and orbed ruler of men.

It thrilled her that he was interested in her, and had invited her to high councils. She'd never had a chief before. That would be like having a king for a lover. He seemed lithe and athletic, unlike Gordon, who was fast deteriorating into soft whiteness. Not an ounce of fat burdened the muscled torso of this barbaric man. She thrilled at the thought of his savagery, and the scalps hanging from the lodgepoles.

How she wished she could talk with him, ask him a thousand questions. She knew, though, she'd write epic poems about him—she was a not inconsiderable poet, and had been published several times, once on the same page as Alfred Tennyson. Yes, love sonnets, odes to friendship and savage lovers, something to convey the innocent manliness of this prairie prince.

She'd been so disappointed when he hadn't detained her after the smoke and welcome yesterday. She'd waited, heart pattering, for some indication that she should stay, but he had simply eyed her languidly when Mister Skye, Gordon and the rest, got up and clambered out. She'd followed, her soul wild with need to stay on and feel his cruel touch. But instead she emerged into the coned village and found her way back to the wagon, and spent a miserable night, feeling rejected.

But now she smiled, her eyes feasting on his hard features, the prominent cheekbones, his obsidian eyes that peered sharply outward but let no mortal discern what lay behind his gaze. In his thirties, she supposed. Young. His jet hair, carefully done in two braids, showed no sign of gray. And no beard. She peered again, curious about the smooth cheeks that appeared not to have been scraped at all. Did these people grow no beards? She wished to touch his cheeks, be his woman. She was curious about that, being his woman. The thought sent ripples of excitement through her. Tonight! Maybe now!

She peered about her at the two shy young women who seemed to be waiting for something. Stunning women, now that she looked at them. How she envied them their dusky beauty. She felt weightless and knew she would confide her joy to her journal soon. They sat studying her, especially her flaxen hair, doing nothing. It surprised her. She had thought Indian women constantly did things; made moccasins, cooked food, skinned hides, sewed calicoes. But these were the chief's wives, and maybe they didn't have to. Lots of servants, like the peerage of England. She had never had to do anything. Always a dozen servants flocked about to dress her, make her bed, help her with her toilet, cook, clean, keep fires burning, run errands, wash, and all the rest.

Plainly these people were superior to anything she'd known in England. What dignity the chief had! With none of the petty little faults that afflicted everyone she knew at home. And how noble the women! Strong and serene and free of all white men's taints and vices. She could see it in their open faces, this vast perfect kindness. She'd never met people without vices before. Her eager gaze traveled from one beauty to the next and to the chief, and she blushed at the thought she had, wondering just how things—happened. It would be beautiful when it came, ecstatic, ethereal, so spiritual rather than animal, because these were people of large soul and exquisite religion and perfect integrity! She closed her eyes tightly, arched her head back, listening to the carillon of the universe, preparing her soft yearning body and soul for all the joys that would transport her onto some true, savage plane her spirit had never penetrated.

She'd been summoned to the great lodge about the time the village emptied itself for the hunt. Bear's Rib's wives couldn't speak words, but made it plain she should come with them, and she had followed at once, walking among young men gathering horses and weapons, past women in begrimed buckskin dresses strapping travois to ponies, past bright children, the little girls in skirts, romping and chattering. She paused once at the sight of Mister Skye and Gordon and the rest, just beyond the village, heading out toward the buffalo.

To delight her prince she'd worn a suit of jade velveteen that matched her eyes, along with a white silken blouse and a black choker with an ivory cameo, which perfectly framed her oval face with its tumble of blonde hair. It had been a hardship to dress herself this trip, but she'd managed. Back in Bury St. Edmunds there had always been several ladies waiting to perform these things. But she'd managed. One had to sacrifice, keep a stiff upper lip. It had all paid off, though: Bear's Rib's gaze had returned again and again to the velvet dress, and each time he'd smiled gently.

Thus they sat for the longest time through the heat of the day. But the shade of the lodge felt comfortable and breezes eddied in below the raised lodgecover. Then at last some sort of excitement thickened the hot air outside, and she heard women's voices, the sounds of ponies, and cries of joy. She peered under the lodge cover, and discovered blood-smeared women arriving. They were leading ponies that dragged heavy travois, the poles sagging under raw, bleeding meat, huge gory chunks of it alive with green-bellied flies, all of it wrapped in mangy hides. It fascinated her, this savage feeding of the village and the excitement that bubbled up everywhere.

Several squaws with travois stopped at the chief's lodge, exclaiming and jabbering in their strange tongue, and that seemed to be what the chief and his wives had waited for. He muttered something and his ladies rose, beckoning Alexandra to come with them. She followed, curious. The women began unloading the travois, and urged her to help them. But she couldn't! Not in her splendid velvet! They tugged at her, and she felt helpless, unable to tell them the dress was her costliest—at least of the twenty she'd brought—and she wouldn't ruin it. But oh, how she wanted to help. The chief was inviting her to help in this noble enterprise!

She knew what she'd do. She slid back into the lodge and began undoing hooks, her nimble fingers loosening her skirts and blouse as swiftly as if she was mad for a lover, and in moments she stood in her snowy chemise and two flounced petticoats, while the chief gazed amiably. Then she stepped out into the blazing sun and set to work, enchanted by the honor bestowed on her. Something for her journal and poems. The squaws dragged huge bloody quarters of a buffalo off the travois, tugged heavy dark hides with blood on them over to a grassy area near the lodge, and Alexandra joined them, proud to be one of the chief's household. In moments her petticoats were smeared with gore, but it didn't matter. She helped one of the squaws stake down a hide, hair down, and then the woman handed her a chipped stone tool of some sort. A scraper. She would flesh the hide, and it would be a privilege. She watched the other squaw labor, stroking the fleshy gore and refuse away from the skin. It seemed so slow and the hide so large. But

Alexandra set to work, scraping diligently, wanting to shine for her chief.

Within minutes her arms ached, but she persevered, enchanted at the thought of noble labor for these noble lords of the American prairies. The chief's other squaw was cutting the buffalo into thin strips and hanging them from a nearby rack to dry. Jerky, she thought. This was how they did it. Tribesmen came and went, and she labored on, oblivious of them, fierce in her zeal to be a worthy Sioux. Day faded, and the redolence of roasting meat filled the village. It'd been a long time since she'd eaten, she thought wearily.

At last the squaws set aside their scrapers and knives and began a meal. Alexandra quit gratefully, her entire body aching beyond endurance. Filth stuck to her, covered her white underthings, gummed her blonde hair. She had no idea what had transpired in her own camp, and she didn't much care. No doubt they were preparing a buffalo roast too. Hump meat would be succulent beyond description, she'd heard, and she intended to find out. From time to time she'd seen the chief peer curiously at her, and she'd redoubled her labors then, wanting to be a perfect savage. Once that creased old medicine man had stared dourly at her and walked off angrily. She feared him vaguely.

The other wives chattered in their tongue, glancing at Alexandra now and then, and she didn't know a word, but she didn't feel lonely. Instead, weary as she was, she felt only loftiness, as if she'd been transported to some finer plane of existence, unspeakably majestic and superior to her conniving, petty, cruel countrymen.

She washed at the tiny creek, yearning for some good English lavender-scented soap. She thought to send for some, but rejected the idea. That sort of luxury seemed sinful to her. She would learn to live just as these magnificent children of wilderness lived, she thought. The chief's wives washed with pulverized yucca root that foamed swiftly when it was immersed, so she borrowed a piece of it and found it made effective suds. She arranged herself as best she could, and by the time the humproast had cooked to perfection she was back in her jade velvet, grinning across firelight to the noble who had smitten her. He returned her gaze enigmatically, nothing visible on his splendid face, which left her anxious and afraid she'd given offense.

They devoured a meal—more meat than she'd ever stuffed herself with—and she learned to let it cool enough so she could eat with her fingers. She felt so drowsy she could barely eat. No one from her own camp showed up to destroy her adventure, and she felt grateful for that.

That night she curled in the dark, curly-haired robe they'd given her, waiting for her savage lover and feeling hard clay beneath her. She knew he'd come sometime. She'd scrubbed in the creek once again after the juicy meal, and then had disrobed silently in the jet darkness of the lodge, her mind transported with visions of ecstasy.

But her savage prince didn't come, and she swiftly fell into troubled sleep.

Mister Skye sat on his impatient blue roan, watching the toil of the squaws in the cottonwood-dotted bottoms below. Actually, he was wondering what to do. The viscount had discharged him—again. It had been the outburst of an empty-handed hunter ashamed of his marksmanship. But it hung there, and Skye was free to leave if he chose. Victoria and Mary would be overjoyed if he did.

He had never guided a party he disliked as much as these. Usually he could negotiate with them face to face, and take the measure of them before committing. But this business had been arranged a year earlier by mail, and he had entered into it blind. It had been disastrous from the beginning, and if Victoria's forebodings were worth anything, likely to get worse. The viscount's station in England had twisted his perception of this wild world where tribesmen roamed free, the writ of courts didn't run, and a lord of England was no more a lord than anyone else. The viscount didn't seem a bad sort, just out of place and expecting a sort of absolute obedience that would endanger them all if Skye ever acquiesced. No doubt the viscount would reconsider back there, among Sioux he couldn't communicate with—not one word—and would send Baudelaire or Galitzin to make amends somehow. But Barnaby Skye wasn't sure he could accept. It was tempting just to let the bloody fool blunder himself, his women, and his retainers into grave trouble, or death. But that very thought largely made up Skye's mind for him.

Below, blood-drenched squaws in old buckskin dresses tugged at dusty hides and sawed at raw meat, loading it onto travois. It was brutal gory work. Already the raptors had collected, whole black flocks of quarreling crows, magpies, red hawks and others he couldn't put a name to. The Sioux hunters had gone back to the village, each leading his prized buffalo runner. Back there they'd celebrate, play the bone game, strut, dance, smoke, brag, and make medicine. The men of every plains tribe Mister Skye had ever seen lived like that, indolently, enjoying gossip and gambling, occasional bouts of hunting, and horse-stealing for the honors that came with counting coup. But the women toiled ceaselessly, cutting and preserving meat, gathering roots and greens, making shelters, tanning hides, sewing clothes and moccasins, cooking, caring for the children, collecting squaw-wood and tending the fires, loading travois, making harness and tack, and most everything else that required grubby toil.

The privileged life of the males had faintly annoyed Mister Skye. It seemed somehow wrong to idle the years away in gambling, gossip, ceremony, and the pursuit of dubious honors, with only an occasional foray required of them. Back in Washington City, dreamers were going to make farmers of them, make them toil like women, but they were only dreamers. These privileged warriors of the plains would either live a subsidized life or die away when the land was settled, refusing to toil like women or white men. Mister Skye hoped it wouldn't happen in his lifetime.

Jawbone grew rank under him, nipping at his boot, so Mister Skye gave him the subtle knee signal that would turn the horse toward the Sioux village. The evil-eyed horse was as ringy and taut-nerved as his wives in this village of their enemies, and showed it in his mincing alert gait. They passed innumerable women driving travois-laden ponies, the poles furrowing the clay under their groaning loads. The village would live fat for a little while, anyway. And the idle warriors would have a wealth of buffalo robes—created through the miserable toil of their women—to trade for powder and ball and knives. It was getting so that a tribesman measured his wealth by the number of wives and daughters he kept busy scraping and tanning robes, he thought. No wonder they all enjoyed capturing enemy women as much as they enjoyed snatching horses.

He reached the busy village knowing what he would do. Unless the viscount were adamant about the discharge, Skye would remain available. He didn't know why he had reached that decision, but supposed it had something to do with old British disciplines long forgotten in this wild land. The viscount would discover himself helpless and in danger without a guide, and Skye hated to abandon former countrymen who were in greater peril than they imagined.

For once the yellow and gray curs didn't greet him noisily. They had all gorged more offal than they could stomach and lay panting in the close heat of the afternoon, unable to stir. The women scarcely noticed his passage among the lodges as they sliced strips of meat for jerking, collected back sinew and backfat, and staked wet hides to the clay for the fleshing. As he rode past Bear's Rib's lodge, his gaze fell upon the astonishing sight of the viscountess in her once-white petticoats, kneeling on a green hide and scraping flesh from it, her blonde hair tumbling over her breast. It amazed him. A noblewoman. A viscountess. Wife of a peer of England, drudging like a charwoman and apparently discovering something romantic about it. She caught him watching and started to say something, but turned her back to him to hide her willowy body and freckled flesh. He grinned, touched Jawbone, and rode to his own camp.

He discovered Mary and Victoria silently building a fire to cook a huge humpmeat roast lying on the grass nearby. They eyed him dourly and busied themselves. Over among the tents of the retainers, the Abbot Beowolf had dropped the tailgate of his kitchen cart and was setting up a spit to cook a vast buffalo roast supper, humming the Agnus Dei cheerfully. The Sioux, unfailingly polite to their village guests, had inundated the viscount's party with the choicest cuts of buffalo, and invited them to the village feasts besides.

His lordship had vanished, no doubt in a sulk, so Skye unsaddled Jawbone and rubbed him, feeling the horse shiver under the massaging it got from Skye's stubby fingers. Then, exactly as expected, he spotted Baudelaire hastening through the heaps of camp equipment like a sallow-faced penguin.

"Ah, Skye. His lordship expressed regret for his tone of voice this afternoon, and wishes you to know that nothing was meant by it."

Victoria stared.

"Mister Skye, mate."

"Yes, yes. Will you accept?"

"Accept what?"

"Continued employment."

"Tone of voice? I heard him discharge me."

"Oh, quite unintended. A moment's disappointment in the hunt."

Victoria set her knife aside and stood, her gaze brittle on Skye.

"Am I to be discharged by the viscount whenever things don't meet his whim?"

"Well, Skye, you understand how disappointed—"

"We are guests here, Mister Baudelaire, and subject to their arrangements. The viscount knew that. He also knows I'll get him to buffler after we get free of the village."

"I'm afraid that's not going to happen soon, Skye. The viscountess is quite determined to stay and enjoy the companionship of chief Bear's Rib."

"They'll want you to leave before the sun dance. That's village religion, not for outsiders. And—Beaudelaire—you won't want to see it."

"Her ladyship is determined—"

"We're leaving at dawn," said Skye.

"But it's impossible. Her ladyship insists."

"My wives and I are leaving at dawn."

"But—we need you. We don't understand a word they speak. Not a word. And not one of us can do the sign language!"

"Then you'll join us when we go. I don't suppose you'll

want to be here in a large Hunkpapa village without a guide.''

"My dear Skye, you're being quite intractable, and it'll dismay Lord Frazier. Surely now you'll wish me to convey your delight to him."

A diplomat of sorts, thought Skye. He didn't know what to do. He hated to abandon these greenhorns to their folly. He wanted to leave this semi-hostile village whose warriors he had killed while battling beside his Crow kin. Every man in the village hoped to do something about it, and none more than that young Sitting Bull, whose agate eyes had been full of it. He wanted badly to please Victoria, who even now stared hard-eyed at him, demanding something wordlessly.

Well, these Britons weren't his kind of Britons, but they were his countrymen even so. "One day, Mister Baudelaire. And against my better judgment. You don't understand how things work here, or why I have my reasons. Let the viscountess indulge herself another day, and then we'll leave, and damned fast."

The viscount's secretary smiled blandly, and hastened off like a flapping crow, without a thank you or a nod.

Victoria wept. "You don't hear me," she said. "Magpie told me truly." The wetness streaking her weathered brown face tormented Barnaby Skye, but he'd made up his mind.

Chapter 11

So it would be. Victoria watched the strange man in the black clothing, with a coarse face the color of the belly of a fish, scurry back to Lord Frazier with the news that Skye would stay on. Now she knew what would come. These Britons from across the sea would take her man with them, and she'd never see Mister Skye again. They had some magic hold on him, like witch medicine, so that he wasn't acting like himself.

Twice now Mister Skye had been free to leave, and twice he had chosen to guide these people. He treated them strangely, as if they were chiefs over him, and didn't seem to be his usual self. And they treated him badly, not like a man at all, but a slave, and he permitted it. Oh, he growled a little, but he permitted it, and that seemed strange to her. When Mister Skye felt the presence of danger, he never permitted his clients to dictate to him, but now he was doing it. Truly, Magpie knew.

"Sonofabitch!" she exclaimed to Mary, who looked as troubled as she was. "Soon they will take him away and we'll never see him again."

She could not imagine her life without him. So many winters ago she could barely remember them, when he still trapped beaver for American Fur Company, he had come to her Kicked-in-the-Bellies village and had seen her. She had passed nineteen winters then, and soon he had found ways to spend time with her, often while she gathered firewood. How she'd smiled! What an honor to enjoy the attention of a happy, famous longknife, unimaginably rich, strong, and full of whiteman medicine. He had loved her. She could tell by the light in his small blue eyes, and the way his gaze had possessed her, lingering on her tall slender form as if to wonder what lay beneath her doeskin dress. In time he had laid before her lodgedoor a gift of a fine flintlock Hawken, a pound of DuPont and another of galena, two Hudson's Bay Four-Point blankets, a fine steel-bladed knife, an awl, and twenty metal arrow points. The next dawn her father had gladly taken these things into their lodge, and the compact had been sealed.

So long ago.

"We will not leave this village for many days," said Mary. "I am not happy here."

Victoria thought that was an understatement. They were both miserable in this village of the Lakotah, ancient enemies of the Absaroka and Shoshones. But as usual, Mary avoided harsh words, and that was a sweetness in Mister Skye's younger woman.

Silently they jabbed an iron spit through the hump roast and set it over the tiny fire, neither of them wanting to talk or even share their misery. She loved Mary, but she couldn't really talk with her any more than she could talk to Mister Skye now. The knowledge of her medicine vision burned too heavily inside her breast. But Mary knew. Indians sensed things that these whitemen were blind to.

Victoria had no way of coping with the impending separation except by withdrawing. She'd started that many moons earlier, when the Cold Maker still raged. Once she was certain of the things Magpie had shown her, she had begun to say goodbye to Mister Skye the only way she knew how, which was separation. She couldn't bear to have him torn from her old arms, so she let the distance come early, like cold fog, so the sundering would be completed before it happened. Now the dread was so large inside of her bony chest that she couldn't talk to her man, even when she tried or he wanted her to. So the gulf deepened as Sun made his passages, and she was almost a widow, though each night Mister Skye rolled into his soft robes and waited for her. But she didn't come to him. When the Britons took him away, she would cut off a finger, and half her hair, just as if she were a true widow.

Two days later it happened again. Mister Skye woke early, just as Sun was painting the world with color, and began at once to prepare for a journey. He saddled Jawbone, and wandered out into the well-guarded village herd to bring back the mares and mules. Victoria's heart gladdened at the sight of him bringing his ponies on a picketline. Could it be? Would they leave now? Hastily, her old heart pounding, she began to dismantle the lodge, unlacing the thong that held it together along the seam, while Mary—sudden brightness in her brown eyes—began filling parfleches with their gear and strapping lodgepole travois to the mules.

Oh, the joy of it! Around her the village stirred, or the women did anyway. There would be more buffalo meat turned into jerky or mixed with fat and berries into pemmican this day; more green hides staked and fleshed; more hides rubbed with buffalo brains to begin the tanning. And probably these Lakotah dogs would erect the forked center pole of the sun lodge they would construct from boughs, like an arbor. But maybe Mister Skye would leave! Sonofabitch, it would be good to escape, to breathe air these dogs didn't breathe, wrest away from the dark spirit-persons hovering here, all enemies of the Absaroka!

Several times she had dourly walked through the Hunkpapa village, a small alien woman hearing and seeing the things whitemen didn't see. She knew enough Sioux to make out what the women were saying, and she knew to read the faces of these dogs. Two faces especially. One was that of a seamed old medicine man, whose name, she learned, was Gray Mole. Named after an Under-the-Ground Person! It scandalized her that a medicine man of these people would name himself for the Underworld Persons. Surely he was a witch. The whitemen—not even her Skye—never noticed the way Gray Mole stared at them all with death in his gaze, and barked harsh things to the young warriors crowding about him. But she saw. Sonofabitch, she knew. And the other one, Sitting Buffalo Bull, who peered at Mister Skye with eyes full of something dark. The youth had vowed to undergo the sun torture at the dance, she'd learned, so that Sun and Wakan Tanka would strengthen him for his task—which was to face Mister Skye, killer of Hunkpapa warriors—whenever his medicine told him to. All this she knew, and it had shriveled her spirit and driven her inside of herself until only an ember of life burned deep within her bony breast.

But maybe now they would leave after all! Maybe Mister Skye had come to himself in the night, just as she had begged the true Absaroka spirits. Maybe they would leave this place now, and these countrymen of his too, with their witch-grip on him that troubled her so.

He grinned roguishly at her, cocking his silk hat and then lifting parfleches into panniers that would end up neatly balanced on their packsaddle.

"We can bloody well be away ten miles before the heat's up," he said. "Suppose you'd like that, Crow Woman."

She didn't dare to smile. If she didn't smile they would remain safely far apart, and that was what she could endure. But she met his gaze.

He peered about the silent camp. As usual, the viscount and Diana, along with Galitzin, the Abbot Beowolf, and Baudelaire, had partied well into the night, tapping the spirits wagon. They'd enticed Mary to join them, and she'd stayed late, Victoria knew.

"I told 'em I'd be leaving first thing," he muttered. "I don't see any sign they're coming along. I suppose that pleases you, old lady."

She turned dourly to her tasks, not wanting his cheer to breech the walls. She hadn't slept for days. Not since they'd all left Fort Union. She'd lain awake with her Green River knife sweaty in hand, protecting Mister Skye and Mary. Now tiredness laced her as she hoisted her little pad saddle over the ribby bay mare. She wouldn't let herself hope until they were a day's ride away from these dogs.

A young Hunkpapa warrior in a loincloth stood watching them, and she saw it was Sitting Buffalo Bull. The youth's gaze never seemed to wander far from Mister Skye, and she knew why.

"I'm ready any time you are, mate," Skye said to him in English. "Give yourself a knife or a lance. I'll meet you with my belaying pin."

She wondered if Sitting Bull understood. At least Mister Skye understood. She eyed her man briefly, pleased to see his warrior instincts hadn't diminished. Then she scolded the thought away from her head.

The one called Galitzin erupted from one of the Englishmen's tents, the one always dressed in brown who was chief of all the bulldogs and ponies. He lumbered across the crackling grass, crying out.

"Skye! Hold up!"

Mister Skye paused beside Jawbone, waiting. And so did Victoria pause, already knowing, the thing that had lightened her breath for a few minutes seeping away so that her body felt like the bars of galena the warriors turned into bullets.

"Skye! What are you doing?" Galitzin cried, out of breath.

"I told the viscount we'd be off at dawn, colonel. He's had the extra day he asked for. My terms were that I would be in command, or I would resign from his service."

"But his lordship intends to stay on. Lady Alexandra insists on it. She can't leave. She's taken to the savage life and plans to write about it." He smiled. "Taken to the chief, anyway."

"Colonel, you don't know what dangers lurk here."

"His lordship insists. He's retained you for a large fee, and expects your loyal, unflagging service, Skye."

"He's discharged me twice, mate. And rehired me twice."

"You'd leave us here, without even the means to understand these savages? You'd do that to your fellow Englishmen, Skye? To a peer and lord of England?"

"I would."

Victoria's heart lifted.

"That's irresponsible, Skye. We can't adjust to your whim every time the breeze turns it. His lordship asks your indulgence for one more day. Surely that's reasonable. Will the sky fall down in one day?"

Mister Skye didn't answer, but gazed out upon the shadow-carved prairie hills, gilded orange by the dawning sun.

"I suppose there's no harm in a day," he said. "Tell the viscount we'll leave tomorrow at dawn."

Woodenly, Victoria began to unpack.

Lord Frazier watched Diana Chatham-Hollingshead lead a little buckskin Indian pony into camp, looking so smug he thought she'd stolen it. She tied it to their parlor wagon and began grooming it, smirking all the while. He couldn't imagine why: the pony stood barely fourteen hands and obviously was mustang stock, with a broomtail and roman nose and narrowset eyes.

"It's a buffalo runner," she said. "I traded for him."

"Buffalo runner?"

"Their prize horses. You saw them run right in beside a buffalo and then duck away before they got hurt."

"Yes, yes of course, but what do you want it for?"

"Hunting buffalo, silly goose."

"You?"

"Of course. Why did I come all this way for? Tiddly-winks?"

"Not a bad reason," he said.

"He cost me my Manton and some powder and balls and caps."

"How'd you manage it?—I mean, you don't know a word."

"I watched the horse work during the hunt. And I saw him picketed before a warrior's lodge. So I got my rifle and laid it before the savage and pointed at the horse. He wanted two rifles—two fingers—and I refused. But I got him. I love being a savage."

"So does Alexandra," responded the viscount drily. "But

don't call them that around Skye. He'd take offense. Of course the ruffian wouldn't know a savage from an Englishman."

"I'm turning wild," she said.

"Not so I'd notice."

"That's because you can only think of that squaw," she grumbled.

"Ah! It'll happen! Soon! Mary has a weakness for spirits. Maybe tonight!"

"I'm a better savage," Diana muttered.

"We'll see!"

They were all tasting savage living, he thought. The trip was turning out well after all, in spite of that bad fright he'd gotten near Fort Union, and a bad hour shooting at stampeding buffalo. But he could take to this life. Skye'd been a problem from the start, but he'd tamed the oaf at last. His English origins had surfaced after all. A sharp word and a glacial glare, and soon enough a dustman or mechanic like that would doff his cap and remember he stood before a dread lord of England who had abundant measures to deal with insolent conduct. Skye had been no different, even though he'd been out in these wilds for years. That silk hat and the Mister were affectations, his way of playing lord over these savages.

But the problem had ebbed away. Between himself, Galitzin, and the wiles of Baudelaire, the beast was subdued, like a spirited dray, and would now turn his useful cunning toward whatever was needed. Whenever Skye wanted to depart, they just put him off another day. They'd put him off three days now and had him licked. Odd what this wild continent did to the dustmen. Not a bit pleasant to observe. Freedom gave a brute like Skye absurd pretensions.

The Hunkpapa village had ceased to alarm him, and now he wandered through it boldly, watching the savages at their daily life and play. How the women drudged! It amused him. Everywhere vast racks of drying jerky blackened in the sun, while squaws on hands and knees fleshed hides or kneaded slippery gray brains into them for their tanning. The warriors had finally settled down to some interesting work, too. They were building a sun lodge, with a high central pole, roof poles radiating from it, and a covering of boughs. He supposed soon they'd dance and prance and wiggle and wave feathers and pound their drums and gargle out howls, and that would be the sun dance. He intended to watch, even though Skye opposed it and muttered. But Skye no longer mattered.

Some of these savages had been just as curious about the whites, and none more so than the boy Skye called Sitting Bull. He'd come over daily to gawk, peering with unblinking solemnity at everything in the carts. He'd even gotten Gravesend to pull rifles out of the armory cart, and Gravesend had even let the savage heft and dry fire them. The youth made Lord Frazier uneasy, and he thought he'd shoo him off next time.

He made his way through the somnolent village, which had suspended its labors during the worst of the heat, to Bear's Rib's lodge. He'd pester Alexandra a bit. She'd gone tiddly for the savage life—a bit beyond what he'd expected, but she was the ethereal sort, and one never could tell. She'd no doubt have stories to tell back in Bury St. Edmunds, just as he would. In fact he could hardly wait to spin yarns. He approached the larger lodge, brightly stained with umber stick figures he took to be battle scenes, and found Alexandra not where he expected, huddled over some miserable hide, fighting greenbottle flies and scraping stinking yellow flesh from it, but standing quietly in the white sunlight while the chief's squaws took tucks in a fringed white doeskin dress she was wearing.

In fact Alexandra quite took his breath away. A blonde Sioux! The white doeskin, soft as velvet, fitted her willowy form tightly, and was gaily decorated with dyed quillwork over the bodice, red and yellow chevrons, while just above the fringed hem of her high skirt, which bared calf and trim ankle, was another red band of quills. She wore exquisite white moccasins, as fine as slippers for a ball, trimmed with rabbit fur. And over her breast lay a corrogated necklace of ivory-colored bones. A flaxen-haired jade-eyed savage! He gaped, feeling an uproar in his loins.

"Oh, Gordon, we're done with the buffalo. My dear chief

has given me a festival gown for the dances, and my sisters are fitting it.''

''You look—ah! Come to the parlor wagon and I'll show you what you do to me, my dear savage.''

She gazed at him levelly. ''I'm not sure I want to, Gordon. Bear's Rib is such a dear. I think I may stay. He's a perfect prince.''

''Really, Alexandra. It's time. Skye says we should—''

''He's a silly man.''

''Oh, I quite agree. But he seems to think the sun dance isn't quite what poor innocents like us should be witnessing.''

''Do you suppose they do something—'' She giggled. ''I must see it.''

''Where is Bear's Rib?''

''Taking a sweat. They have this marvelous idea that if they sweat, they purge their bodies of evil. So they sweat in a little hutch they make, all bare in there. The squaws bring them hot rocks and water. I wanted a sweat too, but they wouldn't let me. And they're going to make me go away to a separate women's hut soon. Oh well. I'll change all that.''

''I'm sure you can change anything, Alex.''

He left her there, a blonde Sioux goddess who stirred wild ripples in him. Oh, for a dusky gorgeous savage! His thoughts turned toward Skye's honey-fleshed young squaw, Mary, and he knew he'd force the matter tonight. Oh, he had his ways! A whole trunkload of trinkets, among other things. And an entire cart laden with kegs of bourbon and scotch, hogsheads of ale, red and white wines, ports and sherrys, and a devilish little liqueur called absinthe, distilled from wormwood, angelica root, sweet-flag root, star anise, and dittany, all of which made the heart grow fonder, as the old joke went. Tonight Mary and the emerald green absinthe!

He found his man, Baudelaire, squatting over a privy trench that Colonel Galitzin had ordered dug, army-style. It amused the viscount to catch his man with black britches down and pasty white rear catching the air.

''Baudelaire, here you are. I've been looking. What on earth do you do all day long? See here, Baudelaire. Make sure the squaw comes tonight for a nip, eh? Make sure of it. And tell the steward—I forget how he's called—tell him to bring the absinthe, eh? And tell Lady Diana to be there. Monkey see, monkey do, eh? And have my parlor wagon aired and the bedding too. Sweetened with sagebrush. I'm savage for a savage, eh? This has gone long enough, her coming for a nip and going back to that lout's lodge."

Baudelaire frowned, a sure sign of displeasure. In fact the man's only sign of displeasure, and the viscount took savage delight in catching him at his duties.

"Your lordship, I hear Skye's insisting we be off, for reasons he knows better than we."

"Ah, it's nonsense. Bear's Rib's getting my lady all fetched up in a ceremonial dress for the sun dance. If he didn't want us, he wouldn't be dressing her. She's gone daffy for him, but so what? It's an experience, eh? The Hunkpapa village in North America?"

Baudelaire grunted.

"The squaw, Baudelaire. And think of something to divert Skye while you're about it. Maybe the bloody oaf will drink once you fetch him some whiskey."

Baudelaire smiled up at him. "Count on me, your lordship," he said. "We will all be savage tonight."

Chapter 12

The lodge of Mister Skye had been darkened so long that Mary felt glad to escape each evening. Mister Skye did not come to her in the night, and because of Victoria's vision, neither did she go to him. The old woman had turned silent, and never chattered or cursed or laughed with Mary the way she used to. They had become worse than strangers because they could not reach across to each other. It shocked her that her man didn't heed the medicine of his sits-beside-him wife. Had he no reverence for the ways of the people? This time he had mocked her vision. She'd watched with troubled eyes as he ignored the prophecy of the spirit-helper.

She didn't like being in the village of the Hunkpapa, foes of her Snake people as well as Victoria's. Her spirit ached to be free, free of them all, the Englishmen and the Lakotah, free out on the endless prairies with only themselves and Jawbone, her man's little household. Never was her own spirit far from dread, knowing these treacherous Hunkpapa could turn on them in an instant. Maybe she wasn't even safe as a guest in their village. Maybe they would even violate the sacredness of the welcoming pipe.

Like blind men walking among rattlesnakes, the Englishmen had settled down to enjoy themselves. But at least they remained cheerful and enjoyed their days, unlike those in Mister Skye's lodge. Each evening the one in black, the one who whispered with soft lips while his eyes burned into her, invited her to have medicine-water with them. And she always did, glad to escape the gloom of her lodge. They gave her lots of things, bourbon and a whiskey with a smoky flavor they called scotch, and wines, some thick and red, others amber, some almost white. They made her giddy each night and made the gloom of Mister Skye's lodge go away.

They always invited her to sit with their chiefs and that was an honor too. The others all kept to their own fire and had no spirits to drink, except once in a long while. But among their chiefs the spirit waters flowed generously, and she never had to ask. In fact they enjoyed making her so giddy she could hardly walk back to her own lodge later. They sat in canvas camp chairs, the viscount in one displaying his crest; and Lady Diana, and Colonel Galitzin, and the strange one, Baudelaire, and the Viscountess Alexandra, who stayed with Bear's Rib now. But she preferred to squat in the way of her people.

"And how is our little Mary?" asked the viscount when she joined them. "Capital, I suppose."

She did not respond. Mister Skye wanted to leave in the morning, before they began the sun dance, but had once again been stymied by the viscount. Now it affected her too, and she thought she wouldn't enjoy this evening.

"I don't know this word capital," she said softly. "I want to go away from here. Mister Skye wants to go away and show you more buffalo. It is bad to be here."

"Oh, ho! We're having a fine time, and your man worries too much, little lady."

"That is why you hired him—to worry."

"Oh! You're a clever little wench. No, my dear, we are, ah, chiefs. Heap big chiefs. And your man may advise us, but only that. We decide. In any case, he's gotten quite tractable."

She stared at him, uncertain of the big whiteman words

but detecting something condescending in his talk. It angered her. And momentarily she raged at her man, at Skye, for bowing before these people from his nation, like some slave.

"Oh, see how you pout," he said. "Well, we're going to have something different tonight. Happiness spirits. See the bottle there, green as grass. It makes us jolly, eh?"

"I don't think I will. I don't want spirits this night."

"Oh, now, that's a foolish girl. Here. Aristides, pour her a generous one. Ah, take a little, you lovely wench."

"No, I don't want to. It is the start of the sun dance and we should not be here."

"My, you're being difficult, little savage. Tell her, Diana. Tell her what the green spirits do."

"Oh, my, they make me hot and I giggle and once I took off my clothes and ran," said Diana Chatham-Hollingshead. "But his lordship caught me easily enough."

"I would not do that," said Mary.

They sat quietly while Baudelaire fussed with things at the cart full of spirits. She noticed a strange anticipation among the whitemen tonight, as if something had been planned. Then Baudelaire thrust a glass brimming with the green spirits before her. "Ah, beautiful lady, this will make you happy," he whispered. "So happy."

"I don't think so. I am afraid tonight."

"It's that Skye again," said Colonel Galitzin. "He puts a damper on things. Drink up, my pretty tart. Ze viscount has gifts for you! A Hudson's Bay blanket. A looking glass. Golden ribbons for your hair. He's been waiting to give them."

"Oh, indeed, little vixen. Have a drink now, and when the world seems better we'll laugh and play. I'm a great tickler. I'll tickle you until you shriek."

Baudelaire held the glass before her, its emerald fluid glistening in the firelight; but she shook her head.

"It is a sacred time," she said. "Even these dogs the Hunkpapa know it is a sacred time to honor Sun, who warms us and gives us all."

The viscount looked vexed. "I say, that's just heathen talk, little lady. Surely your man has educated you—"

"You want me to drink it so you can lift my skirts," she said. "You must ask Mister Skye first. That is the custom."

"Usually when they want to lift my skirts, they ask me," said Lady Diana. "I know just how I'll answer."

"My man will tell you."

"Oh! That takes the fun out of it! Have some green spirits and I'll tickle you and you'll giggle and forget all your troubles."

But she shook her head.

"Well, have some whiskey!"

"No, it is time to honor Sun."

"I say, you vixen. I just may cart you off. I just may have the colonel here pick you up like a bag of wool and cart you off."

"You may cart me off," said the Lady Diana. "If you still can. You're running to fat, Gordon."

He glared at the white woman. "You aren't savage enough. I am feeling savage."

"My poor dear savage," she mocked. "How you growl and snap. Next thing you'll insist upon being called Mister."

They laughed, all except Mary.

"Drink up, drink up!" bellowed the viscount, sipping long and deep.

"I will go to my lodge now," said Mary. She rose, but the colonel's hand clamped her wrist, like a manacle of steel.

"No, his excellency will entertain you tonight," he said matter-of-factly.

She tugged hard, but he only clamped harder with a grip like a bear trap.

"Let me go. I will tell my man."

They cackled and sipped the green fluid greedily.

The viscount's lips parted. "I am feeling savage," he cried.

"Come along, you little red slut. The viscount will give you more than you ever dreamed of," whispered Baudelaire. "It's nothing. A moment of joy. An honor. Few women receive the honor of his attentions."

She struggled to free herself, and found she couldn't. Her

anger transmuted to dread and hate, even as Galitzin dragged her toward the glinting yellow wagon. She yanked hard, stumbled, heard them laugh.

"Oh, a fiesty wench!" cried Diana, giggling.

"Stop." The voice rumbled at them out of the black shadows, and she cried out to it, her spirit flying to meet it.

Mister Skye stepped into the amber firelight like some Viking giant, hairy and naked save for his breechclout and silk stovepipe hat and ugly square-toed boots. He carried only an old belaying pin of battered hickory. He squinted murderously at one and another of the sports, transfixing them with his glare.

"Let her go."

Galitzin obeyed.

"Pimps."

"I'll have you in irons, Skye. Galitzin. Put him in irons. All he's got is a stick."

"Your lordship. That's a belaying pin, and Skye was a—"

"Arrest the brute, Galitzin."

Mary rubbed her wrist where the man had clamped it, wanting to flee away, away, away from here. But she stayed.

Mister Skye turned to the viscount. "Touch my women and I'll kill you."

Baudelaire said, "My dear Skye, it was all a bit of fun. Oh, a bit risqué, I suppose, but just a little amusement."

"You lie well, Baudelaire."

"See here, Skye. You're threatening a peer of England, and I'll have you in irons, one way or another. Take your red slut, then. I don't want the dirty thing."

Galitzin dug into his brown jacket, and whipped out a small revolver. Skye's belaying pin flicked out, as deadly as a steel blade, and smacked it away, cracking the colonel's fingers.

Galitzin howled and began dancing in pain.

And from the darkness a lithe old woman emerged, pointing an old flintlock straight at Galitzin's heart.

"I say, Skye. You're perfectly insolent," the viscount raged.

A wild shriek, eerie even to Mary who had heard it countless times, pierced the quiet, and Jawbone appeared on dancing hooves, ears back, yellow eyes glowing in the firelight, snorting, teeth clacking murderously.

"I am that," said Skye.

On the first morning of the sun dance, Victoria and Mary silently saddled their ponies and rode out of the village, saying nothing to Mister Skye. He watched them go, understanding their need to escape this camp of their enemies as well as these Englishmen. Victoria's dour stare tore at him. It boiled with rebuke for ignoring her medicine and casting them all into some doom she had foreseen. He loved them both, his old sits-beside-him wife, and lovely Mary, each a gift without price for a roaming man of the mountains, sharing his joys and hardships, feasts and famines. Never before had his lodge been darkened by discord, and it tormented him.

He wanted desperately to go himself, just ride out into the breeze on Jawbone, lean into a shaggy cottonwood in a coulee somewhere, and watch cloud shadows windrow the golden grasses. He needed that. Needed to escape this lord of England and his retinue, all the condescension of his class. The viscount had not reached his position through a natural aristocracy of merit, or genius, or industry, but by hereditary right.

Mister Skye's own origins were far from base. He'd been born into the merchant class, son of an exporter and importer, and had a scholarly career ahead of him before he had been pressed into the royal navy by a roving gang of sailors. At least, he thought, his class progressed to some degree—not all avenues were open to commoners—on merit rather than the breeding of sires and dams. And while a debauched lord could fairly well ruin his estate, a lord of England he remained, while the life of any commoner required more character and courage.

Mister Skye was sick of them all, sick of their lechery, their attempts to seduce his Mary of the Shoshone, their nightly bouts of heavy drinking. Not that Mister Skye didn't drink himself, to excess on occasion. He held it to be a weakness in him. But most of the time he didn't drink spirits at all, and so his world held together—until now.

His heart cried for the liberty of the prairies, but he could not bring himself to leave. He loathed his own weakness. The viscount had some kind of grip on him, awakened something servile in him, rooted in his childhood, in an Englishman's respect for peers of the realm. He hated it. He'd lived in perfect freedom here in the American wilderness until this lord had found some way to reduce him, enticed him to ignore his own judgment. He saw himself becoming a lackey, like Galitzin, and it sickened him.

So he lingered sullenly in the village, making a point of stalking hot-eyed through Lord Frazier's entourage, daring Galitzin and his men to do something. They didn't; the sun dance absorbed them. The first day they stood around the great bough-covered sun lodge, chattering and joking, until Mister Skye told them that what they were witnessing among these Sioux was as sacred to them as Holy Communion was to Christians. That didn't quite stop it, but at least they'd been warned.

Each day fasting warriors chanted prayers, heaped gifts to Sun around the forked central pole that supported the brushy lodge, and recited their exploits in battle, often pantomiming the ways they counted coup.

He had no wish to talk to the viscount, Galitzin, or Baudelaire, but didn't mind explaining things to Lady Alexandra, who watched quietly, full of romantic notions. She fascinated him, this blonde beauty wearing exquisite Sioux ceremonial dress, quilled and beaded so delicately that the work could have won a display in the British Museum.

"It's something you can endure now, Lady, but not on the fourth day. I think you'd better not watch then."

"Oh, it is beautiful. These Hunkpapa souls know only light, unlike ourselves. What are they doing now, Mister Skye?"

"They're giving sacrifices to Sun, to appease Onk-te-gi. That's the spirit in the body of all living creatures. If he's appeased, the tribe prospers."

"Oh, that's beautiful."

"You haven't yet seen one kind of sacrifice, I'm afraid."

The youth, Sitting Buffalo Bull, had vanished, and Mister Skye suspected he was fasting in preparation for the brutal fourth day.

Each evening Skye's women returned out of the prairie, and silently slid into their robes, barely acknowledging him. So his lodge remained gloomy, and he had begun to take his food at the cooking cart of the Britons because no one in his dark lodge bothered to prepare it. As the Hunkpapa sun dance progressed his women seemed more and more distant, and he wondered where out there in the great circle beyond the wide valley they lingered, and what they did during the burning days.

On the fourth day of the sun dance a new mood pervaded the village, as tense and solemn as a crucifixion. And now the villagers stared dourly at their guests, with looks that told Mister Skye, at least, that this part of it was to be private. But the viscount and his minions paid no heed. Skye hadn't spoken to them since the night he'd rescued Mary from rape, but now he decided to say something. That was his job. For this they'd employed him.

"I don't believe we're welcome at today's events, Lord Frazier," he said quietly.

The viscount stared, faint amusement rising in him. "Well, Skye, you've decided to start complaining again. We're doing quite well, thank you. I hear it's quite exciting."

"How do you know that?"

"Why, from my lady. She's learned a bit of the blarney."

"Does she know what will happen?"

"Oh, some sort of bloody pain, I guess. My men are all for seeing it, and so am I, Skye. You fret too much." The lord eyed him. "You're wandering free on my sufferance now, so watch your step, Skye. I'll have you whipped yet."

Mister Skye sighed, as unable to cope with these people as ever, and feeling trapped.

Around noon of a blistering day, Sitting Bull emerged from a special lodge made of brush, looking gaunt and solemn, and Mister Skye knew he'd been fasting. He was the only one to have made the vow. Often several men made the vow. And once in a while a woman would sacrifice for Sun, if she wanted something badly. Sitting Bull had painted himself white and black and red for this occasion, turning himself into a ghastly shining spectre. The youth spotted Mister Skye and paused, staring, meeting Skye's gaze with an unblinking one of his own. Then he smiled slightly and walked on.

A profound silence settled among the spectators as they watched Sitting Bull walk into the sun lodge, accompanied by that craggy-faced medicine man, who was now wearing a buffalo-horn bonnet and carrying medicine pouches in addition to the one he wore around his neck. Two others came also, village elders, each with those peculiar scars across their breasts. The Hunkpapa knew what was to come and waited expectantly, and the Britons, sensing something sacred in this, settled into unaccustomed reverence. Children clutched their mothers solemnly, drinking in this sacred event.

Sitting Bull stretched himself on his back, waiting. The two elder warriors, large powerful men with battle-scars on their flesh and coup feathers in their hair all displaying valor, withdrew glinting knives.

"Oh dear no," muttered Lady Alexandra.

Mister Skye watched dourly. They'd all been warned over and over. Several of his lordship's retainers sweated and twitched. The viscount looked pale, determined to endure whatever sights he must behold.

One warrior jabbed his knife horizontally through the chest muscle until its point emerged inches away. Sitting Bull groaned in spite of his best efforts not to. Red blood, brilliant red, bright as death, gouted from the wound and sheeted down Sitting Bull's side and belly.

"Oh! Don't do that!" cried Lady Alexandra.

The medicine man glanced angrily at her.

Sweat beaded on Sitting Bull's brow. The warrior slipped a skewer of glossy bone through the wound until both its ends projected from the youth's chest. Then they repeated the whole thing, jabbing the bloody knife through the mus-

cles of the left breast and following it with a skewer. Sitting
Bull's body turned red.

Lady Diana moaned, and looked ready to flee. Several
of the viscount's men had vanished from the silent crowd,
and Skye glimpsed one heading for river brush, holding his
stomach.

The warriors tied braided thongs to the ends of each
skewer and tugged mercilessly, lifting corded flesh off Sitting Bull's chest until one could see raw red muscle in the
leaking wounds. The youth stood up shakily, muttering
something that Mister Skye understood, even as the blank
gaze of the whole village fell upon him and then the Britons.
Mister Skye stood his ground, thankful that Victoria and
Mary hadn't heard and the others didn't understand. There
were so many young men, in so many villages across the
plains, who had made the same vow, often during a sun
dance like this. And so far it had come to nothing. But one
never knew.

The warriors snaked the two lines up over the fork of the
sunlodge pole and tugged higher and higher until they lifted
the sinewy muscles from Sitting Bull's chest, forcing him
to stand on his bare toes facing the pole. And then they
anchored the ropes that way.

"Hiyah!" cried the young man in a voice that carried
eerily out upon the throng and into the prairie. He began
his slow, spastic dance, sometimes throwing himself backward until he hung from the bone skewers. Around the pole
he went, singing his song, scorning the pain, sheeting blood
from wounds that grew with every vicious tug.

"Good God, Skye, when does this end? Will he die?"
asked the viscount.

"When he pulls himself free after dancing the rest of
the day, mate. The skewers must work through his muscle."

The viscount watched, disturbed. Both Diana and Alexandra fled, the viscountess sobbing as if something inside
her had been violated.

"Skye. What did that chap say just before he began that
dance, eh?"

"He asked Sun to honor his sacrifice of undergoing torture, and to give him strength to fulfill his vow."

"But what did he vow, Skye?"

Barnaby Skye wondered whether to tell the viscount, and finally decided he would. He lifted his silk hat and settled it again in ritual gesture. "To kill me because I once killed Hunkpapa in a battle. And all white trespassers."

Chapter 13

Sometimes Victoria rode out of the village with Mary, but this day she didn't. She wished to be alone, and learn about aloneness. She could not fathom why Mister Skye still lingered there. His countrymen from across the sea had a witch-grip upon his spirit. She could see that but didn't know what to do. Never before had Mister Skye ignored her medicine. Always he had heeded it, and it had saved their lives several times.

She kicked her slat-ribbed mare over to the Yellowstone—she called it Elk River—and turned the horse upstream, her heart empty but her senses savoring the clean summer air and the freedom of the land. She did not know where she would go. She never did. Her intent was to escape, not go somewhere. Back in the Hunkpapa village, the boy, Sitting Bull, lay in great pain, because the ribbons of muscle on his chest had not parted during the terrible dance until well into the night. Big medicine! That much pain would make him a great medicine leader of the Lakotah nations, and one to be feared.

She rode aimlessly along the river trace, small and weathered, hunched over her little pad saddle, and it was only by accident that she saw the warrior ahead before he saw her. Instinctively she slid her pony into the massed cottonwoods and turned herself into smoke. If he was a good warrior he would spot her anyway, because his pony would tell him where she sat on her mare. She felt no fear. With Mister Skye soon to be taken away, her own suns meant nothing. If this one was an enemy of her people, she would shoot him and then go to the Other Side when the rest caught her.

Painted! This one wore only a breechclout and coup feathers tucked into his braided jet hair. He carried a strung bow and nocked arrow, ready for anything. Great chevrons of black and white paint, made from grease and white clay, or fire ash, slashed his face and arms and announced to any observer that this one was on a mission against the enemies of his people.

She slid off her little pony and clutched the bay's nostrils, intending to clamp them shut at the first sign of whinnying. She watched the painted warrior from deep in the cottonwoods, seeing and not seeing, following the sunlight and shadow of his quiet alert passage. Her heart lifted into its fear-rhythm, and she slid out her own Kentucky Longrifle, which had a shortened barrel, and poured fresh powder into the pan to prime it. Out toward the riverbank the warrior paused, sensing something from the behavior of his horse. He peered into the shadowed cottonwoods and didn't see her.

At least she thought he didn't. He was a wise one, and knew the birds weren't chirping and everything had become too silent. She waited, ready to cock the old weapon and shoot. The flint would strike the frizzen and make sparks. The powder in the pan would flash through a little hole, igniting the powder in the barrel and driving a ball into the heart of the warrior. White man's magic, and she respected it.

He slid off his pony and pierced into the dense woods straight toward her, his bow at the ready. Maybe she would sing her death song now, she thought. But her medicine vision was not of this. Closer he came, alert and ready, studying all things. She admired his skills. Closer still, and her heart leapt. Absaroka! Everything told her: his moccasins; the color bands on his arrow; the shape of his bow; the way he had painted himself.

A magpie exploded from a branch and he whirled. Odd that a sun-loving magpie would haunt these shadows. But not odd at all if her spirit-helper had come to protect her. The warrior whirled, followed the flitting raucous bird as it hopped toward the river, and at last he made his way back to his pony and headed back up the Yellowstone. She wanted to cry out after him, this one of her people, but she didn't. Instead she turned her pony deeper into the woods until she reached the broken river bluffs, and steered the mare into a tiny coulee leading upward toward the rough plains. Up there, from a position well hidden by the crease in the slope, she might see.

Near the top, she tied her pony in the deep shadow of a three-limbed juniper, and clambered the last bit of slope breathlessly until she could peer out upon the breast of the earth and down into the river valley ahead. They were there, more than she could count. Maybe two hundred Absaroka, painted for war and stalking the Hunkpapa, planning to avenge ancient wrongs. She squinted hard, trying to name names, but they were a little distant for her old eyes. She sensed these were river Absaroka, not her own mountain Kicked-in-the-Bellies. Still, the People of her tongue, within the hoop of her nation. Oh, to go talk with them! To talk in the language of her birth, and see kin! For there would be many she knew and others she'd heard of. And she could tell them much about the village. They were resting their ponies in the midday heat, and soon would ride again, a long bright column of warriors, painted and armed and ready to die.

She crouched uncertainly, a dilemma pinioning her. Her man and Mary and Jawbone were in the Lakotah village. And the first thing the Hunkpapa would do under attack would be to murder them, and the whitemen too. Every one, but especially Mister Skye, who had fought beside the Absaroka against them. It could happen in moments: the village wolves would spot the Absaroka column; Bear's Rib would gather his elders while warriors sprang to their horses and gathered arms; and the wolves, the village police, would turn upon Mister Skye even before her man knew of trouble. The rest she didn't care about. Let the Hunkpapa do what they would to Lord Frazier. But even as she thought it she felt bad inside. Her man had agreed to protect Lord Frazier and his party. So she must, no matter what her feelings.

She slipped back to her gaunt pony and led it away, carefully keeping a high, grassy hump that was famous as a watching place between herself and the war party. After a little while she slid onto her mare and rode across the prairie-tops, well south of the Yellowstone valley. It would be safer than following the river bottoms. She peered back warily, but no one pursued. Sun had already covered most of his day's journey when she dropped down the bluffs, under the watchful eye of the village wolves, and into the Hunkpapa village. She could see it was preparing to move, with the dance over, the entire flat where the Tongue and Yellowstone conjoined stripped of golden grass, and the odors of long habitation dense in the sultry air. It looked peaceful, but in a little while everything would change, and the shriek of the wounded would fill the land.

She had no time. At any moment the police society would spot the Absaroka and the crier would spread the alarm through the whole village. She kneed her sweating mare straight toward her lodge and found her man there, and Mary, neither of them doing anything except waiting for the furnace heat to lift.

She slid down and padded directly to Mister Skye, who peered up at her somberly, a question in his eyes.

"Absaroka! Painted! Many, many!" she hissed.

Mister Skye sprang to his feet even before she'd finished, and Mary started walking swiftly toward the herd to collect their mules and horses.

"How much time?" her man asked.

"No time."

He squinted at the village, knowing exactly what would happen when the alarm sounded. She could see that.

"Leave the stuff," he said.

Her man trotted toward Frazier's camp nearby, while she caught Jawbone and saddled him. The horse watched her with laid-back ears. Then she grabbed halters and raced toward the herd to help Mary, keeping her pace just slow enough not to draw attention.

When she returned, with two mules in tow, she saw her man roaring at Galitzin. Good. The warrior chief, not Lord Frazier. But the warrior chief wasn't listening, and then she saw the viscount emerge from his wagon with no shirt on, and saw them all talking and waving arms. She squinted at the ridges to the west, and saw nothing. No village wolves scrambling down the bluffs or riding the ridge, shooting off their fusils.

As long as they were arguing, she'd save what she could. She threw a packsaddle over a big mule and cinched it, and then stuffed their things, the pemmican and jerky, powder and ball, spare moccasins, Mister Skye's belaying pin, into parfleches and then into panniers. Mary did the same. They would take everything except the lodge. No time for that. And dismantling it would alert the village. At last Mister Skye hastened toward them, and behind him men stirred, heading for the arms cart where Gravesend began handing out weapons.

"What?" she cried.

"Can't get them to leave quick. They want to take the carts. Half hour of harnessing. Frazier says they've got thirty armed men, some with double-barreled scatterguns. I told him they'd be dead in minutes, scatterguns or not. And I'd be dead even faster than that. He called me a coward and other things. I said I'd stay and defend them—if they'd listen. And you'd try to reach your people, let them know. Frazier got excited, said they'd harness up and head for the ridge and watch, like some tournament."

"You'll die. Why do you do this?"

He sighed. "I have to. It's my job. I was paid to do it, even if they ignore my advice. At least Galitzin's been told. He can organize them. If Frazier lets him. His lordship thinks he'll sit on a ridge and watch an Indian war."

Victoria turned away, her old eyes suddenly blurred. She did not want to look at him or let him see her eyes. Moments later she and Mary rode their ponies up the grassy bluffs, leading the packmules, ever farther from her man.

And ahead were the warriors of her own people, whose presence might kill Mister Skye. The village wolves eyed their passage, whispered to each other, but did not stop them.

Mister Skye watched his women ride away, growing smaller and smaller until they topped a horizon and vanished. He wondered if he'd ever see them again. They'd attracted the attention of the village wolves, who were collecting up there to talk about it.

The village barely stirred. A crowd of young men played the stick game near the riverbank. Old men gossiped. Only the women stirred, packing their belongings in preparation for the exodus to a new campsite starting in the cool dawn. A few hunters were out in the cottonwood bottoms looking for deer, but not very hard because the village was glutted with buffalo meat. Off in the center of the village Bear's Rib sat before his lodge, listening to medicine men decide where the village should go next. Up on the bluffs the policing society spread out once again, but didn't seem alarmed.

Mister Skye turned toward the activity at hand, and saw at once that it looked too hasty. Retainers were wildly sorting out harness and folding up camp.

"Colonel Galtizin," he said. "Slow down the men. Hide those weapons at once."

Galitzin stared at him, rapping a gold-headed swagger stick against his brown britches.

"Colonel. Your safe passage out of here—if it exists at all—is to leave in a normal way, not a panic."

"Who's in a panic, Skye? His lordship wants us to gather on that western ridge so we can watch ze fight. We must hasten or miss it."

Skye grabbed the man by the brown lapels of his hunting jacket and tugged. Galitzin bounced into him, yanked by a giant hand.

"Unhand me, you oaf!"

Skye didn't. Instead he spat words into the face he had yanked inches from his own. "In that village, Galitzin, are about a hundred and fifty able warriors, capable of becoming an army in about a minute, armed and mounted. Add

fifty old men and boys itching to slaughter you. And your
ladies. Add a hundred women who can draw a bow as well
as their men.''
    ''We'll hold them off. Carts make a defensive ring.''
    ''You'll fail. And you'll never see your horses again.''
    Something changed in Galitzin's eyes. At least he was
listening.
    ''Stop the panic, Galitzin. It may be too late. It's been
noticed. I'm riding to Bear's Rib and tell him we've decided
to leave, go buffler hunting again. Maybe—just maybe—I
can make this look natural—if you help.''
    Galitzin didn't reply. Skye let go of the man, and he stag-
gered. A bulldog barked, growled, and bit Skye's boot.
    ''Your disrespect will be reported to his lordship, Skye,''
Galitzin said.
    Skye ignored the man. He strode away, barely containing
rage, and clambered up on Jawbone, who sensed trouble
and clacked his teeth, peering about with scurvy eyes. He
steered his roan straight through the village toward Bear's
Rib's lodge, trying to find a way to make a late-afternoon
exodus seem normal. Behind him he heard Galitzin snap
orders to hide the weapons, and knew he'd won—for a moment. Still, the feverish activity had alerted the village, and
people stared at the whitemen who were frantically gathering their horses and packing up.
    He rode past the lodge of Sitting Bull's family and saw
the youth lying on a pallet before it, his grossly swollen
chest bandaged. It would be a month before the torn flesh
would heal. Sitting Bull watched his passage with raptor
eyes, mumbling something.
    There were no smiling faces in this village now. Sitting
Bull's vow had reminded them all that Mister Skye fought
beside the Absaroka and made widows in lodges here. His
passage past busy women and idling men occasioned stares
and muttering, but he ignored them. The lives of all he'd
been paid to protect would depend on his skills now. He
scanned the bluffs anxiously, hoping not to see a horseman
racing along a horizon, firing warning shots or waving a
blanket. If only the Crow war party would linger a while
more . . .

He dug into his possibles kit and found a pungent twist of tobacco. If he could nerve himself to do it, while his every instinct screamed at him to get out, he'd propose a goodbye smoke with Bear's Rib and his shamans. He didn't know if he had the courage. If the alarm sounded while they were smoking, they'd likely slaughter him on the spot. But only if they identified the enemy as Crows.

He reined Jawbone to a halt a little apart from the circle of village headmen and shamans, and dismounted slowly. He was not a natural horseman, and clambering on or off had never been easy. He took his time unbuckling his holstered Colt revolver, and laid the belt over his pad saddle. It was a sign of peace and trust. He clutched his twist of tobacco, walked to the periphery of the ring, and waited there. These were village leaders, and they were engaged in medicine ceremony, and dressed for the occasion. The selection of a new village site, and even the way to travel there, would be divined by medicine men and war chiefs in congress. The village would need grass, water, trees, and proximity to *pte*, the sacred buffalo.

Time ticked slowly as the headmen continued their divinations, eying Skye occasionally. While he waited, he watched the slumbering hills for signs of the eruption to come, but they lay somnolent in the summer heat, innocent of death. At last Bear's Rib stood and invited him to a place of honor within the circle. Mister Skye settled himself awkwardly—his blocky body never folded easily to the ground—and began at once to say his goodbyes, using what Sioux words he knew, supplemented with his talking fingers.

His party had decided to pull out now, ahead of the village, he said, and head westward on their trip. He brought with him a twist of tobacco for a final smoke, and to honor them for their hospitality.

"Where are the others, the great chief from across the waters, and his headmen, Mister Skye?" asked Bear's Rib. "Have they forgotten us? And why have your women gone away?"

Mister Skye sighed. As usual, nothing of consequence ever escaped a village. By some mysterious telegraphic means, everyone knew everything.

"My women have gone ahead. The ones I guide are busy packing. I will bring them for a smoke soon. But now I have a twist for you, as a gift."

Tobacco was a peace-gift everywhere on the plains, and Mister Skye hoped it might do. He handed it to Bear's Rib, who sniffed its aroma and smiled. He nodded to one of his young women who was hovering near the lodge, and she ducked inside to fetch the pipe.

"It is a strange time to leave, Mister Skye," Bear's Rib observed.

"It will make your passage in the morning easier, Bear's Rib. We will smoke our pipe now instead of in the morning when you will be eager to be off."

Bear's Rib nodded. He accepted the red-quilled pipe pouch, made of the velvety hide from an unborn buffalo calf, and deliberately withdrew the pipe, packing its pink pipestone bowl with the tobacco.

"The woman with hair the color of sun went away after the sun dance," he said as he tamped. "I would trade many ponies for her."

"Ask her man," said Skye. "Perhaps he will trade. He needs good ponies for his carts."

"The carts are strange sights," the chief said, lighting the pipe with an ember passed to him in a green leaf by one of his women. "White men show us astonishing things." He sucked until the tobacco glowed yellow, and then began the ancient ritual, saluting the spirits that dwelled in the cardinal directions, and then *Wakan Tanka*, the One Above, and the Earth Mother below.

Time ground on. Mister Skye studied the ridges. The pipe made its way around the circle of elders, some of whom watched Skye malevolently, Sitting Bull's vow obviously on their mind. And still time ticked on, as each performed the ritual. Mister Skye's nerves abraded with every salute to the spirits, and he wondered if he could endure to the end of this.

Off at the edge of the village he heard the hawing and bawling of drivers, and the creak of carts, and a moment later the viscount's party wallowed across a soft bottom of the Tongue and began toiling up a western slope. The elders watched curiously, some frowning because of this impolite exodus.

The pipe came to Master Skye, and he ritually saluted the spirits, even while he watched the caterpillar of carts toil up a steep grade toward the western horizon, inching away from the Hunkpapa. Now Skye sat alone in a village of Victoria's ancient enemies, and it made his hair prickle. Slowly the caravan topped the bluff and dwindled into small dots while the elders watched.

Bear's Rib took the pipe and tapped it, dumping the dottle, and turned to Skye. "You did not speak truly, saying you would bring the great chiefs to us, Mister Skye."

His eyes plainly expressed distrust, and something more: the power to do whatever he chose with this famous big-medicine whiteman who sat beside him unarmed.

Just then two Hunkpapa wolf-society warriors, half way up the loaf-shaped signal mound to the southwest, discharged their pieces.

Chapter 14

They topped the bluffs and rode out onto a sun-blasted grassy plateau. It hadn't been a long uphill trek, but enough to wind the drays and horses, so Galitzin ordered a halt to let the beasts blow. Lord Frazier sat his pony, absorbing the empty sweep of land shimmering in a white glare. Just north lay the emerald valley of the Yellowstone, coiling between golden bluffs. Far to the south rose low hills, thickly blackened with pine, toothing the horizon. To the northeast he could make out the green valley where the Tongue joined the Yellowstone. Tiny figures down near the Hunkpapa village were scurrying about, gathering fractious horses. He could no longer make out the lodge of Bear's Rib or see that perfidious guide Skye smoking the pipe with the savages, but it didn't matter.

"I say, colonel, isn't that the war party?" he asked, pointing toward a column of crawling dots in the hazy west. The viscount could see that the fight between the Crow and Sioux would occur right around the confluence, with each side unable to spot the other until the last moment because of the dense cottonwoods.

Galitzin pulled field glasses from his kit and watched. "That's what it is," he said. "A large column."

"I say, Galitzin. Let's watch. Head for that promontory, eh? We'll see a rare thing, oh a proper joust! Have them put up the marquess, eh? The ladies and I'll watch. Set a guard, of course. Some of those blokes might ride up here."

"It might be better to withdraw from sight, your lordship."

"Pshaw! Let's see the fight! The Hunkpapa won't fight us, and Skye's squaws went off to warn the Crow to leave us alone, eh?"

Galitzin nodded reluctantly, and commanded the column to make for the level bench near the signal hill. A minute later the viscount's retainers trotted out the gaudy marquess tent from a cart and erected it with its open side pointing northeast. The white and green-striped linen chattered in the furnace wind but in short order the noble tent stood, a protection from harsh sun and the hot gale. Swiftly the men arranged camp chairs within, and settled the viscount and his ladies in them.

"Oh, capital, capital, Galitzin! We've a grand view of the whole spectacle."

"I hope the savages aren't cowards," said Lady Diana. "Do you suppose they'd cut and run? I do so want a fight."

"It'd be a pity, my lady," said Galitzin.

"Savages," said Lady Alexandra. "Blood and gore, feathers and paint, medicine and death. Oh, how they send their ghastly vibrations through me! I shall write an ode!"

"You're being ethereal again, my dear."

Baudelaire supplied opera glasses from the viscount's bountiful supplies, one each for the ladies, the viscount and himself, and they settled down to watch while the canvas behind them rumbled and snapped in the gale like God clearing his throat.

"The Crow column's halted," muttered Galitzin, peering through his field glasses. "They're consulting, I think."

"I suppose Skye would tell us they're making medicine," the viscount said.

Galitzin studied them. "Zey're looking this way."

"Colonel, run up the flags, eh? That'll warn them." The

viscount didn't relish the attention his candystriped tent was
receiving below. "And arm the men, eh? I wouldn't want
those naked thieves around our carts."

Galitzin nodded. A sharp command to Gravesend set men
running, and in a minute the Union Jack flapped from one
pole of the marquess tent, and the viscount's own banner,
a green shield on a white ground, flapped from the other
pole. The colonel posted an armed guard at either side of
the tent as well, just to ward off trouble, and sent the rest
of the cartmen and carts back from the promontory, where
they would be less visible.

"Ah! That's better, colonel. The savages all know the
Union Jack. They've all traded with Hudson's Bay, I imagine."

"What if they come?" asked Diana nervously.

"Why, we'll distribute arms and repel them, my dear.
Gravesend's at the ready I'm sure."

"I wish I had my rifle," she said darkly.

"Watch the show, watch the show! Will you ever see the
like again?" He turned to his aide. "Say, Baudelaire, let us
have some refreshments, eh? Tell the cooks! How can we
watch these savages chop heads off without tea and tarts?"

"I want scotch," said Lady Diana.

"I don't believe we have water," said Baudelaire.

"Well fetch some. Send a man."

"Of course." Baudelaire smiled and vanished from the
chattering, stuttering tent.

Down in the village warriors were leaping onto bare-
backed ponies and urging them toward the river in knots,
while others still gathered arms. Most unwarlike, the viscount thought, observing the clots of warriors erupting every
few moments from the lodges below. And off to the left, in
the Yellowstone valley, the Crow still stalled for some reason, a congregation of them on their ponies collected around
one or two with warbonnets. He swept the whole panorama
with his opera glass, and discovered two or three savages
straight ahead on the lower reaches of the very promontory
from which they viewed this grand event. These faced the
Hunkpapa, and seemed to be their village police, signaling

the whereabouts of the Crow. Ah! What a sight! What a fine yarn to spin back in the clubs!

He wished he had Skye at hand to answer questions. The only thing of any value about that guide was that he knew his savages and what they were doing. But the dustman probably sat back there puffing a pipe in the village.

Off in the heat haze the Crow began to divide into two parties, each under a bonneted chap, he noticed. By George, at least they were organized, unlike the Sioux savages, who all raced hither and yon like headless hens.

"Sketch it, Alex. Have the guard fetch your pad and charcoal, eh?"

"It's too beautiful to sketch. I'd never capture it," she replied.

"Well I'll have them send your things." He clapped his hands sharply. "Guard. You, there. Go fetch the lady's portfolio, eh?"

The Hunkpapa boiled up the Yellowstone bottoms, but were often obscured by the canopy of cottonwoods. Many still straggled out of the village, after snatching ponies from the farflung herd. The Crow, on the other hand, had divided themselves, one wing proceeding down the river straight toward the Hunkpapa, and the other—oh, a surprise!—turning squarely toward the promontory. Why, he thought, the buggers were going to circle around and hit the village from its flank. And they'd pass close enough to give him a dandy look at greased bronze bodies, feathers, painted ponies of every description, the whole bloody thing.

"I think they're attacking us," said Diana nervously.

"Oh, pshaw, they're flanking the Sioux. They'll swoop down on that village from up here. What a sight, eh?"

"Shouldn't we be armed?" she persisted.

Maybe they should. "Galitzin!" he bawled, not seeing the colonel. He unfolded from his camp chair and peered around the edge of the fluttering canvas. There was the colonel, leading a squad of cartmen at a trot, all of them well armed with good British steel, powder and ball.

"Ah, colonel! You're ahead of me. Good thinking, man. Post these blokes round about. If that baggage gets too close, pop a warning shot, eh?"

"Where's the damned wine steward?" asked Lady Diana. "I want spirits. Where'd Baudelaire sneak off to? You can't trust servants to do their duty any more."

"I'm sure he's fetching something, my dear."

"Well, I'm dry as a camel's tit. Tell him to move his arse or I will."

"Where are my puppsies? Where's Chesterfield?" asked Lady Alexandra.

"I think zey took to the shade under the carts, my lady," said Galitzin.

"Have Chesterfield brought! He would enjoy this! He'll snap and growl!"

"I'll send a man, my lady."

"No, you do it. You're master of the hounds."

"As you wish, my lady." Galitzin, sweating in the broiling heat but unwilling to doff his brown tweed jacket, trotted back toward the carts to capture the bulldog.

"Really, Alex. You should be watching this, not worrying about your little puppsie," chided the viscount.

"I want Chesterfield to see it too," she replied coldly. "Oh, the brute strength of those savages!"

They were closing now, around a hundred Crow warriors on thin ponies, each man stripped down to a breechclout, their amber flesh glinting from sweat or grease and slashed everywhere by chevrons of color, vermilion across their brows, white, black, ochre. Some three hundred yards distant they fanned out into a rough line that stretched clear across the western slope of the promontory. At first their piercing cries sounded almost gentle, wafting in against the rumbling breeze. But then the cries grew sharper, like the bark of coyotes under a fat moon, and the thump of distant fusils reached them at about the same time as the ripping sound of balls piercing linen.

He lacked even a moment but he made one. Just as Bear's Rib and the elders sprang to their feet, Jawbone shrieked. Mister Skye threaded through the Hunkpapa, wresting himself away from powerful grips that snared his forearms and ankles. Jawbone knew. The horse bulled in, teeth clacking, front hoofs striking. Mister Skye curled around to the side, quieted the berserk roan with a sharp command, and mounted. His revolver belt had slid to earth; no time to fetch it. He steered around lodges, somehow dodging women, children, old people, and racing warriors, along with curs and loose ponies. Jawbone raced between the cones, tipping kettles, collapsing racks of jerky, scattering embers, pulling picketlines and perforating staked hides.

But Mister Skye wasn't watching where Jawbone took him. His gaze lay on the bluffs and the armed wolves, the police society of the Hunkpapa, who had alerted the village to attack and were even now shouting to each other and urging warriors in the village to ride up the Yellowstone. And who were pointing at Skye as Jawbone burst around the last lodge at the edge of the village and lunged through the muck of the Tongue. They'd stop him if they could. They'd try to keep him from reaching the Crow and fighting beside those old enemies of the Hunkpapa.

He had only his sheathed Hawken. One shot, if the cap was over the nipple and the powder still dry. He let the weapon rest in its beaded buffalohide nest, and headed straight toward the knot of Hunkpapa. He always did that if he could, and it had become a part of his medicine legend. But it was also the direction in which Victoria and Mary and their packmules had ridden earlier, and the route that Frazier's cart train had taken to the top of the bluffs and out upon a broken land above. He felt Jawbone gather his powerful muscles to bound upward as the bottoms gave way to steep-sided slopes. Ahead, warriors bent short bows and loosed arrows, white blurs that flashed close. Already in range. Jawbone knew. He shrieked demonically, striking terror in enemy hearts, the terror of the yellow-eyed medicine horse bounding in berserk leaps to butcher them with his hoofs and teeth.

One warrior fled, but the other four stood their ground, spitting arrows that hissed past like lightning, one glancing off his boot, another nicking his neck and a third notching Jawbone's left ear. He shrieked, a murderous proclamation of what he intended to do in a moment. Mister Skye glanced behind and discovered half a dozen Hunkpapa mounted and pursuing. They wanted Skye. They might stave off the Crow, but not the Crow plus Mister Skye. And every one of them burned with the medicine power of Sitting Bull's vow, sanctified with pain and blood just days before.

The wolf warriors expected him to race up a coulee with a shallow grade and a worn trail, so they fanned out on either side for the coup. But Skye kneed Jawbone left, toward an impossibly steep bluff, broken by sandstone outcrops. Behind, the village warriors gained ground. Jawbone was far from the fastest horse on the prairies, but Mister Skye treasured him for other things, his staying power and sheer strength. The horse danced, eying the barrier and knowing he would skin his hocks pawing upward over ledges, but he never faltered, and his weird shrieks sounded like a gale in high rigging.

Mister Skye stretched a horned hand with stubby fingers over the animal's sweaty neck and withers, an act of love, and the touch loosed a tremor through the great horse. They picked up cover now from juniper and sandstone outcrops, but still the deadly arrows stabbed in, one through Jawbone's mane, nicking his neck. The horse bawled and leapt, just as another deadly shaft sliced air under his belly. The Hunkpapa pursuing him had edged into range now, and an arrow from the rear glanced off rock as Jawbone boomed by.

"Scared you, Jawbone. Everything scares you and me," Skye said. "All I've ever done is keep you afraid, and steer some." Jawbone's battered ears rotated back, listening to Skye's quiet crooning. The mighty horse reached the first ledge, a five-foot leap coming off a steep incline below. He shuddered, gathered, and sprang, lifting himself and Mister Skye's massive bulk upward, hooves flailing, then spattering chips of yellow stone like grapeshot from a cannon, rear hooves clawing stairs out of rock, and then they were over. Ahead lay two small ridges, easy to leap, and a horizon with anything beyond it.

"Ah, horse, I knew you could. Luff to the crest now, and we'll raise the stun'sails," he said, sudden joy sweeping through him.

Jawbone limped slightly and Mister Skye knew the horse had skinned a fetlock clawing up the rock facade. He steered the animal toward the rolling shoulder, unsure what lay beyond. Now, he thought. Now pull the old Hawken with its short octagonal barrel, and be ready. Jawbone seemed to gather another wind and pumped furiously upward, sailing over a low shelf of rock, and then out. The whole world grew, horizons suddenly skidding away and away into hazy infinities. He tugged Jawbone down into a walk, squinting behind him to see what came. Nothing. The ledge had foiled pursuit from the rear. Far off on a neck of level land, he spotted the viscount's caravan, and something else—a bright oblong green and white tent with banners flapping hard in the whistling river of air out of the south. A tent? He could scarcely imagine it. He turned Jawbone that way and kneed the winded animal, squinting about for signs of pursuit.

A tent. Men scurrying about among the carts, unhooking the drays. Camping there, apparently. An infinity from water. Puzzled, he rode north across the scooped head of the coulee, and as he turned the horse into that crease of land, he spotted something he wished his eyes could not witness.

There, invisible in that vee to the distant Britons, were a half dozen Hunkpapa wolf society warriors milling about two small figures hunched over their ponies, figures he knew at once. They all spotted him and shouted, and though he could not make out the words, he knew the message. He didn't need words, eddying hard against the gale. His eyes registered the drawn bows, and the nocked arrows pointing at Victoria and Mary, and he knew their lives depended totally on what he did next. He wrestled back his instinct to boot his mad horse into a berserk run, and lift his Hawken and let it spit, for the instant he tried it each of his women would be pierced by three or four arrows, and by the time he got there he'd find them pincushioned with them, minus their scalps, and their breath.

He hunted for a way and found none. The Britons had seen none of it and wouldn't in this sloping trough of land. He would go die with his women, then. And Jawbone, too. Soon, after the battle with the Crows, every Hunkpapa warrior, every woman and child, old man and infant, would count coup on the corpses of them all.

Yet he lived, and they did too. And he'd been in tighter

squeaks. He turned the yellow-eyed horse toward the knot
of warriors, speaking softly to Jawbone.

"Hold your fire, mate. Hold your fire," he muttered.
"They caught my ladies after all."

And no news of Skye had reached the Crow.

He pulled up Jawbone before them, and felt the animal
quiver, some wild pent-up thing barely contained within.
An elder warrior nodded, triumph radiating from his face.
The prize. On all the plains, no prize like this. Especially
in war with the Absarokas. This warrior was utterly bald—
an odd thing—and murder shone in his eyes. Victoria
squinted dourly at Skye, her own features blank. Mister
Skye slid his Hawken back into its sheath, but the warrior
barked a command, and slowly Skye slid it out again and
handed it to the headman, remembering to slide the cap off
the nipple as furtively as he could. The headman smiled
slightly, and tapped Skye hard with his bow. No coup had
ever meant more.

Skye lifted his silk hat, ran a hand through his graying
hair, and screwed the hat down again, an ancient signal
among them: watch, wait, be ready. Victoria and Mary responded with a faint lift of the jaw. The headman snapped
a hard Sioux word, and they filed down the coulee trail
toward the village. Mister Skye's back itched with the
thought of so many nocked arrows with hoop iron points
aimed at it. But he guessed they'd wait. They had a war to
fight. And when they drove off the Absaroka, a victory to
celebrate. And while they celebrated, the entire village
would count coup a dozen times over, each time more painful than the last, until the final cuts and blows would land
on corpses tied to poles.

Warriors steered them into an empty hollow-coned village where only a few old people remained, along with
some keening women singing their medicine while they
made ready for a sudden exodus if things turned against the
Hunkpapa. Bear's Rib had gone too, though he was the
peace chief. But one remained, still lying on his pallet before his family's lodge, and that is where the headman led
Mister Skye, Victoria, and Mary. They stopped before Sitting Bull, who lay gray with pain, with tight-wrapped calico

binding his swollen chest. He stared up at them, gathered strength against pain, and lifted himself to his feet, clinging to a lance he kept there for locomotion. The young man's wide-spaced eyes took it all in, and a faint joy flooded through his diamond-shaped face. Sun had been kind. Even before he had been healed of his torture sacrifice, Sun had granted him his vow. He lifted his lance and jabbed it toward Skye. The point pierced through his elkskin shirt and drew blood under a rib. It stung viciously, but Mister Skye showed them nothing in his face. Sitting Bull smiled slowly, and jabbed Mary and Victoria as well. Mary wrestled back tears. He'd hurt her.

And Mister Skye knew that was only a preliminary.

Chapter 15

Viscount Frazier leapt up from his camp chair, aghast. The ball had just missed his head. In the flapping cloth at his side a bright hole stabbed sun-glare at him.

"The savages are shooting at us! It's an outrage!"

The women scrambled up too, alarmed.

"Galitzin! Run out there and point at the flag!"

"He's not here. He's fetching Chesterfield," said Diana.

"Run for the carts," Lord Frazier cried. "We've no protection here."

"Oh, it's so savage!" moaned Lady Alexandra. "Balls and arrows!"

The two ladies lifted their skirts and raced toward the carts.

"Tell them to put the carts in a line!" the viscount cried after them.

Arrayed across the slope, more warriors than he could count raced toward the tent. The cartmen who'd spread themselves around the tent began firing, sharp cracks and blue smoke here and there. One warrior's chest bloomed red and he slid slowly from his pony, which broke free and raced laterally, slowing some of the others. The cries of war sifted to the viscount, sounding like the sharp barks of coyotes.

"Shoot the bloody buggers!" cried Frazier. "I'll go fetch Galitzin. Stand your ground, men!"

The prone cartmen were too busy to notice. Most of them had fired their pieces at once, and were now pouring powder down hot barrels, jamming in balls with ramrods, and slipping caps over nipples. The savages never faltered. Those few with fusils seemed capable of reloading on the run, pouring powder and ball down their barrels and seating the balls by rapping the butt of the weapon on their saddles. Frazier watched, astonished and paralyzed until an arrow sizzled past, and then he broke for the rear. Just as he did, a cartman screamed and tumbled back, an arrow clear through his chest with its point protruding from his back.

"Don't do that! See the flag! The Union Jack!" he cried. Oh, where was Skye. The guide knew the tongue of these savages. He could stop them. Down there smoking with Bear's Rib, that's what. He'd discharge the guide for good this time.

From the carts a barrage boomed and found its mark. Half a dozen ponies stumbled and shrieked, tumbling their warriors. Galitzin's work! Lord Frazier turned and ran, lumbering behind the ladies who screamed their way back toward the loose array of carts. Some of the cartmen who'd been defending the tent ran too, knowing they'd be overwhelmed in seconds.

Heart hammering, his lordship fled along with them. Ahead the cook and the wine steward were prying the carts about, trying to make a barrier of them, while Galitzin and the rest loaded weapons. Frazier's legs began to give out, and he trembled, losing ground. Several fleeing cartmen passed him by.

"Bloody cowards," he bellowed. "Defend me!"

One of them fell just as he passed Frazier, his entire face a mass of red and gray pulp. Horrified, the viscount watched the man flop and flail his way downward, dead before he hit the ground.

"Skye! Where's Skye? Tell them to stop!" he bawled, trembling forward on legs that caved and buckled. The women reached the carts and tumbled to earth beyond one, sobbing. Behind, the sweeping line of warriors gained ground. Arrows pierced by. One whipped through his left sleeve, scratching his elbow. Other cartmen passed him, bloody cowards.

Behind he felt the tremor of horses, the snorts, the wild cries. They'd have him in seconds. A vicious feather-decked lance whipped by, stabbing clay just to his right.

Ahead fowling pieces boomed, a great belch of them, and he heard screams behind him. The scatterguns! That bloody fool Galitzin was firing scatterguns and barely missing him! He'd have words with that fool colonel!

Wheezing, his chest hurting brutally, he tumbled around a cart just as a second barrage of the fowling pieces caught the attack and decimated it. Horses screeched, warriors fell, and the rest turned and fled out of range. He clung to a cartwheel, feeling its iron tire burn his hand, his windpipe afire and his quaking body humming.

An arrow smacked earth beside Diana, who lay huddled there. She jumped. The cart offered little protection. "Turn it over," she cried. "Make a wall!"

Galitzin trotted over. "Get a piece from Gravesend," he said to the viscount. "We've turned them for the moment. The fowling pieces. But zey'll come around."

"Keep a civil tongue, Galitzin," the viscount muttered.

"Hurry! We've two dead and six more wounded."

Diana leapt up and headed for the armorer's cart. Frazier peered out fearfully and saw the warriors sweeping around toward the left, flanking the line of carts. Others gleefully pulled down the marquess tent, which sagged and collapsed like something dying. One ripped the Union Jack from its tent staff and danced with it, finally tucking it around his waist, into his breechclout belt. Another picked up the rifle of the dead cartman there. Others shot arrows into the corpse until it bristled with them. The one who'd gotten the piece whipped out a knife, slashing silvery in the boiling sun, and scalped the man, finally holding up a brown tuft of hair and yelling.

Two cartmen struggled to hold the drays, but a wounded horse galloped into the herd, scattering them like tenpins. The entire herd exploded and bolted off to the east, angling away from the closing Crow warriors.

Several cartmen leapt up and began wrestling the carts around to make an ell, even as the Crows wheeled in from the flank. The cartmen tilted one cart over, and it crashed to its side while everything within clattered and tumbled. A dozen men gathered behind this small barrier, but the Crows kept wheeling and the viscount knew suddenly they'd angle in from the rear.

Wounded cartmen sobbed, some trying to stanch the bright blood gouting from arms and legs. Others just lay on earth, leaking their life into it.

Lady Alexandra peered at them, and turned to the viscount. "Make someone help them," she pleaded. "Do something, Gordon."

"Galitzin! Tend to these men. You've bloody well neglected them!"

The sweating colonel ignored him, and continued dragging a cart around. An occasional rifle blast from the cartmen kept the circling Crows off, but their awful barks and yells caught the breeze and sent chills through the viscount.

A piece. He stumbled to the the arms cart and found Gravesend. The armorer handed him a revolver belt with a Colt's tucked in it, then a good Purdey scatter gun, paper cartridges and caps. The weight of the Colt at his belt and the hot steel in his hand suddenly inflated the viscount. He stood tall, his heart slowing, and gazed shrewdly about him, taking stock as a commanding lord should.

Gravesend himself had a rifle at the ready, and used it between the moments when he was dispensing his wares. He rested the barrel on his cart, followed a warrior who had edged too close, and squeezed the trigger. The rifle bucked and the pinto pony out there stumbled and fell, its warrior landing on his feet and racing back out of range.

"Very good, Gravesend," the viscount said coolly. "I'll have a feather for your cap when it's done."

A gang of sweating cartmen tilted the taxidermist's cart up until it tottered and crashed onto its side, forming a little protection on the south side. Cutler, the taxidermist, howled at them for wrecking his equippage. Diana, with a small fowling piece in hand, stationed herself behind it. Alexandra peered about, clucked at the wounded, and headed for the gleaming yellow parlor wagon, situated in a jumble of carts that had not been dragged into the defense.

"Do something for those poor fellows, Gordon," she insisted, and stepped inside.

Viscount Frazier hailed the taxidermist. "I say, Cutler. Help those blokes. If you can stuff and sew skins, you can sew up those poor chaps. Give them some water, eh?"

"There's no water, your lordship. We're a mile from either river."

In fact, the viscount felt parched and he peered about looking for water. It should be in the keg on the cook wagon, and he trotted over to it; but a bullet had demolished the keg, splintering a stave.

His dry throat ached. Wine, then. The spirit wagon. He cast about, not finding it, and then spotted it in the north side barrier. Where was that bloody steward with his key? It had to be locked at all times lest the bloody cartmen steal from it.

"Stauffinger," he roared, not seeing the steward. "Open up. I'm parched!"

Slowly the ruddy wine steward crawled out from under a cart, peered fearfully at the savages who rode back and forth just beyond shotgun range, taunting and working themselves into another assault, and sidled toward the cart.

"Fetch me some port. No, too heavy. Some Rhine. Yes, some light Rhine, eh? And another bottle for the wounded."

"Yes, lordship," he said, his key trembling in the lock.

The viscount peered in and found everything in good shape, although a fearsome arrow point had pierced clear through one wall. The steward snatched two green bottles off racks, uncorked one, let it settle and air a moment, wrapped a white napkin about it and poured a finger of it into a goblet. This he handed to Lord Frazier expectantly. The viscount savored it, decided it was adequate, but just barely. A noxious aftertaste, he thought. "Yes, it'll do. Not very good bouquet, but it'll do." The steward filled the glass and the viscount drank gustily from one. "Now, take this other one around to the suffering blokes," he commanded.

The steward locked up and began his mission, sneaking a long drink himself first while the viscount watched suspiciously.

The wine felt good. The hot British barrels of his double scattergun felt good. The weight of the Yankee Colt's revolver felt good. Galitzin didn't have a perimeter, but they'd managed barriers of some sort. A line of carts on the north; a tipped over cart on the west; the tipped over taxidermist's cart on the south. A jumble of unused carts at the southeast corner. And several enterprising blokes had pulled tents and bedding out of carts and mounded them into two heaps, and lay behind the mounds, at the ready.

The bloody savages hadn't quit, but they'd been scratched by English tooth and claw. They'd lost one warrior at least, and a few others had taken balls. And half a dozen ponies. But it never should have happened. Skye had deserted. The man's squaw was Crow. He could have stopped the whole bloody business with a shout or two, but he didn't. The bloody coward was hiding back there in the Hunkpapa village. Why did all these damned Yanks think so highly of Skye? It didn't make sense. He'd taken the measure of the lout. Maybe he'd shoot Skye for deserting, while his squaws howled. If the deserter showed up, he'd have Galitzin clap him in irons for a whipping. Indignantly, Lord Frazier peered eastward, out toward the Yellowstone valley where that barbarian lingered.

Something caught his eye about a quarter of a mile away, where the grassy plateau ended at the bluffs overlooking the valley of the Hunkpapa. He made out faces just above the grass, tribesmen peering out from below the rim of the bluff. More popped into view, a dozen, twenty, still more. All watching. Crow or Sioux? He didn't know. All savages looked alike to him.

"Galitzin! Over here!" he bellowed, pointing.

The sweat-stained colonel trotted over and stared across the dun flats, muttering. "Who are they?"

"I don't know. If that bloody guide hadn't deserted, he could tell us."

"Where's Skye?"

"In the Sioux village of course. Having a smoke with Bear's Rib."

"I doubt that," Galitzin replied.

"Keep a civil tongue, colonel."

The colonel turned away and summoned some cartmen to barricade the still-open east side, but the faces above the rim of the bluff didn't move.

"Don't shoot. They may be friendly," the colonel cautioned.

Far off to the north, the snap and moan of battle overrode the southwinds to tell them of death and blood and pain. The Crow themselves stayed just out of range, nerving themselves for another assault. They hadn't been seriously mauled. Wounded cartmen groaned in the broiling sun, and no one helped them to shade.

Out of the east a wide line of warriors materialized, trotting over the crest of the bluff. Unlike the Crow, none were painted. Sioux, then, hastily gathered into a defense. They trotted easily, saving their mounts, most of them riding bareback with quivers over their bronzed backs and bows in hand. The Crows spotted them at once, and fierce taunts crisscrossed around the Englishmen. The Hunkpapa stared at the hasty defenses but their real interest lay elsewhere, in the mocking Crow, who outnumbered them twice over. They trotted their ponies northward, away from the Crow, keeping the Englishmen between themselves and their enemies. The Crow raged back and forth, shouting, but unwilling to brave the guns of the whitemen to get at the Hunkpapa.

"Looks like zey're going to flank the other Crows, on the Yellowstone," Galitzin muttered. "Or decoy zese up here somewhere."

Lord Frazier didn't know. Everything had turned oddly quiet. The Crows began wheeling in a wide arc northward, beyond range, to try to pounce upon the Hunkpapa before the Hunkpapa swept down on the rear of the other Crows off to the north.

"I say, Galitzin. It's over for us, eh?"

Galitzin looked disgusted. "We've no water. In this kind of heat, men'll drop from thirst in an hour or so."

"Well, harness up and we'll go to it."

Galitzin sighed, saying nothing.

"Send some blokes out to find the drays, Galitzin."

At last the cartmen tended the groaning wounded, dragging them gently to the only significant shade, beneath the yellow parlor wagon. One chap sobbed and blubbered.

The viscountess watched from her window, annoyed. "Take them somewhere else," she commanded. "It's too savage for me. And fetch me cold water. It's perfectly fierce."

Cartmen stared, and silently dragged their wounded colleagues to the lesser shade of various upright carts.

The silence seemed eerie. The roaring south wind muffled the sounds of struggle off to the north, and Lord Frazier had no notion how it went. He had grown petulant with the discovery he had no horses, no locomotion other than his two feet, and nothing to pull the carts. Bloody damned Skye.

"Galitzin!" he roared.

The weary colonel shuffled up to him. "Sir?"

"Get on with it! They might come back any moment!"

"The cartmen are worn to nothing, sir. They're desperate for water."

"Well, that's regrettable. Have them build a barricade instead of lollygagging about."

"Lord Frazier, I think we'd better retreat to the Tongue. Get to water and safety in the Sioux village."

"Are you daft, colonel? Abandon the carts to those thieving savages? We'd have nothing! Nothing!"

"We may abandon them anyway, sir, without drays."

"Well, fetch the drays. Send a bloke out to find them!"

Galitzin shook his head. "Do you see them? You can look for miles in most directions."

Lord Frazier peered about and fumed. "That Skye got us into this. He should've been here. He knows how to talk to those cutthroats and could have steered them off."

Galitzin sighed unhappily. "We'd better get to the Sioux village while we can, sir. Carry our arms, and whatever we can."

"You're perfectly daft. I forbid it. Send a chap with buckets, then."

"Who'd volunteer, your excellency?"

"Why command it. They're in my service. They owe me total obedience. Tell them duty calls, the duty of any Englishman in service, colonel."

"It's a death trip, sir." He sighed. "I'll go, then."

"Are you quite all right, colonel? You go? I need you. Send some bloke we don't need."

Galitzin stared. Furnace winds eddied across the plateau, whitening nostrils and tongues, parching throats.

"I say, colonel. Have a bit of this Rhine, eh? It'll make you jolly up, take heart. I say, you've no taste for blood, you Russians. Stiffen up, eh?"

He thrust the bottle toward the colonel, who stared at it dubiously, then uncorked it and drank.

"I'll send a bit around to the blokes. Not much. I don't want them tiddly. But it'll wet their whistles."

"It'll make them thirstier, sir."

Lord Frazier peered about him, dreading the sight of a wide line of savages cresting one or another bluff. "I say, Galitzin, here's what we'll do: Put the men in pairs, and assign each man to a cart shaft, a pair to a cart. We'll drag the carts down to the village. We'll save the carts, and have us a drink, and be perfectly safe from those bloody Crow savages."

It delighted him, his inspiration. He'd save the men and save the carts and save the whole trip. And down there, he'd set the chaps on Skye and have his revenge.

"It's only a half of a mile to the bluff. And after that, it's all downhill, colonel. The blokes can do it."

"I'm sorry, your lordship, but they can't."

The viscount glared at the colonel, enraged at this wanton defiance.

"Even if zey had the strength left to load up the carts, right the ones tipped over, and drag them to the trail down the bluff, sir, zey wouldn't have the strength to hold back the carts on that grade. Half a mile of it to the flats. You can't expect two men to slow a cart with a ton or two on it. The carts would run right over them."

"You Russians are fast to show the white flag, Galitzin. No wonder the Czars lose their bloody wars. Smile a little. See Lady Diana there. She's quite enjoying herself, eh?"

Lady Diana had commandeered a bottle from the wine steward, and was guzzling lustily, growing cheerier by the minute. "Kill the red bastards," she yelled.

The sweating colonel nodded. Men lay exhausted in what little shade they could find, while the dying groaned.

The viscount sighed and straightened himself. His fine British scattergun felt splendid in the crook of his arm, and his deadly black six-shooter weighed menacingly on his hip. "I'll go myself, Galitzin. I wasn't born a peer of England for nothing. Fetch me two pails. I'll bring water for the whole worthless lot, and get some help from my friend Bear's Rib, eh?"

He stood straight, wanting to look like a solid bulldog, the queen's own hussar. But Galitzin wasn't looking. His stare was riveted to the north, where once again knots of savages topped the bluffs and rode out on the plateau. This time they weren't in a line, and they were shooting at each other. The fight had swirled up from the Yellowstone, and was about to engulf them.

Chapter 16

Thick silence pervaded the emptied village, and it slumbered in the sun as if great events were distant rather than close. Mister Skye could hear nothing of battle, no shouts or shots on the breeze, no snort and squeal of horses. He wondered about the fate of the Britons. Perhaps they'd been swiftly overrun and only the quiet of death remained.

He could not know, and might never know because he probably wouldn't leave the Hunkpapa village alive. The police society warriors had returned to the upriver clash, but surrounding Mister Skye, Mary, and Victoria were a score of old men, each with a deadly nocked arrow in his bow. A dozen old squaws added to the force, all of them armed with bows and arrows, or lances. And even a few boys too young to fight managed to aim small bows and short arrows at him. He eyed the boys unhappily, knowing the impulsiveness of children. The older ones would hold him for the coup-counting and torture, but the boys might do anything.

Sitting Bull eased himself back onto his pallet, the pain of his self-torture etched in his face. But also glowing in his eyes was victory. It was the biggest medicine ever made in this Hunkpapa village. His chest muscles were obviously much too torn and painful for him to draw a bow for the coup de grace, nor was it necessary. His medicine had brought Skye here, and the whole village knew it. And the competent old men made sure the legendary whiteman wouldn't move an inch.

Mister Skye eased slowly off of Jawbone, who stood shivering, ears laid back, teeth clicking, his evil eyes measuring foes at every hand. He had no weapon at all save for a belt-knife, but Jawbone could be a formidable one. They knew that; all the tribesmen of the plains knew that, and many of those arrows were pointed at the animal. Their victory over Jawbone would be just as important as their triumph over Skye. But Jawbone belonged to Sitting Bull now, by right of medicine.

Still, thought Mister Skye, one word to Jawbone, and the horse would go berserk. But where would it lead? To a whole flight of arrows buried instantly in himself and his wives.

Mary and Victoria did not dismount. An old headman with notched coup feathers stuck proudly in his white hair watched closely and then gestured at the women, repeating the motion angrily when the women did nothing.

"Should we get down, Mister Skye? I am ready to die," Mary said sadly.

"Yes, Mary. We need time."

She and Victoria slid off angrily, and instantly Sioux boys commandeered their horses and the packmules, taking them some distance away. With them went the women's sheathed flintlocks and the rest of their worldly goods.

"We'll see," muttered Mister Skye.

A sharp gesture from the old headman bid them to sit down, thus reducing the chance of flight. They did so, while Jawbone sidled restlessly, almost berserk. The villagers kept their distance from his murderous hoofs and teeth, knowing the legends about him. It had become viciously hot, and Mister Skye sweated profusely in the glare. They would enjoy that little torture, denying their prisoners shade.

On the lip of the bluffs a herd of crazed horses thundered

into the sky, squealing and restless, and then it plunged down the slope to the flats near the village. Familiar horses, Mister Skye thought: the saddle horses, drays and mules he'd bought for the Britons. He wondered if he could make something of that. The herd headed toward its familiar grazing grounds along the Tongue, where the horses had been during the long visit in the village.

Mister Skye watched them intently until they disappeared around a bend in the bluffs, heading for better grass. So the Britons were stuck up there, he thought. Not an animal for those carts and the yellow wagon. Not a pony to ride. It made their prospects much worse.

He wondered if he could slip Victoria out somehow in the night to talk with her Absaroka people who were engaging these Lakotah now. He doubted it. By nightfall, if this village fended off the attack, the three of them would be bound tight to trees, rawhide thongs cutting deep into their ankles and wrists. The whole village would be filing past to count coup, and after that—he didn't want to think about it. He feared pain as much as the next man, and had known his share of it. So had Victoria. But Mary hadn't, and it would go doubly hard for her.

But what about a Crow victory, a Crow rescue? He toyed with hope a bit, and then rejected it. The instant Crow warriors swooped off those bluffs, these old men would bury their arrows in the prisoners. It might save them torture— at the cost of swift death. He lifted his battered stovepipe hat and screwed it down again, his signal to watch and wait. He had no tricks in his kit. So this would be it, he thought. He'd go under now, after a quarter of a century in these wilds. He didn't regret his days here. He didn't lament a minute of the life he'd lived after slipping off of the H. M. S. Jaguar one foggy night into the icy water of the Columbia River across from Fort Vancouver.

"He got no medicine," muttered Victoria. "That sonofabitch Sitting Bull got no medicine. It ain't any good."

He gaped at her. She hadn't said much of anything to him for months, darkening his lodge with her silence. A question filled his eyes.

She glared at him. "It don't happen this way. You'll go away from us later and never come back."

He listened carefully. He had scarcely heeded her before because all those English pounds had scattered his brains. "Tell me your vision," he said.

Something flamed in her old brown eyes, but before she could reply a sharp command from the old headman stayed her. They were not to talk to each other, not to make plans, plot escapes.

She shrugged, smiling faintly. He hadn't seen a smile on her face since last winter, and it affected him crazily, filled him with thoughts like mountain lupines. He began at once looking for ways. He could find none, but talk was always a way. He would make signs, use the little Sioux he knew to talk with Sitting Bull, and see what came of it.

The youth lay on his robe, his eyes joyous even through the veil of pain across his face.

"Tatanka Yotanka," said Skye, "you have made great medicine."

The youth gazed up at him from his bed of robes and nodded. "I made a vow," he replied.

"Soon you will be known everywhere—all the peoples of the plains and mountains—as the one who carries Mister Skye's scalp on your lance."

"Yes. Honor will come, but I will honor Sun for heeding my pain. I have vowed to drive away the enemies of my People, and Sun and Wakan Tanka have heard me. I don't care about honor. It is not for honor I live, but for my People. I live for the People and die for the People. My name will be great, but not because I desired it. Let that be my prophecy."

In a way Mister Skye admired the fanatical Sioux, but set that feeling aside. His life lay in the youth's hands, and he needed to gather what few facts might help him. "You'll count coup on Jawbone, too. Break Jawbone's medicine. You will torture him also."

Sitting Bull gazed softly at the mad blue horse. "No. His medicine is my medicine. After you are dead, he will come with us. He will be free, and no one will touch him. As long as he walks with the Hunkpapa, his medicine is ours, and he will be honored.''

The elders listened intently, and some lifted their bows away from Jawbone, turning them toward Mister Skye and his women. To kill Jawbone after Sitting Bull had said the horse would live to honor the People would be to defy medicine.

Mister Skye watched the elders alertly. A sharp command would send Jawbone careening murderously among them, and none of the old men would pierce the great ugly roan with arrows. It was something to consider.

"We are guests in your village, Tatanka Yotanka. We stayed with you in peace.''

"You warred against us beside the Absaroka dogs. That woman of yours is one. You killed the father of White Weasel and the brother of Running Moon.''

He would not mention the names of the dead, Mister Skye knew, lest their wandering spirits return to plague him. The young warrior looked gray. Even standing for a minute and thrusting the lance at them had been too much for him.

"Jawbone will not let you count coup. He'll kill you if you try. No rope holds him either,'' Mister Skye said.

Sitting Bull grinned and then turned his face away, signalling the end of the talk. The elders would enforce it, Mister Skye knew. Something accomplished, anyway: Jawbone might live.

Off on the bluffs the sounds of war overrode the hum of the southwind. Mister Skye watched alertly, the muffled booms of barking guns eddying to his ears sometimes when the wind paused. Fowling pieces, he thought. Maybe the Britons lived, or some of them. He couldn't really tell.

Then a wide phalanx of warriors—which side he couldn't tell—rose up from the rim of the bluffs and began a swift descent toward the village, while simultaneously a large party of warriors rode down the Yellowstone toward the village, and Mister Skye could scarcely make out who any of them were.

Jawbone shrieked, turning berserk like boiling water flashing to steam.

But Victoria knew. "Absaroka,'' she hissed, pointing at

the rolling line of warriors pouring down off the bluffs.
"Absaroka!"

And probably Hunkpapa coming down the Yellowstone,
he thought. The Crows would reach the village after all, but
from above. He eyed the elders, who were even then responding to the sudden descent of battle, and Mister Skye
wondered how many more seconds he and Victoria and
Mary had to live.

Across the plateau, more warriors milled about than Viscount Frazier had ever seen before. Savages everywhere,
and he couldn't make out whether they were Sioux or
Crow. The bloody buggers all looked alike. Hundreds of
them, racing about on their ponies, collecting in knots, the
yelps and war-cries subduing the southwind. Rarely did he
hear a shot. These blokes used bows and arrows and lances
rather than pieces. He watched one devil tumble from his
painted horse, which galloped off, and other devils jump
off theirs and scalp the downed one.

Amazing!

He peered about. His cartmen had scrambled for protection under the carts, even though Galitzin was yelling at
them to complete the barricades. The east side lay wide
open, and only a single tipped-over cart guarded the south
and west. But the heat lay white upon them, and the weary
cartmen had found shade behind the tilted carts.

Frazier leapt to action, running from one cart to another.
"Make barricades! Get up now and drag the carts, you
chaps."

But no one did. Finally, Galitzin himself, along with Diana and Gravesend, untangled one cart from the others and
dragged it off to the east, making some sort of barrier there
if war should come that way.

"I say, help them!" cried Lord Frazier angrily, but no
one did.

"Them lords and sirs got to wet their whistles," yelled
a defiant voice behind him. "We didn't."

Frazier whirled, but couldn't make out the culprit.

Gravesend trotted back to his enameled blue armorer's
cart and began filling spare shot pouches and powder flasks.

Good man, thought the viscount. Inside that blue cart, which lay in the middle of their hasty perimeter, were twenty or thirty more fine British pieces. That plus two kegs of powder, caps, spare pigs of lead, several casks of fowling shot, and all the rest. Reserves.

He sucked greedily on the bottle of Rhine in his hand, sweating freely in the brute sun.

"Here they come," bellowed Diana. "Blow their balls off."

Odd how bellicose the lady'd become, he thought. That bottle she kept sucking had done it.

"Hold your fire," Galitzin countermanded. "We don't know friend from enemy."

But some cartmen ignored him, and banged away at tiny targets off in the white glare.

Still, a milling clot of savages had gathered to the east, and now rode straight toward their defenses, howling so fiercely Lord Frazier shivered. Frightful! On they came, sundering into two wings and the center, one swirling south, the other north, while the majority plunged straight at them out of the dark east. Cartmen began banging at them, sharp booms and acrid powdersmoke boiling from around the tilted carts.

Arrows stabbed into their refuge, one zipping past the viscount's face. He jumped, and crawled under the nearest cart, one full of Alexandra's evening dresses and a portable chifforobe of linen for her toilet.

Sioux! He recognized two of the buggers as they swept by on their ponies. He knew their bloody savage faces. Village blokes. It enraged him. The warriors circled the barricades, drawing fire from the cartmen, and then it happened: a powerful wedge of the Hunkpapa savages, howling bloody oaths, pierced straight into the fortress, just when cartmen were reloading their pieces. Galitzin banged at them with his revolver, and so did Gravesend, but they swept on, straight toward the blue armorer's cart. Several slid off their ponies, grabbed the tongue and doubletree, and dragged the two-horse cart out of the compound, while knocking Gravesend into the dust.

Nipping the pieces! Viscount Frazier could scarcely believe it. A mob of redmen right there, dragging the cart off! He squirmed around, trying to get his fowling piece free of the spoked wheels to blast the buggers, but by the time he did, they'd fled, leaving Gravesend kicking in the dust. Shots from cartmen followed the buggers, but as far as the viscount could make out, the thieves hadn't lost a man. Galitzin leapt up and calmly emptied his Colt's at the savages, but no ball took effect. Beyond the compound, savages lashed ropes to the cart and then used their ponies to drag it beyond the range of the British rifles. They leapt off their ponies and swarmed around the rear, distributing the pieces and ammunition, until most of them had a weapon. An eerie howl erupted from them, and they turned their ponies eastward, skirting wide around the Britons, going after the Crows with a firepower they'd never possessed.

Frazier gaped at them, scarcely believing it'd happened. Now his blokes had only the pieces, powder and shot in their hands. He suddenly knew why all the warriors in the village had ambled by the blue cart, stared at it, prevailed on Gravesend to show them the pieces, peered into its dark hold, studying the shining weapons, the kegs of powder and shot, the boxes of caps. Lucky a bullet didn't ignite the powder, he thought. And none had stared longer, or dawdled more, than that young Sitting Bull. Thieves, the whole lot.

"Where's that damned steward. I want some booze," said Diana.

Within moments, every savage in sight had vanished over the northern lip of the plateau. Save for the slap of the southwind, the day had become as quiet as death. The crumpled forms of two scalped cartmen lay off to the north where the marquess tent had been. No sign of the tent or the campchairs remained. Not a dead savage darkened the white spaces. The bloody thieves must have trucked off their dead, he thought. If there was war down on the flat near the village, he could not discern it. The southwind hid it or the bluffs baffled it.

Slowly Gravesend sat up, rubbed a knot on his head where he'd been grazed by a warclub, and wobbled to his feet. "Water," he mumbled, staring unfocused at the rest.

Galitzin approached, looking exhausted. "I'm organizing
a detail of twelve men to get water," he said. "We're still
armed, and maybe we can make the Yellowstone. It's a mile
that way. The fighting's over on the Tongue. That's nearer
but full of savages."

"You'd leave me with just a handful to defend my person?"

"Your lordship, the men can't last. The wounded are
dying for want of water. I'm leaving the cooks, the taxidermist, the wine steward, and the wounded, with Gravesend
in command. He'll be all right, after he recovers from that
knock."

"But that's nothing—"

"There's Lady Chatham-Hollingshead and yourself, your
excellency. Between you, you're worth a dozen cartmen.
You alone could handle ten savages, lordship. There's
Baudelaire, too. I don't know where he is, but around
somewhere—and three of the wounded can still shoot. Perhaps you've a better idea?"

"Where is that Baudelaire?" the viscount bellowed.
"Aristides, come at once!"

The pasty-faced gentleman emerged silkily from the yellow parlor wagon, a baby dragoon Colt's in hand. He smiled
blandly. "I was protecting her ladyship," he said. "And
just as well, too, because a savage peeked in while she was
lying indisposed."

"I see. Summon the wine steward, Baudelaire. We'll have
us a dust-cutter, eh?"

Baudelaire nodded blandly. Cartmen stared.

Galitzin snapped orders, and cartmen slowly emerged
from their shelters under the carts and unearthed three canvas camp buckets and a wooden one. Lord Frazier didn't
oppose. The poor wounded blokes groaned for water. A
strong party of cartmen ought to get through and bring
enough back.

"I'll take command. Not Gravesend," he announced to
the remaining men. "Baudelaire, fetch us some chairs and
glasses, and have the awning run off the parlor wagon for
shade, eh?"

He watched the water detail stumble north under Galitzin, and then settled into a chair beside the yellow parlor wagon. An unearthly quiet pervaded the place. He peered mournfully at the forlorn carts, sagging on their wheels and shafts, useless without drays. Each of the carts that had been tipped over had been smashed beyond repair. Four carts ruined. Perhaps he should dock the cartmen, he thought. They did it. He gazed furtively at the wounded, lying half in the shade, half out, and wondered what to do with the helpless chaps, especially without a cart to fetch them along. Give them to Skye, he thought. They would be Skye's problem. He didn't have the faintest idea what to do, but he knew where to start. He'd catch that Skye, tie him to a post, and give him forty lashes plus one. The man deserved worse—the entire hunting trip was a botch—but it'd be the place to start. The thought of raising blood on that oaf's back, and hearing his barbarous howls, pleasured him.

Chapter 17

Mister Skye knew he had to control Jawbone. The swirling battle, edging ever-closer, had driven the mad horse to its brink. It didn't know friend from enemy and would shriek into Hunkpapa and Absaroka both. And the instant it did, arrows would bury themselves in Mister Skye, as well as Victoria and Mary. River Crow were pouring down the western bluffs of the Tongue while the village warriors rushed back from up the Yellowstone. He eased to his feet slowly, his body itching with the dread of pain and death, but for the moment the elders' attention had been drawn to the melee.

"Whoa, boy," Mister Skye muttered low. The wild-eyed horse plotted murder and mayhem, arcing his scimitar nose up and down in terror, utterly unhinged. Mister Skye took one soft step and then another, and still no arrows pierced him, although old men followed with their bows. He caught the single rope that dragged from a crude halter, and soothed the twitching animal.

The horse trembled, and shrieked weirdly, but didn't resist, and something sagged in Skye. Standing up in the face of those drawn bows, walking two steps, and catching Jawbone, had taken all the courage he could muster. He had counted on his medicine reputation—which evoked a fear in the breast of all his captors—and it had held, at least through those seconds, though they watched him closer now.

The fight had become a fluid vortex swirling around the flats near the village, mostly warclub and lance combat at close quarters. Horses shrieked, men screamed, the squaws of the village whined and melted away toward the battle, turning their arrows on the hated Absaroka rather than the Skye family. But the elders held their arrows on Skye. Sitting Bull struggled to his feet and grabbed a lance, sweating with the pain of standing and holding it ready. Crow horsemen raced among lodges, each bent on glory, heading toward Chief Bear's Rib's lodge and the triumph of ripping it down and counting coup.

Jawbone trembled and danced, his feet lifting and falling in wild rhythm, but he did not break Mister Skye's grasp. The old headman guarding the Skyes seemed to approve.

But Sitting Bull, he with the greatest medicine ever seen in the village, thought otherwise. "Let the medicine horse go, Mister Skye," he said in Sioux. "The horse will fight for us. He will kick the dogs to death."

Victoria stared harshly, saying nothing.

"His friends the Absaroka know him," Mister Skye said.

The response enraged Sitting Bull. "He will fight them. My medicine speaks to him. Let him go or he will die."

Once again the elders' iron-tipped arrows turned toward Jawbone's chest.

Mister Skye leaned up to Jawbone's bobbing head and spoke into his ear. "Run," he said. That was not the fight command the horse had heard from its infancy. Mister Skye let go of the rawhide halter rope, wondering if this time the crazed horse would not obey. The battered blue roan quivered, jerked his head crazily, and then trotted off, slowly at first, cutting around lodges, ducking warriors who paused to stare at the medicine horse they all knew and had sung terrible tales about.

The blue horse vanished from Mister Skye's sight, hidden by the concentric rings of lodges stretching toward the pe-

rimeter of the village. The lodges hid much of the battle
too, except where the land rose toward the southwestern
bluffs. He could see no concentration of warriors anywhere.
This seemed to be almost entirely a struggle of individual
warriors, none cooperating with others, which was the way
tribesmen fought. Still he watched, sickened with the
thought that his great horse might lie dying, an arrow
through its chest.

But then he caught sight of Jawbone again, a blue streak
loping easily upslope, far from any warriors, scrambling up
the very slope he had tackled before with Mister Skye on
his back. With giant leaps, the horse clambered over rocky
outcrops, sailing past dark junipers, and with the same
mighty leap as before, he clawed up a yellow sandstone cliff
and paused, triumphantly above. Then, slowly, he trotted
to the crest of the bluff and stood there, his sides panting
rhythmically, staring down on the chaos below. And from
there, high above the fray, he loosed a scream so crazed
and wild, so like the howl of a thousand wolves, that it
paralyzed all below. Scarcely a warrior on either side failed
to recognize that horse and that berserk howl. The Crow
warriors saw an ally—a horse that was a legend among
them—and peered about at once, seeking that horse's legendary owner, married into the Absaroka People.

Mister Skye whirled toward Sitting Bull, who watched
intently, pain etching his face. "Now you will lose the village, and your life, even if you kill me," Mister Skye said.
"He did not give his medicine to you. Your medicine's no
good. You're too greedy, Sitting Bull, and now Sun will
turn on you."

The Crow warriors, heartened by this great medicine sign
above, turned savagely on the Hunkpapa. But the Sioux warriors, terrorized by the sight of this medicine shining in the
sunlight on the bluff, fell back. With a fierce howl, Absaroka
horsemen swept toward knots of Sioux warriors, driving
Hunkpapa before them. In the village squaws wailed, gathered
their children, and splashed into the Tongue or fled to the
cottonwoods.

Even Mister Skye stood, rapt, watching that horse. What
was it about Jawbone? He danced back and forth on that

bluff, light shattering off him like some god-horse from Olympus, neck arched, floating above the ground like an apparition, though Mister Skye knew it was only the spring in the beast's legs, muscles spasmed by a strange madness, that created that effect. If Jawbone had sprung wings like Pegasus and flown and swooped over them all, he'd scarcely have been surprised.

He turned, discovering doubt in Sitting Bull's eyes as the youth witnessed the rout of his people.

"I can stop it," Mister Skye offered.

Sitting Bull stared, darkly, pain flaming in his gaze.

"The Absaroka are my brothers. They will listen if I ask them to spare your warriors and headmen, and let your women and children go free."

"I have medicine," Sitting Bull said curtly. "You will see."

They watched quietly, Sitting Bull, the Skyes, the elders gathered around Sitting Bull's lodge, and it grew plain that the village of Bear's Rib might never rise from this onslaught of fierce Crows. Medicine, thought Mister Skye. These peoples of the plains lived by it, heeded it, consulted it always. Let them discover good medicine in the spirit things of the earth, the spirit-helpers, the totems in each warrior's medicine bundle, the signs given by the sacred buffalo, and grizzly bear, and wolf—let them see the good auguries, and they took heart. Let them glimpse the bad, and their courage deserted them like water from a broken pot.

Fierce Crow warriors steered their war ponies through the village now, collapsing lodges with their lances, braining old men, chasing after the squaws and children who would make good slaves. A few Sioux warriors were scaling the bluffs, obviously defying Jawbone's medicine and planning to kill him and turn the tide, but Jawbone didn't wait. He shrieked, that unholy sound shivering flesh and quaking leaves, and leapt clear off the ledge, onto the Sioux party, hoofs flailing, teeth snapping like rifleshots, and those still in one piece fled pell-mell downhill. Gently, Jawbone scaled the bluff again and stood, triumphant, on its crest, his tail arched, backlit by afternoon sun, lord of all he surveyed.

Something bitter ran through Sitting Bull's face. "Do it," he said loudly. "I will let you go if you save my people. Some other sun, when my medicine returns, it will be different."

Mister Skye waited quietly for the elders to lower their bows. He was not satisfied with them, and did not trust them. So he stood waiting, even as Crow warriors boiled triumphantly through the whole village, upending racks of jerky, pulverizing good buffalo robes, and collapsing medicine tripods, the final sacrilege. Then at last the one he distrusted most, the glint-eyed old headman, set his bow on the ground, a sign of surrender.

Mister Skye breathed easier. Mary and Victoria relaxed almost imperceptibly. He whistled sharply, not sure the horse would hear in the sobbing of the wind. Jawbone pricked up his ears but did nothing. Mister Skye whistled again, and this time the great horse bowed its neck, stepped tentatively, and began a fluid downhill run, somehow turning the jolting passage into a smooth gallop, his iron shoes spraying sparks.

A moment later the horse appeared at Sitting Bull's lodge, breathing heavily, and Mister Skye quietly mounted. He lacked a weapon other than the greatest of all weapons among these people: medicine. He found the Crow headmen gathering and waiting on sweated ponies, exultant with victory over these Sioux dogs.

"Mister Skye!" cried one. "We did not know."

"We were visiting," Mister Skye said, choosing not to say more. "And they held us when you came."

The headman nodded. "Who are those whitemen above?"

"Ones I am taking across the land to hunt the buffalo."

"Some are dead," the headman said.

Mister Skye nodded, absorbing that. By the hand of the Crow, probably, he thought. "I promised the Hunkpapa I would ask you something. You have won a great victory, and the Hunkpapa wail now. It is enough. Let the women and children go. Let the wounded live, unscalped."

"You ask too much. It is good to take the hair of the Hunkpapa. The captives will make good slaves."

"I told the young man there, Sitting Bull, I would ask it."

They debated that, not liking it, seeing it as a defeat in the midst of a great triumph. Mister Skye listened patiently, knowing how carefully these things must be deliberated.

"Our warriors will not like it."

"It was Jawbone's medicine that gave them their power," Mister Skye replied.

"That is so," the headman said reluctantly. "But we were winning anyway. We drove them before us down the Elk River."

It took a while more, but within the hour, it was settled. The Crow warriors counted coup on the Hunkpapa wounded, but did not scalp them. And they let the captives go. Young Sitting Bull watched, mortified, his eyes smouldering with a hate that would last a lifetime. Mister Skye, Victoria, and Mary collected their possessions, including his Hawken, loaded their lodge on its travois, recovered the herd of drays and saddlehorses belonging to the Britons, and started up the long trail to the top of the bluff and the plateau beyond, accompanied by a party of Crow headmen, all of them driving the cart horses and mules before them. An unknown number of Hunkpapa warriors still lurked out in the wild, and some would strike boldly, a last desperate act of redemption. But Skye's family and friends scaled the bluff and headed across the plateau toward the Britons unmolested, while the southwind sighed.

Lord Frazier grew weary of squinting and he ran out of spit to lick his lips, so he repaired to his yellow parlor wagon and found his lady lying abed.

"I say, Alexandra, we've come to a bloody pass. Out here in these wilds, without a dray a pull us. And that bounder Skye, off and gone. A deserter and a coward."

"Oh, the savageness of it! I could hardly bear it, Gordon."

"I thought you liked the savages."

"Oh, I do. They are ever so much finer than Englishmen. I shall write about all that back home. Did you see their nobility? Their bearing? How they stand and walk? Their

beauty? I think they're descended from Greeks. Those ancient Greeks were all swarthy, you know.''
    ''I don't think so, Alex. Asian eyes. They're Mongols of
some sort.''
    ''They're all gods, except when they do naughty things
to themselves. Whatever possessed that boy—Sitting Bull—
to hang himself from his chest, Gordon?''
    ''I haven't the foggiest idea. His headmaster ought to
cane him. Such silly business.''
    ''Savage! So perfectly savage,'' she mumbled. ''I will
dazzle England with my journals. Alfred Tennyson will be
perfectly jealous. Fetch me water, dear.''
    ''Galitzin's getting some. We had a scrape there. But he'll
bring some. And then he'll get us horses.''
    ''Have we none?''
    ''The Crow drove them off.''
    ''Whatever will we do?''
    ''Buy more, of course. From our friends in the village.
They played a little prank on us, taking our rifles. But we'll
get them back. Do you suppose they'll take a draft? They
could cash it at any Hudson's Bay post.''
    ''Well, I wish the colonel would hurry. I'm quite dry.''
    ''There's wine, Alex.''
    ''Summon him, Gordon. I'm perfectly parched.''
    ''Capital, capital,'' he said, rousing himself from his
chair. He poked his head out just in time to see a terrible
spectacle. Off to the east, rising off the crest of the bluffs,
came another savage army. A large herd of ponies—what
miserable beasts they all were—and some creatures laden
with packs and travois, and a knot of warriors, almost naked.
    He discovered Diana staring at them. ''I wish I could
dress like that,'' she said.
    ''They look peacable enough, but we'd better prepare.
That flighty colonel is off and gone, leaving us exposed.''
He peered about. ''Gravesend—ready your men!''
    But the armorer had already deployed what few he had,
including the rubicund wine steward, Stauffinger.
    About when the savages came into rifle range, a stout

bloke on a gray horse pushed forward, and Lord Frazier recognized him at once.

"Why—it's Skye! Hold your fire. It's that deserter, walking right into our hands!"

Oh, the joy of it, the viscount thought. That oaf hadn't run off after all. They'd clamp him in irons for the whipping. Or maybe wait a bit and have Galitzin do it. The savages paused out there, and Skye shouted something, lost in the whine of the southwind.

"We've got your horses," the man shouted.

It was perfectly extraordinary how that bounder's silk topper stuck to his head in the gale.

"Well bring them in," Frazier shouted, testily. "But keep those savages out."

Skye ignored him, and the whole party pushed cautiously into the compound. Horses. Frazier sighed. The bloody guide had done something of value, at last. He couldn't think of anything else the guide had done to earn his piratical fee.

The whole lot trailed in. Skye's squaws, the old one looking sour as usual. Mary smiling. Those mules with their travois. And savages of all sorts, looking peaceable enough.

"Well, Skye, now that the shooting's done, you've crawled out of your hideyhole."

"It's Mister Skye."

"Oh, of course, Lord Admiral Skye."

The guide ignored him. "These are my friends the Absarokas, kin of my wife. We've brought you the stolen rifles and the rest of the truck the Hunkpapa got."

"Well, fine. We were going to fetch it from them in a bit, but you've saved us the effort."

"I don't think so," said Skye, insolently. "The Crows routed the whole village."

"And I suppose you helped them, eh, Skye?"

Mister Skye said nothing, but ran a big blunt hand along the neck of that vile horse. He nodded to these headmen, and they all began handing rifles and shot pouches and powderkegs to Gravesend, who stored them in the retrieved blue cart. The viscount watched narrowly, wondering how many were being held back. These cutthroats would make off with the family silver if you let them.

From under the carts, the wounded watched and groaned. One had slipped into a coma. Mister Skye studied each one.

"Have they water?" he asked.

"Galitzin's gone for some. Took a strong party."

"You've lost men."

"Two out there, and these. Your bloody friends there did it."

"We tried to reach them, Lord Frazier."

"You hid in a hideyhole."

The guide didn't respond. He was watching some specks toiling up the grade from the Yellowstone. "Your water party," he said at last, studying the plateau. The savages did too.

"Skye. Take these savages out of here."

The guide turned and fixed him in that stern gaze that Frazier found so hard to meet. "They've come in friendship. They feel bad about their fight with a party guided by Mister Skye. They've tried to make amends by collecting your horses and weapons. They're here to protect us. There's plenty of Hunkpapa warriors out from the village, and every one's got a burning need to count coup, redeem himself, kill if he can. I'd take it kindly if you'd give these Crow friends some good gifts. A few pounds of powder, some shot, some tobacco."

"You're perfectly daft, Skye. They're murderers."

Skye did something astonishing. He dismounted from that blue terror he rode, stalked over to Gravesend's cart, and dug out a pig of lead, a shot pouch, a fine British fowling piece, and then poured a pound or more of powder into a duck bag. All this he handed to the headman, whose eyes glowed with pleasure.

"Why, Skye, you've stolen our things!"

The guide ignored him, and tramped to one of the enameled carts, the one stowing the trade trinkets, and found twists of tobacco there. These he distributed to each of the dozen savages who'd accompanied him. The viscount raged inwardly, but thought it wise to smile, lest the brutes slaughter them all. He'd deal with Skye later. Oh, would he deal with the man!

Skye talked with the warriors in their Crow mumbo-jumbo, and the savages all rode off toward the village they'd conquered. That old squaw of his hugged one, and jabbered with him a few moments, and smiled. The viscount had never seen the old crone smile. But he spotted tears in her eyes as they rode off with the loot.

Galitzin's water party stumbled in a moment later, and the colonel swiftly detailed men to succor the parched wounded. The wine steward brought one bucket to the viscount and his ladies, plus Baudelaire, who had materialized from under something or other, and they all guzzled thirstily.

"It's better than tiddlywinks," said Diana.

Skye interrupted them. "We'll harness and get off this high country fast," he said quietly. "Not a good place to be. We'll head for the Yellowstone bottoms, mate, and hole up a few days in the shade, close to water. Let the wounded heal. And on the way we'll pick up the dead and bury them down there. I trust you'll lead the services. Church of England, I suppose."

The viscount gaped. The coward and deserter stood there resuming command, reminding him of duties, as if nothing had happened.

Chapter 18

The refreshed cartmen gently tended the groaning wounded, packed the spilled goods into the surviving carts, harnessed the drays, and plunged out of that white hell, pausing on the way to collect the rank, fly-blown corpses of the ones who'd been killed and scalped near the marquess tent. Then the solemn cortege wended its way back to the Yellowstone river bottoms and their dappled cottonwood shade, pushed a few miles upstream, and halted in a blue glade beside the cold water.

Victoria had watched Mister Skye confront the viscount, and it gave her some small hope that he had found himself again. For some reason she couldn't fathom he'd not been himself among these tribesmen of his, as if they had a right to rule over him and even rule the thoughts in his head. She couldn't imagine it; her man had weakened, and it unnerved her.

They made camp silently in a salmon lastlight, all of them too weary to rejoice at their deliverance. Nothing was settled between Mister Skye and the viscount, but for the moment a truce prevailed. Victoria had no meat. She and Mary would make do with greens and roots gathered from the river bottoms, and a handful of jerky thrown into a stew. She would dig for the roots of the sego lily, arrowhead and tule; the bulbs of the wild onion; and hunt the wild rhubarb, pigweed and pokeweed for greens. This time of year, they would find something.

The wind died with the sun, and smoke from several fires layered lavender over the camp. Galitzin, their war chief, set cartmen to digging graves in the moist soil near the Yellowstone where the spades bit easily into the earth. She eyed the canvas-wrapped bodies, knowing they must be buried at once. Three now, she realized. The cartman who'd taken an arrow through his belly had died, too. At least he had his scalp.

Mister Skye picketed the packmules and mares on bluestem near the lodge, and then roughhoused with Jawbone, their way of loving each other, she knew. The ugly roan had saved them again. Many times had the medicine horse rescued them from death. The Britons didn't know that, and Mister Skye wouldn't tell them. They did not understand about medicine. Their religion seemed strange to her. Whoever heard of such a thing as sin? Not even Mister Skye's patient explaining helped.

Around the yellow wagon the viscount and his women lounged, and Baudelaire too, all of them sipping spirits as if nothing much had ever happened and they didn't owe their lives and freedom and possessions to Mister Skye and Jawbone. She eyed them, wondering if they had the faintest gratitude. She decided they didn't. The wine steward, Stauffinger, hovered over them, and nearby the chief cook, Abbot Beowolf, built fires and began some soup and frycakes from stores because they had no meat either. It was all as if nothing had happened.

Mister Skye caught up with Galitzin, who was supervising the repacking of carts.

"Say, mate. There's a lot of Hunkpapa around, itching to get the horses. You'll want to set a strong guard tonight. Picket the horses close and hobble them. Keep a few right in camp, hobbled and tied, for emergencies."

Galitzin sighed. "I'm sure we'll manage, Skye."

Mister Skye caught him by the arm in a grip of such iron that he winced. "It's Mister Skye, mate. And from now on—for your safety, the viscount's safety, and mine—you'll be heeding me."

Galitzin stared aghast at the lése majestè.

"Set your men to watching those horses, or I will."

"Let go of me. If you were a private, you'd be court-martialed."

"I'm not a private. I'm your guide. And things have changed. I'll never again give you the chance to kill yourselves—or kill my wives and me, mate."

The altercation aroused the viscount, who tumbled out of a campchair. "Unhand him, Skye!" he bawled. Cartmen paused, gaping. The viscount wrestled his revolver from his hip and proceeded toward Skye, bawling at the cartmen. Only Gravesend, bull-sized and hard, abandoned his cleaning of the rifles and sprang toward Skye, fists ready.

Victoria slid into the lodge, along with Mary, reaching for the old longrifles there. Many times they'd rescued Mister Skye with them, because whitemen never paid any attention to squaws. She and Mary walked among them almost invisible to them, she knew.

A swift shove sent Colonel Galitzin sprawling, and a well-aimed prod of Skye's square-toed boot caught Galitzin's hand just as it clamped over the grip of his revolver.

"Skye. Stand quiet or I'll shoot," roared the viscount.

"It's Mister Skye, mate," he said, whirling on Gravesend, who bulled in from his right. Gravesend's massive fists rocked Skye, and a deft thrust of the foot tripped Skye, sending him sprawling.

Jawbone shrieked and began dancing madly, the amber light of fires reflected in his mad eyes. Mary and Victoria slid out from their lodge, each armed with a flintlock, plus their swift silent bows and arrows.

Mister Skye rolled and kept rolling in a parabola that landed him on his feet again. The viscount lifted his pistol toward the darkening heaven and shot, a sharp boom in the quiet.

"Stop at once. Don't move, Skye, or I'll shoot. Galitzin, fetch the irons."

But even as he spoke Skye leapt like a panther, all of his massive frame bulling into the viscount, who staggered back, his finger spasming on the trigger and shooting the stars once again. Skye landed on him and in two swift blows sent the Colt flying and spun the viscount around. The ladies screamed.

Gravesend picked himself up and sprang forward, only to be thrown ten yards by Jawbone, who exploded out of the darkness, his massive shoulder slamming squarely into the armorer, toppling him like a sawlog. Jawbone shrieked, wild and eerie, sending chills even through Victoria, who nestled behind a parfleche, her longrifle aimed at the viscount.

"Arrest him!" squeaked the viscount in a voice that lacked breath.

But Skye lifted the man by the front of his shirt until he dangled upright, inches from Skye's face. Fearfully, cartmen watched but did nothing. Something released in Victoria's chest. Her man was himself again. Even now, he held that chief of England in his clutch, making him squirm. Beside her in the dusk, Mary giggled softly.

"Mister Skye," Mary said. "Your hat is over there."

That was a signal to him, Victoria knew. Between themselves and Jawbone, Mister Skye need not fear any rush from the cartmen, Gravesend, or Galitzin. Or Lady Diana, for that matter, who had slid toward the yellow wagon, unnoticed by all except Victoria.

"You lost men," rumbled Skye, holding the viscount inches from him. "You lost your horses. You lost most of your arms. You and your men almost perished of thirst. You made enemies. You came close to being killed, you and your ladies. You've got the wounded now, the dead on your souls. And all of it because you wouldn't listen to a guide who knows the country and the tribes."

The viscount peered back from embered eyes, palpable rage in them from being manhandled.

"You brought it on yourself," Skye rumbled.

"Are you quite through, Skye?"

"No, mate, I'm not. You've toyed with my wife Mary, forcing your attentions on her. If you touch her, Frazier, I will kill you." The viscount managed a faint smirk, but his eyes still blazed back. "I'll not have you tampering with my wife. Or risking our lives."

"Oh, pshaw, Skye. You make much ado about nothing. We had a bit of a scrape and you make a mountain of it. You're a cheeky bugger, telling us what to do after you hid in the village to save your skin. We'd have fetched our horses from Bear's Rib and our Sioux friends and gotten our borrowed weapons back, and that's all there is to it. Where were you? Cowering somewhere. Not a bone in your spine. Some Englishman, Skye! You haven't earned a farthing of your fee. You're a bloody coward. Now let go of my shirt, you dolt, or I'll have you lashed."

Mister Skye did, so suddenly the viscount staggered.

Cartmen gaped. The Abbot Beowolf let his pots boil. Lady Diana edged from the yellow wagon in the shadows, carrying her small fowling piece. Victoria swung her old flintlock around, ready.

"Frazier," Mister Skye rumbled. "Take your pick. We'll leave now, my wives and I, if you say go. If not, you'll follow my command as long as I'm guiding you in this wild land."

"Oh, pshaw, Skye." The viscount stared about, cunning replacing the rage in his face. "Let's wait until morning, eh?"

Victoria studied the lord in the light of the dying fires, and saw deceit in him. She hoped her man did too.

"Now."

Lady Diana edged out of the blackness toward the light, the fowling piece glinting orange in the crook of her small arm. Victoria watched suspiciously. Jawbone snorted, his ears laid back again. From the ground, Gravesend and Galitzin watched and plotted.

"Why, old chap, we'll agree." The viscount smiled crookedly, filling Victoria with loathing and dread. "You just take us to game and keep the savages under control, eh? Don't run off now. I want you handy."

Something relaxed in Mister Skye. "Everyone here has heard that. And everyone here has heard me. But I'm not sure you heard me, Frazier."

"Keep a civil tongue, Skye. Address me as befits your station."

Lady Diana continued to ease around through deep shadow to give herself a clear shot at Skye alone. Victoria waited, not wanting to do anything if she didn't have to. But then Diana lifted the fowling piece, and Victoria pulled the trigger of her flintlock.

The boom startled Viscount Frazier. Instantly he found himself slamming into Skye, who'd grabbed his shirt again and yanked. The viscount's head bounced off Skye's hard chest, even as the guide's thick arm pinioned him close.

"I say, Skye—"

"Easy, mate."

The viscount managed to extricate himself enough to peer around. He spotted Diana limned by the cookfires, frozen, a fowling piece clutched in her hand. She gaped into the darkness toward Skye's lodge. Over there, in indigo shadow, he made out the old squaw, Victoria, a drawn bow in hand, the arrow pointing directly at Diana. And next to the old squaw, the young one on the ground, her piece aimed at Galitzin and Gravesend. That ghastly horse shrieked and pawed grass. One of the bulldogs yapped and growled.

A swift shove from the guide tottered him backward several feet, and the viscount found himself peering into the terrible black bore of the guide's revolver. The man was about to kill him! He, a peer of England! He gaped at these Skyes, the guide and his squaws, holding engines of death upon him, and felt a terror turn over his stomach and squeeze his guts until they drained. His pulse racketed through his veins like a mad snake in his body, and then he trembled—rattled every fiber of his being—and couldn't stop. His hands refused to quiet down, and the tremors turned his own flesh into an uncontrolled rag.

"Lady," rumbled Skye, "set that piece down slowly."

Diana, rage twisting her face, did so. "You're scum, you Skyes," she snapped. "I'll get even."

The viscount peered around at the whole dark camp. Cartmen stood transfixed. Even the wounded had stopped groaning and stared into the wavering amber light and inky shadows. A vast disgust boiled up in the viscount. This barbarous guide and two savage women and a crazed stallion had overwhelmed Galitzin's entire force. It sickened the viscount, this discovery.

"In all my years of guiding, I've never had clients like you," the guide said in a voice so low the viscount strained to hear it. "I supposed this would happen some day, but I've always been lucky. I chose well. Everyone I've taken into the wilds has sensed its dangers and listened to me. I've prowled these empty lands for a quarter of a century. Most of my friends went under. Maybe nine out of ten went under: mostly caught by the Blackfeet, Gros Ventre, Cree, Assiniboin, Cheyenne, Sioux, Arapaho, Arikara, and the rest. The pox, cholera, ague. Mountain fever. Dysentery. Strokes. Heart seizure dropping a man like he was pole-axed. Blizzards, hailstorms, sun. Lightning and wind. Hydrophobia, heat, thirst. Starvation turning a man's guts inside out. Poisoned on bad berries and roots. Clawed to bits by grizzly bears. Mauled by a moose. Smashed by a rank horse.

"Getting lost and not a familiar landmark anywhere. Wandering mad, full of terrors. Noises out of the night that set a man to sweating. Drowning in the cold sucking rivers. Gyp water, poison springs. Froze solid without a hole in sight. Bit by rattlers. Misunderstandings—man couldn't speak a tongue or talk with his fingers and hands, and died for it. White renegades, living wolves. Breeds, too. Accidents—plugged barrels. Wet powder, bad caps, nothing but fizzle in a barrel. Stomped by horses, broke a leg on ice, died of plain terror. Stupidity, too. Leaving friends to hunt alone and never coming back. A mighty lot of them walked out of camp and were never seen again. Some were fools. Insulting Indian medicine and shamans. Torture—oh, I've seen that, too. Tie you up and peel your flesh. Squaws do it. Cut your fingers, one joint at a time, and the more you howl the slower they go. Stick burning brands into you, right into your privates. Gouge your eyes out. Unman you. Scalp you while you still breathe. Lay with captive women until they die. And some, Frazier, die for no damned reason at all. They just do. Oh, I've seen it all, mate, and I've survived. I learned a few things. Mostly I learned to be afraid. I never stop being afraid, right down in my marrow. A man learns to fear out here, or he dies. I learned all that and now I offer what I know to whoever employs me. And they've all been delivered safe to wherever they were going. I've not failed yet. Not yet, mate. But maybe this time."

The guide stopped, letting all this sink in. He had spoken low but everyone in camp had heard perfectly. Lord Frazier realized the brute had come to the end of his monologue. He meant to put him in his place.

"Keep a civil tongue in your head, Skye. You'll address me as you should," he said, still spasming at the sight of Skye's revolver aimed squarely at his chest.

"You didn't hear a word, but the rest did," Skye muttered. "You're the first one who hasn't listened and hasn't become a friend. Well, if you won't be a friend, at least listen."

"A friend! You're incredible, Skye."

The brute grinned suddenly. "That's what they tell me, mate. Take your pick. Discharge us now, or keep us—my wives and me—and heed what I say." Skye slid his revolver back into its sheath and turned his back on the viscount, as if to tempt him.

Galtizin stood shakily, looking pale even in the wavering amber light. "I think we'd better keep him on, your lordship," he muttered. "I'm perfectly willing to follow his instruction."

"Why—why—Galitzin, are you quite well?"

Baudelaire emerged from somewhere. The man had a genius for wiggling under something when trouble loomed. "Your lordship, to keep Mister Skye present is to enjoy future opportunity," he said softly. "Including, ah, rewards—and punishments."

Lord Frazier, feeling calm settle his trembling flesh at last, smiled.

Something had changed. Well, he thought, let it. If this rustic wanted to play lord in a lordless land, let him. For the moment, anyway. Oddly, the cartmen looked like they'd enjoyed it. Well he'd have a sharp word for them at the right moment.

He watched Skye assume Galitzin's command, wandering from man to man, quietly learning the cartman's name and issuing instructions. Two cartmen dug up hobbles and hastened toward the picketed horses out in the dark. Two others found halters and lead ropes and began tugging saddle horses into camp, picketing them close to the tents. That annoyed the viscount, who'd commanded that the horses be kept apart because they disturbed his slumber and their manure stank.

The bloody cartmen were responding all too happily, he thought, watching them transform the camp along Skye's design, tugging carts into a perimeter, shafts sideways to make a kind of barrier against riders.

He was famished. No one had yet eaten. It had been a long, exhausting day. And that sluggardly Beowolf hadn't finished a meal, even now in the July dark. Well, he thought, he and the ladies would have a nip and gossip a bit. He wanted to hear what Baudelaire and Galitzin had to say about Skye's histrionics.

"I say, Stauffinger, make yourself available to my ladies," he said amiably. "And fetch me some scotch with a dash of cold river water, eh?"

The rosy wine steward bustled about while Frazier settled his aching bones into a camp chair beside the yellow wagon. If he had to wait for food, he intended to do it comfortably. But no sooner had he settled into his chair, relishing the thought of a jolt of scotch, than the guide loomed up before him.

"We'd best bury the dead, mate. Grave's dug. Vittles are a way off still."

Bury the dead! The viscount had utterly forgotten them. He peered off toward the river bank and the hole clawed out of the moist earth there, and the shrouded forms still lying there like logs. Three now.

"Oh, have the cartmen pop them in, Skye."

"I think they'd like you to offer words, Lord Frazier. It's something you should do for men in your service."

"It's much too dark, Skye."

"You have a coal oil lantern. Several, I believe."

"Command the men if you must, Lord Skye, but not me. It's been a long day."

The guide waited, letting time tick by, a faint scowl across his scarred face. Really, that battered visage was almost too much to peer at. "Give me their names," he said at last. The viscount didn't know. "I say, Galitzin, who were they, eh?"

The colonel thought a moment. "Milton Ramp, Hardwick Wiggins, and that last one, ah, Abner—no, Adam Quigg."

Mister Skye nodded and walked off, while the viscount eyed him. How he detested that bounder. Stauffinger returned with his scotch, delicious with the cold river water in it, and he sipped, even as cartmen quietly gathered down near the river bank, forming a loose circle around the graves. Mister Skye walked there too, carrying a glowing lamp and a dark book.

The viscount settled back into his camp chair, feeling the honest benefits of the spirits he was imbibing, and watched the Reverend Skye do the funeral.

A cartman held the lantern beside Skye while the guide thumbed through the book—a Church of England prayer book, Frazier realized—and removed his battered silk top-hat.

"Oh God, whose nature and property is ever to have mercy and to forgive," Skye read quietly. "Receive our humble petitions for the souls of thy servants Milton Ramp, Hardwick Wiggins, and Adam Quigg, whom thou has bidden to depart out of this world: deliver them not into the hands of the enemy, neither forget them forever; but command thy holy Angels to receive them and bring them into the country of paradise . . ."

The viscount saw tears streaking the faces of the cartmen, and wished he had done his good English duty instead of preferring his comforts.

Chapter 19

Until now, it never had occurred to Victoria that she might be miserable in the heart of her Absaroka homeland. And she'd never imagined that she would ever want to slide past her own Kicked-in-the-Bellies band like a wolf in the night, but that's all she wanted now. This time she didn't want her father and stepmother, brothers and sisters, her relative Chief Many Coups, and all the rest, to know she was anywhere near.

She hunched over her ribby mare at a place she loved, on Elk River just east of the place the white captains Lewis and Clark called Rivers Across, but she was not glad. Ahead the Birdsong mountains rose razor-edged to slice a cloudless sky. The young Absaroka went there often on their vision-quest, to fast four days and supplicate the spirit ones to come. Mister Skye called them the Crazy Mountains, and called Elk River the Yellowstone, and called the cool lush river valley where her people summered the Boulder, but those were not the names painted on her heart.

The whole river valley before her was black with buffalo, but that did not lift her spirits. Usually her heart would soar when she gazed upon so many of the sacred animals. Some lounged under cottonwoods, while others grazed the golden slopes that broke back from the valley. She wondered where her own Absaroka hunters were, and why they were not making feasts and lodgecovers and robes and moccasins of them.

Never had she felt so alone. No one cared if a small burdened woman sat all alone, miles from her man and the ones he was guiding. Magpie's vision lay heavy in her spirit. She might have rejoiced because Mister Skye had taken command at last, and had cast off the weakness that had beset him among those people of his. Always before, the ones Mister Skye had chosen to guide had become her friends along the trail. But not these ones, who scorned her if they bothered to notice her at all. Always before, she had gladly taken the pale ones to her own village, but now she wouldn't. She would not subject her people to the disdain of these strange ones who confused themselves with the One Above.

Mister Skye had finally won his rightful place among them, and things had gone well, except that they'd found no buffalo day after day, traveling up the river. Because he made them, they guarded the horse herd each night and forted behind the carts and kept some riding horses inside for immediate use. The cartmen liked it, but the chiefs pretended not to notice, or grumbled about small things, especially the absence of buffalo and elk and moose and bear, as if they expected to find those four-foots right along the hot river bottoms this moon of the ripening berries.

She did not like these people, and that weighed on her. But she couldn't bear to be around them, so each day she rode ahead at dawn, and didn't slip into Mister Skye's lodge until dusk, and didn't eat with anyone. She made do with roots and berries, and sometimes a bit of meat she brought down with an arrow and roasted on a tiny fire far from the caravan of carts. She knew she brought darkness into Mister Skye's lodge, and her man grieved, but she couldn't help it. Magpie's vision grew heavier and heavier inside of her breast, and the only way she could cope with the idea of eternal separation from Mister Skye was to start it now, riding alone and apart—a woman without home or husband.

Still, she automatically continued her scouting, as she had always done, squinting over the brow of hills for the tiny movement that might mean Siksika dogs, or maybe Lakotah, or—as now—the great buffalo in their shining light summer coats, many shades brighter than their winter blackness. And here were what she had been seeking, many more than she could count.

She faced a decision: to ride back and tell them, or let them come up in a few hours. Something tugged at her, something deep in her spirit. She wanted to stampede the creatures away, yell and shoot and gallop until they all rose up, rear-end first, and began a great gallop that made the earth tremble under their hooves. Send them away, far from the white men. But she didn't. She willed herself to turn back and find Mister Skye so the viscount might have his hunt. Still she wished that these Britons would never see the sacred animal they came to shoot, and that they would swiftly go across the sea again because they found nothing here to kill.

She sat her patient mare, bewildered, tugged by so many things that her head couldn't hold them. What would Mister Skye want her to do? He was her man, and she found her greatest joy in making him happy. At least until the lodge had darkened. The mare switched her tail angrily at big black deer flies that bit deep and tormented creatures whose blood ran hot. How could Victoria sit there in the land of sweet visions, a land of prairie and fragrant sagebrush foothill and rushing icy creeks and thick cottonwood groves, and not be joyous? Not even want to see her own family and clan?

She knew she should ride back and tell her man, but she couldn't. Slowly, she permitted herself to know what she would do. She had never done such a thing, but now she would. She turned her little mare south toward the grassy benches that hemmed the valley, riding into the hot wind. She passed dark clots of buffalo, most of them sprawled on the golden grasses, their weak eyes missing her and their ears deafened by the wind. As long as she stayed downwind, they would barely pay her any attention. She had never done this thing, and she began to chant a strange sad song, begging that the spirits of those that walked the earth might understand.

From a bench south of the river she could see the entire herd, dark masses almost inert in the midday heat. All of them south of the river. She wanted them to cross. A gray wolf skulked behind her, and then another. Every herd had its wolves, preying upon the old and the injured and very young. They eyed her brightly, knowing what she would do, and she looked back and called them brothers.

At the bench she circled westward, quartering into the southwest wind, and the wolves followed, an arrow-shot to one side. And still the gusty breeze favored her. Soon it would carry the message of her to the sacred beasts, tell them that a horse and a withered Absaroka woman rode up the wind. She paused on a knoll where she could see the entire sweep of the Yellowstone country; the great mountains that roofed the world glistening far to the south and west; the Birdsongs across the river, still creased with white here and there; and broken country lying between and around. Her heart lay heavy. Down near the green sweep of the river, with its silver thread, crows fought over some morsel left by a coyote or wolf, black flocks cleaning up after the fanged ones had finished.

The white people had called her own the Crows, but they had got it wrong. They weren't the Raven People either, but the People of the Great Bird, and this was the heart of their home. Other times she might have been transported into a kind of ecstasy at the panorama before her. It had never failed to suffuse her spirit with things unspeakable, feelings beyond words that flowed out to the tips of her fingers and tingled there. But not now.

She touched her moccasins to the flanks of her pony and steered it westward again, quartering deeper into the wind. Far to her right a sentry cow stirred, turned her massive head and sniffed the eddying air, and lifted her face. The cow circled restlessly, testing the air in other directions, and turned again toward Victoria. The wolves settled on their haunches and watched, panting in the heat.

Victoria rode across the wind again, and saw more sentries rise and sniff the relentless breeze. Others, dozing quietly through a cloudless afternoon, sniffed and humped up upon their feet, scything their heavy heads back and forth. Several calves sprang up and trotted toward the center of the herd. Victoria sang, letting her words ride down the wind.

"This day I am sending you away, sacred ones. Sending you away from these hunters from across the sea. This day I do a thing I will not tell to my man. I will hide from him what I have done. I will save you for the Absaroka, for the Peoples who come to you for meat and robes and the covers for their lodges. Go away, sacred ones, and hide yourself from the ones who come up the river. Hear Many Quill Woman."

More stood and sniffed the wind restlessly, alert but not moving. She turned the pony and kicked into a light, lithe run, jarring down the grassy slopes, into the wide golden bottoms, rolling a black wall of buffalo before her. Her brothers the wolves trotted beside, still a wise arrow-shot away, sending their own scent down the wind. A dozen or so bearded bulls broke into a lumbering trot, and then others, and finally the entire herd bolted toward the shivering river, racing with a muted thunder, narrowing into an arrowhead that pierced through a fringe of bright cottonwood along the bank, and thrashed into cold water until it frothed white with the passage of an army.

"Ayah, sacred ones!" she cried as the great herd twisted into the river, swam, struck bottom on the north bank, and splashed out, snorting and shaking off water but never slowing as it snaked up a distant golden flat along Big Timber Creek and vanished among the cottonwoods. The wolf-brothers patrolled the south bank hungrily but didn't swim, and she knew they'd hunt another supper soon.

The earth ceased its trembling, and a great quiet, save for the moan of the wind, settled upon the sun-drenched valley. She had sent the sacred ones away. And by the time the slow cart caravan arrived, even the sign they left behind would have turned brown in the hot air.

She turned her winded pony, rimed with dry sweat over its withers and hips, back toward the river trail snaking close to the southern benches.

She saw him then, his silk hat cocked against the wind, sitting Jawbone, taking it all in. She had never known his anger, and wondered how it would taste in her mouth and feel in her ears. She turned the little slat-ribbed mare toward him while he watched, and drew up before him, awaiting words that would land like warclubs.

"I love you, old woman," he said, and she wept.

"Let's go up yonder," he said gently, and turned Jawbone upslope. She followed, scarcely caring where he took her. He steered up to a bench, and then a second one further back, where golden grasses rippled beneath them, making the land pulse and tremble. On the second bench he slid off Jawbone and gazed silently at the vista, studying it for signs of life and danger but enjoying it too. She could not see through the blur of her brown eyes.

"I imagine your people are up there," he said, pointing toward the Boulder valley and the great blue mountains rising to the south. "They usually are about now. Cool and sweet, plenty of deer and antelope."

She nodded silently.

"I imagine you miss them, this close. All your clan."

She nodded.

"Here now, let's sit down a spell," he said. He slipped his burly arm about her frail shoulders and eased her to the hard clay, facing toward where the Boulder tumbled into the Yellowstone amidst a dense canopy of cottonwoods far below.

He didn't say anything for a while, but let the hot breeze toy with his graying hair and tug at his silk hat. She sat quietly, comforted by the arm about her shoulders and his great paw of a hand encasing her arm.

"The carts are two, three hours back. I left Galitzin in command but told him to heed Mary with any sign of trouble. He's not a bad sort, and he agreed."

She liked his presence, even if she dreaded it. Many moons had passed since he had even touched her because of the darkness in their lodge. She resisted his hand and arm; she should be separating herself, learning to be alone. But she could not take his arm away.

"You never told me your medicine vision, Victoria. The one last winter."

"You never listened."

"I suppose I didn't," he said slowly.

"It is too late now."

"I am listening."

She didn't want to tell him what Magpie had shown her. So she sat still, liking and not liking the closeness of man and woman.

"Sonofabitch!" she muttered.

"Magpie took you up into the hills above Fort Laramie last winter and showed you something. You were gone so long I thought you'd frozen to death."

She did not want to talk about it, so she said nothing, huddling deep into the hollow of his arm and chest.

"I didn't pay it much heed," he said. "You didn't tell me and I was busy with the outfitting. Took some doing to get the ponies and the rest. Next thing I knew, you weren't saying anything and my lodge was dark and sad as death. Even Mary—you must have told her."

"You wouldn't hear," she said. "Just some old savage woman's notions. Goddam."

"I wasn't listening," he agreed. "But I will now."

He wanted to know now. But it was too late. She shook her head.

"You were fixing to ride right past your people. I saw that, Victoria. They're likely half a day away. Usually around here you turn into a girl, beaming at the whole world like sunlight, itching to slip into the lodges of your pa and his new wife, and your brothers and sisters . . . but not this time."

She felt the tears and could not fight them back, so she burrowed her head into his shoulder so he might not see her foolishness.

"You're thinking the viscount and those people aren't fit company for your village."

"Sonofabitch!" she spat. "They treat you bad. They treat me bad. Mary, too. What did they do that they can treat everyone bad?"

"Born to it. Born lords and ladies."

"But what did they do? Were they great war chiefs?"

Mister Skye shrugged. "Their ancestors, maybe. That's the way my country is. Divided up. The lords, the freemen, and lots of peasants who weren't even free until not long ago."

"Goddam, I don't want them in my village. They're damn dogs, like Siksika."

He held her tight, until she could feel the thump of his heart beneath the elkskin shirt she'd made for him. "You go visit your people, Victoria. I'll push along slow, up the Yellowstone, and after a good visit you'll catch us easily enough."

"Sonofabitch," she muttered. "When they hire you they hire me."

He didn't say anything, and they sat quietly, closer than she wanted to be, peering at the restless land, windwhipped and shimmering. Off to the west, an eagle floated lazily in an azure heaven. From where they sat they could see a few buffalo well north of the river, dots upon broken piney hills. They would not be visible to the caravan, toiling along the bottoms.

"My spirit-helper summoned me on a cold day, when the air cut through my bones, even in my robes. I was out gathering sticks. She landed on my shoulder and then hopped to my head and pecked. Who ever heard such a thing? The magpie is a bold bird, but not so bold as that.

"So I went away into the hills with only my robe and fasted. The nights were so cold I didn't think I'd live through them. But Magpie summoned me, and she is my protector and friend, so I knew I would not die."

She didn't want to talk of it, but at last she had Mister Skye's ear, and their lodge was dark.

"Magpie shortened the time because I was cold. She came the third dawn, and I saw—I saw—Goddam."

Far off, the eagle flattened its black and white wings and plummeted downward.

"They will catch you in their talons like that eagle," she said. "I saw lions catch you and take you away across the water, and I could not go along. Not I, not Mary, not Jawbone. They took you away on a fireboat across the water, and I never saw you again. I was worse than widowed. I cut off my hair and a finger and grieved, but soon I died because you never came back. And they kept you there in a cage until you died, even though you wanted to come back to us. Soon they will do this thing.''

Mister Skye seemed puzzled. "Why would they do something like that, Victoria?''

"Goddam, I don't know!''

He sat quietly, saying nothing, his mind obviously at work. "Was this a warning? Did your spirit-helper say this might happen? Or did Magpie show you the future itself, something that was bound to happen?''

"I don't know! I saw it when Sun came the third morning.''

"You didn't tell me.''

"How could I? You were full of pounds and dollars and buying ponies and getting rich. I don't think you hear me now.''

He sighed, lifted his stovepipe hat and screwed it down again. "I am listening. I don't know whether Magpie had come to warn you what could be, or show you what will come.''

"It's too late! Mister Skye's lodge is dark and soon we will all be torn apart. I don't want to live after that, Mister Skye.''

"But there's no reason," he said, puzzled.

She pulled free of him. She didn't mean to let him hold her; that had been too good, and she had to push those things away as sternly as she could. "Your lodge is still dark," she said angrily.

"Victoria—beautiful woman—''

She stood bitterly. She'd told him her vision and he didn't believe. So it would be.

He clambered to his feet slowly, while the southwind toyed with his iron hair and whipped the fringes of his shirt. "I have listened to your medicine, Victoria," he said with a strange quiet dignity. "You are Mrs. Skye and will always be. I am not going back across the sea to England, no matter what. Don't let your good heart carry something so heavy. The viscount may be a lord there, but he has no power here. He can't command the law and the sheriff and the courts here. There are none, and he's powerless. He can't carry me in chains down the Missouri, through St. Louis, up the Ohio, and all the rest, Victoria.''

But he didn't comfort her. She watched glinting dots toil toward them far to the east. The caravan, the handiwork of Viscount Gordon Patrick Archibald Frazier and his men. They would reach this place in a while. Not soon, but a while. The sight of them filled her with loathing and dread, and that added to her shame. But now Mister Skye knew, and understood why his lodge was dark.

Chapter 20

Not a buffalo. For days they'd toiled up the broad valley of the Yellowstone without seeing the shaggy beasts. The viscount fumed. He had come clear across the Atlantic to shoot them, and he'd scarcely had a shot. He'd seen more from the river packet than he had in his entire journey with that incompetent guide. Millions of the bison on the north American continent, and Skye couldn't lead him to one. The viscount thought he'd have done better engaging some Hudson's Bay guide in British possessions.

Their food stores had declined alarmingly too. He'd been counting on abundant buffalo to feed those ravenous cartmen and all the rest. Instead, they'd made do with an occasional mule deer and antelope. He could never accustom himself to chewing on those prairie goats, but it was that or starve some nights. It took at least three deer a day to feed this throng, and four were better. Skye and his wives brought in most of the meat, and that annoyed Frazier all the more. He'd come on a hunting trip, and those savages brought in the meat. Once in a while the squaws dug roots and plucked greens, and had instructed Beowolf, so they had occasional stews full of strange tasteless things that needed dosings of salt. But none of it was as satisfying as a boss rib of bison. Several times he and Diana had saddled up at twilight and chased after the stags that had come down to drink at the river, but the slippery deer had danced off faster than these dismal cobs Skye called horses could follow. So Lord Frazier had skulked back to camp fuming, his hunting trip a ruin.

July slipped into August, and still their menacing guide pushed upriver. They rounded a great bend in the Yellowstone and plunged through a throat of rock, into a vast north-south valley hemmed by spines of indigo.

"Not far to the geysers and hot springs, mate," said Skye one evening as the cartmen made camp.

"Address me civilly, Skye."

The guide grinned insolently. "Sorry, sir," he said, his face belying the apology. "A man should be addressed civilly."

That had been the way with Skye since the beginning. He had no respect. At least the man had run an untroubled camp since that—episode. But at what a cost!

"Skye. I want buffalo. I went to great lengths to employ a guide who'd take me to buffalo, but I saw more of the beasts from the deck of that riverboat than I've seen since you joined us."

Skye peered back at him, his silk hat jaunty on his unkempt skull. "Yellerstone's not the best buffler country, mate. We could swing north to the Judith country—rich with the bluestem they like—and I'd show you buffler by the thousands. Or we can head up the river toward the geysers. There's moose, elk, grizzly up there, and sometimes buffler too."

"You're asking me to choose, are you? That's a novelty, Skye. Letting your client choose."

The guide smiled blandly. "Two, three days more and this valley'll narrow down into rugged country, and we'll start climbing. That's about as far as the carts can go. No roads through that high wilderness, and no ways to drag carts across those mountain streams. The geysers are up there, all sorts of steaming bubbling pots. And big game, mate. Bull moose with racks wider than your outstretched arms. Grizzly ba'r, if you're inclined, but I don't suggest it. Balls take no effect in them.''

''You mean we can't take our carts and my wagon up there? Why didn't you tell me?''

Skye didn't reply.

''We'll have to ride in on horses, will we?''

''Three or four days on horseback, sir. You may wish to leave most of your men in camp and bring a small party up on horseback, with the packmules for supplies.''

''We'll have to sleep on the ground?''

''Tents, camp foods, sleeping on the ground, mate.''

''But what will Alexandra—and Baudelaire. Oh, well. I'll leave them behind. A pity. I think the geysers would excite my lady's sensibilities. She's a poet, you know, Skye.''

''If she'll ride, I'll make her comfortable, mate.''

''I say, Skye. This mate business grates on me. No, Lady Alexandra doesn't ride much. She usually doesn't adorn herself in split skirts.''

''I thought to leave Gravesend in charge of the carts and men at the lower camp, and take those who wish to go, plus three or four cartmen for packers,'' Skye said.

The viscount had turned testy. Skye did that to him. ''Do what you will. But get me to game. I've brought Cutler— my taxidermist—clear from Huddersfield to cure the pelts and save the heads, and he's not had a bit of work—thanks to you. All right then. Take us to moose and elk and grizzly if you must. I suppose a stuffed grizzly in my guildhall will look as fine as a buffalo. And Skye—I'll say it again. Keep a civil tongue and mind your station.''

Skye nodded, and rode off on that berserk jade he called a horse.

His lodge remained dark. He'd never known a time when his women had turned silent as death, their faces like obsidian. Mary, too. They rarely even cooked, and stayed away from him as much as possible. In the night she turned from him, and drew her robe tight about her. His young Snake woman seemed as distraught by Victoria's medicine prophecy as old Victoria. Maybe more so, because the child stirred within her. At least he had a reason for all this now.

He took to riding out at dawn each morning, ostensibly hunting but actually just wanting to be alone. He had no home any more. All the Skyes went their separate ways each dawn. Galitzin now ran the caravan competently since Mister Skye had insisted on night defenses, especially a guard for the horses, so the guide felt less and less need to stay close. He'd never guided a party who'd scorned his services, and he felt no compunction about drifting off each day rather than suffer the constant mock of the viscount's cronies.

But mostly he grieved. Victoria slid off into the night, even before dawn, avoiding his company, believing heart and soul in her medicine vision, and preparing herself for some sort of separation Magpie had foretold. It left Mister Skye uneasy about the vision itself and the grip it had on his two wives. They shunned him as if he'd done something wrong, but he couldn't fathom what it might be. Riding out alone was his only solace.

He didn't hold with Indian visions—too many had been nonsense—but he respected medicine, understood the power of its grip upon the people of the plains, and used it ruthlessly to foster a certain perception of himself. He couldn't even talk to his wives in reasonable terms. That evening, after Victoria had finally told him what burdened her, he'd tried to tell them he had no intention of going away. They'd stared at him somberly, and his lodge remained dark.

This dawn he saddled Jawbone before the rest of the camp awakened, as usual, intending to slip away as he had for several days. He had no answers, but lone-riding with his faithful Jawbone offered some small balm, especially in this upper Yellowstone valley he always enjoyed. But before he could flee once again, Lady Diana Chatham-Hollingshead popped out of the yellow wagon, in riding attire, and approached.

"I'm going with you today, Skye," she said. "I'm having my buffalo runner saddled."

It didn't please him. In fact, the arrogance of her class pierced him. She hadn't asked. It had been an announcement. She'd supposed she had a perfect right; supposed he'd be pleased to have the company of a highbred lady. He wasn't pleased. In fact, she awakened an ancient loathing that cut back to his childhood and infected his merchant father as well as himself. It was not enough to be a freeman in England. Not enough even to be rich or to achieve great things, or give splendid gifts to mankind or the Crown or the Church. Never enough!

"Very well," he said, reminding himself she was his client.

A night guard brought Lady Diana's mount to her, and they rode off. From his lodge door, Mary stared.

This day's solitude would be ruined, he knew. And he'd have to remember to address her properly: my lady. He steered Jawbone east of the much-diminished Yellowstone river, across benched flats that shouldered the vaulting mountains. The sun rose behind the giant crags to the east, shining on another world up there while the valley was still bathed in lavender. He'd planned to shoot a good buck or two to feed the camp, and nurse his loneliness while he did it, but now he was stuck.

She kicked her coyote dun forward, until she rode beside Mister Skye. Jawbone didn't like it a bit, and laid his ears back.

"I don't think you like us, Mister Skye," she said.

It struck him that she'd addressed him as he wished. He felt like saying plenty—about lords and ladies, about the viscount, about class and caste, but he bit it off. "Someone has to bring in meat," he said evasively.

She laughed. "There's several good hunters among the cartmen. Gravesend, for instance. No, try again. You detest us, and we detest you."

He glanced at her and found her face lit with amusement. She lacked beauty, having rather blocky features, but she possessed a fine radiant face and a bright mien that gave her a rich handsomeness anyway. "Whatever you say, my lady."

She bellowed at him, a laughter so loud it'd scare off the game he sought. "The thing I like about you, Barnaby Skye, is that you don't m'lady me. Gordon needs sirring and your lordshipping, but I don't."

Mister Skye was determined not to let that pleasure him, and focussed fiercely on the obvious fact that she'd intruded on his morning, and on his peace.

"Won't talk, eh? Gordon says you're an Australian, and no doubt right out of a penal colony."

"Let him think it."

"Where are you from, Mister Skye?"

"If we talk, we'll miss spotting the game. Drive it off, especially this hour when sound carries."

She peered up the valley, still indigo and lavender in its dawn shadow, and misty far upriver. But high above, snow-streaked peaks caught the sun and glowed like embers under a bellows.

"I admire this valley. One of the choice places in the western wilderness," he rumbled.

"Where are you from, Mister Skye?"

He sighed. "London."

"Were you sent to Australia?"

"No."

"Ha! Gordon's wrong. He thought you'd been a common crook, a footpad or a thief sent to the colonies. But he also says you were a seaman and I think he's right."

"I was."

"Gordon says that's a common trade."

"It wasn't what I intended."

"What did you intend, back in London, Mister Skye?"

She annoyed him, probing so much. Yet something responded in him. Her fine clipped English stirred ancient memories: faint visions of narrow streets, half-timbered houses, and always the scent of the not-distant sea sweeping in on breezes.

"I don't seem to be getting anywhere, do I? I've been watching you, Mister Skye. You're a mystery to me. You never touch spirits, do you? You never join us. Mary joined us."

"Was I welcome to join you?"

She laughed. "You have me there, Barnaby."

"It's Mister Skye."

She laughed, a waterfall of music in the cool dawn. He'd forgotten what the music of laughter sounded like.

"I touch spirits."

"But you haven't. The viscount's got a whole cartload still. Scotch, ah, there's a drink to get tiddly with. It improves my shooting too. Give me a good dose and it steadies my hand."

"When I touch spirits, I roar like a grizz, stomp on stars, ride bull moose up the canyons, bugle like a rutting elk—"

"And what else?"

"And make water." He guffawed. "Like the Yellerstone."

"You are a man of many parts."

He hoohawed.

"But you don't touch a drop. It must be our company you don't like."

"I don't touch drops. I touch jugs. Since I don't trust Galitzin to do anything sensical, I don't touch anything. But I'm getting a gawdalmighty dry in me."

"Do you really bugle like a rutting elk?"

"More like a bull moose."

"You'll have to show me," she said lightly.

"I'm dry."

"I'll fix that. I'm a famous boozer and I'll drink you under the table."

She made him uneasy, even though she was good company. He couldn't relax. And mixed into it was the constant sense of her breeding and his lack of it.

They rode quietly a while, topping several grassy benches that seemed to form pedestals for the mountains. She didn't banter, and he felt grateful for that. At the topmost bench he turned Jawbone south and rode up the valley, letting himself absorb its grandeur. Ahead a few miles rose a huge conical peak, still snowstreaked. A splendid hotsprings purled out from its base, cascading into pools, each one cooler than the one above. Victoria's people loved to bathe there. They came summer and winter, but especially winter, enjoying a delicious soak in the steaming water when the land lay burdened with snow. He'd had many a soak himself to drive the cold and numbness from his bones, lolling in the hot water amidst steam so thick he could scarcely see his toes.

But now he studied the valley, his alert eyes focusing slowly on the surrounding country, reading it and the sign it offered him. This had always been a great thoroughfare for wandering tribesmen. For eons they had come this way en route to the obsidian cliffs up a way, a mountain of black glass that flaked into the finest arrowheads in North America. But today he saw nothing. The land lay as somnolent as the horse-latitude sea, sun gilding the western slopes across the valley and driving the blue shadow ever eastward as it climbed above the eastern range.

"What do you see, Mister Skye?" she asked softly.

"The Sargasso sea."

"I've never seen a valley like this. In England things are small and close. Here, everything is—reckless with size and beauty. A reckless giant made this place."

A glint caught his eye, and he studied the east bank of the Yellowstone far away. "They're starting off," he said, pointing to the shining dots, crawling like beetles along the river.

"How can you stand to be so far away? If it weren't for you, I'd shudder to be here."

"I've lived a quarter of a century in this. It's home—much as anything is home."

"You were a sailor before this?"

He nodded and touched his heels to Jawbone. He didn't really want her probing or even getting too friendly. She wouldn't scruple at much, he knew. Her class rarely did. "Hotsprings a mile or two ahead. Maybe two. You can wiggle your toes in the warm water," he said.

"Hot water!"

"Yas . . ."

"A bath! Oh, how I miss baths."

"Ah—I'll fetch my Mary to keep an eye—"

"A bath!" she cried, heeling her buffalo runner into a canter.

He cursed himself for mentioning it and followed behind her on Jawbone, sniffing mingled sage and juniper and pine eddying sweetly down from the high country.

She held her pony to a rocking-chair gait until at last they burst into a scoop of land where the waters purled. Usually he surveyed places like this carefully, hidden in shadow, but he'd had no time with this noblewoman racing ahead. He fumed at her recklessness. But this time things seemed to be safe.

"Oh!" she cried, sliding off the dun. She stabbed her finger gingerly in a glimmering little stream, and cried out. "It's warm! Is it hotter higher up?"

He nodded, following helplessly as she dashed ahead, dragging her pony toward a pool partially scooped from the slope and partially dammed by tribesmen some time in the distant past. He peered about nervously, wondering whose eyes surveyed them here. A long shoulder of mountain separated them from the valley now, and its distant caravan.

"I'm going to. Here, Skye, tie my horse." She thrust the reins at him and began at once tugging at her slender riding boots.

"Ah, Lady Diana, I'd better—"

"Oh you ninny. You dither too much!"

"I think—"

"We're going to have fun, Skye. Take your duds off."

She popped her second boot off and wriggled out of her brown riding jacket. Her split skirts came next, and then she undid her silky blouse, until she sat in her chemise and drawers.

"Ah, that's just fine, Lady Diana. Wet your toes—"

"You're a goose, Skye."

"Ah—"

She pulled her chemise off, baring lush brown-tipped breasts and golden flesh, and then dropped her drawers and smiled. "See," she said. "I don't have the best figure, but I still turn a man's head."

Mister Skye gaped at her curvaceous breasts and taut wide belly, and felt a rush of desire he couldn't help. She knew it and posed seductively, her gaze riveting him.

"Take those buckskins off, Barnaby. I don't think you've had a bath in years. You need a bath. You stink. Your hair's greasy. But keep that awful silk tophat on. That'd be the funniest thing I've ever seen. We'll do it in the water with your silk hat on."

"I'll stand guard," he replied primly.

"Stand guard! Against what, Skye? Take your chances. The same as I am."

"I'm married and love my wives, Lady Chatham-Hollingshead."

"Your wives. All two!" She gusted with laughter and slid gracefully into the pool, the shimmering water gliding over her loins and breasts, up to her neck. She rolled and played in it like a dolphin, splashing hot water in sunlit rainbows.

"Oh! Glorious! Paradise!" she exclaimed. She wallowed about in the water, dipping her dark hair into it, sputtering and laughing. "Drop your breechclout, you idiot."

"Sonofabitch!" bellowed Victoria from behind, where she sat her ribby pony.

Chapter 21

Barnaby Skye could delay no longer. He'd gone dry, so dry his juices didn't flow and his soul stiffened like sunblasted rawhide. He'd put it off, fought it off, but now it pounced upon him and he knew what he had to do. In all his days he'd never had such an awful thirst as this.

Without a word he turned Jawbone back to the caravan, leaving the noble lady to her bath and ignoring the hard look in Victoria's eyes. His old Crow woman had come at just the right time. He wouldn't have resisted Lady Diana's voluptuous charms. It had all been too much, with his own lodge darkened, his wives cold as an arctic storm.

And then Victoria had ridden in. His woman hadn't laughed. She should have laughed. She came from the bawdiest tribe on the plains, a tribe whose wild women had made mountain men blush. But Victoria had just hunched on her ribby mare, cursing, reading the faces, and that was all it took. Something collapsed in Barnaby Skye, and he turned Jawbone toward the caravan, leaving the women to their own devices.

He trembled with his need, and Jawbone sensed it. He

laid back his ears, hating Mister Skye for it. But Mister Skye had slipped far beyond help. He would take his journey now, and say goodbye to lords and ladies who loathed him and subverted the discipline he established; goodbye to Mary and Victoria and Jawbone, his own family, or what was left of it. He didn't care what happened. The whole hunting trip could fall apart and he wouldn't care. In fact he wished it would.

He rode over the grassy shoulder and spotted the caravan instantly, off in the northwest, toiling up the right bank of the Yellowstone along the first grassy bench above the river. The sight of the enameled carts with their heraldry blazoned on the sides enraged him. They didn't belong here. The viscount didn't belong here, and neither did his ladies, Galitzin, Baudelaire, and all their retainers. Let them take themselves, their oriental carpets, linen tents and all the rest back to England.

He rode dourly down the grass, hoping he'd be discharged and free, hoping for oblivion. Jawbone acted strange under him, snarling and clacking his big molars, sensing what would come. It enraged Skye, this censure from a horse, and he thought to whip the beast or kill it, and then felt shocked at his own wild rage. He spotted Mary ahead of the caravan, riding her dark pony and herding the pack mules and horses that dragged their lodge and lodgepoles on travois. Something steamed within him. He'd throw her out. He'd get rid of Victoria too. He'd toss their worldly goods out of his lodge, every last thing they owned, throw them out, cast them loose, divorce them Indian-fashion, cut free of his damned women and all their damned superstitions and hoodoo. It was over. He'd gather up his packmules and git, out to the high lonely, away from his dark lodge and these asinine lords and ladies and their whole retinue! But not until he pillaged a certain wagon. The thought of it turned his tongue dry and parched his throat.

"Take them to the hotsprings," he snapped at Mary as he passed her. They could all go there, these lords and ladies, and prance around naked in the hot water. She stared at him, recoiling from the harshness in his voice. "Victoria's there. So's the fancy lady."

She nodded gravely and turned her pony to the east, tugging on a picket line to swing her packhorses off the river trace.

"Follow the squaw," he snarled at Galitzin as he passed the colonel. He wouldn't call Mary wife any more. He rode down the caravan, passing drays and carts, scattering bulldogs. Jawbone minced along with laid-back ears, menacing everything around him, but Mister Skye paid no heed. His thoughts focused on a single gorgeous cart near the rear, and the fleshy man walking beside it. He passed the yellow wagon, drawn by four mustangs, and saw no sign of Lady Alexandra. But the viscount sat beside the coachman, eyeing the banks of the river with a small field glass.

"No game, Skye. My hunt's a ruin, thanks to you."

The guide ignored the man. The viscount no longer mattered. "We're heading for a hotsprings, Frazier. Your bawd's already there."

"I say, Skye—"

"Discharge me, Frazier," Skye snapped.

Lord Frazier winced, and then withered under Skye's glare. "I think I might. I've endured enough of your insolence."

"Say it, Frazier."

The viscount looked pained. "You tempt me. But I'll wait a few days. Take us to the geysers. Get me to the moose and bear and elk you promised, and after that we'll find our way back down the Yellowstone without your, ah, assistance. And after this, if you've anything to say to me, tell it to Colonel Galitzin. I won't suffer your rudeness any more, Skye."

"It's Mister Skye, matey. When you start calling me Mister, I'll start calling you Sir." He hoped that would get him fired. "Meanwhile, you're whatever I feel like calling you." Angrily, he heeled Jawbone off, leaving his lordship to his glassing of the riverbanks for deer. Things had come to a fine pass. His lordship didn't want Skye's words reaching his tender noble ears.

Near the back of the procession he spotted what he'd come for, creaking along like a mirage, an oasis splashed across a desert sky, with gaudy palmtrees and shimmering brown waters. Grimly he steered Jawbone toward the apparition, knowing he'd take by force whatever he needed.

"Mister Stauffinger," he said with controlled politeness. "I have come for refreshments."

The rosy-fleshed steward looked dubious at first. "I'd better ask his lordship," he said.

"Open," roared Skye in a voice that brooked no disobedience.

"We'll have to stop and I'll get too far behind," the man complained.

"Keep going. Hand me the key."

"Oh, his lordship would—"

Skye glared at the man until the steward wilted under his stare. Stauffinger swung to the rear and unlocked the double doors of the creaking cart, nervously eyeing both Skye and Jawbone.

Skye steered Jawbone behind, and peered into the darkness. "What's in there?"

"Wines, two barrels of scotch, a hogshead of American corn spirits for the cartmen, and—"

"Any empty jugs?"

"Why yes—"

"Fill two with corn whiskey."

"But his lordship hasn't—"

"I'll do it then," said Skye, heeling Jawbone closer.

But Stauffinger scurried into the creaking cart and began drawing the whiskey from the bung in the hogshead, filling one jug and then the other while Skye studied it.

"Hand them to me," Skye roared.

"I—I'm afraid of your horse."

Wordlessly, Skye slid off Jawbone and grabbed the jugs, feeling the cool heavy porcelain in his big hands, and enjoying an ecstasy that stole into him even before he uncorked one.

"I'll be back," he roared, as the steward clambered out of the squeaking cart and locked the doors. Behind, other cartmen and the horse herders gaped.

Ahead, the caravan veered to the left, abandoning the river trace to climb a grassy slope leading toward the conical peak. He watched, knowing the squaw was taking them to the hotsprings. The two gray jugs felt good in his palms. He clamped them to his belly with both hands, full of juicy joy. He kneed Jawbone away from the caravan, and the evil horse responded sullenly, lashing his tail and sulking with every step. It didn't matter. He'd lodgepole Jawbone too. He'd had all he could take. Off to the south, puffballs hung on peaks, and by late afternoon they'd turn into mountain showers. But here in the golden valley of the icy Yellowstone, the benign sun coddled him and warmed the jugs in his horny hands.

He veered away from the gaudy carts, feeling cleansed by every yard of distance he put between himself and the loathsome caterpillar wending up a shallow coulee toward the springs. He stuck to the shoulder of the nameless mountain, wanting high ground. He would find a place high above, a place with a few pines to sough in the breeze and a warm boulder to lean against, a vast view of the upper Yellowstone valley before him, and maybe the hotsprings off to his right. That's where he'd slide off Jawbone and go away into his own world for a while.

He rode ever higher, sometimes in sight of the caravan snaking toward the springs below. Once he rode across a dish of land where he could see the hotsprings. A tiny white figure still lolled in the waters, but Victoria had vanished. Not far, he knew. She wouldn't leave the noblewoman alone in that wilderness. But it didn't matter. Nothing down there mattered.

He found a drinking place beside a tiny alpine lake and sighed happily. Tension leaked away from him as he slid off the horse, clutching the jugs, and turned Jawbone loose to graze. He could wait no more. A great boulder rose like a breadloaf before him, and he sank gratefully to earth before it, and settled into it. He eyed the jugs, wondering which; finally uncorked the left, and lifted it to his lips. The stuff gurgled into his parched mouth burning like fire, and he gasped, choked, and laughed. His lordship had bought raw whiskey for his cartmen. He swallowed again, gasping, feeling fire burn out his insides. And then, slowly, the thing he'd needed began to creep through his tormented body and soul.

"I quit," he bellowed, lifting his jug toward the sky.

* * *

The competent Colonel Galitzin had known exactly what to do, much to Lord Frazier's relief. It wouldn't do for the cartmen and retainers to be about while a peer of England and his ladies were disporting themselves at the hotsprings. So the colonel had established two camps, the one for Lord Frazier at the springs, and the other for the cartmen, half a mile down and slightly around a bend. The runnel ran tepid down there, but what did it matter? The cartmen could dam it into a little pool, and make do. The important thing was to keep their mean eyes and thoughts away from the ladies and himself.

There'd be some slight inconvenience because the Abbot Beowolf would have to cook at some distance, and the wine steward, Stauffinger, would have to bring his wares. But that was proper and necessary. Lady Alexandra had demanded that canvas walls be erected about the pool, but Lady Diana, lolling perfectly bare in the pond when they'd arrived, had scoffed at that. Lord Frazier suspected she rather enjoyed making a spectacle of herself, even in front of the mechanics. Baudelaire and Galitzin, of course, would camp at the springs. They were the souls of discretion, and if they saw the ladies cavorting, not the slightest hint of it would ever pass their lips.

The hotspring purled out of a meadow near the foot of a vast pineclad slope that vaulted upward to cloud-shrouded high country. It lay in a natural vee that opened to the north, protected by a root of the conical mountain, perfectly private, except, of course, to his dear Alexandra, who couldn't imagine disrobing out of doors. And indeed, there remained one little problem. Those savage squaws of Skye's had erected their cowhide lodge right there at his lordship's camp. It was a perfect breach of manners, insolent in its very nature. They didn't belong here, but seemed to think they did.

"I say, Galitzin," he yelled. "Tell them to be off."

The colonel sighed. "I'll try. They do what they choose."

"It's unthinkable. I haven't seen that lout of a guide all day, but he has no business here. Tell them to mind their manners, eh?"

Lord Frazier refused to speak to any of the Skyes. They'd become so insufferable to him that he left communication to the colonel. The light had turned dusky, and he looked forward to a plunge before full dark, but he'd be damned if he'd bare his flesh before those squaws. The water felt delicious to his immersed hand, and he could barely wait to plunge into it. He watched the colonel approach the savage women, talk and point down the slope, and finally turn away.

"They say no, they're here to protect you," the colonel said.

"We can take care of ourselves! We don't need the bloody common squaws!"

"That's what I told them. They said no; with the cartmen so far away, we needed them all the more, and they are staying."

"Blast!"

"I can remove them by force, your lordship."

"Then that lout of a guide will make a fuss. Oh, well, Galitzin, the evening's ruined. Lady Alexandra won't unhook a shoe with a commoner around. I suppose we'll just suffer their disrespect."

"After it's dark, sir, she might—"

"No, never. Not with that pig of a guide watching. By the way, have you seen him?"

"Gone all day, Lord Frazier."

"Deserted us. It tallies."

"The cartmen say he compelled Stauffinger to give him some spirits."

"Ah! Theft. I knew his boozy nature would show itself. He's London dregs, penal colony stuff. I'll cane him personally if we can catch him."

"Ah, your lordship, what are we to do about food?"

"Have Beowolf bring it. Have him stop a hundred yards from us first, eh?"

"We're down to nothing. Skye didn't bring in any meat."

"Deserted us, Galitzin. Stole spirits and abandoned us! Tell Gravesend to start hunting at once. But not around here.

If he peers over that ridge, he'll be flogged. Send me spirits, Galitzin. I'm famished. Have Stauffinger leave some with us and then retire to the lower camp.''

It was tempting to have that monk of a cook and the wine steward stay and wait on them, but that would be unthinkable. They'd see and hear things not meant for common eyes and ears.

Lord Frazier had worked himself into a temper because nothing was going well. Still, a lavender dusk had lowered upon the hotspring, and soon enough he and his ladies could have their delicious sport.

Far above him, on the grassy shoulder of mountain that hid the camp from the Yellowstone valley, something bawled like an old buffalo bull. He'd heard the very sound from the deck of the river packet. Buffalo! Up there in the settling dark! Meat! That grating noise had scarcely subsided when wild bawling laughter erupted—the laughter of a man or a spirit, he scarcely knew which. But sure enough, the bellowing seemed human, Skye's squaws stared upward, a frown etched deep in the old one's brow. Skye? Was it Skye, drunk as a lor—ah, oaf? A horse screeched. He knew the horse. Only one horse in creation screeched like that, the bag of bones called Jawbone. Its shriek shivered through him, and no doubt woke the dead for miles around.

Lady Chatham-Hollingshead giggled. The viscount stared at her, still lolling in the pool. Why didn't she fetch a robe instead of displaying herself shamelessly to commoners?

"It's Skye," said Baudelaire.

"Warn him off! Tell him to head for the cartmen's camp, eh?''

Far up a grassy shoulder, a horse and rider appeared in the dusk, the rider bawling and bellowing and weaving about on the angry animal.

"It's Skye all right, flying his true colors," Alexandra said shortly. "Make him go away. I want a bath.''

But the insufferable bellowing and bawling continued as the horse picked its way down into the narrow flats.

"Sonofabitch!'' muttered the old squaw.

Jawbone sugarfooted forward, with that hog on his back

weaving to one side and then the other, righting himself at the last moment before tumbling in a heap.

"Frazier!" bawled the guide. "You and me's going to have us a toddy!"

The very thought of it drained the viscount's energies from him. He peered about for Galitzin, and remembered he'd sent the colonel to the lower camp. He'd have to deal with this brute himself. He and Baudelaire, who was worse than useless in moments like this. He spotted his aide peering from the wagon window.

"Frazier, you old coon, fetch a cup," Skye bawled, the rasp of his voice shivering the air. "Tell the ladies to join us. We'll have a little spirits, and then have a splash."

The viscount gaped.

"Shed your skins, Barnaby," yelled Diana from the hot pool. "The water's divine. Hurry up before my flesh puckers."

The viscount was aghast. Skye's squaws stared angrily.

"Everything but my hat."

Mister Skye sagged over the near side of Jawbone, righted himself, teetered toward the off side, shrugged too late, and tumbled in a heap while Jawbone snarled and shrieked.

"Goddam," said Victoria.

Ponderously, Mister Skye hoisted himself from the grass, rear end first, and peered at him. In one massive hand, he clutched a gray jug. He wobbled uncertainly, while Jawbone skittered sideways angrily, snorting and clacking his teeth.

"Go eat," said Mister Skye. He lifted his battered silk tophat and screwed it down again, and turned to the viscount. "Have a slug," he said, proffering the jug.

Lord Frazier recoiled.

"Won't booze with a commoner, eh?"

The viscount refused to speak. Let Galitzin convey messages if there must be any.

"Ah, paradise," Skye said, uncorking the jug again and quaffing juices that gurgled out of his mouth and dripped on his elkskin shirt and over his grizzly bear claw necklace. "Ah!" He belched like a dyspeptic Turk.

Tenderly he fondled the jug, lurched down, daintily placed it upright, and teetered back to his feet again. Then he veered toward the pool, while the viscount followed, speechless. At the rippling pond, with lavender lights lifting from it in the dusk, he peered about serenely, set his silk hat on the ground, fumbled with the laces of his crude square-toed boots until he could wrestle them off, releasing a vast noisome odor, fought his elkskin shirt off, baring a massive chest with hair going gray, unbuckled his heavy belt, which supported his leggins and breechclout, along with his revolver and knife scabbards, and let it all fall.

"Ah!" he said, retrieving his silk hat and screwing it down over greasy gray-shot hair. He maintained a perfect dignity, even wearing nothing over his hairy flesh except a black silk tophat.

"I knew you would," said Diana.

"I think I'll retire to the wagon," said Lady Alexandra, but she didn't move, and watched Skye, her gaze riveted on his massive frame. Something excited her. "Oh!" she exclaimed.

Lady Diana whooped and splashed water at Skye.

Mary giggled. Just like a squaw, thought the viscount. Then Victoria giggled too, the pair of them grinning like strumpets. Had those savages no decency?

"Come on in, yer lordship," bellowed Skye. He turned slowly, tread his lordly way to the pool, and toppled in like a felled oak, landing in the pond with a crash that sounded like a plugged cannon exploding, and shot tidal waves of hot water roiling over the banks. The tophat bobbed. Mister Skye surfaced and gently settled it down upon his dripping hair.

"Diana, come out of there!" the viscount demanded.

"Tiddlywinks," she retorted.

It enraged him. "You—you—in there with a common criminal?"

Lady Alexandra started dithering and muttering.

"A common sailor, you mean. Royal Navy," bellowed Skye.

"I thought so—I thought so!"

Mister Skye splashed mightily, spraying showers of hot water into the dusk. Lady Diana whooped and splashed too, soaking the viscount's pants. He danced back from the bank.

Mister Skye belched joyously and bugled like a bull elk. Then he roared, shivering the dark slopes. "Pressed in on the banks of the Thames; jumped ship at Fort Vancouver."

The news froze Viscount Frazier. "What did you say, Skye? You deserted the queen's navy?"

Skye bawled at the distant ridges. "Overboard with a belaying pin, foggy night, second watch."

"You deserted her royal majesty!"

"Naw, she deserted me. Press gang snatched me at age fifteen, just as I was about to start at Cambridge. Made me a bloody slave, a powder monkey. Your bloody queen and her bloody lords don't care anything about that."

"A common deserter. A thug and a lowlife!"

"A freeman, yer holiness."

"Oh, tiddlywinks, Gordon." Diana wallowed over to the deserter who stood in the pool, ludicrous in his silk tophat, steaming water lapping his waist. "Let's all have a splash."

"I think I will," whispered Lady Alexandra in a strange squeaky voice.

"Goddam," muttered Victoria. The squaws trotted toward the inviting dark water.

Lady Alexandra Frazier and the two squaws began pulling and tugging and unhooking and squirming.

But Viscount Gordon Patrick Archibald Frazier, peer of England and seventh of his line, refused to budge. He had the man now—deserter, traitor to the queen. But it would take some planning.

Chapter 22

Victoria endured. She would not sleep. She'd never quite grown used to sitting awake all night, but whenever Mister Skye crossed over to the Other Side, she watched over him ceaselessly. For as long as she'd known him he had taken these occasional journeys, and been helpless as a newborn. She couldn't fathom why he drank the spirits. Mary drank too, sometimes. And that left only her, Victoria, Many Quill Woman, to guard over the lodge of Mister Skye.

She sat crosslegged outside of the lodge, a thin two-point blanket drawn close about her to ward off the sharp chill of a mountain night. Her man snored peacefully, a white mountain under the buffalo robe she'd roughly thrown over him, afraid someone would see tenderness in it. Earlier, he'd wallowed to the bank of the hot pool, let more of the spirits gurgle down his throat, and then had fallen asleep in the water, bobbing on it like a great otter. She and Mary had pulled him out and covered him, setting his silk hat at his side. And she'd settled into her own blanket to watch through the night, as she had countless times before.

She would not weep. Neither would she sort through the

confusion that snared her. It had been a dark evening, sinister with portents that she felt in her flesh and soul. She didn't want to watch over Mister Skye, but ancient habit made her do it. Soon he would be taken away, and nothing would remain of Mister Skye's lodge. She had felt something new this night, some fierce power radiating from the viscount, who'd prowled around the lip of the hot pool like a panther looking for a way to pounce.

No sooner had Mister Skye fallen asleep in the water than the ladies abandoned the pool and hurried off through the dusk to their yellow wagon, mincing barefoot through grass and clutching their skirts and linens. A swift silence settled around the hotsprings. Even Galitzin and Baudelaire had vanished to the cartmen's camp far away, leaving only the lord and ladies, and that little bulldog, Chesterfield, who trotted along with Lady Alexandra everywhere. The ugly mutt lay in moonshadow under the yellow wagon.

She sat with her old muzzle-loader across her lap and Mister Skye's heavy dragoon revolver close by. She and Jawbone. The horse cropped meadow grass angrily, his temper even more vicious than usual because Mister Skye had gone to the Other Side. The horse was staring now, his ears pricked forward, but in the light of the small moon she couldn't see anything upslope. If it was thieves from other tribes, he'd bugle and begin that unearthly howling. Many a night his bloodcurdling shriek had awakened them in time to avert theft or murder. But he wasn't shrieking, and whatever was up the slope did not have a human spirit. She watched anyway, waiting to see the creature that engaged Jawbone's attention. Usually she loved this place, a favorite resort of her Kicked-in-the-Bellies, but this night she dreaded it. Evil lurked and danced, and she knew it was the spirts of the dead that had gone to the Beyond Land without the scalps and ponies and weapons and eyes and limbs they needed over there. She watched sharply, half-afraid of the spirit people.

So far she'd had health. She was actually a year younger than her man, but her flesh had withered sooner and she'd grown small and light, while he stayed the same. But maybe this evil night the spirits would cast a spell upon her body and make her sick. Maybe that was good, to die before Mister Skye was taken away from her.

Something lurked out upon the slope. She couldn't see it, but she sensed it. She squinted into the slit-mooned murk, seeing not even a hint of motion. Nothing stirred. A few embers still glowed in the remains of a tiny fire Mary had used to make a broth of jerky, and she wondered whether to build them into a flame again. She thought she would. The thing out there wasn't human, but a creature. She creaked to her feet intending to find squaw wood. Little of it remained here where whole villages camped. But Mary had left some she'd gathered earlier, so Victoria fed sticks into the coals and blew gently until a cold flame awakened out of its womb of ash and cast a somber glow into the night.

Goddam! she thought. This was a night when the dead danced. Nearby, Mister Skye snored suddenly and rolled, a shuddering mountain under the curly black robe. A beefy white calf flopped out upon grass. And just beyond Mister Skye sat a small wolf on his haunches, its eyes dancing a phosphorescent orange in the wavering light.

Startled, she slid back to her blanket and her battered rifle there, keeping an eye on the bold animal, which stared brightly back at her, its muzzle oddly turned and jaw hanging. A wolf. Not a large one. Solid gray, except for a black diamond rising over its brow and into the ruff of hair back of its ears. A strange mark, she thought, suddenly afraid. She'd never seen a wolf like that. It panted, its tongue slavering even in the chill of the night. One of its yellow eyes seemed larger than the other, or radiated more light from the guttering fire. It sent fear piercing through her, though she couldn't say why. She'd never known a wolf to venture so close. The creature watched her while she studied it, slowly easing her rifle around, and then deciding Mister Skye's Dragoon Colt would be better for close work.

Chesterfield came alive over at the glinting yellow wagon and growled. The little bulldog stood up, bulbous-eyed, and muttered like distant thunder. Then the dog yapped and barreled toward the wolf, which leapt lithely toward the smaller bulldog and bit it, breaking its neck with one crunch of its heavy jaw. Chesterfield's yowling died along with the writhing dog. The wolf sat back on its haunches again, panting.

"Chesterfield," said a woman's voice from within the wagon. "Do stop annoying us, dear."

The wolf turned, listening to the sound emerging from the yellow wagon, and walked lazily toward Victoria and Mister Skye, slobbering strangely, grinning at her madly. And then she knew. Madness! Hydrophobia, Mister Skye called it, though her people called it spirit-madness. Hydrophobia! She had heard the whispered stories in the light of a hundred campfires. The fearlessness. The slobbering. The bite that always killed. The wolf grinned at her, reading her mind, laughing at her because a bad spirit possessed it, peering out from its mad eyes.

Kill it! She clawed for Mister Skye's holster and found it, and lugged the cold steel from its sheath on his belt, but the wolf was trotting toward Mister Skye's bare white calf. Too late, too late. She whipped her weapon around, cocking the heavy hammer, just as the wolf snarled savagely and sank its fangs into Mister Skye's flesh. She shot, the explosion blinding in the night. Mister Skye roared, flailing legs, erupting from his robe.

She searched for the wolf but it had vanished into the gloom, its evil spirit hiding in the darkness. She heard talk in the yellow wagon and saw it creak on its leafsprings. But even as she watched, a terrible realization sliced through her: Mister Skye had been bitten, and he would die.

Mister Skye clambered to his hands and knees, fighting off his own fogginess, rumbling and muttering. Victoria gaped, seeing death upon him, seeing the slow, mad, crazed dying that would possess him in about two moons, maybe less, until he slavered his life away, foaming at the mouth, unable to drink, spasming and convulsing, berserk and tied down to keep from harming himself and everyone else.

"Sonofabitch," she wailed.

Skye stared at her, alert now, no longer over on the Other Side.

He stared at the four fang holes piercing his calf. "Hydrophobic?" he asked quietly.

She nodded, tears welling up.

Swiftly he yanked his Green River knife from its sheath, paused, and then slashed across a fang mark until blood welled up freely. He groaned, but didn't hesitate. The knife ripped into his own flesh across the other small wounds until all four bled copiously, the red blood gouting to the earth. He sobbed, anguish shaking him.

"Heat the knife and the iron spit, Victoria. We've only got seconds."

She was never sure what he meant by seconds. A white men's concept. But it meant little time. Wordlessly she plunged the knife in the coals along with the iron cooking spit, grateful she'd built up the fire. She heated the metal, barely aware that the viscount had crawled out of his wagon.

"Get back in, mate," Skye commanded. "Hydrophobic wolf."

Viscount Frazier gaped.

Her man found a stick of squaw wood and clamped his teeth over it. He gripped two more pieces in his massive hands and lay back. "Don't spare me, woman," he demanded, an urgency in his voice she'd never heard before.

She didn't. She jammed the smoking blade down into the first fang wound to cauterize muscle, recoiling as his flesh fried and the stench of charred meat assaulted her nostrils. Mister Skye's body jolted, he screamed, and his spasming legs rocked her away and catapulted the knife from her grasp.

"Goddam," she muttered, crying, unable to find the blade in the dark.

Far away, in the direction of the cartmen's camp, she heard shots thumping through the night.

Skye groaned and then sobbed. She saw tears glinting on his face. She found the knife and stabbed it into fire again, her heart hammering, and pulled out the smoking iron rod. Somehow, Mary appeared beside her, still wearing nothing, and stared, horrified, her eyes welling tears of her own.

"Hurry," muttered Skye. "If it gets into the blood, I've gone under."

* * *

About the time that the viscount finished lacing up his boots, Colonel Galitzin loomed out of the night.

"Your lordship, there's trouble," he said.

Testily the viscount pulled aside the canvas flap of the parlor wagon, leaving his ladies staring at him in the darkness, and stepped down to earth. Galitzin seemed to be half-dressed, in boots, a nightshirt, and brown tweed jacket.

"I say, colonel, you're a sight." The viscount chortled at the spectacle.

"We've had a wolf. Hydrophobic, we think, your lordship. He bit Cutler about ze face."

"Bit Cutler?"

"On the neck. Sank its fangs into his cheek. We tried to shoot it, but it vanished in the dark."

"Cutler? the taxidermist?"

"Yes. I fear he faces a horrible death. There's none worse, or drawn out so terribly."

"I see. Anyone else?"

"No, Lord Frazier."

The viscount eyed Skye, who lay groaning and sobbing beside the small fire before the lodge a few yards away. That mad nag, Jawbone, stood beside the guide, screeching and carrying on.

"Did you take any measures?"

"There are no measures. Poor Cutler—he's doomed. It'll take a while, and the last will be frightful."

The viscount sighed. "Skye was bit. First thing I knew he was stabbing himself, and then his squaws were heating a knife and cauterizing the holes. Savage nonsense, I think. I don't suppose it'll save him."

"I can't imagine it."

"Now I'll have no one to preserve my trophies, Galitzin. What a piece of bad luck, eh? Losing my taxidermist. I suppose we'll have to put up with his howling, too. Keep him at the end of the caravan, as far from my wagon as possible. I don't want to listen to all that howling."

"I think he'd welcome a visit from you, sir. He knows his fate."

"That's your business, Galitzin. You're in charge of the blokes. And say, Galitzin—when Skye begins to rave, snatch him from his squaws and throw him back with Cutler. And then drive the squaws away."

"Why not just send them packing, your lordship?"

The viscount peered through the darkness toward the two Indian women, hovering over their groaning man. "I say, Galitzin, I found out something this evening that changes everything. The drunken fool's a deserter. He was in the Royal Navy and jumped ship at Fort Vancouver. I've got him now, oh, I've got him! I knew it; I knew him for a scoundrel. I want him with us just in case he lives, just in case all that cutting and burning works. In truth, Galitzin, I'm a bit disappointed he got bitten. I had better plans for him."

"They might just leave us, sir, and go off somewhere to let him die."

"Don't permit it! Keep an eye on them, Galitzin. I'm charging you with it."

"Very good, Lord Frazier."

"We'll know if the hydrophobia takes soon enough. And even if it doesn't, I've made new plans."

Lady Alexandra poked her head out of the wagon. "Chesterfield, sweetie, Chesterfield. . . . Where are you, my little poopsie."

The bulldog didn't come.

"Chesterfield!" she cried nervously. "Find him, Gordon. Find my little poopsie."

Galitzin pointed. Off a few yards, barely lit by the flickering fire, lay a mound of hair. They trotted over and found the bulldog dead, its neck snapped and its throat ripped open, its bulging eyes turned milky.

"Gone!" exclaimed the viscount, poking the soft little body with the toe of his boot. "Killed by the wolf. While protecting his mistress." A sob rose in him. "Was there ever such a noble pup, colonel? It touches my very soul, the courage of this loyal little bloke. I wish men were half as loyal." He sighed heavily, absorbing the terrible reality of death. "Tell the lady, Galitzin. And then fetch men with a spade and we'll bury the little chap with honors, eh?"

Grief pierced him as he stood in the eddying nightbreeze,

watching Galitzin walk over to the bed wagon and say something to Alexandra. Her shriek shattered the night, and the sobs that followed wracked his soul.

"Oh my little poopsie!" she cried, sobbing and gulping. "Oh my baby, my baby."

The lady shuddered and wept, and finally withdrew from the door of the carriage and tumbled back into their bed, her sobs rising muffled from within. The viscount felt her pain deeply, and resolved to bury the manly little bulldog with all the honors due him. He was a true English bulldog, fierce and loyal and noble, the best that England could make.

"Galitzin," he said softly. "We'll wait for dawn. We're going to have a proper burial for that noble creature. We'll lay him to earth with a prayer and raise the Union Jack and fire a salute. And I'll say some words, eh? And, blast it, colonel, you could have broken the news to her more gently. Have you no sensibility?"

The colonel didn't respond, but stood in the wavering firelight looking sheepish. He annoyed the viscount. Was there no competent help anywhere on earth? Why did retainers all turn out to be boneheaded and coarse, if not crooked? He had no answer to it, but knew it had to do with breeding. The world's ruffians, like that groaning Skye over there, were simply brutes.

"Galitzin. Take Chesterfield with you. Sew him into wagonsheeting for the burial. I don't want him lying there when dawn comes up. The sight would grieve my ladies. Do it up proper, Galitzin, or it'll be a mark against you."

"Very good, sir."

"Post a guard, Galitzin. Why wasn't a guard posted? The pup might be alive if there'd been a guard."

"You sent us all to the other camp, sir—"

"No excuses, Galitzin. Negligence. I detest negligence."

"You had the Skyes guarding, sir."

"You should have been. Nothing but an old squaw watching for trouble."

From beyond the fire, the old woman stared at him, along with the young one, who sat shamelessly unclad beside that cowardly oaf who groaned and wept and kept running those big paws of his along his bloody left calf. Well, he was done for, and a pity. He deserved a worse fate.

Galitzin picked up the dead bulldog awkwardly and made off into the night with it, while the Skyes all watched. It grew quiet, save for the constant sobbing and grunting of that lout. The viscount walked over there, as far as he dared with that vicious yellow-eyed horse snarling at him.

"I say, Skye. If you're going to groan and weep all night after butchering your own leg, take your lodge away, eh? It'll ruin our sleep. But not far, mind you. We're still retaining you, Skye, and I won't have you sneak off."

The guide peered up at the viscount, from a face raked with pain and weariness. "If there's any chance at all with hydrophobia," he said hoarsely, "it's by bleeding the wounds and frying the flesh around them. Saw it work once. Saw it fail many times, back in the trapping days."

"Whatever," the viscount said. "Now be a man for once, Skye, and stop the blubbering."

Skye didn't respond. The calf looked ugly, with black holes of charred, fried flesh pocking it, while blood and gore caked the whole swelling limb. The guide turned silent, his mouth clamped shut even though his eyes still leaked.

Jawbone snarled and clacked his teeth. The viscount thought to shoot the animal as soon as Skye died. If Skye died. If by any chance that drastic treatment kept him alive— well, all the better.

The viscount wished it would happen that way. Skye living. That would change the whole trip. Instead of heading up to the headwaters of the Yellowstone to hunt and see the geysers, they were going to head north. He would insist on it. Somewhere, perhaps two hundred miles north, lay the boundary, and beyond it, the Queen's possessions. And beyond that, the Hudson's Bay Company's Rocky Mountain House in Saskatchewan. Once they hustled Skye across that line, the viscount's word would be law, and when they reached the Hudson's Bay post, he'd give the command that had tickled his fancy all evening. He'd clap irons on Skye and haul him back to England as a deserter from the Royal Navy, and see to it that the scoundrel rotted away the rest of his days in a dungeon.

If Skye lived. The viscount earnestly hoped he would.

Chapter 23

Victoria wept. Loss engulfed her. Mister Skye would die. Shame pierced her too, because she had failed to drive the wolf away, even though she'd been guarding her man. It'd happened so fast she scarcely had time to act. But mostly she wept because her man would die, and she would be alone and a widow, and the lodge of Mister Skye would be cast to the winds.

Dawn came slowly in the blue valley where the hotsprings purled. She sat in the dark lodge beside her man, who lay half-covered by a buffalo robe, groaning occasionally. His swollen calf projected from the robe, because the slightest weight on it was more than he could bear. After things quieted outside, he'd crawled in beside her and Mary, silent and somber. His trip to the Other Side hadn't lasted long this time, but it was too long—much much too long.

The knowledge that he would soon die crushed her so much her lungs didn't pump right. Her man, gone! Not because of arrows or gunshot or knife or a stumbling horse, but because of the bite of a mad wolf. She had darkened his lodge these past moons, darkened his life, darkened

Mary's because she couldn't bear to become a widow. She'd fled to the hills each day, not talking to him, not doing her work, not hugging him. And now her selfish deeds were upon her head. She had made him unhappy; she had driven him away to others; she had not helped him deal with these strange people; she had thought only of herself and her own future.

She slumped in the gloom, not wanting sleep but weary, feeling tears streak down the seams of her weathered cheeks, registering the unsteady breathing of her man and his occasional groans. She felt his heat and knew he'd become feverish from the brutal knife-work and cauterization. He had settled himself on his robes and said only one thing: "I'm going under."

He might last one moon; two moons; three moons. That was the way of hydrophobia. His fate would hang over their lodge like a thick snow waiting to avalanche, filling the next moons with dread and finally terror as the disease pounced on Mister Skye. She knew what she had to do. Even as gray dawn began to filter through the umber cone of cowhide, she knew she would darken his lodge no more, and make his last days as happy as she could. They would be unbearable, those last days. But she would do what she could; she owed it not only to Mister Skye, but to Mary too. She reached out in the murk and found his sweated palm, and held it tightly. He moaned. But it was a beginning, and he would know his lodge was darkened no more. She sobbed, knowing how good it was to hold her man's hand.

Mary saw, and smiled somberly. They had both heeded Victoria's medicine vision, the gift of Magpie, and now all that seemed an aching mystery. Had Magpie's guidance been wrong, or was it yet buried behind mysterious veils that would be drawn apart, one by one? How could the Englishmen take Mister Skye away to a place across the sea if he no longer lived? She could not fathom all this, and set it aside as something beyond her frail knowing. She knew only that she'd failed her man and that she would pour out her love upon him during his last days, so he might go to the Spirit Land comforted.

"I think we should leave these people now," said Mary softly from across the lodge.

Mister Skye's voice startled them. "I've been thinking on it. We're close to Victoria's people and I'd like to go under there. With old Many Coups telling jokes."

"Ah!" exclaimed Victoria. "You are here."

"Need a day or so. My leg hurts so much from that carving I can't ride. Puffed up now. I'll tell the viscount we're quitting—I'll write him a draft for the balance—and we'll cut free of them. They'll find their way up the Yellerstone, I imagine."

Victoria's tears welled up again at the sound of his somber voice. Impulsively she squeezed his clammy hand and held it fiercely. "I've darkened your lodge. I won't darken it any more," she cried.

She waited for him to say something. He caught her small hand in his and held it tightly. "I'm glad of that, Victoria. Makes it easier to go."

She wept bitterly, remembering every day of every moon she'd darkened his lodge.

Mary crawled over to them from her robe and held his other hand tightly, and in that sweet dawn quiet they banished darkness from Mister Skye's lodge forever.

"You are hot," said Mary softly.

"I'm some fevered. But that'll pass unless my leg takes to mortifying."

"Oh, why did it happen?" Mary cried.

"My weakness," Skye said somberly. "My weakness for spirits, that did it. I knew it would do for me some day. For twenty-five years I've lived careful as a doe, except for the times when I take spirits. I always slept light as a cat, ready to leap. Recent years, Jawbone helped, like a sentinel in the night—if I wasn't too far gone with the spirits . . ."

"No, not you. I was watching. I always watch when you are gone to the Other Side." She fought back tears again.

He clutched her hand tightly. "I know, Victoria. Saved my life more'n I can remember. Watching over me. Don't you blame yourself any."

He was reaching to her, she knew, and it warmed her a little.

"I don't want to go under. I want to see my child. I've fought off wolves and bears, snow, freezing, starving times, thirst, ambushes and thieves—all of it. I didn't expect to have a hydrophobic wolf cash me in. I can hardly make it real—that I'm going under."

The dawn light intensified outside of the lodge, and she could see him now, see the vicious wounds, scarlet and charred black, each the size of a brass trade dollar, pitting his purplish calf.

Daylight triumphed but they didn't stir. The disaster had drawn them together again, for a last forlorn time before they scattered to the winds.

"Worried about Jawbone. Don't know what'll become of him," he muttered. "He'll turn outlaw around anyone else. Victoria, maybe you could take him out to a band of wild ones up in the Pryors, let him run free after I go under. I'd like that."

"Don't talk of that," she replied crossly. A helpless anger welled through her. She had no medicine for this, and no shaman of her people did either. The tears rose again, unbidden. Mister Skye gone. Jawbone gone. Mary gone.

Colonel Galitzin's voice eddied in from outside, and they heard men busy themselves with morning tasks. Apparently the whole caravan had been pulled up to the hotsprings, and morning chores were underway. But it didn't matter. Within their little world inside the cone of skin they did nothing, wanting only to share a reconciliation that was precious to them all, even if laced with sorrow.

Sun struck the lodge, turning its eastern flank into a wall of amber light that radiated on those within.

"Are we ready, colonel?" asked the viscount, outside.

"Bring Lady Alexandra, your lordship," Galitzin replied.

Victoria slid her hand out of Mister Skye's, tugged a soft doeskin dress over her small frame, and tied her moccasins. Then she stepped through the lodge flap into a glaring sun, and blinked. Off a little way, beyond the rippling pool in the meadow, the cartmen had gathered around a small grave chopped out of the turf, along with the lord and ladies and all the rest, it seemed. Lady Alexandra wore a black dress with a veil over her face. And Lady Diana as well, looking solemn.

Had the cartman died so fast? Puzzled, she walked toward the gathering, her gaze settling at last upon a small canvas sack resting on the yellow meadow grasses. She found a place at the rear edge of this solemn assemblage and waited.

"We will begin with a prayer," said the viscount earnestly, opening his black book. He cleared his throat portentiously and read, and she wondered at the smallness of the man they were burying. Then he closed his book and handed it to the lady, whose eyes brimmed with tears. Victoria had never seen Lady Alexandra cry. But now she grieved, along with the lord and the other lady.

The viscount paused, pregnantly, waiting for a hush in the assemblage that would amplify his words.

"We have come to bury a great Englishman," he began sternly. "Never was there a nobler breed, a more perfect expression of the courage and daring of our island race, a finer example of the faithful steward, the loyal soldier, the sentry who never abandoned post or duty—than the one we lay to rest here today.

"Chesterfield was no ordinary dog. He was a noble dog, of a noble English breed bred on our own little island for its loyalty, courage, daring, and honor. Let us think about Chesterfield now, and how he dashed, full of fury, into the jaws of his giant adversary, the mad wolf, to protect his mistress Viscountess Frazier, and gave up his little life doing it for her . . ."

Victoria listened, astonished, as the eulogy droned on and Lady Alexandra wept softly, a steady flow of tears sliding down the alabaster face under her veil.

"We will have an oil rendered, and it will occupy the place of honor in my guildhall," the viscount went on. He wiped a tear from his eye. "We will have a great medal struck, both silver and gold. We will petition the Queen, God save her soul, for a decoration for this noble breed, our own Chesterfield . . ."

At last the viscount wound down, and with a curt nod to Galitzin he stepped aside so the cartmen could lower the little gray sack and shovel sod over the little grave. This they did while the lord and ladies watched, and added a cap of rock clawed out of the bluffs above to mark the place. Then the viscount led a final lengthy prayer, commending Chesterfield to earth and his dog-spirit to God. And at the last, ten cartmen lifted their fine rifles and fired three volleys that echoed slowly and somberly across the valley, into the rising mountain beyond.

"Sonofabitch!" she muttered, and slid back to Mister Skye's lodge.

"What was all that about? Cartman die?" Mister Skye asked, from his robes.

"No, Mister Skye. They buried Chesterfield."

The viscount commandeered Colonel Galitzin's black and gold kangaroo leather-wrapped swagger stick because it suited him. With every passing moment he felt his military soul burgeon in his breast. It lay buried in him, that hawkish blood of his warrior ancestors. The Lords Frazier had been generals and chieftains, marshals and admirals, coming alive to the howl of bagpipes, lancers, archers, and cavalry.

The hunt was a ruin, but it didn't matter. He had a nobler mission now, to bring a foul deserter to England to taste the queen's justice—if that drastic surgery saved him from the hydrophobia. It'd be a lesson to every skulking limey in her majesty's vessels of war. Not even the distant wastes of North America could hide a traitor to the Crown. He'd come to these wastes on a lark, but high duty called now, and fired his blood with visions of liege-duty to his queen and his country.

He rapped sharply on the guide's silent lodge, feeling cowhide give under his baton. "I say, Skye, let me in."

The flap parted and the older squaw squinted out. The viscount didn't wait, but pushed in, finding the lodge filled with a soft brown light from the translucent cowhide skins. The ruffian lay at the back in his buffalo robe, except for the swollen left leg, which bore evidence of ghastly self-mutilation, its burnt-black wounds suppurating yellow fluids. The scoundrel peered up at him sharply.

"I say, Skye. We've a change of plans. Instead of going

further up the Yellowstone to hunt, we're going to start north to British possessions—to Rocky Mountain House, the Hudson's Bay post on the Saskatchewan River.''

Mister Skye absorbed that, keeping silent.

"Have you nothing to say, Skye?''

"It's a long way—longer than you imagine,'' the guide said at last. He looked feverish, now that the viscount could see him in the dim light. "Up past Bug's Boys, all three tribes of them . . . Piegan, Blood, and Northern Blackfoot.''

"They trade with Hudson's Bay, don't they?''

The ruffian ignored the question. "Why?'' he asked. "Why go there?''

"Because I wish to,'' Frazier replied coolly.

"Long way home. You can't take your carts from there back east. It's packtrain, canoe and portage.''

"I'll deal with that when I get there. I'll have an HBC escort, no doubt.''

"You didn't answer my question, Frazier.''

"Keep a civil tongue, Skye. I don't choose to answer it.''

Skye sighed softly. "I won't make it. Going under, one month, two, three. Go ahead, Frazier, but don't count on me. We're resigning. I'll give you a draft on my accounts carried by the sutler at Fort Laramie. I'm going to choose the place where I go under.''

"I won't permit it.''

"We're doing it.''

"I need you for a guide.''

"I'm going under. And any Blackfoot can take you there. They'd kill me anyway.''

The revelation delighted the viscount. So Skye had his enemies up there!

"As you wish, Skye,'' the viscount said, carefully. "We're leaving in an hour. Perhaps you'll come with us as far as the great bend of the Yellowstone and help us ford.''

"Galitzin can lead you now. I can scarcely get out of my robes.''

The viscount nodded, his mind made up. He peered about the lodge. Skye lay naked under the robe. The squaws had set their weapons near the lodge door, along with his Hawken. That's all he needed to know. The old woman stared at him, as if transfixed, as if reading his mind, and the younger one peered at him also, rank hostility in her savage face.

"Very well," Frazier said, backing out into bright sunlight.

It had to be done at once.

He found Galitzin organizing the departure from the hot springs, and rapped sharply on the colonel's shoulder with the swagger stick.

"I'm taking Skye prisoner, colonel. The bird was about to fly the coop. Go away to die, he said."

"Prisoner, your lordship?"

"Of course! Deserter! We're going to Rocky Mountain House on the Saskatchewan. HBC post."

Galitzin gaped, absorbing that. "Without a guide, sir?"

"Skye, if he lives. If not, any Blackfoot. They've been allies of England all along. We'll have a royal reception from the northern savages."

"Have you a right, sir? To take Skye, I mean. Zese aren't British possessions."

Frazier glared, and smacked his swagger stick in his palm with a resounding crack. "The eye and arm of the queen reach anywhere on earth, colonel! Go find Gravesend and the best ten cartmen you've got, and issue them arms. And then do your duty."

The colonel nodded, and trotted off to collect the men while the viscount stood watching, snapping the swagger stick sharply against his britches. He fancied that the cracks, which sounded like rifle shots, stirred the fiery blood he'd inherited from the first Lords Frazier.

Minutes later cartmen filtered around Skye's silent lodge, armed and ready. The viscount watched, approving, feeling the power of steel. A stiff morning breeze hid their movement. Not even that vicious blue roan horse paid any attention.

"All right then," he whispered to the colonel. "Skye's naked in his robes. Their weapons are heaped just inside the lodge flap, to the right. But his belt with the dirk and revolver's a bit closer to hand. Skye's at the rear. Don't announce. Just send Gravesend and some others in.''

The colonel nodded, saluted smartly, and deployed his men quietly, with whispers and gestures. The three who were to plunge in formed a wedge and drew their revolvers. Others surrounded the lodge, rifles at the ready.

"They'll rush at the crack of your stick, your lordship," the colonel whispered.

The viscount felt a strange joy well up in him. All about the camp men paused to watch, and a deep silence stained the bright morning, except for the groaning of poor Cutler, lying bitten and no doubt dying in a cart off a way.

He peered about and then cracked his swagger stick sharply in the palm of his hand. It sounded like a cannon-shot. Gravesend leapt, piercing into the Skye lodge, followed by the two others.

He heard a muffled roar, and the cursing of the savage old woman, and a few thumps, and soon enough the lodge-door belched out a squaw, the old one, who sailed through and tumbled into the grass. The younger one followed, on her feet, her arm pinioned by a burly cartman. And finally, Gravesend pulled Skye out, naked and white and so weak he could barely stand. The deserter stood in the sunlight, blinking, absorbing the armed men, the pieces aimed at him, the captivity of his wives. In the light his calf looked ghastly, swollen into a tree trunk, scarlet and black.

Gravesend motioned, and a cartman ducked into the lodge, pulling out Skye's Hawken, the squaws' flintlocks, Skye's belt with its sheathed revolver and knife, and finally Skye's robe.

"I suppose you want an explanation, Skye."

But the guide said nothing, staring at them all from small blue eyes burdened with pain.

"You're a deserter! And I'm taking you to the queen's justice! If you die of hydrophobia, justice will be done at last. If not, you'll taste the justice of a good English court and an English dungeon."

"Sonofabitch! Magpie said it true," muttered the old squaw.

The statement puzzled him, but it didn't matter. "Keep

a civil tongue, old woman. Next time you profane the air, you'll be whipped.''

She stared at him, almost shrinking before his eyes.

He nodded, and the cartmen dragged Skye off. The fevered guide didn't resist, but mustered what strength he could while Gravesend and another cartman marched him toward the distant cart where Cutler lay, a tumbril now devoted to carrying the two hydrophobic men to their doom.

"Fetch his robe but keep him naked," the viscount commanded. "He won't go anywhere naked."

Skye paused before the viscount. "Hope you'll let my wives pack up the lodge, mate. They can guide you, even if I can't. Make sign talk with the Blackfeet."

The viscount had been wondering about the squaws, whether to confiscate in the name of the crown their shabby lodge and ponies and drive them off or not, but now he realized they'd be useful. He nodded curtly, and the cartmen released the women.

"One thing, Galitzin. Take Skye's clothing. Don't let them pack that."

The colonel nodded and began supervising the squaws. He found Skye's silk tophat and grinned, setting it on his head rakishly.

The cartmen helped Skye into the tumbril and threw the robe over him. Skye stared sharply at Cutler who lay beside him, his face and neck a gashed ruin from the rabid wolf, and sighed, knowing. Cutler stared back, his gray eyes wet.

And the viscount watched, exultantly.

Chapter 24

Barnaby Skye lay in the bouncing cart, his mind upon medicine rather than the violent jolting that rocked and bucked his bruised body. At least the cart had bows and a ragged canvas wagonsheet over it to keep sun and chapping wind and rain off him, as well as the icy night air of September.

The caravan had retreated down the Yellowstone to the great bend, and had forded just below there at a place Victoria knew of, and now pushed north up the Shields River valley, an ancient Indian route that would take them ultimately to the lands of the Blackfeet, up near Canada, on the eastern flank of the Rockies.

In the week of travel his fever had died and the swelling of his leg had diminished, and he had recovered strength, at least temporarily—until whenever the hydrophobia pounced on him. He could walk now, and even resume his guiding, but he decided against it. If they knew he was strong enough to escape, they might well clamp him in the manacles Colonel Galitzin had with him for disciplinary purposes.

He wanted only to die free, in a place of his choosing,

with Victoria's people. It seemed to him he had a good chance at that, if he and Victoria and Mary could slip away in the night. He'd do it naked if he must. Victoria's people would take them in.

The first two days, while he still lay fevered, Victoria slid over to him at dawn or dusk and they talked in Crow to keep Cutler or anyone else from understanding. But the viscount had heard about it and forbidden Skye's women to go anywhere near him. Still, they knew how to signal to him and he knew how to answer, and they might yet arrange the escape, a last melancholy trek so he could die in peace.

He feared for his women. Once this party reached Blackfoot country, anything could happen. The viscount might well turn them over to his Piegan hosts and his wives would either be tortured to death, as enemies of the People and especially as Skye's wives, or else made slaves and treated almost as badly. Somehow they had to escape. He ached to tell Victoria to flee while they could, but he had no way to talk with her now. And she and Mary were resolutely sticking with their man, rather than considering their own fate.

Jawbone had followed along puzzled and unhappy, sometimes edging close to Skye's cart. But he'd learned to accept the people in any Skye party, and still accepted these Britons, not grasping that friend was no longer friend. Mister Skye feared for his horse; feared what might happen if Jawbone took a notion that all wasn't well; feared that the viscount might simply have the horse shot. The thought was so unbearable to him that he resolved to do something at all cost, even if he were murdered in the process. He would tell Jawbone to go! And hope the horse would obey this last heart-rending command.

Beside him in the jolting cart, Cutler sat up and peered out the rear.

"It's coming," he said. "I can feel it."

"Hope it's not, mate." Skye studied the taxidermist, noting the fang wounds in the man's neck and the furrows gouged across his cheek and brow and ear by the mad wolf's crazed biting. He didn't know much about hydrophobia, but he knew a victim took the disease faster from a facial wound than one lower down, like his. A man bitten around the face might die in two weeks. The disease seemed to attack a man's throat, torturing it until he would no longer drink, even if he lay famished for want of water.

"It was rabid," Cutler said. "I'll never see England again. If I go mad, Skye, kill me. Don't let me suffer."

Cutler had struck a nerve. If the taxidermist did go mad at the end, he would quite likely bite Mister Skye, dooming him to an earlier death. Mister Skye stared bleakly at the man. "I won't let you suffer the last," he said slowly.

"It's revenge. The animal kingdom revenged itself on me," Cutler said. "I preserved their hides and stuffed them with straw, and now they're having their revenge."

"I don't follow the reasoning."

"How'd you liked to be pickled and stuffed, Skye?"

The faintest amusement crept into Skye's thoughts, but he pushed it aside. "You didn't kill them. Hunters killed them and brought them to you."

"It's revenge," Cutler insisted. "The mad wolf wanted me pickled and stuffed and mounted." He sobbed, and Mister Skye could think of little that would comfort the doomed man.

"Maybe the wolf wasn't rabid," he muttered, which evoked only a scornful snort from the taxidermist.

Mister Skye lay back in the cart, pondering once again the nature of Fate. His imminent death lay like a stone upon his soul, infusing his every thought with desolation. He'd weathered it all for twenty-five years in these wilds, surviving with caution and cunning, only to die from—this. He desperately wanted to live. He peered out upon the azure sky and loved it madly, its transparent blue. He gazed at the vaulting mountains hemming in the Shields River, the soaring Crazies to the east and the rising hills of the Rockies to the west—and ached within, for they were his wild home. He smelled the sage, pummeled by the mid-day sun, and it was incense in his lungs.

It was all more than he could bear, but not the least of his sorrows. For soon he'd never see his dear Victoria again, she of infinite resources, who always gave—and still gave— the whole of herself to him, for his pleasure and comfort and safety. And his dear young Mary, of the golden flesh, laughing and lusty and eager to give her love to him—a hallowed gift—and receive his. Gone. Soon a swift dark wall would arise between them all, terrifying and impenetrable, and they would be drawn farther and farther into a blackness, taken away forever. He sighed, loving life more than he'd ever loved it before.

They nooned on an oxbow of the lazy little river, in a place where the breezes made the yellow grasses shimmer, and the blue peaks of the mountains danced under a golden sun. There'd be no food, he knew. Now that the Skyes were no longer hunting, there'd been precious little of it—not enough to feed a large caravan. Gravesend and the other hunters, including the viscount and Lady Diana, had proved inept, and the caravan had slowly begun to starve on half rations the last few days.

He heard voices outside of the canvas walls of his prison, and then Frazier and Galitzin appeared at the back of the cart.

"Skye, step out," Frazier commanded.

"Weak," Skye responded.

"Step out or we'll drag you. I suppose you're not too weak for a few lashes."

Galitzin dropped the tailgate. Mister Skye reluctantly pulled himself to the rear, not wanting them to see the healing. He slid to the grasses, clutching his robe about him. Galitzin yanked it off.

"There!" said the viscount, pointing his swagger stick at Skye's calf. "Healing over. Swelling's down. No flush in his skin any more. Take him to do his duties, and put the manacle on. I won't have this fish jump back into the water."

"You might attend to Cutler," Skye said softly. "He's feeling thirsty and feverish."

"Yes, yes. And from now on, Skye, don't speak unless spoken to. If you speak, we'll devise appropriate punishments. Don't talk to your squaws, the cartmen, or Cutler either."

Fury welled up in Skye, and he could barely contain it. He could strangle the viscount before they could claw him off and shoot him. But if he did, they'd brain Victoria and

Mary next. He walked barefoot toward the riverbrush, wary of rattlers, ignoring the stares of cartmen watching his naked progress. Galitzin followed behind, revolver drawn. The viscount stood at the cart, snapping his swagger stick against his britches. Far off, he spotted Mary and Victoria observing solemnly. Victoria lifted a hand and ran it through her ebony hair, an ancient signal among them: watch and wait.

Jawbone whickered and approached, and he felt a sudden terror.

"Away!" Skye cried at the eager horse. It paused, unhappy, ears flattened back, and reluctantly turned to graze.

"That's one lash for talking, Skye," the viscount announced. "Galitzin—when you're done, shoot that horse."

Something terrible flooded through Skye. Had it all come to this?

"Away!" he yelled at Jawbone. "Away!" He roared it hoarsely, his voice choked in his throat. Jawbone stopped grazing, peered at his master, and whickered. The sound was love, Mister Skye knew. Love that Mister Skye returned with his eyes and outstretched hands.

"Ten more lashes, Skye."

"Go!" cried Skye. "Go!"

Victoria rode toward them, an old squaw no one paid the slightest attention to, until her little dark pony stood a few yards from Jawbone. "Come," she said softly, and the ugly blue roan followed, slowly at first, and then ever faster as the old woman heeled the ribby mare into a gentle trot.

Mister Skye watched, the faintest hope rising in him. Sometimes Jawbone obeyed her. But not usually. In the distance, Victoria drew up beside Jawbone, took his ear in her hands, and said something. The horse trotted, and then loped, and then stopped about a thousand yards distant.

Galitzin laughed. "Your ugly brute didn't go. Too bad for him. And there went your escape plans, Skye. We'll have some rifle practice when I'm done with you."

Barnaby Skye watched the small form of Jawbone standing on a distant mound, and hot tears welled up from his eyes.

A few minutes later, after he'd done his duties in the river brush, Galitzin escorted him back to the wagon and clamped heavy hobbles around his ankles and locked them. The rusty steel bit at his tender legs, and the chain links rattled with his every movement. But Galitzin wasn't done.

"Hold out your wrists," he commanded.

Skye thought to bash the man, but thought better of it. He slid his thick arms forward, and Galitzin clamped lightweight brass cuffs over his wrists, and pocketed the key.

"That should stop any thought of running off," he said. "If you resist, I'll chain you to the cart, too. Now stand quiet while I get the whip."

Nothing in Victoria's life had prepared her for the next moments. The crack of Colonel Galitzin's lash across the back of her man pierced across the campground, each terrible blow vibrating in her own small body. It pushed her to madness. She could kill Galitzin. In a pocket of her high moccasin, beneath her voluminous skirts, nestled a Green River knife they hadn't found. She could do it—whitemen rarely noticed the movement of old Indian women—but she would die for it. They'd club her with the butts of their rifles, cave in her skull, and toss her unburied into the brush for coyote food. So she stood and trembled, berserk within but rigid as stone to any observer, across the camp where they'd pushed her, with only the ripping sound of the whip across Mister Skye's naked back in her soul.

He didn't cry, at least as far as she could hear at her distance, but absorbed the blows silently. They waited for him to resist, so they could kill him. The viscount himself stood near Galitzin, revolver in hand, waiting for their erstwhile guide to roar and fight. She feared only that he would, in despair, since he would soon die anyway. At last they finished and threw her man back into the cart. His crime had been talking, begging his horse to save itself.

"Savages!" she spat.

From out on the bench where Jawbone stood she heard a whicker, and a whinny, the love-noises of Mister Skye's faithful horse, reaching toward his master. The noise paralyzed her. Soon he'd trot back to camp, and his doom. Even now, Galitzin was commanding his cartmen, forming a squad of them to shoot their fine British pieces at Jawbone.

She watched, paralyzed, as they formed smartly into a line, lifted their rifles, aimed at the distant roan, and waited for the command to fire.

The viscount laughed. This would be sport, and would destroy Skye's outlaw horse as well as one more avenue of escape. "Aim high, lads. He's far up that slope. We'll have dogfood, anyway."

Jawbone stood, facing them, whickering, uncertain, pleading, loving, wanting to come to Mister Skye's lodge. He lifted his head and shrieked into the noon sun, and then trotted down the slope toward them.

The viscount laughed again. "Hold your fire, lads. He's making it easy!"

But a cartman shot, and they all did, a ragged volley that battered Victoria's ears and left blue powdersmoke drifting off in the zephyrs. Something hit Jawbone. He screeched and began bucking, berserk, confused. He knew the sound of rifles and knew pain, but this volley had erupted from his own camp, his master's camp. She saw blood then, even at that vast distance, rivering over a shoulder.

"Goddam!" she cried, her eyes welling up tears.

"Damn you!" cried the viscount. "I didn't give the order. Now you've driven the outlaw off!"

The cartmen hastily reloaded while the viscount raged. But Jawbone didn't flee. Confused, he milled about, out there on the sunny slope, bleeding scarlet, whickering for Mister Skye, unable to come to grips with murder.

She couldn't stand it. Beside her Mary slumped to the ground, sobbing. Cartmen grinned. Victoria whirled toward her lodge, trotting toward her ribby old mare. Too late, too late. She'd die now, time to die, time to sing her deathsong and go to the Beyond Land. She clambered painfully up on the mare, bareback because she had no time, using the halter rope for a rein, and kicked her mare with her moccasins.

Nearby, the cartmen were finishing their reloading, and Galitzin was rebuking them for driving Jawbone off. She trotted past them, an old, small squaw, hunched over the withers of her mare, rode straight past them, trotting toward Jawbone.

"Stop her!" Viscount Frazier roared.

A few ran after her, but she lifted her mare into a lazy lope, leaving them behind. She heard the harsh bark of rifles. The snap of bullets. A good time to die. Only let her lead Jawbone away first. Tears blinded her. She deliberately rode toward the flank, drawing fire from Jawbone, then jagged back the other way.

"Stop that squaw!" Frazier roared. "Can't any of you aim?"

In truth, she'd progressed three hundred yards on her loping mare, becoming smaller and smaller to them. But then her pony shuddered and stumbled, and sagged slowly into the grass. She wept, feeling life falter in her faithful old mare that had carried her for so many winters. The mare caved to earth, landing with a lurch that threw Victoria sideways, slamming her into clay. She gasped, winded, too stunned to move.

Jawbone raced toward her, coming back into the range of the terrible rifles. She sobbed.

"Go!" she cried. "Go, Spirit Horse!"

But Jawbone screamed, some wild bleat erupting from its throat, and bulled toward her, even as ragged shooting lifted puffs of dirt around him. Behind, men came running now.

She'd lost her wind, and her limbs felt like bars of lead, but she willed herself up and stumbled toward the great horse, the medicine horse, the storied horse of all the plains and mountains. "Go!" she screamed, sobbing, her eyes so wet she could not see.

He whickered and dashed toward her. Now she could see the wound, a vicious crease just below the withers that leaked a sheet of bright blood. She wept. A day to die. A bullet caught her blouse, ripping fabric, the force so terrible it spun her. She sprawled, leapt, and ran again, small and hunched. Behind, they came closer, and she heard the roaring of the viscount, like a rabid bear, shattering the air.

A ball parted Jawbone's forelock, grazing his skull between his ears, and he shrieked, bewildered, bucking and snorting.

"Go!" she cried, panting, her breath cauterizing her lungs and throat.

But he didn't. Berserk, teeth clattering and snapping,

yellow-eyed and evil, leaking blood and foaming at his mouth, he limped toward her, a demon beast, a monster from the Under-Earth spirits, limping and blowing until he pulled up beside her, trembling, and shrieked, deafening her with his trumpeting.

"Go!" she panted. But he stood, trembling. She peered behind, terrified, as men lifted rifles. She grabbed his mane and clambered on. He shivered as her old legs slid across his cut flesh, and then they exploded away, even as murderous bullets pecked and probed the space they'd vacated. She steered him by leaning, just as Mister Skye did, this way and that, zigzagging, becoming ever smaller to the cartmen behind, until at last she slowed him down on a knoll. His sides heaved and he trembled, bobbing his massive roman nose up and down, wild-eyed, brimming evil and love.

She let him catch his wind. She hunched lightly on his bony back, feeling him tremble under her. If she could hold him still a while, the blood oozing from the wound would coagulate. She reached her small strong arm forward and ran her palm tenderly under the mane, along his sweated neck, calming him.

"They are no friends now," she said to Jawbone. She talked to him, trying to convey meaning to him, knowing that Mister Skye talked to him constantly, with English words, because the terrible horse seemed to fathom something of it. "He is alive," she said. "But maybe not for long now. The mad-spirit is in him, waiting to burst out and kill him. We can't go back. They'll kill you and bash my head in and throw me away."

She hunched in the zephyrs, unaware of the caressing breeze, weeping. "I wished to die with him, so we might go to the Beyond Land together," she said, feeling tears river down her seamed cheeks. "But now we must go away from them, Jawbone. He asked me to do something, and now I must do it."

She watched the tiny distant figures trudge back toward the noon camp. They congregated around the black heap of what had been her mare, and shot their revolvers into it. Victoria bled inside. But she was safe, and so was Jawbone.

Mary wasn't, and neither was her man. She wiped her eyes, trying to think what might happen, but she couldn't think. Perhaps they would murder Mister Skye for this. Perhaps not.

Beneath her, Jawbone calmed, and stopped shivering, except when buzzing flies landed in the long bloody crease. Mister Skye wanted her to take Jawbone high into the Pryors, there in the heart of Absaroka, and release him among the wild ones, where he'd be a great stallion-chief among them and make his blood to flow in many colts. She could do that. She could slip away now, before they tried again. Only one horse in camp could keep up with Jawbone, even wounded, and that was the buffalo runner Lady Diana had purchased from the Sioux. Maybe Lady Diana would come with a gun and shoot her and Jawbone. But she didn't think so. Victoria didn't dislike the lady who hunted and rode and wouldn't bend to Lord Frazier's will.

Not yet. Not until after her man died from the mad-spirit fever. Then she'd take Jawbone on the long sad journey to his home. But now she would shadow the caravan, out of sight mostly, stalk it like a cat, watching and waiting for the time she could help her man, help Mary, help them escape. It'd be hard. She had only a knife for getting food.

She spat. "Sonofabitch," she exclaimed to the zephyrs and the warm sun. "I can outsmart them all."

Chapter 25

Mary found herself alone, with all the burden of holding Mister Skye's lodge together. Never in her young, happy life had she experienced such desolation as she felt now, her man doomed by the madness-fever and a prisoner in chains, lying naked in a jolting cart. And old, wise Victoria gone too, in a sudden, desperate flight to save the medicine horse.

At least Victoria and Jawbone lived. They roamed ahead a few miles, invisible to these blind whitemen, but visible to her. Victoria had deliberately walked Jawbone along soft river sands and moist earth, leaving Jawbone's tracks and sometimes her own Crow moccasin prints for Mary to see. And Victoria had left the mark of her digging stick in the earth, as she gathered cattail roots and arrowhead and sego lily along the bottoms of the Smith River, which they followed north into a jumbled, wild land broken by sinister yellow coulees and tattooed by long black arms of jackpine reaching toward the canyon.

Mary discerned a limp in Jawbone from the way his prints marked the soft earth, but at least the horse lived. It brought a bit of gladness to her, even though everything else lay dark upon her bright spirit. She ached to tell Mister Skye, who lay in torment back in the rear cart beside the one who was dying of the fever. But they watched him day and night and kept him chained like a beast, and prodded her away whenever she tried to slip close. Raw open wounds festered on his back where the whip had lacerated his skin. They'd seen each other from time to time, but he'd said nothing, staring at her silently, unable even to lift his hand to greet her. But at least he knew she was present, and knew Victoria was not.

She kept the lodge and lodgepoles on the travois now, not erecting it at each night's camp the way she and Victoria usually did. These people had ceased to feed her, and had taken away her hunting weapons, her bow and quiver, and her flintlock. A little jerky remained in a parfleche, but she refused to touch it, knowing it might save their lives if they could escape. Instead, she did what Victoria did, gathering buffalo berries and bitter chokecherries and digging up edible roots, surviving somehow.

The foreigners themselves weren't any better off. They all proved to be inept hunters, driving away game with their noise, not understanding the spirits of the creatures they stalked. They were poor marksmen even when they did occasionally spot a distant deer or antelope. And so they starved, grew cross and mean, and blamed the Skyes all the more for their dilemma. She sensed they'd stopped feeding Mister Skye at all, letting him starve and grow weak, hogging what little meat they shot for themselves and the remaining bulldogs. How foolish they were, even when they shot meat. Didn't they know of the succulent marrow in the bones, or the goodness of a tongue? Or the broths one might make of the things of the belly that they threw to the dogs? How strange whitemen were. In spite of all their medicine, guns, and metal, they didn't know the earth and its creatures. They looked straight at muledeer without seeing them, ignored the four-footed creatures at every hand, the ones they called skunks and raccoons and badgers, scorned coyotes and wolves as food as if they were unclean, and scarcely bothered to gather purslane, milkweed, cattail, wild onions, wild grape, pokeweed, rhubarb, or anything else that lay thick across the land these last days of summer. Neither did they fish for trout. They could not even fashion traps and deadfalls to snare rabbits.

She listened to the cartmen complain about half-rations and then quarter-rations, and the weakness that smited them, and she knew it wouldn't be long. She slid out each dawn, a wraith invisible to Colonel Galitzin's guards, and gathered her berries and roots and greens in the Smith River bottoms, devouring as many as she could in the pale gray light, and then filling a small duck pouch of Mister Skye's with them. She had to try to reach him in the night; nourish him.

With each passing day the luck of the hunters turned even worse; the country seemed utterly devoid of game, even though they worked through a rich jumbled foothill land with all sorts of forage for the four-footed things of the earth. Once they passed a grassy valley where buffalo had grazed and wallowed and rubbed against the bark of cottonwoods not long before, but the white hunters didn't even know it. Mary knew it, and knew why the buffalo had gone away. Victoria, ahead, drove them away, as well as every other four-foot her sharp old eyes spotted. She was fighting her own war her own way against these inept whitemen, making their hunters return each day with nothing but shame upon them. Secretly Mary exulted, but it was a bitter pleasure, knowing her man lay in chains, doomed either to death or a dungeon.

One chill evening the viscount approached her. She watched his measured tread with hatred and terror, wanting to flee from him like a wild thing flees from evil.

"I say, woman, we're having a bit of bad luck hunting. You'd think a wild place like this would be full of game. Not even a buffalo. The men have had all they can bear of it."

Mary said nothing, meeting his arrogant stare with the steady gaze of her own bright brown eyes.

"I'm giving you your flintlock and a bit of powder and two or three balls. The savage has his skills, I suppose. Beginning at dawn, you'll ride out for meat. Each evening you'll return the piece to Colonel Galitzin."

"No," she said softly.

"What? What?"

"You heard me."

"I'll make you. I'll whip you until you do."

"No," she said.

"You're a prisoner, you know. An accomplice of the deserter. We can turn you over to your enemies the Blackfeet if we wish."

"No."

"You must be hungry. Or maybe not. I'll have my men search your parfleches. If you've got jerky in there, we'll confiscate it. You've been getting by on something, that's plain. If you want to keep your dried meat, you'll hunt."

"Perhaps I will waste the powder and shoot at the sun, Frazier," she said, curtly.

"Keep a civil tongue. You're a savage and don't know who it is you're talking to, but that's no longer an excuse."

She thought a moment. "If I hunt, will you feed my man and take the chains off?"

From the kindling realization in his face, she knew at once she'd made a grave mistake.

"No, I won't. But you will hunt each day, and each day you fail to bring in meat, he'll be whipped. Five lashes a day ought to move even the savage paramour to hunt."

"Give me the rifle, then," she retorted slowly. "And powder and three balls. I will make meat. With the first ball I will shoot you. I think you will taste bad. With the second, I will shoot Galitzin. And with the third, I will shoot Gravesend. After that the cartmen can kill me."

"By God, you little savage. I think you would."

She smiled scornfully at him, and he whirled away.

A little later she heard a shot from the direction of the horse herd, and walked that way swiftly, wanting to know what it was. She found a dark corpse of a mule humped obscenely in the grass, leaking blood on the clay and twitching its last. A Skye mule. One she used to carry the parfleches on a pack saddle. Even before the mule breathed its last, cartmen began slicing down its belly, desperate for the mule steak they'd devour that evening.

She turned away, feeling the hopelessness of her fate. Not

that it mattered now, with Mister Skye dying. But she hoped to escape, hoped to give birth to Mister Skye's child which lay inside her belly, and tell the child some day about the great one who had sired it. Let them shoot the mules, then. She could slip away on foot any time unless they chained her too. But as long as Mister Skye lived, she would accept her fate among these ruthless men.

They celebrated that night with an impromptu party. The hardy, stringy mule meat didn't last long among so many starving men, but it filled them; and Lord Frazier, his ladies, and Galitzin and Baudelaire, drank themselves into a silly glee beside the yellow wagon, while the cartmen ate, snoozed, and neglected their duties. She watched them closely, biding her time as the night thickened. The crickets chirped their last hymns of summer, and one by one the men dozed off and neglected their three campfires until only embers remained.

She dared not wait too long. She slipped through the nippy moonless dark to the rear, where the cart rested on its tongue and cumbersome wheels, its slant making life miserable for the two within.

"Mister Skye," she whispered.

"Mary!"

"Eat this first."

She handed him the duck bag full of berries, and listened to the soft clink of his chains as he devoured handfuls of them.

"Needed that. Perishing of thirst. They forget to take me to water."

"Do you hurt?"

He sighed softly. "Can't sleep on my back. Can't sleep anyway with these irons, and the slant of the cart."

"Victoria and Jawbone are safe, ahead. They hurt him and he limps. She's driving away game."

"Do they know it?"

"No. They are blind and deaf."

"They shot our mule. They're down to that now."

"Are you—sick yet, Mister Skye?"

"Sored up some from the lashing. But my legs are healing. I'm strong as I ever was, but . . ."

She waited, afraid.

"Cutler's took the fever. Throat's swollen up, and he's going fast. That wolf was hydrophobic, Mary, and it'll be my turn soon. I'm going under. I'm done. Don't wait around to fetch me away. You and Victoria slip off while you can, because any time now we'll meet up with some Piegans, and then you can't. Forget me, Mary. Go, now. Save your lives! Don't let the Blackfeet get Jawbone! I'm glad you and Victoria and Jawbone . . ."—his voice broke in the dark— "you three'll get loose. Just remember me, Mary. I loved you all."

"I am staying close to you," she replied stubbornly, not letting him sense the tears welling into her eyes.

The taxidermist, Albert Cutler, died on a cold morning, but the cartmen didn't discover it until evening. Mister Skye felt pity and relief. The man had thrashed and foamed and spasmed, his throat virtually swollen shut, in such obvious torment that the sight terrorized Skye and made him dread what was to come. At the last, Skye had wrapped himself in the buffalo robe, skin out, as a sort of armor against the man's slobbering. He feared being bitten, which would only shorten his own life. But Cutler slipped into a coma, lying inert and hot until fever took him off.

Barnaby Skye watched and wondered how he might kill himself before that final torture. He'd try to escape, he thought. They'd shoot him down, and bullets would be better than the sort of misery Cutler had been forced through. The taxidermist had been a decent man, lamenting that he could not return to England and be buried close to his parents there. Toward the end he'd choked out his goodbyes to Skye from a throat that barely worked, and then sobbed through convulsions that spasmed and twisted his helpless body. It would have been a mercy to shoot him then, he thought.

They'd had a bad time of it that day, working through rough country never before traversed by wheeled vehicles. Often they were forced away from the bottoms of the Smith River to crawl over a headland or escape a gorge. The two-wheeled carts did well enough but the heavy yellow parlor carriage didn't belong in this sort of country. It careened half-uncontrolled down slopes, and had to be dragged up other slopes by double-teaming.

Mister Skye lay beside the dead man, feeling the cart tilt downslope one moment, and uphill the next, rolling with every jolt of the wheels, sometimes feeling his irons bite his flesh. He felt, actually, healthy enough with his blistered and gouged calf healing and the hydrophobia not yet showing itself. But the days had become increasingly miserable, and sheer starvation kept his stomach rumbling and slowly weakened him. Some days he scarcely even got water. The late September nights bit at him under the loose buffalo robe. His nakedness magnified every eddying breeze that pierced the robe to torment his flesh. Skim ice had shown in buckets at dawn, and winter would pounce on them any time—sooner than they realized, he knew. He'd seen many a blizzard in this country, this time of year.

He felt, at bottom, a terrible helplessness. Being naked, unarmed, chained like a beast was only part of it. He couldn't even speak without risking more lashes across his aching back. Not even Mary and Victoria paid the slightest attention to his will. He'd commanded them to escape while they could, but Mary stubbornly stayed close, risking herself and the little one that would be the only thing Skye would pass on to the world. His mind turned endlessly to that tiny bit of life growing in her belly, the bit of life that he would never see, but which would be something of himself for the future. He had no other future but that, and as long as Mary insisted on staying close, she jeopardized herself and that small miracle within her.

He could not be angry with her. Everything she did now was pure love. She'd managed to feed him berries and roots each night at terrible risk, and whisper a few things to him before slipping off into the blackness. But the moon was pregnant again, swelling each night, and in a few days sentries could spot her in the silvery light. He welcomed her nocturnal visits more than anything else, even as he worried about her fate.

By noon it had clouded over, high streamers out of the northwest first and then a heavy overcast with a whiff of snow in the wind, and he knew he was in for it. There'd be the usual equinox storm common to these parts, snow at the higher elevations, icy rain below. Snow here. The thought of his own lodge with a hot fire at its center and his wives close by ravished him. Robe or not, he'd come close to freezing tonight in the drafty exposed cart. He toyed with the idea of hobbling, chained, to Mary's lodge tonight after they'd all settled down. Surely tonight she'd erect it, lifting the heavy rawhide-bound tripod of lodgepoles first and then adding the rest, nine others, and then wrestling the cumbersome, leaden lodgecover over the poles, prying it higher, lacing its seam, inserting the windflap poles and adjusting the flaps, finding rocks and setting them in a ring around the lodge to anchor the cover to earth so wind didn't slide in—either that or staking the cover down if they hadn't taken away her hatchet; hauling robes and parfleches from the pack animals, gathering wood for her fire . . . together Mary and Victoria managed it with difficulty; alone, Mary would stagger under the burden of it.

If she couldn't do it, he prayed she'd bring him a blanket to slip around himself under the robe, and then pluck it off again just before dawn. A lot to ask of her.

Mid-afternoon he heard shouting, and then the caravan halted on a steep slope, the cart beneath him pitched forward so steeply that he could barely keep from sliding into its front planks. Cutler's inert form, cooling beside him, did flop forward and roll until the cart-wall stopped it. In irons or not, he couldn't stay in this position long with blood bursting his head. He hauled himself to the rear, dragging the robe with him, and eased himself clumsily over the tailgate, tumbling into sandstone detritus on the steep slope. His cartman had vanished. He settled himself on the earth with the robe about him, knowing he risked another whipping. How easy it'd be to crawl off, he thought. The quarantined prison cart always trailed the rest by a hundred yards or so. The herders followed, driving loose stock, but not always. Sometimes they trailed the loose horses far to the side, or even pulled ahead. He could drop off some morning and his absence wouldn't be noted for hours. Not that it would do him much good, bound hand and foot in irons.

Down below, in the bottoms of a giant coulee that dumped toward the distant Smith River, the yellow parlor wagon lay on its side, its undercarriage shattered and its off-side wheels a ruin. No one seemed to be injured; at least both the ladies stood nearby, gawking at it. Cartmen struggled with the tangled four-horse team. Two drays were on their sides, pawing the ground, thrown down by the tongue and harness. A ruin, Skye thought. They'd failed to lock the wheels properly going down that slope. Or maybe they'd locked the wheels but failed to add a drag, a log on a chain behind for a spare brake.

He pulled the robe tight about him, aware of the cruelty of the ruthless wind, and grateful that no one saw him out of his prison up on the slope. No one but Mary, who glanced upward with troubled eyes. Below, both the viscount and Galitzin shouted orders while cartmen eviscerated the shattered parlor wagon, toting wardrobes, bedding, chamberpots, field desks, lanterns and wigs toward carts emptied of foodstuffs earlier. The lord and ladies would either move into a cart, or camp out. By the time they'd finished, the castiron skies had darkened noticably, and he could see Galitzin motion toward a small flat in the coulee bottoms, apparently a place where they would spend the night. Cartmen spread out toward their vehicles, including the one who teamstered Skye's prison-cart. Skye, still unobserved, hobbled to the rear and clumsily threw himself as high as he could over the tailgate, feeling the wood bite into his belly, and tumbled back into the cart, bruising his shoulder.

The cart jolted down a grade so steep he slid helplessly into the front wall, pinioned next to Albert Cutler's stiff blue body. The cartman was having a time of it in spite of locking the creaking wheels. The cart skidded on its iron tires, hurrying the dray that pulled it, alarming Skye with its uncontrolled lurches. But at last the cart pulled out onto a small flat hemmed by towering ridges, a flat lying squarely in the coulee bottoms. Mister Skye didn't like it a bit, especially with a fall storm brewing and himself in chains and unable to swim, or even walk at any speed other than a painful hobble.

The viscount's dour visage appeared at the rear. Frazier

noted the body sprawled grotesquely at the front of the cartbed, and sniffed.

"I say, Skye, you could have told us."

Mister Skye said nothing.

"Speak when you're spoken to, or you'll taste the whip again."

"He died this morning," Skye said.

"This morning, your lordship," the viscount corrected.

Mister Skye nodded. "May I address you about a matter of some importance for your safety—your lordship?"

"No. I'll fetch Galitzin. We'll have to bury this fellow, and far from camp. Terrible pity, and all that. The sooner the better. Your turn next, eh, Skye?"

The guide nodded.

The viscount turned to leave, and then remembered something. "Say, Skye. I'm confiscating your lodge. We had a bit of a mishap here, and my ladies and I need it. I'll give the savages credit—they invented a snug tent that could handle a fire, eh? We'll be cozy."

"I believe my wife needs it, sir."

"Oh, pshaw, Skye. Those savages can manage in any weather. In any case, it's yours and I've taken it for the Crown. She can bed under a cart."

"I have a suggestion concerning your safety, sir."

The viscount stared, his face pained. "I've already told you no. Galitzin is perfectly competent. And one more impudent word from you and I'll fetch Gravesend and the whip."

Chapter 26

Victoria sat Jawbone atop a vast shoulder of land, near the edge of a ponderosa forest that blackened its upper reaches. The long-needled pines cut the sharp wind but offered no other comfort. She had only the thin summer clothes she was wearing when she fled with Jawbone.

The object of her attention, far below, was the Englishmen's camp on a golden flat in the bottom of the coulee. The castiron clouds and late hour made the light tricky, so she wasn't certain what she was witnessing, but she sensed things as well as saw them, and trusted in that as much as in her eyes.

Beneath her, Jawbone twisted restlessly, itching to gallop down there to his master. He'd become so fractious she'd been forced to cut a thin coil of doeskin from her skirt with her Green River knife to fashion a loop rein, tied over his ugly nose. Even as she sat lithely on him, near the edge of the forest where she could observe without being noticed, she felt the evil horse's muscles ripple, and knew he was thinking black rebellious thoughts about her slender control over him. But she had to keep him here; death awaited him below, so she cursed him soundly, that being the only language an evil medicine horse could comprehend, yelling whitemen's blasphemies first in one ear and then the other, while the horse pawed pine needles and snorted.

The damp wind cut into her in spite of the trees, and she knew the storm would pounce soon. She had no shelter at all. This time of year, this kind of storm spat either snow or icy rain, and murdered the unwary. She might make a crude shelter of boughs or find some cranny in a bluff. But she scorned that now. She would endure until the last heat left her.

That day she had ridden far ahead, down the giant ridges toward the valley of the Big River, the Missouri, and peered into the distant haze, seeing the long tendrils of the storm sweeping across an endless sky. She knew trouble would come soon. But on the last ridge she discovered a more profound menace. In a sheltered hollow on the Smith River, not far from its confluence with the Missouri, lay a giant village. Siksika! The word filled her mouth like spit. She didn't know which ones, Piegan, Blood, or northern Blackfeet, but she knew instinctively it was one or another.

She'd peered around warily, hunting the Mad Dog Society warriors, the village police who'd be patrolling even this far away, along with its hunters. She saw nothing, but sensed she hadn't been seen there in the shadow of the pines. The Englishmen would encounter the village the next day or so, and that'd be the end of Mary and Mister Skye. Those Siksika dogs would discover Mister Skye in chains, his medicine shattered, and demand to have him, count coup—the whole village—and then torture him to death. They'd take him from the viscount, no matter what the viscount said or did. And Mary'd fare no better. Neither would she or Jawbone, if she were caught.

She'd run out of time. Not a trace of blue smoke marked the village. Instead, the sharp wind blew it off and made the village wobble and dance in her eyes, and brought it closer because the air was so clear. The Siksika village writhed in the distance, like a snake ready to strike, and she knew she'd have to act that very night because there'd be no tomorrow. She'd eyed the advancing palisade of clouds anxiously, and trotted back up the Smith River canyon toward the caravan.

What she saw in the Englishmen's camp alarmed her just as much as the village of the Siksika dogs. They'd picked a site that would flood if it rained hard. A wall of icy water could roar down the cavernous coulee. The cart that held Mister Skye—how well she knew its sagging sheet and its green bones of wood—had been unhitched squarely in the dry watercourse, where it tilted crazily on its tongue and two wheels. Nearby, the wrecked yellow parlor wagon lay on its side like a smashed grasshopper, its wheels spinning in the wind. And just behind that her lodge was being erected, but not by Mary. Cartmen wrestled the poles up and laced the heavy cover over it, while the lord and his ladies watched, their backs to the icy wind. They had taken it from Mary. She peered about for Mary, not seeing her in the slate light, as anxious about her as she was about Skye. The lord and ladies would be snug tonight with a fire to warm them—unless the coulee ran, and then they'd learn another lesson, and fast.

That disappointed her. She wanted the lodge. Mary had ceased erecting it these past days, and that suited Victoria perfectly. She would have to carry Mister Skye on a travois because his legs and hands were chained together and he couldn't ride Jawbone. But the Skyes' two travois had always been made from the lodgepoles, and these had been commandeered by the viscount.

She would have to make a travois before dark with only her Green River knife. And out of crooked, twisted jackpine instead of the slender lodgepole pine. She peered about, knowing at once the task lay beyond her. And yet she had to have some way to carry her man away in the night. He could lie over Jawbone's back, like a dead body, for only minutes.

She heard a shot clatter up to her on the cutting wind, and saw another mule slump. For several days now they'd eaten mule—the Skyes' horses and mules. That was the bitter price she'd paid for driving off game. But she could steal animals tonight from the stupid guards, especially after the storm hit. They'd crawl into their tents and tell themselves no savages would prowl in such a storm. She felt a gust of bitter air cut through her blouse, and shivered. The storm might be a blessing—if she lived through it. It'd cover her tracks.

Below camp, men scratched at the bottoms with spades, and she realized the cartmen were digging a shallow grave. Was it Skye's? The very thought clutched at her. She watched tensely, wondering, seeing the evidence of death. Two men shoveled, and two more broke the breast of Earth with pickaxes, and others gathered loose sandstone for a cover. Probably it was for the other, the one who stuffed animal skins with straw. They would not be so kind to Mister Skye, but leave him for the coyotes. She waited, transfixed by the spectacle. At last, in a thickening gloom, four of them approached the cart that held Mister Skye, and pulled a body from it, one man grasping each limb. Not Skye. Even from her vantagepoint high above, she could discern that. They toted the flopping body to the shallow hole and dropped it there and began piling the yellow clay back in with no ceremony at all. It shocked her. Did no one down there care about the brother they buried or wish to say words or weep?

In the last of the murky light they finished with the grave and carried the pickaxes and shovels back to the tool cart, resting them on its dropped tailgate. She watched, a desperate idea forming. On the grassy flat several campfires blossomed orange, guttering wildly even behind rock barricades cartmen built to hold off the wind. They'd eat their butchered mule half raw tonight, she thought. Or entirely raw if the rains deluged them. Except for the lord and ladies, of course, who had discovered the comforts of her lodge.

She did not see Mary. And the figures below had become black blurs, indistinguishable from one another. It troubled her. She had to know where Mary would be. She needed to know where the Skye parfleches lay. She wanted to know which cart Mary would crawl under after losing her snug home.

She cursed and spat, wondering what it all was for, this desperate plan of hers. Mister Skye would die soon anyway.

She could leave this instant, turn Jawbone south and reach her own Absaroka people, if she could find them, and if she could endure the icy cold. But she wouldn't. She had only one goal, and that was to take her man away from here, with Mary and Jawbone, and flee to a safe place so her man could die of the mad-fever among friends.

She'd risk her life for that; readily die for that small thing. Her medicine seemed an aching mystery now, this vision sent by Magpie of Mister Skye being carried off across the waters, never to return. He lay dying instead, his lodge lying apart because of mad-fever. Sonofabitch, she couldn't understand these things.

A gust of cold air sliced right through her blouse, so that its tendrils froze her ribs and robbed her breasts of warmth and nipped her calves. Jawbone turned crazy under her, sawing air with his head, and she realized he was about to whicker his piercing greetings to the herd down there. She yanked a rein to turn him, and slid off, pinching his moist nostrils just as they erupted. He bobbed his massive head, fighting her hand, yellow eyes looking murderous, but she held on.

"They kill us!" she snapped at him. He seemed to calm down, and she released his nostrils. Then he shrieked.

"Sonofabitch!" she yelled at him, kicking him fiercely with her moccasin. He backed off.

Below, an animal neighed. Frightened, she peered into the deepening gloom, wondering if they'd noticed. Everything had melted into blackness now, except for what she could see from the glancing amber of the fires. She waited angrily, ready to kick the evil horse again, but nothing much happened. She felt numb and walked to the lee of the horse, pressing into his high warm withers to warm herself. He let her.

That's when the sleet hit. One moment there'd been damp cold wind; the next, a wave of stinging pellets that soaked her miserable calico blouse in moments and sucked life from her with each passing second. Below, men abandoned the cooking and hastened into their dark tents. Even from where she stood, she could hear Galitzin's larger tent chattering and rumbling in the gale. In moments the sleet had mur-

dered the fires, except for the one that glowed in Skye's
lodge, where the lord and ladies lay comfortably in the
bright cone, no doubt enjoying a mule supper.

It wasn't late but blackness engulfed the camp. She
couldn't wait. She needed just a bit of light to find her way
around. So much to do there. And the storm would kill her
in minutes. Kill Mary if she lay outside. Kill Mister Skye
under the bowed canvas with both ends open to weather.
She clambered up on Jawbone's slippery back, feeling the
ice soak through to her loins, and steered him urgently down
the slope, with only the translucent glow of the lodge, in
the blurry distance, to guide her.

Stringy mule loin didn't appeal to Lady Diana. As she
gnawed at the miserable meat her formidable temper boiled
higher and wider. Gordon had turned perfectly daft, heading for Canada, abandoning the hunt, alienating the Skyes,
who had been the steady provisioners for the entire party,
all because that splendid man Barnaby Skye had once
jumped one of the Royal warships. She liked Skye, totally
male beast that he was. And at the moment she was ready
to strangle the viscount, who sat across from her in the
warm lodge, looking smug as he gnawed a revolting gray
haunch.

Beside him sat Lady Alexandra, who'd abandoned her
meat after a few bites and stared unhappily at the fierce little
blaze in the center of the lodge. She'd turned as dour recently as Diana, talking of home and snapping at Gordon
Patrick Archibald Frazier, who had been growing odder by
the day.

Outside, volleys of sleet rattled the lodge, and gusty winds
thundered around the ears that drew the smoke off, shivering them like angry sails. Diana found herself fairly comfortable, except for an occasional billow of smoke that didn't
escape into the blizzard. The viscount had dug the inner
lining out of the Skyes' belongings and had commanded
that the cartmen tie it up to the lodgepoles and anchor it to
earth with stakes. She was, she knew, far more comfortable
than she would have been in the unheated wagon.

"Well, aren't we snug. These savages don't live half badly," the viscount said jovially between bites.

"This meat's disgusting. It's getting cold. We should be halfway down the Yellowstone by now," Diana muttered.

The viscount turned grave. "We have higher purposes inspiring us now."

"I would think that decent meat for ourselves and the men is a high enough purpose. I haven't had a decent meal since—since you put irons on Skye. Really, Gordon, you're perfectly daft, and I'm perfectly tired of it."

"That mule is disgusting," Alexandra said. "Why don't you do something? Why doesn't Beowolf cook something? Why doesn't Stauffinger bring wines any more? Why don't we have greens? I need greens but no one brings them to me. Really, Gordon, this is quite enough, and I shan't put up with it. Take us home at once."

The outburst surprised Diana. Lady Alexandra had never displayed temperament before.

"The men are complaining, too. They're all half-starved and angry. Maybe they'll run off," Alexandra added.

"I hope they do! That'll put some sense in you, Gordon," Diana snapped.

Slowly the viscount set his Wedgwood plate aside and dabbed at his greasy lips with a linen napkin. He looked pained, and Diana feared he would begin one of his lectures, which he'd delivered to them frequently these last weeks. He sat crosslegged on a feather mattress salvaged from the yellow wagon, looking ruddy from the summer's outing, his eyes piercing and bright.

"I'm going to bear this criticism with some nobility," he said, his face infused with suffering. "And I don't suppose you ladies understand the half of it."

"Oh, hell, Gordon, stop it. Stop it!"

He turned to her, his eyes ablaze. "I'm doing it for England. Have you no loyalty? No thought of England? No love of the Crown?"

"We're starving. The men are miserable. Just because Barnaby Skye chucked the Royal Navy long ago you've wrecked our summer. He was pressed in. Doesn't that mean anything to you? Stop being a silly goose and let's go home. He's half-dead anyway.''

''Never,'' said the viscount sternly. ''They all say they were pressed in, and even if they were, that's what brutes like him deserve. It's no excuse for deserting. I say, we'll proceed. I'll take him to Canada and justice, and even if he dies, his last thought will be of an English dungeon and my resolute purposes.''

''I'm quitting. I'm going to find that poor squaw we stole from this lodge from and have her take me to Fort Union.''

He stared at her, aghast. ''You can't do that. I forbid it.''

''I'll do what I choose.''

''I'll prevent it. And don't pity that squaw. Savages can survive in any weather. And she willingly allied herself with that deserter.''

''I do pity her. Here we are in her warm lodge. And the men are freezing in tents or under wagons. I pity them all.''

''The low classes endure well. Don't waste your frivolous sentiments on them.''

She knew what she'd do the moment the storm abated. She'd find the squaw, pay her well, saddle up the buffalo runner, gather her own weapons from Gravesend, and ride for Fort Union. To hell with this mad lord.

A gust of icy air billowed down the smoke hole, bringing sleet and woodsmoke with it. The viscount coughed.

''Blast!'' he exclaimed. ''Wind's shifting.'' He stood up and walked to the doorflap, and pulled it aside, letting in a gust of air. ''I say—Galitzin. Galitzin,'' he yelled. ''I say, adjust the flaps, eh?''

No one answered him. The viscount bellowed into the night but his voice drowned in the wind.

''Worthless help. Why is it help has gone bad these times? I've never seen retainers so insolent. We'll do something about it when we get back. This American wilderness subverts their good conduct.''

Angrily he donned his tweed coat, a hat, and gloves, and crawled into the night. She watched the smokeflaps move in the dim light high above, and then they stopped chattering and driving smoke back down. The viscount crawled in, coated with white, and huddled over the tiny fire.

"These savage lodges are clever, but they take doing," he muttered. "It's a bit nippy out. I'll have words with Galitzin tomorrow. It's a stain on his record, this indolence."

"I want some booze and some tiddlywinks. If I can't eat because you're being such an ass, I'll booze. And then we'll have fun. I'll play squaw, long as I'm decorating a teepee. Where's Stauffinger? Your hunting trip's turned into a crashing bore."

"Oh, tiddlywinks," Alex said. She smiled for the first time in hours.

"I'm going to get so crocked it'll be noon before I remember I'm here," Diana announced. "I suppose he's in one of the tents. I'll get him to unlock—"

"Don't you do it. Call Baudelaire. He's our domestic man."

She ignored him and clambered past the doorflap. A stinging barrage of icy pellets sliced into her as she peered into a whirling white murk. She could barely see the tent shared by Galitzin and Baudelaire, much less the little hovels beyond.

Angrily she yelled at the shivering tent. "Baudelaire. I want scotch," she bawled. "And now."

A dark head emerged from the tent flap, stared, and then retreated. "And hurry!" she snapped. She'd have her booze. Nothing else would do. As long as that ass she'd come with had wrecked the hunt, she'd have her booze.

Back inside the Skye lodge, she tossed sticks on the fire and tried to drive the numbness out of her limbs. If those servants didn't bring the scotch, she'd wring their necks tomorrow. She thought to roll herself in blankets on one of the feather mattresses and guzzle until she passed out.

But Lord Frazier had risen, and stood near the center of the lodge, smoke coiling around him as if he were emitting it, and snapped that swagger stick he'd plucked from Galitzin smartly across his palms, cracking it almost in rhythm with the volleys of sleet outside.

"You need moral instruction, Diana. There'll be no, ah, frivolities tonight. No scotch. No, ah, tiddlywinks. From now on, we shall contemplate higher matters."

Scarcely hearing, she stared at the stranger he'd become.

Wordlessly he thumbed through a morocco-bound book, one of several salvaged from the wagon. "Ah, here!" he exclaimed. "Now listen and let it be a lesson. This is from King Richard the Second: 'This other Eden, demi-paradise, This fortress built by Nature for herself against infection and the hand of war, this happy breed of men, this little world, this precious stone set in the silver sea, which serves it in the office of a wall or a moat defensive to a house, against the envy of less happier lands, this blessed plot, this earth, this realm, this England.' "

He peered at her, eyes burning, his countenance triumphant. "You see? For this we live. For this we suffer. For this we'll devour mule meat and starve, endure rain and sleet and a harsh continental winter. For this we'll show our steel, our backbone, our fierce execution of duties. For this we'll take Skye in chains back to our sceptre'd isle and show him, and all the brutes of the world, what it means to be one of us, an Englishman."

"Gordon, you're such a goose," said Alexandra.

Chapter 27

Mary did not exclude murder from her thoughts. She huddled against the northwind, hoping they would leave her good four-point blanket capote alone as they pillaged. They scarcely noticed her as they led the last Skye mule away to be shot and began erecting the lodge themselves. Lord Frazier intended to occupy it—he and his ladies—now that they had no wagon.

She made her spirit lie very still within her, though every fiber protested. She wished to shout at them that they were desecrating Mister Skye's home, that they took what was not theirs. But instead she huddled against the blast of arctic air and watched, knowing they didn't have eyes for squaws except when they lusted. Mister Skye's big medicine lay scattered upon the trembling grasses, just like his possessions. Galitzin found their small hoard of pemmican and jerky in a parfleche and exclaimed. But the viscount commandeered it.

They'd already pillaged the parfleche that contained Mister Skye's clothing, and had long since distributed it to ragged cartmen. Skye's moccasins, especially, had been snapped up by cartmen with tattered boots. And Mister Skye's grizzly bear claw necklace, filled with the shining gray talons of the king of the mountains, hung from the viscount's leathery neck, a perfect symbol of medicine shattered and medicine won.

"I say, what's this?" asked the viscount as he withdrew Mister Skye's battered belaying pin. "A belaying pin. Hickory, I imagine. Royal Navy. The scoundrel stole it. There's a bit of evidence I'll just cart along." He set it in the grass.

She heard a shot and saw the mule sag and then collapse heavily. Even before life fled, cartmen began eviscerating it. The last mule, she thought. But she had her mare, and Victoria had Jawbone somewhere. The Britons had eaten the rest, grumbling all the while. The light had gone gray, draining life from the world. No four-foot remained to drag the travois. But it didn't matter to the viscount. He'd throw the lodgecover and poles into a cart after this.

She eyed the battered belaying pin, remembering how Mister Skye used it as a weapon in the days of his medicine. She thought she might use it too, once, before they swarmed over her. Once to crush the skull of Viscount Frazier.

"The squaws' stuff," Colonel Galitzin said as they emptied a parfleche. Mary's own doeskin skirts and calico blouses tumbled to earth, along with her double winter moccasins, the outer ones with soles of rawhide cut from a bull. "Capote there—nice little trinket for the ladies. Something to parade in around London, I suppose."

Her winter capote. She could no longer repress the turmoil within her. Mister Skye had bought her the blanket at Fort Union, thick wool with four bars in the corner, creamy wool with green stripes at either end. She'd carefully cut and sewn until she had a fine capote with a hood, against the times when Winter Man came from the north to torment her.

"It is mine," she said.

They peered over to her amazed, unaware that this squaw of Skye's had been watching.

She walked resolutely toward these men, aware that her medicine had gone bad, and theirs was good. She would take it from them. She would need it.

"There now, little lady. We have it. You're Skye's wife and the man's a criminal."

"They are mine. All these. And those are Victoria's. I will take them." She reached for her winter moccasins, but the viscount yanked her away, his cold hand powerful on her arm.

"Your medicine is bad," she said softly.

"The savage mind at work. Here now, you're looking for a bit of warmth to crawl into tonight. Take a robe. I'm going to trade the rest at Rocky Mountain House. But you can have that one."

She followed his pointed finger to one that had been Victoria's. "I will take my capote, too," she said, but the viscount dragged her away again. "And my moccasins."

"We're taking them. They'll be a great curiosity in London. All this truck. Beads and feathers and dresses of hide. That elktooth blouse you have here, that's a sensation. Maybe I'll donate it to the British Museum. You've got moccasins, little lady; you don't need any more."

She clutched her robe angrily, watching them pillage the kitchen things; the copper kettle, spider, the iron spit they used to hang kettles. The whiteman's bowls and plates.

"Maybe your medicine is bad sometime soon," she said.

The viscount responded thoughtfully. "Keep an eye on her, Galitzin. Who knows what evil lies in the savage breast?" He turned to her. "Why aren't you fetching us greens? Helping the men? In fact, why don't you just go back to wherever you came from? We don't need you now."

"I will stay."

"Then you'll work, little lady. And you'll walk. Tomorrow we'll have that worthless mare for breakfast."

She stood her ground as the light thickened, and watched them pillage all that had once belonged to the lodge of Mister Skye. She didn't know what the British Museum was, but with each discovery of things she and Victoria had quilled or beaded, or woven feathers into, or tanned, the viscount babbled about what a sensation they'd make in London, and what a contribution they'd be to the museum's collections.

She watched the cartmen stake down her lodgecover, col-

lect firewood, hang the liner, tote in the viscount's feather-
beds and blankets; watched the viscount's shivering ladies
duck inside. Tonight would be miserable, but at least she
had the robe. A thought came to her. Maybe two robes.
She wrapped the robe about her, skin-side out, and
walked swiftly down the coulee to the Smith River bottoms
a long way distant, and there found a stick. She had to feed
Mister Skye something, anything, because they gave him so
little now. And feed herself. She felt faint with a hunger
that wouldn't let go of her. But it was too late. The cruel
dark snuffed her vision, and she could see nothing—no roots
or berries. She wanted cattails at least, and found none here
where the river cut through rock and hammered an opposing
bluff.

She ached to find Victoria too, but the older Absaroka
woman wasn't here. It had turned too dark to see hoofprints
or messages that Victoria often left in plain sight for Mary.
She remembered the old woman wore nothing but summer
things, a hip-length blouse belted at the waist, a doeskin
skirt, and low summer moccasins with no warmth in them.

Sleet and blackness hit her simultaneously, a stinging
blast of it, followed by gusts that laced her face. She had
to get back before she was lost! No food at all this time.
Wearily she toiled back to the camp, steering by instinct,
climbing steep slippery meadow, somehow hewing to the
watercourse up the coulee that might run later. Ahead, finally, she discerned the vague, bobbing light of the lodge,
the only light because the wet sheets of sleet had doused
the campfires. In just moments she'd felt her body go numb
with the cold, and knew she in her robe was better off than
Victoria, who rode almost naked to the ice.

Not a cartman remained out in the weather. She glided
swiftly through camp, the gale whipping through her robe
and piercing to her thighs and belly. She sensed the horses
nearby, their rumps into the storm, tugging at their pickets.
Galitzin had learned: he always kept two or three hobbled
and in camp now, to chase after the others. She noticed one
tethered to Galitzin's own tent, looking miserable as sleet
whitened its body and lodged in its dark mane.

No one. It pleased her. She stumbled through the bitter

air, feeling the sleet lace her neck and collect in her hair until she came to the cart set apart, a little lower than the others, a black forlorn thing whose sheet chattered in the gale. Its front end opened north, letting wind and sleet whistle through. She found the tongue and slowly twisted the cart sideways, its creaking wheels yielding bit by bit until she had one side athwart the wind. Then she felt her way to the rear.

"Mister Skye," she breathed.

"Mary!"

"They are not watching tonight." She crawled over the tailgate and slid beside him in the icy dark.

"Don't get close or you'll take the hydrophobia."

She ignored him, found his heavy form on the slanting bed of the cart, and pulled herself to him. His hand found her icy one.

"Want to hug you but I can't," he said.

She knew. She felt the icy brass between her breast and his. But at least she could make them warm. She pulled her own robe over his, the skin sides to the weather and the warm curly fur tight against their flesh. She tucked both robes carefully around their feet, and drew them over their heads to make a small cocoon that might hold a little heat.

"You are so cold," she said softly, just barely clinging to calm.

"I am that. I'm feeling well enough, but this cold might have put me under. Not much I could do. You saved me, Mary."

Tears came, and she hugged him, giving him what little heat she possessed. Slowly the double robes warmed them while the thundering wagonsheet above held off the sleet and most of the northwind.

"Mister Skye, they've taken everything. The lodge now. The viscount's in our lodge. I don't even have winter clothes."

"Not much time left," he said slowly. "You'd better get out while you can."

"They're eating our horses. Only my mare is left. Tomorrow I walk or ride a cart."

"Mary—you hitch up with Victoria and get out."

"I didn't find roots. I'm so hungry. You're hungry."
He remained silent and she knew how starved he felt.

"Need to hug you goodbye," he said. He made a loop of his arms, stretching the chain that pinned his wrists. She felt what he was about and slid into the circle, and felt his massive strength surround her, along with his broken medicine.

The footing became treacherous as the sleet turned the gumbo slope into a greased chute. Jawbone skidded and floundered, his hoofs flailing, but he pressed on eagerly because Victoria steered him toward his master. Only a faint amber glow from the lodge gave her direction. Closer in she discovered a second glow, often shrouded by the whirling white flakes that began to replace the sleet. A coal oil lantern in Galitzin's large wall tent, she surmised. Probably for warmth. He and the privileged Baudelaire weren't suffering.

She'd never been so cold. Sleet and snow whipped out of the blackness, plastering her entire body, hair and face, thin calico blouse, hands, skirt, legs. It had soaked through her meager clothing instantly, turning it into a sodden clinging sheet that magnified the cold and sluiced heat from her. Her feet turned numb and then she ceased to feel anything except a strange white pain there. Her bony hands fared little better, though she buried one, then the other, in her armpits. Her fingers ached and then died, sensation abandoning them so she could not know whether she held her makeshift rein or not. And at last, near the camp, spasms convulsed her, a violent shaking she could not control.

I will do it, she thought. I will not let Cold-Maker win. She steered Jawbone past the cart where Mister Skye lay. He resisted, turning his head and threatening to screech, but she guided him resolutely toward the cartyard, keeping a sharp eye on the huddle of dark tents where cartmen lay awake in blankets and shivered through the miserable night. She needed to find the tool wagon. If it had been left just as she saw it from above, they would have a chance; if not, all would be lost.

So opaque was the blackness that she could not tell one

cart from another. They lacked color and form and looked utterly unfamiliar, alien beasts faintly limned in the lodge-light. She hunted desperately among them, ignoring the shaking that wracked her, wanting the one with the tailgate down. At last, despairing, she slid off Jawbone, landing in a heap in icy grass because her feet never felt the earth. Then, leading Jawbone, she worked cautiously among the carts, stumbling once over a tongue or a shaft. She located one of the food carts and found it empty. She stumbled into the cart that held the spirits and found it locked tight.

Her strength ebbed even as the convulsions of her slim body defied her will. Soon she would no longer be able to walk. Her cheeks still stung, but she was losing feeling in her arms. Then she lurched into a sharp projection that bit her hip, and found herself at a cart with an opened tailgate. She crabbed her hand around until it caught on something she couldn't feel.

"Sonofabitch!" she exclaimed into the wind. Her arms refused to lift the heavy thing. Panting, she began running in place, making her heart pump hot blood into limbs that no longer worked, and slowly she felt life, a thousand painful prickles, course down her arms. Her hand clasped a wet pickax. And then the spade.

She carried them over her shoulder, not able to hold them in her hands, and slid through the camp watching sharply. At Galitzin's tent stood a picketed horse, which lifted its head sharply and whickered. Jawbone whickered back, and Victoria froze. Nothing happened. She studied the colonel's glowing tent in the shrouded dark, and still nothing happened. Maybe these whitemen heard only the bitter wind, or maybe they were just too lazy to check during a storm.

She hastened toward Mister Skye's cart, plunging back into utter blackness on the edge of the camp. Jawbone followed, shaking his head and bobbing it in some eerie horse mood she couldn't fathom. She tripped over the tongue and fell, the spade and pickax clanging as they flew from her grasp.

"Sonofabitch!" she bellowed.

"Victoria!" The muffled voice of Mary lifted from

within, and that instantly solved a major problem. Victoria had had no idea where Mary lay, and hoped Mister Skye would know.

Warm hands pulled her over the front of the cart and drew her down under two robes. She lay shivering while Mister Skye and Mary pressed her tight. From outside, Jawbone whickered, and Mister Skye barked a sharp command at the animal. They couldn't see him, but sensed his ugly head close by, perhaps poking into the cart.

For a long time she lay between them, feeling her tremors slow, even if her body still felt like ice and her arms and fingers refused to work. But time flew.

"Goddam it's cold," she muttered. "I tell my arms and fingers and feet to go and they don't go. They got a mind of their own, worse than Jawbone."

"He's all right?"

"Got a crease across a shoulder. He's coming fine. Limped a few days."

"Victoria—take him to your people. Set him free high in the Pryors. Let him breed the mares. That's all I want. All I've got left."

She listened to her man, dreading to refuse him. "This morning I found a big Siksika village ahead. They find this camp soon, maybe tomorrow. We got to go tonight—use the storm."

She waited for his objections but didn't hear any. Her man seemed to be in an odd mood. Maybe he'd given up too soon, waiting for the madness-fever to eat him.

"Good enough way to die," he muttered at last. She lay so close she felt his warm breath as he muttered. "I'm not much for walking barefoot in chains. You got a pony and travois?"

"It's too cold," Mary said. "You've got nothing to wear. Mister Skye's naked. They took everything in our parfleches. We have nothing. Not a blanket. Not a moccasin. Not even pemmican."

"Goddam, we got to go—now!" she whispered fiercely. "I got ways."

"Two buffler robes and one horse," Mister Skye said.

"You git to your people with Jawbone and leave me. It doesn't matter if I die now or in a month."

"Mister Skye," she whispered fiercely—but outside the darkness danced and bobbed. She pulled free of the two robes and peered out, seeing a coal oil lantern swinging on its bail. Someone was coming.

"Coming!" she hissed. "They check. Hide Jawbone!"

Lithely Mary slipped out the shadowed rear of the cart while Victoria slid deeper under the robes. Mister Skye swiftly wrapped the robes tight about her, concealing her under the dark curly hair.

The light bobbed, making shadows dance, and even under the robe Victoria could see its steady approach. Then, she knew, the whole interior of the cart blazed white above her.

"Gravesend," muttered Mister Skye.

"Just checking. Show me your hands."

Mister Skye reluctantly drew his arms out of the robe and let the light fall on his chains.

"Show me your ankles, Skye."

Victoria worried that her own moccasins would be exposed, but her man worked slowly, tugging the robe back until his ankles lay bare in the wavering light, and the chains around them shone.

"That do it?"

Gravesend laughed. "You ought to pitch the robe out and just freeze up, Skye. That'd beat dying of hydrophoby, or rotting away in a British gaol. Not that you're going to live. We buried Cutler, and that's how it'll be, Skye."

Gravesend lifted the lantern and vanished into the swirling white. Victoria peeked out and saw downy flakes boiling down, making walls in every direction. The sleet had turned to snow, and the wind had ebbed.

Moments later Mary clambered over the tailgate and crawled, shivering, into the robes again.

"Jawbone's safe?"

"Yes. Right here. The snow hides him good. The man could not see more than a little way."

"They'll be back," he muttered.

"We go now!" she hissed.

He sighed but did nothing.

"Outside I got a spade and pickax."

She felt him listen in the dark. But he said nothing. She'd never known him like this, giving up, not trying. It was the madness-sickness coming to him.

"We take the pickax and land it on a chain. Make the point go through a link. Pop the link. Then you can walk. You ride Jawbone away."

"Barefoot and naked."

"No! I fix that too!" She slid a hand down to her Green River knife in its moccasin sheath. "Here! Feel this!"

His hand closed over hers, and the knife. But he said nothing.

"The wagonsheet. I'll cut it off. And keep the cord too. I'll make three ponchos, slice a neck hole. There's lots more canvas than we need. We'll take it too. For a tent. For leggins. For—after we get away, I'll make what we need—moccasins, leggins."

"Horses?" said Skye, a change in his voice.

"Jawbone. And I'll steal Galitzin's. It's picketed at his tent with a saddle on it. We put the saddle on Jawbone for your feet."

"Bare feet in a blizzard. You figure I'd make it in just a canvas poncho? I'm bare-ass naked."

"Goddam! You want to die your way or their way? The Siksika, they see your medicine's all goddam busted up, and they take their time torturing you."

He was weighing it, she knew. "You'd have a robe too. Me and Mary, we got the other one and ponchos."

"You'd both ride Galitzin's horse?"

"Yes. We're light. We bust your chain, make ponchos, take the rest of the wagonsheet, take the two robes, steal the pony, take the pickax and spade. We go maybe half a night. Then maybe dig us a dugout. And now it's snowing to cover the tracks. In a few suns we're with my people."

"We're half-starved, Victoria, and weak as pups."

He seemed to be objecting, but she heard something else in his whisper.

"You want that goddam viscount to throw you in a

shallow hole like they did the other one? Cutler? You want that? While he gloats and laughs and they all have a drink?''

"You warmed up?" he asked.

"Yes!"

"Well, don't figure on staying that way," he said, tossing aside the robes. "Where's the pickax?"

Chapter 28

Mister Skye poked his head out of the wagon, feeling snow slice across his cheeks and seeing nothing. At last he made out a dim blur, so veiled and subtle through whirling snow that he wasn't even sure whether it was light from his lodge or from Galitzin's lantern within his tent. He could not see his own hands or the ground beneath the cart, even though white snow accumulated on the grass. He knew, with a sudden black epiphany, that the thing Victoria proposed was impossible. They needed light.

He pulled back in and drew the robes about him. "I need light to drive that pickax into the chain. Got to sit in the snow, legs apart, drive that point into a link. I could spend all night pounding at it, like some bloody fool. Victoria, you'll need light to cut that wagonsheet into ponchos."

"I can cut the wagonsheet from the cart in the dark," Victoria muttered. "It's tied down with puckerstrings."

"Maybe we can harness the cart and drive off," Mary said. "They always leave the harness next to the carts."

"You think you can fetch two drays from the picket line

and harness in this kind of dark? You'd get lost out there. I can't help in these chains.''

She said nothing and Mister Skye sensed her discouragement.

"Sonofabitch!" Victoria exclaimed. He felt her crawling about on the tilting bed of the cart, and then a sudden gust ripped in from the north, and canvas flapped like a shivering trysail. He felt the cart creak again, and suddenly the canvas sagged, free of its anchors, riding over the bows. A blast of arctic wind instantly destroyed their snug world.

"Now we're in trouble," he muttered. "Can't put this back together in this blackness and cold."

"Damn right," the old woman snarled. He heard her clamber out, cursing and muttering, felt the wagonsheet drop from the cart, and then heard the clink of metal.

"All right, get out," she snapped. "Bring the robes."

He sighed. Something desolate had crept back into him, paralyzing his will. All right then. Death by freezing would be better than death from hydrophobia. But he wasn't quite ready for death.

"Hurry up—you freeze your ass."

He grabbed a robe and sensed that Mary had grabbed the other. He heard the tailgate drop, and knew the old woman had made it easy for him. But the chains impeded all movement, and his linked wrists kept him from pulling the robe close. His feet landed in snow that bit at them swiftly. Then he felt her small hand.

"Come," she said.

She dragged him forward while he hobbled, his steps reduced to mincing because of the ankle irons that scraped and chafed him. Then he stepped onto the wagonsheet.

"Sit on that, and hold them tools," she whispered at him. "Mary, help me pull."

He felt himself sliding over snow and grass and rock on the wagonsheet, straight toward that single dim source of light that lay veiled by swirling snow. The sheer audacity of it amazed him. He worried then that any of the cartmen would step out to make water and spot them; that Galitzin or Gravesend would hear and rush out; that his women would suffer endless pain for their efforts to free him. And still the women tugged relentlessly, dragging him straight toward the lodge and the light, which slowly enlarged so that he could see the forms of his women, and even see his leg chain.

They circled wide around Galitzin's glowing tent and the saddled horse outside. He wondered where Jawbone was, and spotted him ghosting along, and worried that the horses might greet each other. But it didn't happen. His women dragged him well around behind the lodge, opposite the doorflap, and then stopped. Snow eddied down, and he felt a deepening numbness even though his robe hung over his shoulders.

"You got eyes. Do it now," she whispered. They had halted scarcely twenty yards from the lodge. He could see his chain, but couldn't make out one link from another except for a wet glint.

"Mary," Victoria whispered urgently. "You go get that horse and put the saddle on Jawbone. Then you look around the camp and find what you can find. Horsemeat, maybe."

Mary nodded and glided into the snow, swiftly walled from their sight.

Mister Skye crabbed forward until his bare ankles and feet rested in the snowy grass. Then he grasped the wet pickax, feeling his numb fingers clamp the slippery wood. One end tapered to a point; the other tapered to a chisel two inches wide or so.

"Hurry!" she snapped at him, anger suffusing her voice.

He lifted the pick and arced it down sharply. The act caused his knees to lift and his legs to buck, and the pick buried itself in the unfrozen clay.

"I hold your legs," she whispered. "Be careful."

She crawled clear over his lap, pinning down his legs. He was conscious of warmth.

He arced the pick down again and missed. He pulled the point out of the earth savagely, and arced it again. It struck metal and clanked. He waited, expecting the lodge and tents to disgorge men. Nothing happened. Snow whirled, numbing his face. His ears hurt. His feet had turned prickly.

Viciously he struck at the links again and again, missing, clanking, pinging, but not sundering a link. He lost his breath, sobbed, and struck again, feeling the clay trap the point and not let go. His hands had quit hurting, and he could no longer feel the pick in them, but he kept on, naked in the snow, seeking the eye of the needle and never threading it.

He rested, wheezing, his heart racing. They were in for it now. They couldn't go back to the cart. The best he could imagine was to have Jawbone drag the canvas with him on it far enough away so that maybe they could bust the chain in the morning. The snow might cover their exodus. But he knew they'd not make half a mile that way, and would be found swiftly at dawn.

Smoke from the lodge whirled back down on him, searing his lungs. Within, someone stirred, the shadow lapping the cone's translucent side. Putting wood on the fire. Then a figure loomed outside, vaguely male. Frazier. About to make water.

"Goddam," Victoria muttered, swiftly lifting the white wagonsheet up around them both, making them virtually invisible through the veil of snow. They watched closely, waiting for whatever came. Mister Skye worried about Mary. Frazier walked toward Galitzin's tent.

"I say, Galitzin, we need more wood. Fetch some sticks, eh?"

They saw the colonel emerge and stand, a blurred figure beside the viscount. He talked but Mister Skye couldn't hear what they were saying.

"Well, fetch it then. And tomorrow load a cart with wood. I won't have this sort of neglect," the viscount snapped.

Galitzin ducked back into his tent, and emerged carrying his coal oil lantern on its bail. He walked through the snow toward the carts and disappeared back there, hidden by snow and the various conveyances. Frazier dashed back into the lodge, and Skye watched his shadow bob across the cowhide.

Galitzin appeared a while later, carrying two lanterns, both lit. At the lodge he summoned Frazier. Skye couldn't see what transpired because he was on the rear side, but in a moment he watched lights dance within. Galitzin had given the lord and his ladies both lanterns and had returned to his darkened—and colder—tent.

A quietness settled over the snowy camp. If anything it seemed darker without the faint glow from Galitzin's tent adding to that of the lodge.

"That lord sure don't leave nothing for his brothers," Victoria whispered. "They'll be warm enough with two lanterns."

Barnaby Skye thought about warmth. His ankles and calves had gone numb again and he'd lost track of his bare feet. He turned the pick around idly, until its chisel edge faced the ground. He arced it down angrily, and felt its edge strike metal with a thud. Suddenly excited, he reached forward, found the chain with his hands, but his fingers had lost their touch. Then he sensed Victoria's hands probing along the chain, and she muttered something.

"Ah! You cut a link but it ain't open yet. One side cut."

"Victoria! Help me. I'm going to drive the chisel edge into the ground until the point sticks up. Then I'm going to lie on my back with my legs up in the air. Fit the weak link over the point and I'm going to jerk my legs down."

He didn't wait for an answer. He drove the pick down, burying the chisel point. He felt her lift his legs and guide the chain until the weakened link lay over the point. He jerked his legs downward—and nothing happened.

"Yank down, Victoria!"

He felt her try, felt her fail, heard her curse. He sobbed. He felt her tremble, knew the cold stole her strength from her, just as it robbed him. She yanked. They yanked together. The link didn't yield. He fell back exhausted, feeling snow collect on his goosebumped flesh wherever the robe failed him. Felt his butt freeze on the wet duck canvas.

Defeated. He'd take a few more whacks at the link with the chisel point, and that would be the last of it. Freeze up and die, then. Tonight. He lay panting, nothing left in his cold, starved body to give to this desperate enterprise.

"You sure that link's cut on one side?"

She snarled at him in Absaroka.

"Drag me," he said. "Get Mary and Jawbone."

She nodded. But even as the old woman began to unfold,

they spotted a form gliding toward them in the snow. They froze until they knew it was Mary. She was carrying things. She looked like a ghost with furry snow clinging to her robe and hair. Gently she set some things down on the wagonsheet, and Mister Skye strained to make them out in the murky amber. A horse collar. A cylindrical thing—his old belaying pin, the hickory covered with snow. An excitement built in him.

"Goddam!" the old woman cried. She hefted it, pleased. "Maybe you fix us, Mary."

Mary looked mystified.

Swiftly they positioned themselves again. Mister Skye settled on his back, legs up, while Victoria settled the weakened link over the point of the pick. Then she whacked the chain. He felt cold iron jerk his leg. She tried the other side, her hammering making sharp cracks in the night. He peered fearfully toward the lodge.

She paused, feeling the pick point and the weakened link with her fingers. "It's coming," she announced. She hammered again, each blow cracking woodenly into the night. "Mary—Don't just stand there. Get that horse."

Mary started—and froze. Ahead, Galitzin poked his head outside, curious about the sharp noises. He had only the glow of the lodge for vision now, and Mary edged softly away from his view. Snow whirled, but the wind no longer whipped and roared, drowning noise. The colonel clambered entirely outside, and peered about.

"Gravesend," he roared.

From obscure darkness a man loomed, and the two conversed in low tones Skye couldn't make out. More men appeared, some relieving themselves and others collecting around Galitzin's tent in light so obscure Skye couldn't even count them. Beside him, Victoria eased the white wagonsheet upward to conceal them. In the whirling snow they'd be invisible even from a few feet, with the sort of light they had.

Someone, Galitzin probably, approached the lodge. "Your lordship?" It was the colonel's voice.

Skye saw shadows flitting across amber cowhide, then heard muffled talk around the other side of the lodge. He heard fragments of talk, and the words alarmed him: lantern, pounding sounds, patrol, check the squaw, Skye . . .

They were going to patrol. They'd find Mary up and around; read her moccasin prints. Discover the cart with no sheet, and Skye missing. He knew they'd run out of time. He saw the lantern now, illumining Gravesend's burly features. The armorer formed a party of six cartmen and plunged into the snowy night toward the horse herd, probably intending to check that first. Galitzin crawled back into his blackened tent.

Only a minute or two, then. Victoria threw back the wagon sheet, found the weak link and once again settled it over the point of the pick and cracked the belaying pin over it sharply, the sound like a rifleshot. He sensed her hands feeling the link and exclaiming, and then some gentle tugs, and his legs fell free, chain dangling from each ankle.

"Ah!" she cried, too loud. She sprang up. He did too, onto feet that had ceased feeling. He walked stiffly, joyous, hearing the chain-ends clink softly. But she was already smoothing out the wagon sheet to make ponchos.

"Hold the damn thing," she growled. "This here is hard work." She began sawing savagely at the sheet, muttering and cursing, finding that her small knife didn't easily sever the tough duck canvas. He peered about as she sawed, seeing nothing but whirling white, worrying about Mary, worrying about getting the horse they needed desperately. It occurred to him he was half-starved, mad with hunger. He stood, dancing, making his dead feet hop and whirl, jumping crazily on free feet, wanting his hands freed to. But that must wait.

"Haw!" he roared, and then chastised himself. Much too noisy.

He saw shadows bobbing about within the lodge. And then, near Galitzin's tent, the vague figure of a woman leading a horse. Mary!

Victoria sawed away fiercely, muttering, and then she lifted up a large rectangle of canvas with a slit in its center. "Try this," she whispered.

But he couldn't, not with his wrists still chained. Clucking, she lifted it up and pulled it over him, jamming his head through the slit, tucking the front side between his chained arms. It didn't warm him at all. In fact, the wet snow on it stung his flesh and chilled him anew. But still it was clothing of a sort. She found the cordage she'd salvaged and tied it around his waist, pinning the poncho to him.

Mary drew up with the bay horse and swiftly undid the cinch, intending to transfer the saddle to Jawbone. Skye knew the saddle, a good English make with tie-down rings fore and aft, and light, slender stirrups. He was glad of the stirrups, knowing they'd help support his iron-weighted legs.

Shouting. They'd been found out. Skye squinted into the blur, discerning the bobbing lantern ghostly in the distance, near his prison cart. Men running. Men boiling out of small tents that shed snow in heaps when they were jarred. Galitzin bolting out of his larger tent.

"Sonofabitch," Victoria muttered. Swiftly she jammed her Green River knife back into its bullhide sheath on her ankle, and snatched up the wagonsheet. "Let's get."

Mary threw the saddle onto Jawbone, who screeched when she did it. The other horse sidled backward, tugging at its reins and then pulling free of Mary's one-handed grasp.

Mister Skye dove for the reins, but the horse sidestepped back, closing toward the lodge.

Mary returned to her saddling. Victoria clawed at Skye. "Don't. Let me. Them chains spook him."

Skye stopped at once. If anyone could catch the spooked horse, which sidled closer and closer toward the lodge and light, toward the viscount, who carried a fowling piece that glowed amber, it would be Victoria.

"Stop!" bawled Galitzin, but he was facing and yelling the wrong direction, tricked by eddying snow.

"Mister Skye—come. I'll help," whispered Mary.

She drew him to Jawbone. He needed help. He couldn't feel the stirrup. His legs trembled and wouldn't lift. She guided a cold bare foot into the near stirrup. Jawbone felt the chain smack him, and squealed. Then she lifted, and he found himself sprawling atop Jawbone, trying to stay on his slippery back, finding the cold wet saddle, and dropping onto it. She ran around to the off side, found his bare foot and jammed it into a stirrup. He felt nothing except an anchoring of his numb legs.

"Stop!" cried the viscount, and this time they were shouting in the right direction. Just beyond, men tumbled out of the flurries, one carrying a dancing lantern. Off behind the lodge, Victoria caught the horse and threw herself up onto it, teetering over its wet back for a long instant. And then she righted herself and steered it back from the light, the dark horse much more of a target than Skye's blue roan.

The viscount lifted his fowling piece toward them and fired, a shocking report in the night. Shot seared past. Now men boiled toward them and Skye saw sidearms on several, including the colonel.

"They're out there. Stop them, blokes."

Shots.

Mary tugged desperately at the pick, but the clay of Earth Mother wouldn't surrender its prize. Viciously she yanked, and this time the pick popped up, spinning her backward. She thrust it toward Skye, and then the wagon sheet. He grasped everything in his chained hands.

Men twenty yards off. More shots, white flashes in snow. Mary running toward Victoria's horse. Mary pausing to catch the remaining buffalo robe lying in a heap. Mary picking up the belaying pin. Men closing on Mary, bulling in. Mary clawing at Victoria. Victoria clamping Mary's arm, dragging her up. Horse sidling away from running men. Shots, white flashes. Jawbone sliding into deeper gloom. Jawbone shrieking. Shots whipping close.

The dark horse plunged past him, Victoria and Mary riding double. He followed, plunging into absolute inkiness without knowing where they were going except that it was uphill and the northerly winds quartered at him from the rear.

Behind, volleys of shots, white flashes, shooting blind. The shouts grew faint.

"Talk to me. I can't see you."

"We will talk," said Victoria, just ahead. "You talk too."

They set the horses into a quiet walk. The horses minced, unable to see, groping into a murk.

"Free, I guess," he said. "They can't follow. And we don't know where we're going. Victoria, can you cut more ponchos by feel? We might as well, before we freeze solid."

They stopped only a short distance from the camp, but it could have been a hundred miles in a night like that. Mister Skye sat Jawbone and held the rein of the bay horse while Victoria and Mary worked in the blank dark, muttering and mumbling. He heard the faint sound of a knife sawing at canvas. He clamped the pickax in his numb hands, knowing it'd free his wrists in the morning. He loved the pickax like a brother.

He felt someone wrap his feet in canvas and tie the bandage. He felt someone lift his poncho off of him and then slide a buffalo robe over him. The robe had fresh slits in it for his head to go through. He felt warm fur slide over his shoulders and then his chest and back like an angel's caress. Then he felt hands pull the poncho over and tuck it between his chained wrists. Then he felt the loving hands of his good dear women tie his makeshift clothing tight about him. He could make it to the Kicked-in-the-bellies now.

"We'll go now. Keep the wind at our back so we go south. You talk, Mister Skye, yes? We'll talk. We got to talk for a long time now."

"I'll talk, mates," he said. "I could eat a grizzly ba'r right now."

They laughed, or was it crying?

Chapter 29

Escaped! Lord Frazier gaped at the wall of snow that hid that deserter and his squaws from good British justice. He could scarcely believe it. How had it been done? He glared at those around him, wondering who had betrayed him. Galitzin, maybe. The colonel had the keys to the irons.

"After them!" he cried. "I want them stopped. For God, for England, for the Queen!"

Cartmen gaped at him.

"Really, now, Gordon, don't be silly," said Lady Diana. He whirled to find her standing there in dishabille, a blanket wrapped around her.

"You've taken his side," he accused.

"It's snowing. It's black as ink. The man was pressed into the navy, made a slave. And it happened a quarter of a century ago. Really Gordon, you're so silly."

She enraged him, "Into the lodge. I'll speak to you later. Not in front of these retainers. He deserted. If we let him perform these criminal things, then every other dustman and lowlife in England will too."

She laughed, and it infuriated him. Around him cartmen

smiled, their grins hideous to him in the swirling snow and yellow lantern-light.

"Your lordship, the man's as good as dead from hydrophobia," Galitzin said.

"That's not it, not it!" the viscount cried. "He's dying the way he wants, escaped and free. He must die in irons. And speaking of that, Galitzin—how did he get your key?"

"He didn't." Galitzin pulled the keys that locked several of the carts—the armorer's cart, the spirits cart, the carts carrying silver and china for the lord and ladies—as well as the simple skeleton key that unlocked his irons. He jangled them before the viscount's nose, most rudely, the viscount thought.

"Someone has betrayed me, and the crown," he announced darkly, while surveying the villainous faces about him. "Well, get on with it. We will bring them back. If they resist, they'll die. I don't suppose they have weapons."

"Your lordship, it isn't practical in this—"

"Practical, practical. Here is a lantern. Out there are tracks in the snow. Take spare oil for the lantern. Saddle up. Take a squad, Galitzin. You shall lead it. I shall come along. I want every man saddled in five minutes. I want Gravesend to issue sidearms and rifles and rounds."

"With one lantern, sir, the men could hardly find mounts, or saddle—"

"Do it!"

Lady Diana laughed. "Gordon, dear, come play tiddlywinks. You'll get over it."

He paused before her, noting her amused smile, her insolence. "You are perfectly worthless. Trash. Go join Skye. If you return to England, it shall be in shame."

The amusement vanished from her face, and she stared at him contemplatively. "You've changed, Gordon. For the worse."

"Your lordship, what are we to do for rations?" Galitzin asked. "The men are starving and weak. A horse a day is vile fare."

The staring cartmen suddenly turned solemn, and the viscount noted it. "Bring Skye back dead or alive; then I'll stop the caravan for a few days and we'll hunt. Every last one of us. But only if you bring him back, and his squaws for good measure. They're all horse thieves. Stole Galitzin's mount."

Diana started laughing again. "And just what were we, eating Mister Skye's horses and mules day by day? Be consistent, Gordon."

"Out of my sight, you—"

She chuckled, obviously enjoying it. "Oh, pooh," she said. "I'm glad Mister Skye's free."

He could barely stand it. Had she not been nobly bred he would have ordered ten lashes. But he didn't wish to give the cartmen ideas. Instead he pulled his revolver from its sheath. "Go saddle," he said coldly.

Reluctantly, cartmen dispersed to their small tents to pull on clothing.

"And saddle a mount for me," he roared.

It took an hour. Lord Frazier stalked around his lodge, raging, fuming, checking his revolver and his rifle; glaring at Lady Alexandra, who cowered in her blankets, and ignoring Lady Diana, who dressed in her hunting attire as if she intended to go along.

Then, at last, he heard that bloody fool Galitzin outside the lodge. "We are ready, your lordship," the man proclaimed.

"It took you long enough," Frazier muttered. "I hope the tracks haven't snowed over. I don't suppose you thought of that—or did you?"

Lord Frazier peered about him. Ten cartmen wrapped in blankets sat their mounts. Galitzin sat on a gray, holding the lantern by its bail. Diana sat on her buffalo runner, looking ready for a hunt, snow collecting on her split skirts.

"You're not going."

"I wouldn't miss the fun for anything, Gordon."

"Dismount."

"Make me, dear."

He thought he might. But it was unthinkable to tell a cartman to manhandle a noblewoman.

"Have you spare oil for the lamp, colonel?"

"A tin."

"Very well then. We will all do our duty."

Galitzin touched heels to his mount and the viscount fell in beside him, the two of them studying the ground for the snowed-over dimples that remarked the passage of Skye and his squaws. The cartmen strung out behind.

He and Galitzin picked up the trail easily enough, the dimples left by the passage of two horses. And no blood. He'd been hoping for blood in the snow.

"I am a man of iron, eh, Galitzin?"

"A determined leader, sir."

"Where do you suppose the scoundrel's going?"

"South of course, sir. As long as zey have a little north-wind on their back zey'll manage it—unless the wind shifts. I think it's out of the northwest, myself."

"Very good, Galitzin. Even if we lose the tracks, we'll head south. By the way, did you leave anyone in command at the camp?"

"I'm sure Mister Baudelaire—"

The viscount snorted. "A pimp in command."

The strangeness of everything subdued them. They drove through a low tunnel of whirling white, scarcely knowing whether they were climbing or descending, walking the edge of a cliff, or circumventing a forest. There was only the fast-filling string of dimples in the lantern-yellow snow, sucking them through nothingness.

"Faster," he said at last. "The trail's dim."

Galitzin set them into a trot, and behind he heard horses wheezing, gear clattering, weapons rattling in their sheaths, and the jingle of bridles. The sound satisfied him. Good British steel.

They clambered up a vast slope and then the trail vanished where wind had scoured the snow. It alarmed him.

"We'll go until we strike snow again," Galitzin said. "Then I'll halt the column while I work to either side. I'll pick it up."

"Excellent, Galitzin."

They crossed the barren ridge into snow, and in a few minutes Galitzin spotted the trail.

"We might lose them, your lordship."

"Pshaw. They're going to go south to the band of that older squaw—what's her name. We'll just press ahead and intercept. They'll cross the Yellowstone about where the Shields joins it. They must be weak as pups, and the oaf is probably half-dead by now. Canvas wagonsheet won't warm him, eh? How do you suppose they took it? Did you miss a knife?''

"I've learned not to underestimate the savages, your lordship.''

"Very good, Galitzin. But that old squaw must have hidden a dirk.''

Diana drew up beside them and it annoyed him, but he said nothing.

"We're catching up, aren't we. We have the lantern, but they have to feel their way along,'' she said.

"We'll have them soon,'' Galitzin replied.

She sighed unhappily, and the very sigh curdled the viscount's thoughts. An insufferable woman.

They rode relentlessly, while snow caked on their clothing and cold bit their toes. The temperature had barely dropped to freezing, the viscount knew, but the fall storm came fanged with wetness and bitter air. The ride had become eerie, a steady plodding across a white island in a black sea, without the faintest guidepost.

The light wavered, and Galitzin stared at it. "We'll stop and fill the reservoir,'' he said. He tugged his horse to a halt just as the light blued and vanished. Instantly the blackness closed in around them, clamping them in a stygian vise.

"I say, Galitzin, you brought some matches—''

He heard Galitzin rummaging in a leather pouch slung over his shoulders, and then white light blossomed in his hand. "I've plenty. Bring me the tin, Wiggins.''

It took them a few minutes, while the viscount chafed. Once Galitzin lit a match so the cartman could see where to pour the coal oil. He spilled some, and the viscount caught a whiff of it in the air. But at last the colonel struck a sulphur match again, cupped the bright flare, and the lamp sprang to life. Galitzin carefully replaced the glass chimney, and they started off again.

But while the colonel refueled the lamp in the dark, the viscount thought he spotted something. He peered into the night, straining his eyes to catch it again. And yes, there it was. Off behind them and to the right, he saw two or three stars just off the horizon. He realized even then that the snow had diminished, and so had the wind. There'd be little more snow or wind to obscure Skye's tracks, and just enough on the ground to leave an indelible trail. He exulted. The Divine hand, reaching out on behalf of mighty England and the Queen once again, as always.

"Look over there, Galitzin. Stars. It'll clear off in a few hours. And the snow's stopped. Now we have them."

The snow died and the wind died. Victoria knew the snow had stopped because it no longer stung her hands or dampened her cheeks. With the death of wind came the death of direction. She had no idea whether they progressed southward or meandered. She could not see the trail behind for reference. The horse would follow the path of least resistance.

"Talk to me, Mister Skye," she said. They'd neglected the contact.

"I'm here," he said, behind her. "Jawbone knows to keep up."

"I don't know where I'm going."

"We might head downhill. Any coulee should take us to the river. I'm used up. Hope we'll find some shelter down in the bottoms."

The thought gladdened her. She was used up too. She had Mary's warmth pressing her back, but the horse's hard backbone sawed her in two, and her legs ached.

"Are you cold?"

"Feet ache. My legs feel the way they did when I was making beaver. I'd climb out of those icy creeks and they'd hurt for a day."

He never talked about the aches in his bones from all the years he'd trapped beaver. He'd kept his hurts to himself, but she knew every scar in his battered body tortured him through the winters.

The earth tilted to her left, and she felt the horse's gait change, jolt more, on a downslope. She felt the darkness thicken even more, if that were possible, and felt the presence of forest, though she couldn't see a tree. Then a branch brushed her, and she felt its shower of snow. She turned the horse into the downgrade, and felt it skid slightly.

"I am going down, Mister Skye."

He didn't answer.

"I'm going down," she said louder.

"Feeling bad," he muttered, and the words relieved her as much as alarmed her. "Like to stop. Can't stand my hands chained up any more. Can't stand my feet hurting."

"Soon!" she cried. "Not now."

The medicine vision had returned to her, Magpie's prophecy scorching her mind even as she peered blindly into nothing.

"We're safe," said Mary. "I need to stop too."

"No! sonofabitch!"

"Magpie talkin'?"

"Yes!" In truth, her mind crawled with the vision, almost as if Magpie were there in the dark, on her shoulder, showing her Fate.

"Funny thing," Mister Skye muttered behind her. "That medicine vision was plumb right. The viscount fixing to haul me off. But how come I'm free? How come I'm dying of hydrophobia instead of being carted off to England?"

"Are you dying?" she cried.

He didn't answer for a while. "Don't want to go under. I want to see the baby." He paused again. "Die free. Die without these chains on. Die with you—" His voice broke hoarsely, and she heard him sniffing and muttering back there. She ached to hug him, dismount, help him off, bury themselves in the robes and hug. But it could not be. Something crabbed at her.

Victoria felt Mary's hands tighten around her waist. The horse skidded down a sharp defile, careened into a trunk, and righted itself. She felt the lash of needles.

They pierced into deeper forest. The horse picked its way along, stumbling frequently, its hoofs barking logs and rocks, skidding on wet unfrozen ground covered with needles. She peered upward through the canopy and saw stars off to one side, and sensed the night blooming open. A while later the heavens were clear. Cold deepened, hurting her. She could make out the snow on the ground, dim in starlight. Not much. The September sun would demolish it in a few hours.

They bottomed out onto a flat, emerging from the pine forest at the same time. They sensed looming shoulders of the earth catapulting upward, lifting horizons. Probably the Smith River, coiling in oxbows toward the Missouri.

"Northstar back off to our left. Dipper," muttered Mister Skye. "We're going southeast."

These whiteman's directions meant little to her. She took her directions from places. Now they were going to a place she loved.

"See!" cried Mary.

Victoria peered about, seeing nothing at first. And then, far away, atop the black ridge, just where it touched the open heavens, she saw a tiny bobbing light. They stared as the little light slid off the horizon and down into the blackness of the slope.

"Magpie's right, Victoria," Mister Skye said quietly. "They've got a fresh trail in snow to follow. But we've got a light to watch for. Armed to the gunnels, I imagine."

"That viscount—he's got one thing in his head."

"You have any notions, ladies?"

She peered sharply at him. He sat Jawbone, a ghostly figure in the dark, but visible now. She had never known him to surrender himself like this. The onslaught of death had robbed her man of will.

"You got that pickax?"

"Not much of a weapon, Victoria."

"Get down," she yelled at him. "I got to do something."

He obeyed, sliding clumsily off Jawbone and falling, unable to right himself with chained hands and legs that had ceased to function. She helped him up.

"Come here," she said. She lifted the pickax from the snow and steered him toward a downed tree. "Now get down. Put your hands out. Make that chain tight across the log."

"In the dark? You'll hit my—"

"Goddam, just do it. That chain, it locks your spirit worse than it locks your hands."

"But it's too dark—"

Mary said, "Do it, Mister Skye."

He stared from one woman to the other. Then he settled himself over the log, his arms out, the chain taut over the bark.

She lifted the pickax, turning it to make use of the chisel edge. A faintness undermined her, and she remembered how long it had been since any of them had eaten. She aimed carefully, and drove the heavy tool down. The chisel buried itself in wood. She yanked it loose, muttering to herself.

"Careful, Victoria," Skye muttered.

She drove the pick down again, and felt it drive into the link, burying chain in the rotting log. She tugged the pick out, and pulled the chain up. It fell apart, the links of drawn wire easier to cut than the forged links of the leg irons.

Mister Skye stared, seeing liberty in the starlight, and slowly drew his arms apart, chain-ends dangling from each wrist. He did not speak. Slowly he stood up, lifted his gaze to the infinities above him, lit now by a rising quarter moon, and stretched his freed arms upward, wanting to touch the stars, reaching, arching his back, straining his arms, his reaching fingers lifted to touch the music of creation. Then at last he lowered his thick arms and turned to her.

"Victoria. Mary," he whispered, and the two words made love.

She hugged him. They both hugged him. Then they turned toward the bobbing lantern, now visible, now obscured, as the viscount's men worked down the trail toward the bottoms.

"The river," said Mister Skye. "We'll head north, downstream in water. They'll look to the south."

Swiftly they mounted, gathering their few things: the pickax, spare canvas, and belaying pin. Liberty infused Mister Skye with an energy she hadn't seen in him. She grunted, satisfied, knowing she'd acted wisely.

He took the lead, steering Jawbone into brushy bottoms, and she and Mary followed on the dark horse, pushing now through whipping branches. Then, ahead, Jawbone stopped abruptly. She could hear water.

"Damned cutbank here. Ten-foot drop, looks like. Maybe more, hard to tell. Go back. We got to cut south a bit— make them think we're heading south."

They pivoted and worked their way back from the bank, pushing through clawed brush. When they broke out on meadow at last they whirled south, alarmed by the bobbing light, now three-quarters down the black slope and only minutes away.

They trotted furiously along the bottoms. Then Mister Skye pushed Jawbone back into the brush, cutting for the river again. On the trail above, a horse heard them and whinneyed. Victoria's horse squealed back. Discovered, then. This time they struck the riverbank at a place where the water undulated three or four feet below the cutbank, wobbling the stars that rode its surface. They stared, not knowing how deep the river lay. It could be a pool, and they could drop into a spot that would drench and kill them. The water boiled evilly by, oily in the night.

Behind, they heard distant shouts and the motion of horses as the viscount's men reached the open bottoms. No choice. The cartmen didn't need their lantern any more, and were closing fast.

"All right, you bloody horse," Skye said, kneeing Jawbone. The great beast poised on the lip of the cut-bank, shuddered, and then let himself slide in, his fore-hoofs plowing down clay, slowing the descent in some small way.

Jawbone struck water, staggered under Skye's weight, and righted himself. The river scarcely reached his pasterns. Only inches deep.

Mister Skye laughed softly. "Come along, ladies," he whispered.

Victoria and Mary had a bad time with the dark horse. They kicked and cursed, while just beyond the brush the noise of horsemen pierced to them.

"I will make him," said Mary. She turned, the belaying pin in hand, and cracked it over the horse's rump. The animal careened forward, dove off the cutbank and landed with a splash. It staggered, almost dumping its bareback riders, and then stood in starlit water that didn't reach its hocks.

"I hear you, Skye!" the viscount called. "Surrender now, or we will shoot to kill. All of you."

Chapter 30

Mister Skye sat quietly on Jawbone, listening. Beside him, Victoria and Mary sat waiting on their dark horse. Beyond, walled by a thick band of dense brush, his pursuers collected on a meadow. He heard the mutter of horses and talk, and then the movement of horses. Up and down the stream, he surmised. They were fanning out.

The Smith River ran in great oxbows here, walled by brush and contained by steep cutbanks in spots. Across the slender river a six or eight-foot cutbank loomed, trapping them in the water. If they could scale that, they could vanish in the brush on the far side easily enough. The cartmen had light enough from stars, a slim moon, and a few inches of snow, but it was tricky light, and all three Skyes wore white ponchos cut from the wagonsheet. He doubted that all the cartmen would shoot to kill, but he couldn't count on that. He felt like a fox beset by hounds, with only his guile to protect him.

Jawbone stood quietly, ears laid back, ready to shriek. Skye, enjoying the lush pleasure of freed hands, ran one up his neck, under the mane, quieting the horse. Downstream

lay a high cutbank with dense brush on top. And across the
oily river there, a low bank, maybe three feet. Something
they could negotiate if they had to. He signaled to the
women and gently turned Jawbone in the water, letting
the animal pick his way along, step by slow step, toward
the moonshadowed pool of blackness below the bluff. Victoria's horse, less disciplined, splashed, and he heard her
cursing softly.

"Mister Skye." The voice was a woman's and rose from
some distance, beyond the brush. "Will you marry me?"

He paused, astonished.

"I'd love to be your third wife—even for the—the little
while left."

He turned. Victoria and Mary sat grinning at him.

The viscount yelled at her. "Have you no decency?"

"Mister Skye—" Diana called again. "I don't know if
you're there or hearing me. They've divided into two parties. Galitzin went down—"

"Stop that," roared the viscount. "You're betraying the
crown. I'll see you brought to justice!"

"—and Gravesend went upstream with the rest."

He heard a sharp crack, like a slap or the blow of a
swagger stick across her face, and a small scream, followed
by groaning and weeping. He used the noise to dash swiftly
through the water. As they slipped into the shadow below
the cutbank the river deepened suddenly, and Jawbone
plowed water rising to his knees and hocks. Skye peered
around swiftly. Safe enough for the moment, with an escape
into brush across the river, and up the steep fissures of land
beyond. From both sides now he heard crashing in the brush
as cartmen spurred horses into the red willow and chokecherry and hackberry that massed along the creek.

"Skye," yelled the viscount. "We have you. Surrender
or die. We'll have mercy on your squaws if you do. Otherwise—death to all of you. Prepare your villainous heart to
meet God!"

Mister Skye said nothing.

"You're not armed, Skye. You haven't the faintest
chance."

Mister Skye thought he might be armed at that, but the

thought lay bitter in his soul. He knew then what he'd do, if he had strength enough after being starved for weeks and now chilled to numbness. His women wouldn't like it.

He nodded to them and began pulling his poncho over his head, luxuriating in the liberty of his arms. Then he pulled the buffalo robe off too, wrestling with its heavy weight. He rolled the robe into a compact cylinder, and tied it behind the low cantle of the British cavalry saddle he rode, and slid the poncho over him again. He wanted freedom.

"Goddam," muttered Victoria. "I tell you about medicine and you don't care." She sounded angry.

Mister Skye held out a hand toward Mary. Wordlessly she reached over and handed him his belaying pin. Then he quietly slid off Jawbone into the river. He ran a loving hand down Jawbone's neck, steadying the great horse. Icewater blasted his feet and calves and knees, but he was used to that. For years he'd braved the bitter waters of the north setting his beaver traps, seeing how the sticks floated day after winter day. The old pain flared at once but he ignored it. New pain from wounds barely healed bit at him too. It didn't matter.

He stood listening. Horses and men beat the brush above and below. A pancake cloud, silverlined by the moon, skidded across the sky and would darken the land in a moment. Good. He began a slow, quiet plowing against the current, feeling his way along the slippery bottom until he found a spot where roots gave him toeholds up the cutbank. In a moment he crouched numbly in brush, feeling his near nakedness in the bitter night.

He enjoyed what he was going to do. If he died doing it, that would spare him a worse death shortly. Audacity had saved his life several times, and ultimately had become part of the legend of Barnaby Skye told in the council fires of the western tribes. He'd grown aware of the legend and used it, called it medicine, and turned his medicine legend into a powerful weapon. Even now, he knew, his own women hunkered in the moonshadowed lee of the cutbank, wondering if he had gotten back his medicine.

"Very well then, Skye. You've signed your warrant."

Good of the viscount to announce where he stood, Skye thought. He slipped gingerly forward, knowing how to stalk, how to test the ground ahead for sticks that might snap, branches that might whip. He focused on one thing, the viscount, and scarcely registered the cold on his flesh. Off to either side he heard the thrashing of horses and the voices of men. He might die at that. Most of the cartmen were near.

He slipped into a dense grove of young cottonwoods, their naked branches praying to the moon, and steered through them warily, afraid of snapping a stick. But his medicine held. He pushed gently through brush he knew would look red by daylight, and then found himself peering out upon the rough flats—and the lord and lady, both sitting their horses. He had drawn his revolver and pointed it at her.

"Go ahead and shoot, Gordon," she said mockingly. "Mister Skye! Take me to your bed." She laughed. "I'm mad for you, Skye. I'll be the third wife, Skye!"

She obviously enjoyed taunting the viscount. And she was obviously missing the sudden murderous calm that settled across the lordship's face, something Skye sensed even in the dim light.

A volley of shots split the night, shots from downstream, where his women hid. Shouts drifted to him, and more shots, and violent crashing in brush. Alarmed, he squinted into the murk, seeing nothing, worried about Victoria and Mary. Had the cartmen shot his women in cold blood?

The viscount and Lady Diana stared northward, wondering. Whatever the viscount had intended had been arrested by the commotion. Skye considered slipping back through the brush to his women, then decided to wait. Off in the north he saw Galitzin's lantern bobbing, and the blurred forms of men and horses. Some rode; some led their horses. Skye could scarcely make them out. But then his gaze settled on something that roiled his stomach and caught his breath in his throat. Over one led horse lay a body. A gray thing bobbed and dangled and leaked blackness. Mary! Victoria! Oh . . .

They came swiftly now, cartmen trotting, until they reached the viscount.

"Get back out there, I say," yelled Galitzin.

"No, we'll eat!" cried a cartman.

"Do your duty first. The lord insists."

A cartman paused defiantly. "The bloody hell with that. We'll eat and be damned."

Men slid a slain doe off the nervous dancing horse. Skye gaped, a sudden tremor rattling through him.

From the south, upstream, men trotted back, drawn by the commotion.

Galitzin waved his lantern. "I command you to do your duty. You can eat later," he said. "There'll be severe discipline—"

"Shut your scurvy mouth. We didn't eat today. We've downed stringy horseflesh for a week. We'll—"

The viscount's revolver blasted. The jostling cartmen froze in place. "Two things," said Lord Frazier. "I'll shoot the first bloke who touches that doe. And second, I'll shoot any man who doesn't go back out immediately and hunt down Skye. Get Skye. Then eat. If he escapes, you won't eat. I'll confiscate the carcass."

Men gaped. Any one of them could have lifted his rifle and shot the viscount, but they didn't.

Diana laughed. "You're such a goose, Gordon. These chaps don't want to hurt our Mister Skye. They like him. He and his ladies brought in meat. They kept us all safe and got us out of some bad scrapes. There's not a one who'd shoot at Skye."

"I beg to remind you that a lord of England has measures," the viscount replied coolly. "Colonel Galitzin, make note. This one here, that one there, the ringleaders. We will deal with insurrection as it must be dealt with, with the lash and the noose."

From the edge of the brush Mister Skye watched the cartmen acquiesce. He was so relieved that the body was that of a doe that he trembled. He'd watched that body in the stealthy dark, watched and felt his soul die. Now he crouched transfixed, seeing the surly cartmen yield their wills to the one they'd always called lord.

The soft voice just behind Skye galvanized him. "Up with those big paws, ye bloody oaf."

He whirled, too late. Just behind him in the brush stood the armorer, Gravesend, with a cocked double-barreled fowling piece pointed squarely at him.

Gravesend grinned from behind the weapon. "And drop the hickory stick, sailorboy. Now, or—never, eh?"

Slowly Mister Skye let the belaying pin tumble to earth, and stood.

"Cassocked like a bishop and ready to pray," Gravesend said. "All right, matey. For'ard march."

Mister Skye turned and walked, emerging from the brush and exciting the mob a few yards away.

A sudden hush fell over the cartmen. Lady Diana Chatham-Hollingshead watched bleakly as Gravesend prodded the erstwhile guide into the circle of lanternlight. Somehow, though she couldn't fathom why, the act seemed shameful. Something loathsome was happening. Like the assassination of a king or the murder of Thomas a Becket. The cartmen sensed it, and looked solemn.

Gravesend halted Mister Skye before the viscount. "Here's the bishop, your lordship," he said cheerily.

The viscount nodded benignly.

Skye stood pale in his poncho, naked otherwise except for the tied-down canvas that shrouded his feet and calves. She'd seen him in similar condition many times these past weeks, ever since he'd been captured and his clothes taken from him. By good English models Mister Skye didn't look like much. His torso formed a great barrel, and it rested on massive haunches, tilted slightly forward. He wore his graying hair shoulder-length and loose, like any mountain ruffian. The great body under the poncho was blocky, like her own, and perhaps that is what always started something pattering inside of her when she glimpsed it. She'd long since recognized that sensation as lust, but now, as he stood helpless before his tormentor, she felt no such passions, but only a sadness, and that stain of shame she'd noted.

"Well, Skye," said the viscount blandly, some deep

pleasure in his eyes. "You departed without a stitch and now return in a burial shroud." He smiled.

The guide did a strange thing. He didn't speak, but he rumbled in a most peculiar way, almost as if in some sort of pain. Maybe he was, she thought. His flesh must suffer in the icy air.

"Galitzin, go find the squaws and shoot them. And that bloody horse once and for all. We can't be fending off rescues and plots and all that."

"As you wish, lordship. Come along, come along."

But no one followed. She saw at once the cartmen had no intention of shooting squaws, and half of them looked to be on the brink of rebellion.

"Go along," said Lord Frazier sharply. "I will suffer no insolence." He snapped his swagger stick against his britches smartly.

It occurred to Diana that she held fate in her hands. Or would, as soon as she eased her fowling piece from its sheath hanging on her saddle. She managed it without difficulty, because Skye remained the cynosure of all eyes, and she sat her buffalo pony well back in the darkness.

But Skye saw, and his sharp quick gaze surprised her. For an instant their eyes locked, and he nodded slightly. Then he made that strange noise again, roaring like a grizzly bear, and she saw spittle collect at the corner of his mouth. Sick! Hydrophobia! The sight desolated her. Others saw it too, and muttered.

"Your lordship, you've caught me. I'll shake your hand, then, and we'll be off," Skye said amiably. He stretched his right arm forward. The locked manacle and severed chain shone amber in the lantern light.

The viscount sniffed, stepped back, and glared. "Shake hands with a lord, would you? And you, the scurviest scum alive?"

Skye grinned, and lowered his arm slowly.

"How'd you sever the link, Skye? We'll make sure it doesn't happen again."

"Take a look yourself, matey," Skye said. He held his hands forward, letting the links dangle.

The guide was certainly acting strange, she thought. Pity

seeped through her. She'd come to see this man in a new light during their long passage through a dangerous wild. She'd discovered education in him, and courtesy, and a commanding way of dealing with crises along the trail. She'd thought him a barbarian at first, and found him an eminent citizen of a wild kingdom. By degrees, she had learned to admire him, and particularly his grace under pressure, the thing she called courage.

The lamp shattered. One second it stood on the snowy ground shedding gold; the next, it flew apart, glass splintering, and the whole scene blanked black. Her light-blinded eyes could see nothing.

Men exclaimed.

"Goddam," muttered someone, and it sounded like Skye's older woman. Diana scarcely understood the whirl of motion about her.

"I say! Take your bloody paws off me!" the viscount roared.

She heard scuffling in the dark.

"All right, mate," roared Skye. "Tell them."

The viscount whined.

"Tell them or I'll bite you."

"Bite me?"

"Right at the base of the neck. Here. Right here." Skye's voice. Somehow close to the viscount.

"Bite me? Bite me?"

"Like the wolf." Lady Diana heard an awful gnashing of teeth. From somewhere out in the darkness, close by, that awful horse screeched.

"Bite you," said Skye. "Sink my teeth right in. Chew your flesh and spit it out."

The viscount made some sort of noise that sounded like a gargle. Then, "Don't kill me, Skye. Don't bite me. Galitzin. Gravesend, don't try anything. Not a thing. He'll give me hydrophobia."

Skye roared, and the sound shivered Lady Diana. The man had turned into a hydrophobic lunatic.

Jawbone shrieked.

She could see a little now that the lantern-blindness was fading. Skye stood behind the viscount, pinning him within his massive arms. His face was poised just over the viscount's right shoulder.

"For God's sake!" cried Lord Frazier. "You're oozing hydrophobia."

Skye laughed wildly, and the sound echoed up the coulees.

Diana watched a dark form edge around behind Skye. Galitzin, intending to brain the guide. She lifted her fowling piece, and then knew it wouldn't work. She needed a revolver or a carbine.

"Colonel, one more step and I sink my teeth into this meat."

"For pity sake!" cried Lord Frazier.

"Gravesend, you might hit me—or the viscount—but before I die, I'll sink my teeth into his lordship."

Diana watched Gravesend, over on her right, falter. Then something hit him. He fell, poleaxed, tumbling in the snow. Diana had the distinct impression she'd heard the sound of hardwood striking the skull. And at last she made out the wizened figure of Skye's woman, holding something like a club in her hand.

Skye laughed, his bellow eerie in the night. "I suppose most of you cartmen would be pleased if I bit," he said amiably. "Set down your pieces, and we'll palaver a bit."

They hastened to do so.

"Lady Chatham-Hollingshead, please keep your scattergun on them."

"Don't bite," cried the viscount. "I'll do anything."

"Of course you will, mate. To save your hide. All right, Gordy, or is it Pat or Archie? Here's what you'll do. You'll say 'Damn the bloody Queen,' eh?"

Diana waited, some wild amusement welling up in her.

"Say it, matey, or I'll bite. I'll count to three and bite, your holiness. One, Two—"

"Damn the bloody Queen," croaked the viscount.

"Why, matey, you're a deserter!"

Cartmen laughed. Diana chortled.

"Sir, you are an abomination," said Colonel Galitzin.

Skye addressed him benignly. "First brave thing you've said or done, colonel. And I respect it. You've been a toady from the beginning, bowing and scraping. No wonder the Czar's hussars promoted you, and no wonder your army's full of lickspittle officers. Where'd you learn English, Galitzin? Cambridge?''

The colonel muttered something.

"Here's what you do, Galitzin. You're taking charge. Somewhere inside of you is a competent officer. You'll march your caravan up to Fort Benton on the Missouri—the Blackfeet'll steer you—and my friend Alec Culbertson will see you all down the river. Tell him I said hello—and goodbye.''

"Very good, your excellence.''

Barnaby Skye roared. Jawbone shrieked.

"Don't bite!'' cried the viscount.

"My lady,'' said Skye, and Diana realized suddenly he was addressing her. "The viscount was about to do you harm a few minutes ago. You are welcome to come with my wives and me. Not, as you may suppose, to become my third one, but because we offer you safety and friendship. I am going to Victoria's people to die. They will see you safely to Fort Laramie.''

She didn't hesitate an instant. "Bye, Gordy,'' she said.

Skye continued: "I'm going to borrow a few things, Lord Frazier. That tweed jacket for one, and those lace-up boots. My feet have forgotten what warmth feels like. And a few arms, of course. We'll have to disarm you. And a good horse. We'll take a haunch of that doe, and leave the rest for your men. Unless you'd prefer I bite you. And then you can trot off to Alexandra's featherbed and Baudelaire's comforts.''

"Anything, anything. Don't bite!''

Chapter 31

The waiting seemed worse than the dying. That fall had been glorious, with mild days and frosty nights and azure skies. It grieved Mister Skye to know that he was enjoying these things for the last time. As the cottonwoods and aspens turned golden and lost their leaves, he saw his own doom in the naked limbs that pressed against an enameled sky, and it lay in him, haunting and dark. He felt well through the Moon of Falling Leaves, but that meant nothing. Hydrophobia lurked and waited and inspired false hope and wild relief—until it sprang.

They had found Victoria's Kicked-in-the-Bellies band on the Stillwater, and had been warmly welcomed by Chief Many Coups and all the people, who counted Mister Skye as one of their own and who honored his feats of battle beside his Absaroka brothers. They listened raptly to their story of the viscount, which Mister Skye told in halting Crow, while Victoria embellished easily in her own tongue. But when he'd told them of his wolf-bite, the death of Cutler, and his own certain fate, they saddened and began their mourning.

That afternoon, the great medicine man Red Turkey Wattle had examined Mister Skye's calf. Wordlessly he felt the puckered scars and pink flesh where the swift knife had bled each fang puncture and Victoria had fried the surrounding flesh, leaving a wrinkled red pocket and unending ache in the calf. The skeletal shaman peered up from rheumy eyes and said only that he would fast and seek a vision in his lodge for four days. Mister Skye thanked him, but did not delude himself into believing it would alter his fate.

The whole band vied to reprovision the Skyes. Young women hiked high into the mountains to the south, to a grove where young lodgepole pines grew dense and slender after a fire, and cut new lodgepoles. Older women tanned cowhides from the fall hunt, then laced them together into a shining lodge. Others made luxurious winter moccasins for all the Skyes and Lady Diana too, with thick bullneck soles sewn to softer uppers. Victoria's step-mother fashioned a splendid elkskin shirt for Mister Skye, with dyed quillwork across the chest and long fringes under the arms. Young men brought them meat, choice buffalo hump and boudins, haunches of elk, and soft rabbit pelts for moccasin lining and warmth. Older men, proud of their bow and arrow-making, honed seasoned chokecherry into fine bows for Victoria and Mary and supplied them with carefully wrought arrows with hoop-iron points. And so the Skyes were made new with an outpouring of gifts from the Absarokas.

Mister Skye felt well. In fact, he had never felt better, apart from the ache in his calf. But that new ache mingled with ancient ones that cried at him in the onslaught of each winter, aches from the days he waded hip-deep in icy streams, setting beaver traps, pulling wet, drowned beaver from their watery tombs. The Kicked-in-the-Bellies had chosen a dazzling place to while away the fall. Their vast pony herd fattened on rank golden grasses that grew along the river flats. If they chose to winter near here, hoary cottonwoods would offer fodder for the ponies. Beyond the flats, tumbled foothills dotted with juniper and jackpine vaulted toward the purple mountains to the south, already snow-tipped and beyond mortal reach. Often, Mister Skye took all this in, staring at the tawny collection of lodges, the drying racks of meat, the transparent sky, and the noble mountains, and wept.

But he did not let any one see his tears. Not even Victoria and Mary. All three of them huddled close in their new lodge each night—and waited. As long as he felt well, he tried to be of some use. He made a point of taking Lady Diana around the village and introducing her, and she responded with childlike joy. He wanted to be alone with his women during his last days, so he introduced Diana to Pine Leaf, the legendary old warrior woman of the band, graying now but greatly honored, and powerful in the councils of the whole Absaroka nation. Pine Leaf had never married, but for years she had been the lover of that scamp Jim Beckwourth, and knew English perfectly.

"My lady," she said graciously, "I'd be delighted if you would stay with me. We'll hunt. You love the hunt and have a fine buffalo pony. So do I. We'll see who hunts best!"

"Pine Leaf, I'd be delighted!" Diana had said, and Mister Skye was pleased. Almost every day from then on the pair rode away at dawn, and returned in a crisp fall evening with spare ponies loaded with elk and deer and quarters of buffalo, outstripping all the young men of the band in their successes.

Mister Skye watched approvingly as the young noblewoman transformed herself into an Absaroka huntress, swiftly mastering the Crow tongue, dressing herself richly in Crow attire, and letting Red Turkey Wattle give her a Crow name, which was Grizzly Sow Woman.

"Am I a grizzly sow?" she asked Mister Skye.

"You're more fetching," he replied.

"I'd like some cubs."

He laughed.

"I don't want to go to England."

"Then don't. But I'd better warn you, the winters are often starvin' times."

"Many Coups has asked me to be his fourth wife. It must be my blue blood. Do you think I should?"

"You'll make up your own mind, Lady Diana."

"I'm Grizzly Sow Woman." She laughed, and then

turned somber. "I'd hoped it might be you, Mister Skye. I've never known a man like you. You're so full of—innocence! Innocence."

"I jumped ship."

"Oh, Barnaby. They pressed you in. You were going to go to Cambridge, like your father."

It startled him. "How'd you know that?"

"When you drink, you babble on and on."

"Do me a kindness, Grizzly Sow Woman. Keep that to yourself."

The trees lay naked, and ice formed along the edges of the Stillwater, and Mary's child grew in her belly, making her large, and still the hydrophobia did not pounce. He dared to hope a little, but found hope worse than the surety of doom. With hope came an ache for living that he'd ruthlessly driven from his soul. But he could no longer contain his hope. Each day he examined himself anxiously, and each day his body replied with bright strength and ease. His women had stopped weeping at night, clutching him, and saying goodbye; now they peered at him shyly, contemplatively, sharing his hope but not daring to express it.

His lodge was no longer dark, at least in the sense of divided souls and hearts, but death lurked at its doorflap and Mister Skye's great medicine lay in balance. He felt an unfamiliar helplessness. It chafed him that he could do nothing. But at least he could die well. He lavished love on each of his wives, making them smile, letting them bask in his caring. And he roamed the village each day, bringing a kind word to old men and encouragement to young hunters and warriors, and a gentle flirtation to women young and old. Yes, he thought, he could die well. That alone was left to him, dying well.

One cold day a French trapper named Jean Gallant rode into the village on a shaggy winter-haired pony, and presented himself to Many Coups first, then Mister Skye. He'd come, he said, at the request of Alec Culbertson, bourgeois at Fort Lewis—soon to be renamed Fort Benton. The British, he said, had arrived half-starved and petulant at the American Fur Company post, along with a Blackfeet escort, and had negotiated for two mackinaws to float them to Fort Union. There they would embark on a waiting Chouteau keelboat that would float them down to St. Louis.

"Monsieur Culbertson, he ask me to find out if you live, and I will say zat you do. And he ask me to give this—" he reached into a sack he was toting—"to your good widows." He pulled out a battered silk tophat. "Zee colonel, Galitzin, give it to the bourgeois."

Mister Skye roared. "My medicine hat! I've got my medicine again. Good as new! Burnt and bled the hydrophobia out. Haw!"

Victoria plucked up the battered hat and set it rakishly on his head, grinning.

"Sonofabitch, you got your medicine," she bellowed.

Author's Note

This story, like each of my Skye novels, is pure fiction. But it follows history loosely. This story was inspired by the exploits of Sir St. George Gore, eighth baronet of Gore Manor in Ireland.

In 1854, after outfitting at Fort Leavenworth, he set out on a three-year hunt across the American west that became a legend in its time. His caravan was composed of four six-mule wagons, two ox-wagons, and twenty-one Red River carts. One wagon was filled entirely with the best arms England could manufacture, made by Purdey, Manton, and Richards, and numbering seventy-five rifles and a dozen shotguns. Another contained nothing but fishing tackle. He had greyhounds and staghounds with him, as well as one hundred twelve horses, eighteen oxen, some milk cows and various mules. One of his horses was a Kentucky thoroughbred called Steel Trap, which got to live indoors during the winter encampments, enjoying corn meal fodder.

He had a personal wagon with a collapsible roof (which inspired the parlor wagon in my story), a fancy green-and-white striped tent, a luxurious rug, washstand, brass bed, and other accoutrements of civilization. He even brought a telescope with a six-inch lens for star-gazing. And of course he had a large retinue, about forty men plus several guides, including Jim Bridger for a while. These included cooks, secretaries, dog-tenders and even a professional fly-dresser.

Unlike my fictional viscount, Gore knew how to hunt, and he slaughtered game in prodigious quantities. By his own estimate, he killed two thousand buffalo, sixteen hundred elk and deer, and a hundred bear. Most of this meat was left to rot on the prairies. His chosen method was to shoot standing up, his weapon resting on a forked stick, while his gun-bearer stood beside him with a reloaded rifle. Even in those days when game seemed inexhaustible, his slaughter aroused indignation among the western tribes as well as back east in Washington, where officials pondered ways to curb his hunting and stop his illegal trading with tribesmen.

Like my fictional viscount, Sir St. George Gore eventually prevailed on Major Culbertson, of American Fur, to help him head back to St. Louis on mackinaw boats. Culbertson, glad to get rid of Gore because his profligacy had enraged the tribes, swiftly built the mackinaws, and sent him on his way after several contretemps.

I am indebted to John I. Merritt, whose *Baronets and Buffalo*, Mountain Press Publishing Company, contains a brief, excellent account of the Gore hunt. It became the germ of my novel. As is commonly the case with Old West material, the historical reality is wilder by far than anything rising from a novelist's imagination.

HISTORICAL NOVELS
OF THE AMERICAN FRONTIERS

DON WRIGHT

☐ 58991-2 THE CAPTIVES $4.50
☐ 58992-0   Canada $5.50

☐ 58989-0 THE WOODSMAN $3.95
☐ 58990-4   Canada $4.95

DOUGLAS C. JONES

☐ 58459-7 THE BAREFOOT BRIGADE $4.50
☐ 58460-0   Canada $5.50

☐ 58457-0 ELKHORN TAVERN $4.50
☐ 58458-9   Canada $5.50

☐ 58453-8 GONE THE DREAMS AND DANCING $3.95
           (Winner of the Golden Spur Award)
☐ 58454-6   Canada $4.95

☐ 58450-3 SEASON OF YELLOW LEAF $3.95
☐ 58451-1   Canada $4.95

EARL MURRAY

☐ 58596-8 HIGH FREEDOM $4.95
☐ 58597-6   Canada 5.95

Buy them at your local bookstore or use this handy coupon:
Clip and mail this page with your order.

Publishers Book and Audio Mailing Service
P.O. Box 120159, Staten Island, NY 10312-0004

Please send me the book(s) I have checked above. I am enclosing $_____
(please add $1.25 for the first book, and $.25 for each additional book to
cover postage and handling. Send check or money order only—no CODs.)

Name _____

Address _____

City _____State/Zip _____

Please allow six weeks for delivery. Prices subject to change without notice.

MORE
HISTORICAL NOVELS
OF THE AMERICAN FRONTIERS

<u>JOHN BYRNE COOK</u>

THE SNOWBLIND MOON TRILOGY
(Winner of the Golden Spur Award)

☐	58150-4	BETWEEN THE WORLDS	$3.95
☐	58151-2		Canada $4.95
☐	58152-0	THE PIPE CARRIERS	$3.95
☐	58153-9		Canada $4.95
☐	58154-7	HOOP OF THE NATION	$3.95
☐	58155-5		Canada $4.95

<u>W. MICHAEL GEAR</u>

☐	58304-3	LONG RIDE HOME	$3.95
☐	58305-1		Canada $4.95

<u>JOHN A. SANDFORD</u>

☐	58843-6	SONG OF THE MEADOWLARK	$3.95
☐	58844-4		Canada $4.95

<u>JORY SHERMAN</u>

☐	58873-8	SONG OF THE CHEYENNE	$2.95
☐	58874-6		Canada $3.95
☐	58871-1	WINTER OF THE WOLF	$3.95
☐	58872-X		Canada $4.95

Buy them at your local bookstore or use this handy coupon:
Clip and mail this page with your order.

Publishers Book and Audio Mailing Service
P.O. Box 120159, Staten Island, NY 10312-0004

Please send me the book(s) I have checked above. I am enclosing $_____ (please add $1.25 for the first book, and $.25 for each additional book to cover postage and handling. Send check or money order only—no CODs.)

Name _____

Address _____

City _____ State/Zip _____

Please allow six weeks for delivery. Prices subject to change without notice.

Printed in the United States
77080LV00002B/211